1

Anno Luce.

Liam Sweeny.

Anno Luce.

Published by;
JTT Publishing.

ISBN 13: 978-1-906529-03-1

JTT Publishing books may be ordered through all internet booksellers, or through your local book retailer.

Printed in the United Kingdom.

To my mother and father, without whom I'd have neither the ability to write, nor the desire.

... and to all those who were affected by Hurricane Katrina.

JESSICA,

YOU'RE BEAUTIFUL.

Chapter One

He came to the shelter disheveled and weary, his leather cap adorned with an enamel pin that read; *Gone Fishin'*. He reminded me of a New York City cabdriver, with the stains of the entire world on his threadbare, tweed coat.

I made my assumptions ... *A late-stage alcoholic.* But no, that wasn't right. His eyes were too clear, not reflecting a life of hard-drink. And they were intense too. Late-stagers had a shiftier gaze. *Mentally ill?* If that was true, it certainly wasn't apparent. His mannerisms were calm, fluid almost, and when he spoke, I could sense balance.

Working at a homeless shelter introduces you to all types, and the Mt. Calvary Mission was no exception. After a while, you begin to feel like you can read the person before you. Hundreds of intakes reveal patterns, and eventually you see the pattern that fits the person, not the other way around. But with this one, no pattern emerged. When he spoke, the words he chose showed a remarkable vocabulary, almost poetic in its meter - and his confidence level was strange.

Most of the people I encountered on intake are what best can be described as 'broken souls'. There's a blunted fear in their demeanor; afraid to die, but so beat up by life that the fear of death was only just there. This man had none of that. He seemed to project a personality that made me feel that, in a benign way, the intake was of *me*.

It was warm that February evening; unseasonable, even for Southern California, and as usual I had my sleeves rolled up. Alejandro Ortiz, the Assistant Director of Mt. Calvary, always yelled at me about rolling up my sleeves on intakes. This was thanks to a crooked, home-job tattoo of a cross on my forearm, courtesy of my drinking days.

Alejandro's cool though, we go way back. He only does it because Zee, our director and boss, doesn't want us to 'promote a particular religion.' Apparently he's never looked up 'Mt. Calvary' in the ol' Oxford.

During the intake, I noticed the man looking at my forearm. Mindful of lurking directors, I pointed to it and said, "... A souvenir of my young and stupid days."

He smiled jokingly. "The universe is old, so you'll always be young," he replied. "As for stupid, well, I won't tell anyone if you don't."

He was all right.

Over the next few months I would get to know the unknown man; his life and times, struggles past and present. During that time I would realize who he was, and would attempt to understand that the one I've prayed to my entire life was now a homeless man named Yashua King.
A man who in a short time would become known to the world as the second coming of Christ.

I was never what you would call an overly-religious person. I was an overly political person. Though my causes were always, in my opinion, true, I'd more or less irritated, aggravated, agitated, or bored more people than I knew. I couldn't help it. I could never understand how most people weren't concerned with the world around them.

I was a Roman Catholic, of the lapsed denomination. I never went to Church. I prayed occasionally, but really more of an on-going monologue. I knew God listened, even when I was ranting.

I'd been working at Mt. Calvary Mission for four years. It started out volunteer, just a few hours a week, but the place just grew on me.
One out of three of the guys that came in there was a veteran. Some people there were alcoholics, some had mental illnesses and still others were victims of; 'one paycheck away.' We'd even seen families with young children in there.

Everybody who worked there got involved. I'd had people staying in my house on sub-zero nights. Once we paid for a coffin and burial plot for a guy who was there named Ed Martin, who, by the time of his death, had become a dear friend to us all. I remember at the funeral we played 'Cocaine' by Clapton, which was Ed's favorite song. The Director didn't say anything.

San Miguel Ridge, our home-sweet-home, aka, *The Mount*, was an 'Economically-disadvantaged, fiscally-challenged urban area.' Or, as I liked to put it, a slum. A *big* slum. And what always cracked me up was that five miles away there were multi-million dollar mansions and pedicured lawns. I knew people who lived in some of them. They'd always ask me; "*Why don't those people get jobs and fix up their houses?*"

For starters, most of them *did* work, and a lot of people there didn't have enough money for basic phone service. Try to get a decent job without a call-back number. Forget computers and internet (virtually non-existent in San Miguel.) Poverty has a cruel way of keeping people holding the pot.

But, I digress. Though impressed by Yashua, I, of course, had a job to do. I was able to obtain what little physical information about him that I could. He said that he was born in 1945 in Ethiopia, to a Jewish mother and an American father. He said that Ethiopia kept poor records at the time, and his birth certificate had been lost. He told me that his father was an archaeologist, but that he was separated from them both at an early age. No kidding though; he didn't look a day over forty.

Apparently he never attended college. He professed to be self-taught. He said he'd been to so many countries I stopped him at around twenty. For income, he'd supported himself through odd-jobs, (he mentioned landscaping,) and the generosity of others.

Not much to go on when having to deal with bureaucracy. Yashua had no birth certificate or Social Security Number. Luckily, I knew someone in the Department of Social Services, and after the intake, I sent him an email. It was worth a shot.

Another curious detail was that he didn't ask for anything. Usually people who came into the Mission would ask for something after the intake; cup of coffee, maybe, or a new pair of socks, a shower ... *something*. Yashua asked for nothing.

He almost didn't get in. Our mission remained open, in part through donations, and in part through a federal grant we were eligible for. However, a few months prior, the grant fell victim to budget cuts and it was really hurting us to take in new people. The lack of obvious defect that had piqued my curiosity hurt Yashua's chances for admittance.

I went to bat for him though. I told Alejandro that since he had no records in the system, he wouldn't be able to get a job, an apartment or anything. We could help him get those things, and he could be one of the few success stories we'd see. But the battle, I realized, wasn't between me and Alejandro. We were tight. It would be between him and the director, who was just tight generally.

Now, I'd like to say that the director wasn't a bad guy, really. He was in it because he cared. But he went to umpteen universities for social-work related things, and he was a little, well, 'schooled.'
I'm no enemy of higher education; I have a degree in philosophy myself. But colleges and universities teach through the analysis of large aggregate amounts of data, or abstract concepts. In dealing with social issues like homelessness on a day-to-day basis, you find that there's no one case that mimics the general, or 'average' condition.

The director was catching on to that, slowly, but often he fell back on institutional thinking, and 'official policy'.
I can understand and appreciate the need for adherence to policy. We all have bosses, and he was no different. But there are times you're clearly 'off the radar,' and if you have to bend the rules at those times, it shouldn't kill you. It killed him.

We gave temporary shelter to all who came in for three days, and every two days, Alejandro met with the director to review the cases that came in during the two days prior. It was two days, not three, because we liked to have at least one day to make preparations if we couldn't give them a longer stay. Yashua came in on Friday, so I gave Alejandro my pitch before he took off for the weekend. Alejandro had to meet with the director on Tuesday for intake-reviews, and he said he'd see what he could do.

On that Tuesday morning, the strangest thing that had ever happened at the Mission - up 'till then anyway - happened.

I was busy as usual, at my desk, air-drumming away to a Mahavishnu tune, blasting out of my crappy CD player, when Alejandro added the 'shave-and-a-haircut' to my front door. He peeped in and said, "Dude, you're not gonna believe this one."

"Tell me Jimmy Jamz ain't runnin' around naked again?" I said. Jimmy was our resident streaker. It wasn't his fault; he had problems.

"No, you'd believe that," said Alejandro, "just come here." He left, leaving the door cracked as he walked toward the main office.

I pressed stop on the CD and went to the office. Alejandro was sitting down, looking at a letter.

"Who's trying to screw us this time?" I asked, only half-joking.

"Well if they are, we're gonna enjoy it," he said, and handed me the letter. "Read this."

I looked at the letter. Linen paper, something I'd never seen any letter addressed to *us* printed on. The sender; one Jeremiah Ovitt, Esq.
Okay, a lawyer. *'Good screwing?'* I thought.

It was written to the director. (Alejandro handled his mail.) The address was in Jerusalem. It was dated Saturday, just three days before. It read:

Dear Sir,

I am writing on behalf of the estate of one Kaleb Faste. Mr. Faste has recently passed, and his estate is currently being administered by our office. Mr. Faste was a wealthy man. I am writing to you because in his will, there is an unusual request.

Mr. Faste was in America, in your area, many years ago. Upon one occasion he found himself homeless. Mt. Calvary, back then, had taken him in and helped him secure passage home to Jerusalem. He had never forgotten this, apparently, and has bequeathed to your mission an amount of $1 million dollars. Please call my office so that we can discuss this matter in more depth.

Sincerely,

Jeremiah Ovitt, Esq.

"A little early for April Fools, aren't you?" I asked, not taking it at all seriously. Alejandro had gotten me on many good practical jokes before.

"I would have never thought of this," he said, and handed me the envelope it came in. The postmark was indeed Jerusalem, dated Saturday. First class. Although its arrival from Jerusalem three days after it was sent was surprising, I couldn't deny its validity.

Quite reasonably, I was stunned. I'm usually a man of many words, but I couldn't find any.

"Ain't that some shit?" Alejandro said, and I could tell he was stunned too.

I finally found words. "I guess now we can get a *real* air conditioner?" I said, pointing to the fan-and ice bucket we'd crafted to beat the heat.

Alejandro laughed. "Or a truckload of ice…" he said.

"Did you tell Zee yet?" I asked (the director's name was Zebediah; we called him 'Zee' for short.)

"Not 'till he gets here," Ale' said. "If I tell him on the ride, he's likely to veer off the road and kill someone."

"Dude, we're partyin'!" I said.

"Righteously!" Alejandro scratched his chin.

Zee took it suspiciously at first. He said he wasn't going to say anything until he talked with Mr. Ovitt, *esquire*, which he did shortly after.

The call took about fifteen minutes; he came out of the office ashen white. And Zee was black, which made it seem even weirder. Apparently it was confirmed.

"Well, gentleman, we're going to DeGregorie's tonight," he said after a long pause. We went to DeGregorie's about once a year. At about this time, I realized that Mt. Calvary Mission had been resuscitated.

Dinner at DeGregorie's was beautiful, and indeed righteous. I got way too drunk, as I'd cut down from my days of youth. I had Jack Daniels, straight; my poison-of-choice. Zee always loosened the tie at DeGregorie's, but that night he truly became one of us. Like a crazy all-nighter that bonds a group of friends, the feast at DeGregorie's really brought us on the same page.

Alejandro said something after dinner that made me think. We were talking about the letter and he said, "One the new guys, Yashua King, was sitting at my desk, and he saw the envelope. He told me that he'd been there before. I didn't believe him, but he knew right where the address was in Jerusalem. He also said he knew Hebrew and Arabic, sat there and spoke in all three. He pronounced the names of a few things that were in Jerusalem, supposedly."

Alejandro sipped his drink. "It was funny," he started, "Yashua said; 'The world doesn't truly know its significance.' He didn't elaborate further though."

I digested this, along with linguine, clams and whiskey. I shared a cab with Zee for the ride home. I made the request to him that we 'keep' Yashua, in light of the recent windfall. With money no longer an over-riding whip, he agreed. Alejandro is officially tasked with these sorts of requests, but it was one of those nights, I knew he wouldn't care.

I slept like a baby that night.

The next morning I awoke to a beautiful spring day. I noticed a funny thing when I looked at my arm to check my watch. The home-job tattoo looked a little bit different. The cross was still there, but it looked like it was coming apart beneath the skin. It was crooked to begin with, but now it looked more pronounced.

'*Better get that checked out,*' I thought as I dropped back down to commence an extra hour of beauty sleep.

We had a meeting to officially address the gift. I can attest with all truth that pay raises were not mentioned until after every other factor had been discussed, and it was really an afterthought. I think we were all just happy to know we were actually *getting* paid. Zee gave us all a raise, but only enough to cover paying the debts we all had. We avoided the excitement of expansion and concentrated on meeting the immediate needs of residents already there. Zee said the best thing to do was to strengthen the center's current programs, and when physical expansion came up, it was in terms of simple accommodation areas. We didn't want an expansion that *reinvented the wheel.*

Of course, as excited as we were, the show went on. We had busy, hectic lives to begin with, and 'busy and hectic' they remained.

That day I had a mixed schedule. In addition to intakes, which occurred as people came in, I was also an advocacy specialist. That meant meeting with the residents periodically, assessing their situation, and making sure they got what they needed. When we knew we were getting the money, we immediately opened the doors to all incoming.

We'd always had more beds than we'd needed. Our inability to accommodate everyone before was an issue of money for food, clothing ... the basics. The windfall allowed us to 'open the flood-gates.'

So, naturally, Yashua King was allowed in. I didn't even have to ask Zee, really. Yashua was my first advocacy session that day.

We liked to bring people into the 'Green Room.' It was a room we set up especially for meetings and was nice and comfortable, with plants all around. It was also the one room with a window that had a decent view of something other than garbage and abandoned buildings.

I brought Yashua in, and he looked around, bemused. He walked up to one of the more battle weary plants, I think it was an African violet, and he stroked one of the leaves gently. He mumbled something under his breath, and smiled.

'*Okay, maybe he is nuts,*' I thought. Not that I'd hold it against him or anything.

"It's an African prayer," he said.

"I'm sorry?"

"In African cultures, there are prayers that are said for a sickly plant," he explained. "I was reciting an ancient Mali blessing."

"Oh, okay," I said. *'Alright then, he's only neurotic.'*

Again he smiled. Gotta admit I thought he was reading my mind. Or maybe my facial expression. To break up that awkward moment, I motioned for him to sit down.

"So how's it been today, Yashua?" I asked.

"I'm well," Yashua said. "Everyone here has been most kind to me."

"We kind of see ourselves as one big, dysfunctional family," I said.

Yashua laughed. "Well they say you can make a perfect machine out of imperfect parts."

"Ya' sayin' we're perfect here?"

"Not perfect," he said, "but good enough."

"Thank you," I replied.

I continued on with the session. "Well, Yashua, this is the part where we try to find out where you're at, and what you need in the short-run and the long," I said. "These are regular meetings, every two days, and if you need anything in between then, I'm always around." I brought my pencil to my notebook. "The first thing I'd like to start out with is ... where you're at right now. Obviously, in the short time I've known you, you've shown yourself to be an intelligent, well traveled person," I said, looked at my notepad, then continued. "You say you don't drink, or use drugs, and I believe you. You don't show any signs of that. You don't appear to have a debilitating mental illness or disability. I don't understand why you're not working?"

"My work never ends," he said, after a pause. "I have called many of these structures my home. My work is here as well."

I was puzzled. "Are you saying you're here to work?" I asked.

"You said it," he replied.

I thought for a second, and then said, "Ya know, we might

be able to actually hire you, but we'll have to know what your work experiences are."

"My references have been lost through the years, and as for being paid, you're hospitality is all I seek," he answered.

I always bitch about Zee's inability to handle the occasional monkey wrench, but right then, I knew how he must've felt sometimes. I genuinely felt that Yashua had come there to work. I couldn't understand how that kind of an arrangement would work out, or that it wouldn't turn into a pile of shit.

"I can't promise they'll let you, but I'll bat on this one," I told him. "They'll probably do it just to shut me up. I have to know though, what exactly would you want to do?"

"Bring some spirit back to the people here," Yashua said, his hand waving through the air.

I started thinking about my inability to roll up my sleeves. Zee would have a fit if Yashua started preaching to people.

As if on cue, Yashua said, "You have what's called a counselor here?" he asked.

"We don't have one officially."

"Perhaps now you do."

I saw where he was going with it. That could work out.

"Okay," I said, "that's what I'll try for."

Then I added, at a lower tone, though no one could have heard me anyways, "Just for the heads up; Zee, the director, is a bit funny on promoting any *one* religion. He's a good guy ... I'm just letting you know."

"The Word has many forms, and not all have to mention a Name," Yashua replied, and I nodded.

'*He'll keep below radar,*' I thought to myself.

As the session ended, when I was asking him if there was anything that he needed, I told him we had the newspaper up front everyday if he wanted to read it. He declined, saying the news just depressed him.

"Amen, brother," I said to which Yashua simply laughed.

Thus ended the session, and the next day I discussed the proposition with Alejandro and Zee, securing the arrangement. With minimal prodding, I might add, as Zee and Alejandro both liked Yashua.

     After work I went to the doctor's office and waited in there for over an hour before he saw me.
Dr. Jones his name-tag said. *'Must be a new guy,'* I thought.
     "How can I help you today?" he asked.
     I rolled up my sleeve. "This tattoo here is moving. It was crooked to begin with, but it's moved around in the past week."
     He looked at it, and swabbed it with alcohol. "How long have you had it?"
     "About ten years," I replied. "I did it with a needle-and-thread ... with India ink."
     He looked at me funny just as I knew he would, then asked, "And ... it just started moving a week ago?"
     "Yeah, I can't figure it out."
     "Are you feeling any itching or burning? Tingling or ... anything?" He pressed on it as he questioned me.
     "Nope," I said, "...nothing."
     "How are you feeling otherwise?"
     "Fine," I said.
     He held my arm up to the light and looked at it intensely. He then said, "For right now, I'm going to draw some blood and run a few tests. I can't think of anything definitive at the moment. We'll make an appointment for the following week. Say, next Thursday, same time?"
     "How about Friday?" I asked. "I have plans for Thursday."
     "Friday it is," he said. "Call the office if it gets worse."
     "Thank you, Doctor ... Jones," I said, and grabbed my coat.

     I walked into the 'City Dump' (*my apartment*) shortly after ten that night. My apartment was what you'd call, *eclectic*, with a wide assortment of styles and themes, classical, contemporary, Burger King, Marlboro, you name it. If it existed on Earth and was cheap, it was represented in my pad. I kept saying I was going to tear through my apartment and clean up, every New Year's Eve I said that. The only things that had made it to the trash then were the pictures I had of Jeannie, the love (lost) of my life. Our

relationship encountered a snag. His name was Brett. Looks, money ... I couldn't touch him. It would of upset me a whole lot more but for the fact that she was a real pain in the ass anyways. *Congratulations, Brett! You've just won yourself a high-maintenance bitch!*
But ... it still sucked getting dumped.

I'm a big news freak. My apartment was a repository for newspapers, magazines, and the assortment of odd books. I even got Spanish papers, though my Spanish wasn't the best. All the Canadian and British papers, you name it. I had cable, but I only watched news channels.

I grabbed an oversize mug and poured myself a cup of cold coffee from the pot. I threw it in the microwave long enough for it to burn me when I tried to take it out. I grabbed the fat and the sugar, made myself a nice cup of lovely, plopped down on the couch (leather - the only splurge I'd made in years.) and turned on the TV. CNN was on.

They were showing the 'Moral March' on Washington, DC. A million and a half people that time. The year past, it had been less than half a million. The leader of the March, the Rev. Joseph Biggs, was talking in front of the Lincoln Memorial.

"Today we gather here in the name of Jesus Christ, our Lord and Savior, to call upon our government to instill the values, Christian values, American values, to this the greatest nation on Earth!"

The crowd erupted in brain-dead cheers. *"We will continue to march, and to protest, and to grow, until the McPherson Bill is passed through both houses, and signed by the President of the United States!"*

He was acting like he was Martin Luther King or something. What a joker.

I turned the TV off, disgusted. The McPherson Bill was a lousy attempt by radical Christians to institute biblical law. They'd had three marches on Washington and rallies in every state. And the Reverend Biggs was a real peach, too. He talked about morality, and he owned a power plant in India that had been spewing toxic waste into the air there for two decades. Lots of people got sick. Many died. Not a dime from him came though, and he was worth billions. He only closed the plant down when he got busted by a journalist.

He was the kind of guy who believed that only people who believed in the same things *he believed* in were going to heaven. He'd openly condemned Jews, Muslims, Buddhists, Hindus, everyone but Christians; *his* kind of Christians, which explained the power plant. I'd heard him rant on about it, and I couldn't call it anything else but hate and dogma. In the name of Jesus, too. I was sure God had a place for the Rev. Biggs. I hoped it was a hot one.

But surely I shouldn't have thought that. I really just had hoped he'd wake up someday, and realize that in his fervency he'd made a lot of different people hate each other. Or maybe people should've woken up and stopped listening to a man who was obviously delusional.

Lacking anything better to do, I decided to go to the mission. It was late, approaching twelve, but I frequently put in late hours. We all did. I figured maybe I could catch up on some paperwork. I hit the road.

Jefferson Highway connected the city of Anno Luce to all points north. I frequented this passage. I lived in Silverton, which was about ten miles north of the city limits. It was an okay place, Silverton. The garbage was collected and the rent was cheap.

The city of Anno Luce had about 150,000 residents, both legal and otherwise. We were the last such populated city before the Mexican border.
Driving down Jefferson, it was a beautiful place. The buildings weren't as large as in a big city; the tallest one was the Paradigm Building at fifty stories. But the architecture was amazing. Hard to believe, driving by, that you were a part of that environment.

Anno Luce was so named for an old festival of the region, from when it was still Mexico, called *Anno Luce*. 'Anno Luce' meant 'year of light' in Latin, and apparently it referred to the number of years since God had said, "Let there be Light." The festival traced to an earlier Native-American ritual of a similar theme. The Anno Luce year was worn as a number around everyone's arm during the festival. It's something like four thousand years different from ours. The early American settlers named the original settlement

Anno Luce in part to please the people who were already there when they arrived. Of course, Anno Luce is a Latin name, not a Spanish, or Native -American name, but compromises were made.

The 'Exit 3' ramp led to Barker St., which ran right across the Mount. The nickname came from Mt. Olympus, which was what people in the 70's used to call it, sarcastically. The Mount was rough. Every week there was a murder or shooting, and there wasn't anything there except bodegas, gun and liquor stores, and churches. It got worse the higher up you were. We were about three blocks down from the top, so we saw our share, but not as bad as the 'peakers.'

I didn't worry too much about the neighborhood. Most people on the Mount knew they might be homeless at any time. So we were considered neutral figures.

I went to the door and swiped my card. *Bzzt.* Open sesame. I walked in and saw Eddie Kelly sitting at the front desk. Eddie was one of our volunteers. He was a retired insurance salesman. He said he volunteered at night because he was a night-owl, and it gave him something to do in the wee hours. Good man.

"What are you doin' here at this hour?" he asked.

"Bored. And you?" I asked.

"Same thing," he said.

I laughed. "All quiet on the front?"

"Pretty much," he said. "Yashua is still up. Does he sleep all day or something?"

"No," I replied, "he's up all day."

"'Cause the past two days, he's been up the entire time I've been here," Eddie said. "He's a great guy, don't get me wrong, but he said he never sleeps. He says; *'I'll have rest when I'm passed on.'* It's weird."

"So what does he do at night?" I asked.

"Well, he talks to people, mostly," he started. "I can say that we haven't had the usual night-time unrest around here. He also prays over people when they're sleeping." Eddie paused. "I hope no one wakes up when he's doing it and flips out."

"Well you're on the helm," I joked. "Everything will be A-Okay!"

"Yeah!" he said, and laughed as I took off down the hall for my office.

I went to sit down, brushing yesterday's paper off my desk, and out of the corner of my eye I saw the headline; '5th Day of Moral March in Washington.'

"Damn, he's everywhere." I mumbled as I looked ominously at the stack of evaluation assessment reports filling the plastic tray I bought at the dollar store.

They were mostly filled out, except for generic stuff - check this, circle that ... things I didn't need to fill out during the evaluations. Some people would do it right then, lightning fast, but I always thought that came across as impersonal. I just let them pile up until the last minute.

I grabbed the one on top and as I did I heard a knock at my door. "Come in," I said loudly enough to be heard. (*I never asked who it was when someone knocked on my door.*)

It was Yashua. He was dressed in a brown bathrobe, as I recall the ugliest one we had, complete with cigarette burn-holes in it.

"Yashua! How are ya?" I said, motioning him to have a seat in my only other chair.

"I'm good," he said. "Yourself?"

"Shootin' fish in a barrel," I said. "Life's easy."

"It's too bad more people don't see it so," he said, and glanced down at the paper, by now on the floor. He looked back up and said, "I couldn't help but hear you say 'He's everywhere.' We're you referring to him?" Yashua pointed to the article about Rev. Biggs.

Now I knew I didn't say it that loud, only to myself really, but he had some ears. Those walls were thick; I couldn't hear anything through them.

"Uh," I said, flustered a bit, and then thought, 'Ah, *what the hell,*' and said, "Yeah, this guy. What do you think of him?"

Yashua seemed pretty reasonable. I was interested to hear what he had to say.

"He leads many who fail to lead themselves," Yashua said, "He cannot forgive, and tells others to follow him." He flicked the newspaper. "Needless to say, I'm not a fan."

I laughed. "Thank God," I said. "I know you're religious and all."

"Spiritual." He corrected me.

"I'm sorry, spiritual then. I just meant I didn't know if you liked that guy or not."

"No," Yashua said. "He's blind to me."

"Agreed. I just hope that the people who follow him wake up before they drive this country over a cliff."

"They won't," he said. "They'll follow him right off that cliff."

Yashua looked right at me. "Let me ask you something."

"Shoot."

"What made you stop going to church?" he asked.

"Who says I don't go to church?"

"You don't call a tattoo of a cross 'stupid' if you're going to church every Sunday."

He had me there. *Where to begin?* Should I start with the clergy sex-abuse scandal, which I felt hadn't been properly addressed, or the fact that everyone at church was thinking about going out to lunch or dinner that day.

"You're right," I began, "I haven't been to church in a while. I don't know, I just have a lot of problems with churches these days," I flustered to explain. "I have faith, and I try to live right ... but sitting in church every Sunday is tough for me. I don't know why."

Yashua looked at me and smiled. "Barnabas, some people go to church looking for hope." He picked up my small trophy from 'Play for Hope' (*A musical benefit for childhood leukemia.*) "... And some walk through those doors to give it."

I always hated it when people called me Barnabas, which is my real name. I always tell people it's Barney, but it's Barnabas on the birth certificate. I didn't seem to mind Yashua calling me Barnabas, though. He wasn't making fun of it like the kids in school did.

I caught what he was saying about Church, though. It made me think. "I see your point," I said. "I think I'll go Sunday."

"I think I'll go with you," Yashua said. "I know of a small church a few blocks from here, with a wonderful service."

"Sounds like a plan."

"Do me a favor and don't wear any gold," Yashua said.

"Okay. Out of curiosity, why not?" I asked.

"The Church symbolizes the worship of the Presence of God. None should wear gold before Him."

That actually made sense. "Okay, I can see that one. I'll leave my gold Rolex at home then." I smiled.

"You do that," Yashua said as he turned his head at something. "I'm needed," he added and got up to leave.

"We'll have to have more of these conversations," I said.

"Of course," Yashua said, smiling. "Perhaps one day I'll *really* tell you something."

I smiled back. "Yeah, maybe the history of Jerusalem."

"Indeed," he replied.

Yashua left. I sat for a while, thinking about going to church on Sunday. I have to admit, I was actually looking forward to it. It would at least get my mind off of Jeannie.

I got to work on the evaluation assessments. Even though I wait until the last minute, I was fast with them, and it only took a little over an hour. I grabbed a soda from my mini-fridge, and checked the cap. They're having a contest for a cruise to Jamaica. 'Kickin', mon.' No luck under the cap though, so I turned on the tunes while I drank down that corrosive sweetness. Jerry Goodman could rock that electric violin, man.

After the 'pop' I turned everything off, and packed up. About 2:30 in the a.m. Not bad. I usually left around then when I came in late. And, fortunately, I had the next day off.

So, a nod to Eddie, a go at my fritzy starter and I was in the wind. I cranked down my windows and blasted 104.7 KALR, *Anno Luce Rocks*. Oddly enough, the song blasting as I sped down Jenkins Street was 'Cocaine' by Clapton.

Chapter Two

I woke up Thursday around noon. '*The big day*,' I thought to myself as I cracked my back. No doubt I was psyched to be playin' out. I play guitar, blues mainly. I didn't normally play out; didn't have time, but I met this girl Jen at the diner, and was feelin' the rebound thing. We were talking about a song on the radio, and I told her I played. So she invited me to an open-mic night at La Junta, a club in the northeast pass. A wee bit more upscale than any place found on the Mount. I was thinking of going in there, playing my heart out, and sweeping the lovely Jen off her feet.

No, actually I was thinking about my amp not blowing up. When I play, I bare it all, its beauty and its ugliness. Amps can generally handle the 'beauty' and 'ugliness' by themselves. Both, over long periods, take their toll. I would've hated to go to that thing, and right before I ripped, *it* ripped. The speaker, that is. '*Satriani doesn't have to ever worry about this shit.*' My first thought. '*Satriani can afford a back-up rig.*' My second thought.

I sat up out of bed and went for my axe; a vintage 2003 Fender Mexican Stratocaster. Would've rather had the American Strat, but ya got what ya got, so I picked it up and started practicing. Practicing for me wasn't very structured. I saw guitar as a hobby, so I'd just goof around for ten minutes, playing blues lead to accompany nothing, and work on the occasional composition. So that's what I did. I spent half-hour that day 'cause I was gonna play that night.

I got pretty close to the 'upper zone' - that next level of playing; always reached for, seldom attained. You always hit it when you're not trying. And once you're hitting it all the time, the level goes to the next-higher level. The Top Zone, I guess, is never meant to be reached, just strived for. That day, I hit one riff that just smoked. Right near the zone. I had to put the guitar down after that. If I was corny, I would've gestured the 'sizzle.'

As usual, I clicked on the TV, that great American 'electro-babysitter.'

CNN greeted me. The bar at the bottom said, 'Late Breaking News.' That always grabbed my attention, even though the odds were good it was something stupid. I turned up the volume. Darren Freeman, the anchor, was questioning someone in a box in the top right corner, a woman wearing a bright red slicker.

"So, Janice, we're hearing that this was a magnitude seven quake?"

"Yes, Darren, that's right," Janice said. "... But we're getting in word that the quake was apparently followed by another quake, that one a magnitude six point three, that just occurred on the Italian-Austrian border, about seventy miles northeast of Venice."

"Was that an aftershock?" Darren asked.

"It's difficult to say," Janice said, over sirens that could be heard in the background. "From what I've been told, it seems to be too far away to be an aftershock of the original quake."

"Can you give us any indication of the damage there right now?" he asked.

"Well Darren," Janice turned around to look behind her, "I'm here at the Acropolis, and behind me, *far behind me*," she motioned back to shadows and smoke, "...is the Parthenon. The Greek authorities won't allow us beyond where we're standing now."

I could roughly make out ruins, but they just looked like Greek ruins. "The Parthenon has suffered severe damage, as did ... so I'm told, much of the ancient city of Athens. People who've been in the city tell me it's been all but destroyed."

"Are they estimating casualties at this point?" Darren asked.

Janice hesitated; it seemed like the connection was bad. She finally heard the question and replied. "No, Darren, they're saying it's way too early to estimate casualties. There will likely be a very large number though. The quake affected several hundred square miles ... it's difficult to say in the end what we're going to see."

"Thank you, Janice," Darren said.

"Thanks, Darren."

"Janice Crenshaw, our senior correspondent in Athens tonight," Darren said as she cut out.

'*Wow*,' I thought.

Makes you think about how precious life really is, ya know? One day you're walkin' down the street, next thing you're whole life's upside down.

I felt bad for people when things like that happened, though I can't say I always gave as much as I could. I guess you get desensitized to it after a while, and it doesn't seem like it mattered as much if it happened somewhere you'd never been. I don't know. Needless to say, I thought about it, but it didn't exactly consume me.

At that moment, my all-consuming passion was playing well enough to score a date with the one called Jennifer. As far as what I knew of her, she was smart, funny, easy going and beautiful. She worked at a Crisis Center. She was a musician, which was cool, but I didn't know what she sounded like. I met her at a poetry meet at Luella's Diner, a place known for its politics and its Manhattan clam chowder (*Coffee's alright too, but Joe would kill me if he heard me say that.*)

She read an interesting poem she wrote about the division of wealth in America. She had me right there. When I went up and talked to her, I found out that she played acoustic guitar. I told her I played, and she invited me to the open mic. She said she might puke on the set because she hated the Northeast Pass. That was cool. So I agreed to show up.

So there I was, actually picking up the guitar again, not caring if I jinxed myself by tappin' the good groove early. I was still just fartin' around though. I never knew what I was gonna play 'till it came outta me. So I just practiced tricks a little bit, proposed, forwarded, and seconded the motion to grab a cup of coffee at Joe's Coffeehouse, down the road.

Joe's was a fine institution; small, cozy, and tucked away from Route 30, the only other highway in Silverton, except for Jefferson Highway. Joe McGee, a short, stout Irishman with a winner's circle up top and a thick, trimmed red beard, was a gentleman and a scholar, though never both at the same time. Joe was what I'd call my 'ground.' Joe never held anything back, tact wasn't his thing. Great guy to talk to, though. I always made sure to have an extra twenty minutes to stop in for some Joe (no pun intended) before I went to work.

I walked in that day, and set my windbreaker on one of the pegs by the front door. Joe was his usual cool self, looking at the sports page of the L.A. Times.

"Joe!" I said.

"Norm!" he said, in full 'Cheer's' mode. 'Asshole.' I laughed.

"Does that mean I can run up a tab?"

"Sure you can ..." Joe said, "Down at Dirty Dan's."

"Hell no," I replied. "I think they pee in their coffee." We were referring to Dan's Café, down in Los Manos, a suburb of Anno Luce. And yes, Dan's really was dirty.

"Yeah, but I'm sure they'll let you run up a tab," he said.

"That's okay; I just got a raise anyways."

"Yeah, I read about that in the paper," Joe said, shifting through his stack of papers, not really looking for it. "Jerusalem. Well you can thank me dear Auntie Bridget for that one."

"When we get a check from Ireland, I will," I said and he laughed.

"Usual?"

"Or what passes for it," I answered with a grin.

He poured me a cup of Kenyan. I get straight coffee at the convenience stores when I have to, but Joe's Kenyan is by far the strongest mud on the planet. Love that stuff.

"Hear about those quakes?" I asked, knowing, of course, that he had.

"Yeah, it's a shame. I heard Athens is in bad shape. All that history. Ya know, when we get quakes here in the states, our oldest and most famous landmarks, the man-made ones, are only three hundred years old. Here we think about damage by insurance estimates. Now tell me, who's gonna insure the Parthenon? Met Life?"

I laughed. "Maybe, I mean, you can't rebuild it, so even if they filed a claim, it would never have to be paid."

"Maybe you should get a job at Met-Life," Joe said.

"I'd probably hang myself with the tie I'd have to wear."

"Everyone's gonna talk about the historical damage," I started, "but what about all the people that are probably dead? I saw on the news today they don't even know how many they're looking at."

"People die," Joe said.

"Joe, that's cold, even for you."

"People die. It's true," Joe said again. "It's only a tragedy when humans have something to do with it. God had your day mapped out before you were born. You just have to *live life well*, as if today's that day."

"Yeah but you grieve when it's a friend, or someone you have a bond with."

Joe stirred his coffee with a pencil. "You grieve the loss of friends and family because you miss them being around," he said. "It's not because you think death destroyed them. It just put them a little bit out of earshot. See, the Irish have a healthy respect for death."

"Drink that much whiskey and you should."

"That's low, even for one so low as yourself." Joe didn't get offended with drunken Irish jokes, unless they sucked.

"Eh, just breakin' up the monotony, my friend," I said. "Don't want the patrons to be fallin' asleep, listenin' to your catalogue of aches and pains…"

"Oh, don't even go there," Joe said, laughing. "For each one I got stories."

"And issues!" I added, quickly.

"Yeah, maybe I should start a newspaper. I'll call it … The Naked Irishman."

"As long as there aren't any pictures," I joked, then plunked my buck on the counter. "Well, Joe," I said, as I got up and stretched, "this is where I say it's been a pleasure doin' business wit' ya."

"And this is the part where I take your money and plan my trip to Aruba." Joe snatched the bill.

"You'll burn to a crisp," I said as I headed for the door.

"Take it easy, Joe."

"Yeah, Barney. You too."

I went back home and went through the routines to get ready for La Junta. I wanted to get there early, but not too early. I wasn't thinking of fashionably late or anything. I just didn't want to spend more time there than I had to. Not my crowd. Too uptight; too rich, too flashy and too showy. My preferred crowd didn't take themselves so seriously.

Amp? Check. *Guitar?* Check. *At least two cords?* Check. I had put new strings on the axe about a week ago. They were broken in by now, and still relatively new. *Emergency strings?* Check. I was guessing it to be an acoustic open mic, so I didn't bother to grab effects pedals. I only use them when absolutely necessary. Too many pedal disappointments when playing out, I guess. I grabbed my lucky Pez dispenser, and threw it in the back of the amp. Long story.

I packed the gear into my van, an old Econoline. I took off for the nearest oil spill (gas station,) to fill up. I picked up a paper and took off south on Route 30 for La Junta.

Anno Luce was as beautiful as ever, with the fresco of twilight painted across the city skyline. Flyin' down Jefferson with the window down, crankin' *Birds of Fire* (again, the Mahavishnu Orchestra was insane), The Paradigm Building spiked from the ground like a thorn of steel, concrete and glass. The building is completely conical; I believe it's the only one of its kind in America. It's sixty stories to the tip, but about 50 stories of office space. I'd never been in there.

Paradigm is a tech company that specializes in Cellular Automata Virtua, or 'CAV', as they call it. CAV was just a souped-up version of virtual reality.
Anno Luce was an enclave for the artificial intelligence community. Pretty far off the American radar. But I can tell you that at least five corporations had headquarters in Anno Luce and dealt with some part of computer 'intelligence.' As I said, Paradigm dealt with CAV. There was AZURA that sold data modeling software. There was ArcEpic, which dealt with programming for use in

psychology. There was ZNexus, which worked with nano-scale wiring grids; all the stuff that you'd need if you were creating artificial life. I knew they were up to something, probably no good. I only hoped it would blow up in their faces.

I turned off Trinidad Avenue and onto Johnson St as La Junta came into view. La Junta was a nice looking place; pueblo style, all lit up with blue and red light. Its décor was never my problem with it. I parked as far back as I could, though I couldn't exactly hide an Econoline. I went to the door without my gear. I liked to go in first when I went out to a jam.

The inside of La Junta was amazing, I have to admit that. Polished chrome, black walls that almost made you feel like it was all a big stage. All kinds of lighting equipment strung up atop the large dance-floor. The whole place was etched in marble and chrome.

I can tell you I was in natural unease as I walked in. It was dim, as I would expect, and I eyed around to look for Jennifer. I didn't see her, but I did see at least three people that I knew and couldn't stand. Two of them I went to school with, and one I knew through work. Derrick Teymon, the one I knew from work, was a Councilman for the 12th Ward of Anno Luce; our ward. He'd been gunning to take down our Mission because we were the 'voice of last resort' when there were problems in the neighborhood.
One time, there was a tree on Sheraton Lane that needed to come down. It was always dropping branches, and the thing had to be about eighty feet tall. We called Teymon about it, and he said he'd get the city to look into it, but we got nothing. Having gotten the run-around before, we decided to have people gather the limbs when they fell (they were *always* falling,) and we had the neighborhood kids paint them. We then called a press conference at the mission and announced that they were for sale, to help hire a private company to take the tree down.
Yeah ... we did that.
Needless to say the tree was taken down by the city the next day. And that's just one thing we'd done to him. We weren't political, though. Mt. Calvary had a long history of having to make noise for the neighborhood, through many years and many council

members. Teymon, like the rest of them, had wanted our institutional head.

The other two, Brad Carr and Judy Myers-Carr; I went to school with them. They were both pretty rotten in high school, and they'd not changed growing up. They never said hi to me when they saw me. Oh well. Brad was a broker, and Judy was his drink-at-home wife.

I finally spotted Jennifer, who was ravishing. She was over by the stage, pulling cords out of a denim duffle-bag. She was talking to some guy in a ... I don't know ... it looked like a beret. Not military either. Like a French beret.

'Weird,' I thought as I walked up to them to say hi.

"Jennifer," I said.

She looked up from her duffle-bag and stared at me, blankly.

"I'm Barney. We met in Luella's."

She acted like she remembered, but I knew she didn't. "Oh yeah, Barney, hi! I'm glad you came out tonight. Now, you play?"

"Guitar."

"Oh, okay! Great! Just sign in and pick a time." She pointed to a small table off to the right.

"Okay," I said, and before I turned to go and sign in, the guy next to Jennifer said; "Just one thing. Everybody comes here; they wanna be Eddie Van Halen. But if you're too loud, we'll have to turn you down." He accentuated the point by pinching his fingers.

Jennifer laughed and gave him that look like; *okay, she's into that guy.* Wow. What an idiot. *Eddie Van Halen.* Ya know I probably had almost ten years on that fake *Inspector Poirot.* And the way he said it, like he was cute or something. With the exception of the fact that the girl I was into was into such a tool, it would have been better than comedy.

So I was in the situation. The place sucked, enemies at tables five and six, and Jennifer was gaga over an imbecile. Should I just leave? That would be the easy answer. But I'd not been through the life I'd been through by always doing what was easy. So, I signed my name, incidentally on the first spot.

I went to my car and grabbed my gear. It was small, yet

powerful, so it was portable, yet heavy. I got the stuff in, and put it all under one of the tables. I went to get a soda. I wasn't worried about my stuff. That crowd wouldn't touch equipment that looked as beat up as mine. I paid the bartender five bucks for a soda with no ice. (The no-ice was my request. Ice costs them less than soda, and I want the most for my five bucks.)

Jennifer and Frenchie (His real name was Gene) started the evening. Now I gave them the benefit of the doubt musically. I don't pick music apart because I don't like the player. Tools and imbeciles (and the women who love them) can still make beautiful music. I just wasn't feelin' it there.

For starters, if you're playing acoustic, you gotta have movement. I love acoustic when you can hear the fingers flyin' on the strings, something to give the rhythm a pulse. Her playing was kind of thin there.

But that wasn't the bad part. Jennifer's playing was at least good. Gene was playing bongos. *Miserably.* He must have been trying to give it some kind of African rhythm. Now, I've heard African rhythms. Real live ones, and not at a show either. We have a West African enclave on the Mount. I've many times heard traditional rhythms. Gene was guessing.

They played a few songs, like five or something. Jennifer was loud when she read at Luella's, but she was singing softly here. I couldn't hear the words she was singing. She sounded alright vocally, but she needed to project.

At the end of the five songs, she said, "Okay, we've got a few musicians who are going to come up for you tonight." Gene handed her the list. "First up," she said, "is Barney Sheehan. Let's give him a warm welcome."

The 'warm welcome' would've frozen my soda. I think I heard two claps, one of which was Jennifer's.
I set up quick - I made sure I had that one down in less than two minutes.

"Do you want percussion?" Gene said to me as I was setting up, pointing to the bongos.

"No thanks. It might break my concentration," I said. *For sure.*

"Yeah, it's not for everybody."

'*Is there anybody it's actually for?*' I wished that thought had slipped through my manners.

I went to turn on the amp. Nothing. '*Shit!*' I thought. '*Not now.*'

I slapped it on the side, and it let out a piercing shriek. '*Uh-Oh.*' That got everyone's attention. Gene got within earshot and said, "You do that one more time, you're out."

"Sorry," I said. I was getting a signal, but it was low. '*Great, I'm gonna look like a fool in front of Teymon.*' I realized that the signal was too low to be heard by anyone except me. This was a crisis.

Then suddenly I was at perfect volume. Not only that, but when I hit a minor seventh chord, it was the best quality I'd heard in it since I bought the amp two years ago. '*Miracle.*'
So, not to waste any more time, I turned to face the crowd, who I couldn't see because of the stage lights, and then I let the one-man symphony roar.

I was in the zone. I couldn't marvel at it and keep it up, so I just stayed there a little while. I built it up to a crescendo, paused for a hair, then, looking in the last direction I knew Frenchie to be in, I slapped on the guitar to make our enclave proud (wished they were there.)
I didn't want to end on that; it would have been insulting, so I tapered it into a funk riff I was working on earlier that day. I played that kinetically for a few measures, and then stopped it all abruptly.

Nothing at first. Then I heard clapping. From everywhere. I was still in a daze, musically. I walked off stage and saw Gene first. The beret was hard to miss, I'm sorry to say. He was smiling and clapping too. I suddenly felt sorry I showed him up with the African slap-beat.

Then I saw Alejandro and Yashua. They were sitting at one of the back tables. I saw that Yashua's arm was in a sling. I rushed over.

"Wow, man… " Alejandro started before I cut him off.

"What happened?" I asked, and pointed to the sling. "Are you okay?" I asked Yashua.

Yashua nodded yes, and Alejandro added, "He's fine. He had to get a few stitches, that's all."

"What happened?"

"We had an..." Ale' hesitated, "...incident, at the Mission this morning. Yashua was in the lobby, talking to Jimmy Angel, and this guy comes walking in, sees him, and lunges at him. I didn't even know he had a knife."

"A *knife!?*"

Alejandro continued. "Yashua put his arm up, and he got cut once, and when I grabbed the guy, he got loose for a second, and he cut Yashua the second time. After that I was able to restrain him."

"He got cut twice?" I said.

"Yeah, neither was too bad though. They didn't bleed as much as I thought they would, and we got him to Ascension General real quick."

"So, you just got stitches?" I asked Yashua. He smiled, actually, and said, "Yes. Seven of them."

"Didn't even wince," Alejandro said. "Seriously, he's a trooper."

"You said this happened this morning. How come you didn't call me at the house? I was at home," I said.

"I tried. It's been disconnected. Did someone forget to pay his phone bill?"

"Aw Jesus," I said, "I didn't have the cash last week. I sent in a payment yesterday! I didn't think they'd disconnect me."

"We tracked you down ... wasn't easy though," Alejandro said. "I finally thought to stop at Joe's, and he told us where you were going."

"So, who was this guy?" I asked.

"That's it, *Guy*. Guy Francis. That's what his library card said. I was surprised he *had* one!" said Alejandro. "He was strung out on something, or out of his mind. He just sought Yashua out. He was uttering gibberish, like he was trying to speak some foreign language, but it was just gib'. You know me and languages."

Alejandro knew several languages, even dialects of some languages. "It didn't sound like anything I've ever come across."

"Yashua," I said, "You know languages, right?"

"Yes. And he was speaking Aramaic," Yashua said, calmly.

"Aramaic?" I asked. "Like ... Aramaic as in the Bible?"

"Yes," Yashua replied.

"Probably not exactly like Biblical Aramaic," Alejandro said. "I mean, I know there's *Syriac*, which is a modern Aramaic, but surely it's lost the proper pronunciations from the Biblical version..."

"No, it was perfect," Yashua pointed out, again, very calmly.

"C'mon ... nobody remembers those pronunciations," Alejandro said.

"In ancient Israel, there were a group of men known as the Essenes. Are either of you familiar with them?"

"Yeah, they were the ones with the Dead Sea Scrolls."

"Well, yes," Yashua said. "They also held a spiritual tradition of worship that survived over millennia. Women were not allowed into this sect, so this tradition was carried on without anyone being born into it. Tradition can withstand years, and real, *Biblical* Aramaic has indeed survived. You just need to know where to find it." He smiled.

"Okay, so, even if it does, it's obviously rare. How in the world do two strangers intersect that both know Biblical Aramaic. I mean, you don't know that guy, right?"

"He is indeed unknown to me," Yashua said.

"So then how do you explain it?" Alejandro asked Yashua.

"I don't," he said, and took a sip of his soda. "Fate is under the Dominion of God, and since God is beyond explanation, so too is Fate."

"So, what did he say to you?" Alejandro asked.

"I'd rather not get into it," Yashua said. "Nothing nice."

We sat there for a little while. "I wanted to get Yashua away from the Mission for a little while," Alejandro finally said. "I figured we'd come and check you out."

"What'd ya' think?" I asked.

"Incredible!" Alejandro said. "I knew you had it in ya'."

"Truly inspired," Yashua added.

"Hey, guess what?" I said to Alejandro. "That girl Jennifer

likes some guy." I looked over to where they were sitting.

"Oh, the one in the beret?" he asked, looking where I was looking.

"Yeah, that's corny, isn't it?"

"Just another fish in the sea," Alejandro said. He knew I was hopin' to get with her.

Picking up on the vibe, Yashua said, "The one for you will not sing so softly."

I laughed. "Thanks, both," I said. "Oh, Ale', I saw Teymon here."

"Did you have a chance to piss in his martini?"

"Nah, I didn't have to go," I said. Alejandro and Yashua both laughed.

"What do you say we blow this pop-stand?" I said. "This place is boring."

"Where to?" Alejandro asked.

"Luella's is open 'till two-thirty,"

"We roll!" Alejandro said.

I went over and made my good-byes to the fair Jennifer and her French Connection, and Alejandro helped me lug my gear out to the van. With Luella's on the evening horizon, we concluded our stint in La Junta's.

Chapter Three

Luella's was great. Yashua continued to amaze me. The level of knowledge he possessed, on arcane bits of history, politics; I mean, he knew things to a level of detail that almost made me think he was making it up, but he was very matter-of-fact. I believed him. We were there until thrown out at two-thirty. Then we all called it a night.

Off to work the next day, as my alarm clock sounded the ol'

'Get out of bed you lazy jackass!' at the crack of eight-thirty. Work at nine. I always cut it close. I had my routine though. I got it done.

I got to the Mission just after nine fifteen so I must have been lagging a little that day. It happened, now and then. No one there cared unless it was half an hour or more.

I got in the door in time to see a police officer at the desk. '*Oh no, not again...*' I thought, and picked up the pace.

The officer, Seneda, his name was, was just there to find out whether Yashua was going to press assault charges on Guy Francis. Apparently despite the advice of Alejandro and the officer both, Yashua refused. He said that the man's *storm had passed* and that he was forgiven. By now this didn't at all surprise me, and I don't think it surprised Alejandro either. But we had to look out for Yashua, and Guy could've come back. I said that to him, and he replied; 'Guy Francis would trouble him no more.'

In reality, we couldn't force Yashua to press charges, but we could have pressed charges ourselves. Perhaps not for assault, but for something. In the end it was Zee's call, which made it Alejandro's call, since Zee wasn't there that week.
After thinking about it for half a minute, he decided that if Yashua wasn't going to press charges, we wouldn't either. This was after much insistence from Yashua, because Alejandro wanted to do it.

However, we'd always, in the end, gone along with the wishes of our guests, and even though we had reservations about Francis being on the street, we had to make that hard call and go along with Yashua.

After that, it was pretty much an unremarkable day. I have to say it was the first unremarkable day that week, so the mood was pretty light. In fact, I 'assassinated' Yashua with silly string. We had a game we played in the office called '*Contract Killer.*' We all had silly string, and we had to 'do a hit' on someone who was a member of the office. Yashua was, well, kind of staff by then, so that day was his day. (In light of what I would learn about him later, I felt *really* bad about it. He just laughed, though.)

Other than that, nothing, all day. In fact, all the way through the weekend things were more or less dull. I did my intakes, Alejandro did his thing, and Yashua talked to people. I was quite

impressed with the fact that the three people Yashua was assigned
to (we only gave him three cases to start with officially, though he
talked to everyone,) were all late-stagers, and they had not failed
any breathalyzers when we'd administered them, which was
nightly. Rare indeed. But I'd stopped questioning good things.

Sunday, as I had promised, I got up at nine-thirty to get
ready to go with Yashua to Church. I took care of the three 'S's, and
then dressed in my finest, which wasn't saying much. A decent,
button-down, blue shirt, slacks, not my usual jeans. I had a tweed
coat I'd secured from Goodwill. Looking sharp.
I remembered what Yashua had said about gold, and checked to
make sure I wasn't so adorned.

I hopped out of the house around ten after ten. Yashua told
me the service was at eleven-thirty, so I knew I'd have time to get
there. Yashua said *a few blocks from there*, but the place was across
town, at least a twenty minute drive by Anno Luce traffic. I drove
down Jefferson with actual radio silence. I hadn't been to church
since before Anna, so I was nervous.

Anna was a friend I had lost. At one time we were going
out, but we broke up. We had our fights and bitterness, but I
always still loved her, and cared about her. We were friends when
she died. She died in a car accident, so it was unexpected. She was
young and healthy. I was in the car with her, but I awoke in the
hospital. She didn't. It was Alejandro who had to tell me. I couldn't
believe him at first.

Walking into the funeral home on the day of her wake
brought the full sum of reality to bear on my perspective. I can't
even say I tried to keep my composure. Her mother, far closer to
Anna than me, was calm, and strong, and I had to walk out. I'll
never forgive myself for not being able to be stronger that day.

We used to argue about each others flaws. But her death
taught me that what I found to be such pressing flaws in her when
she was alive, became what I missed the most when she was gone.
I identified her by those flaws. Her flaws made her unique. And
seeing those flaws in others reminded me of her.

So I went through a real bad time. I was in college then, and

I tried to focus on my studies, *for her,* but I eventually dropped out. I went back, but not before spending a year unemployed. I didn't get out much then, afraid I'd run into some girl that looked like Anna, or sounded like her. Oh yeah, it was that bad. I never blamed God directly, but I was very confused by it all. I knew in my heart she was in a better place, so in the end I felt the need to move in a direction she would have been happy with. So, Philosophy degree in hand, I made my way to Mt. Calvary Mission.

I think I would've headed down that road anyway. But Anna's death, I don't know, lit a fire or something.

But enough about me; back to Church. As I said, I hadn't been there in four years, so I was a little nervous. Radio silence. The Anno Luce skyline loomed ahead.

I arrived at the Mission just shy of ten-thirty. I walked in and saw Yashua, who came over and said, "I need to pray now. After that we'll depart."

"Okay, but it takes twenty-minutes to drive there. We'll have to get going."

"It takes no time to walk there," Yashua said, and went to his room.

'Walk there?' I thought. 'Is he nuts?' Anno Luce is small, population-wise, but the land area is rather large, close to thirty square miles, so I couldn't fathom how we were going to get there walking, period, much less in under twenty minutes. But hey, I figured, the most it meant was that I'd not have to go to Church.

Yashua prayed for about fifteen minutes. He got out, and in no particular hurry, grabbed his overcoat and said, "Let's go."

Though I had no expectation of actually arriving in the church by eleven-thirty, I nonetheless endeavored to the attempt. Yashua and I talked. I spoke about Anna, and the questions and confusion that I, to that day, still had, and he told me that 'one life's end begins the next.' I kind of understood ... kind of. But Yashua told me more about himself, stories about places he'd been to, and others about him growing up.

"We're here," Yashua said.

I looked to a small church in a store-front. There was a homeless man sitting out front, I knew that because I knew him. His name was Taylor.

"Hey Barney!" Taylor said as he rose up and walked over. "You joinin' us for Church today?"

"Sure am, Taylor," I said. I couldn't believe we were there already. We couldn't have been walking more than ten minutes. We were clear across town. Amazing.

"How are you, friend?" Yashua said to Taylor.

"Doin' all right," Taylor said, grabbing his lapels.

We walked in. It was small, of course. There was a statue of Jesus, about four feet tall, and a couple of candles dotted around. They were different colors and mismatched. It looked like they were using whatever they could pull together.

"What faith there is here," Yashua said, looking around, "could not be replicated in the most palatial edifice the kings of the world could commission."

"I feel a lot of warmth here," I said, and I actually saw a few people I knew from the Mission. This was like La Junta's in reverse.

"This is the root of true faith, and fellowship," he said and went to sit down. "Come," he beckoned.

We sat down and I looked at the hymnals - old, of course. And the books weren't the same either, so I figured they were just able to scrounge these books together.

"No statue can equal the time these people have spent gathering this collection of hymnals. They have next to nothing, and for what little they have, they go to these lengths to thank God. They are continually being tested, as Job was, and each day they pray, and they thank Him. The world could learn from them."

"Yeah," I said. "This gives me hope."

"So, today you gain hope," Yashua said. "The next time, so you may feel to give it."

"Yeah, I think I could swing something," I said, smiled, and the Reverend Johns took the lectern.

The Reverend Johns was Arthur Johns. He had actually worked with me on occasion with Christmas dinners. He was a shorter, wiry guy with a salt-and-pepper beard. He was always remarkably dressed, never expensive or too flashy. A light brown felt fedora adorned his head every time I'd seen him.

"Brothers and sisters, we are once again on this day gathered together to remember the one who had come in the name of our Lord, who's name was Jesus, whose root was all of justice and humanity. Yea' though we struggle, and toil, and face many obstacles, and battle many demons, we walk always in the example of He who came to illuminate the path of righteousness."

"Amen," said one man in the crowd. "Praise Jesus," said another.

"Now, this week, we mourn the passing of our brother Daniel Jenkins," Rev. Johns continued. "Let us have a moment of silence for the passing of our brother, into that better world."

I knew Daniel Jenkins too. He used to panhandle in front of the Mission. He was a real decent, friendly guy. He refused our many offers to put him up, and he was so friendly we didn't bother him about the panhandling. That was why I hadn't seen him around for the past couple of days. I'd miss him.

The Rev. Johns then said, "We were not able to have a proper funeral, but I would like to eulogize for a moment."

More 'Amens' were uttered from the crowd.

"Daniel was a wonderful companion to us all. He had his troubles. Many did not know he was caring for a sick mother as well as himself. By the grace of God he was able to make money, panhandling each day so he could buy her food and medicine. He often went without himself. He taught many of our neighborhood kids to read in his life; many who, otherwise, would not have ever learned. He lived every day for those around him, and loved the Lord with all his heart. May the Lord receive His servant home, on this day."

"Amen!" and "Hallelujah!" filled the room.

The Rev. Johns paused, and then began to address the room with a new composure. "Brothers and sisters, as you know, I've been keeping abreast of Paradigm's desire to bring about artificial life, life *without* the Breath of our True and Ever-Living God. I must tell you, brothers and sisters, what I have to say is not good."

We all perked up, myself included. '*This ought to be interesting,*' I thought.

"I have learned that Paradigm, in conjunction with the companies AZURA, ZNexus and ArcEpic, have announced the introduction of the HIPPO." I heard a chuckle.

"Laugh not," Rev. Johns said. "HIPPO is no animal. It stands for *Human Interactive Peripheral Polymorphic* systems. Now, I quote here from the C.E.O. of Paradigm." He pulled out a newspaper clipping. "...'This system will be able to create a state of bliss, completely free of drugs, that can not only be enjoyed by one user, but by multiple users, sharing the experience together.' He goes on to say that; 'The device consists of a transceiver, and two electrodes; one worn in a headband, and one in a wristband.'"

Yashua sat there with a thousand yard gaze. I don't know what he was looking at. I just thought the sermon was a little bit extreme. It would be yet one more drug-like thing people could get addicted to.

"Beware the mark of the beast, for it has been foretold in Revelations to be a mark upon the forehead, or upon the wrist. We here in Anno Luce may very well be at the root of the bringing forth of the Beast. We must be strong, and pray that in his Divine Judgment, we must ask our Lord to hold His Hand in releasing this evil upon the Earth."

He paused briefly, then went on, "And if, Lord, in Your Divine Wisdom, You see that it is time, then we pray that none may fall victim to it, and lose their way."

Again, more *Amens* and *Hallelujahs*.

"And Lord, if any of Your children can fight this, may You give them the strength to keep steady their hand, true their mind, and sharp their spirit."

"Amen," said all.

"And as always, Lord, please extend Your traveling mercies upon us as we leave this place of gathering today, and continue, as always, to allow us the capacity to love and serve You, and each other."

"Amen."

I was genuinely touched by the service overall, but I was especially intrigued by the 'HIPPO' thing. I had seen something in the paper about it, but hadn't paid it any mind. On the way home, I asked Yashua what he thought about it.

"That, *thing*, will be the full and total enslavement of Man. Take heed to his words, for they are true," he replied, bluntly.

"Yeah, but won't it just be like one more drug?" I said.

"Drugs alter the mind in a pre-defined manner, specified by their chemistry," Yashua replied as Anno Luce seemed to just fly by us. "No drug is perfect, or covers all bases. And tolerance develops. But this machine is different. It perpetuates an all-encompassing state of bliss. This machine will be more than addictive; it will perform the functions of a man-made God."

I thought about it. It was a reasonable conclusion. "Well, wouldn't the government control it eventually, like other drugs?" I asked.

"They won't waste an opportunity to make people docile," Yashua said.

I had to agree with him there. "What about the Morality Brigade people, like that Rev. Biggs. Won't he be screamin' about it?"

"He gives it his blessing! Soon, he'll say it is God's gift to the world." Yashua had a sad look in his eyes as he spoke.

"And the world will buy it, too."

"Not everyone," Yashua said as he glanced at me. "You won't."

"No, I've had my share of perpetual bliss," I joked.

"You'll be hunted."

"Probably," I said.

"They might not have Silly String," he said.

"You're not pissed about that, are you?" I asked him.

"No, it was a clean hit," he said, and smiled.

We arrived back at the Mission just as fast as we arrived at the Church. Which turned out to be about ten minutes.
Later that day I drove to the Church, using the same route we took, and looked at my trip odometer. Five miles. This meant we were walking thirty miles an hour. *Impossible.* I drove back, and again, five miles. And that way was the closest thing to 'As the crow flies'

as you could get in Anno Luce. I couldn't figure it out.

I drove home and soaked in the tub. I kept thinking about the Paradigm thing. After I got out of the tub, I went to my computer. I didn't have the internet cable connected, but I had all kinds of software I was able to pirate from friends. One was a CAV program. Mike Jones – Jonesy - used to work for Paradigm. He wrote software for them, low-level stuff though. But he was able to get a few goodies snuck outta there, one of which was sitting in front of me.

Zygote 3.4, as the program was called, consisted of a series of rules and algorithms that could be applied to a pattern to create a screen display. Very easy use, I would add. You pick a rule, and a pattern, and hit 'Start.' It did the rest. I made quite a few psychedelic-looking screen displays with it. But that night I was looking at it a bit differently.

Cellular Automata Virtua, at least in the form I knew it, created those displays continuously. They changed on their own; no element of the display was pre-recorded. It, well, *self-generated*. Literature I had read on CAV said that it was essentially a recreation of the world of Physical Laws, affecting a pixel as opposed to a person, or object, or whatever.

Each pixel was an individual unit. Like our world of physical things. Each pixel followed a 'rule' to determine what its next color would be. Just like the Physical Laws and constants, and the rule was based upon the colors of each of the adjacent pixels at the previous cycle. In laymen's terms, you were affected by the world that immediately surrounded you.

CAV replicated the physical world for a group of pixels, your screen, and recreated, in color, a *living process*; 'alive' in the sense of physics, and in some cases, biology. CAV had no 'intelligence' to speak of. Any activity, no matter how ordered and carried out, was 'uni-focus', one process over-all, so it had the intelligence of a bacteria, at best. The 'intelligence' part was a whole other area of study.

I had, to that point, been studying CAV more out of academic interest, but now that I *really* looked at it, I came to a conclusion. '*Yashua is right!*' I thought. This very program replicated, or attempted to replicate, existence. I had hoped that they wouldn't be successful at creating artificial life, but I was thinking of it as a person. Viewing it as a man-made God, it had become more than a hope; it was a plea.

I looked at Zygote, and closed it out. I moved the icon to the Recycle Bin, turned the computer off, and went into the living room to watch some TV. As always, Darren Freeman was the star pitcher on the mound.

"John Mills, reporting live from Venice," he said, as a remote box blinked out in the top right.

"We now go to Janice Crenshaw, who's been in Athens since the quakes began. How is it out there, Janice?" he asked.

"Well, it seems to have generally calmed down. We haven't felt any aftershocks since Thursday. Friday began the rescue effort, which is continuing today, and will likely continue for quite some time."

"Now Janice, I've heard that there were a number of sizeable aftershocks on that day, with, almost a, *pattern* to them? Can you tell us about that?"

"Yes, Darren. Apparently there were fourteen aftershocks. They occurred within a short time of each other, starting about an hour after the second quake. They seemed to follow two major fault lines, and they seemed to be," she paused, "perpendicular ... almost to the fault."

"I'm not sure what you mean," Darren said.

"What I mean is, if you were to draw a straight line from the first aftershock to the next, it would be perpendicular to the direction of the fault. It would actually bridge the fault lines."

"Now, have they ever seen that before?" Darren asked, puzzled.

"No, this is the first time," Janice explained. "They say they'll hope to learn the cause of this soon, but right now they're far too busy with what it left behind."

Janice paused before she carried on her report. "These quakes actually tore the fault-lines to some degree, Darren. There's just a lot of devastation here."

"Now, Janice, we know that Athens, and Venice, and

countless other historical cities have been severely damaged. I mean, from a historical perspective, how much have we lost?"

"Darren, Athens is destroyed. Venice has sustained severe damage. There are just countless cities that have been around for hundreds, in some cases a thousand or more years ... that have been effectively wiped from existence."

"I see," Darren said in a lowered voice. "Janice, as you may have heard, in a press conference today, the President has pledged $15 million dollars in aid for this. From where you are now, what do you think the international response is going to be to the President's pledge?"

'Well, Darren," Janice said, "I know the people of Athens are appreciative of any help coming from the international community, but to be honest with you, I'm not sure the President truly understands the magnitude of what just happened here. The Greek and Italian governments alone are spending over $200 million dollars *a day* for the rescue effort alone right now."

"Do you think America should be pitching in more?" Darren said.

"I can't tell you that specifically," Janice said, "but I can tell you that Syria has pledged $50 million dollars, and the Republic of Togo, which is a small nation in West Africa, has pledged $15 million dollars," Janice said, looking behind her.

She was on a street in Athens, or what remained of a street, anyways. The street itself was only just visible beneath the pile of twisted steel and structural remnants.
I could see men working, and I saw a red cross on a white sheet. I could hear noise in the background, but it was hard to tell what it was.

She turned back to the camera and said, "So, there is a sense that the U.S. could send more."

"Thank you, Janice. Janice Crenshaw, in Athens this evening," Darren said. He then turned to a different camera angle, and said, "With us this evening in our studio are Professor Jeremy Rubin, professor of language and Greek mythology at Syracuse University, and the Reverend Joseph Biggs, A minister of many denominations, Leader of the Righteous Brigade, who just concluded the five-day 'Moral March' in Washington DC. Good evening to you both."

'*Damn. Everything in reach is hard enough to break the TV.*' I thought of turning it off, but hopefully Professor Rubin would be able to shut him up. It was worth a look.

They both said good evening, and Darren said, "Professor Rubin, let's start with you. Obviously, Athens is a center of world history. What will the likely effect be of its near, or complete destruction?"

"Well Darren," the professor said, leaning in with his hands clasped, "What we're looking at here is the loss of the physical reference for what may be called the birth of western civilization. You have to remember that this city is over 2,600 years old, and at one time was a state in-and-of *itself*. The first democracy, 2,500 years ago, was an Athenian democracy. Plus, look at the sheer architectural loss alone. The Parthenon, destroyed completely. The Theseion, demolished. The Olympieum, gone. The Erechtheum, only a corner of it's standing. And we're only talking about pre-Hadrian historical sites here. This city was a symbol of our past that we'll now only see pictures and videos of."

"Certainly," Darren agreed, and then he turned to Rev. Biggs. "Now, Reverend Biggs, I heard that you issued a press release announcing that this was the work of ... God?"

The Reverend Biggs sat up, and I swear I saw him puff out his chest a little. "Well, Darryl," he said.

"Darren,"

"Yes, I'm sorry, *Darren*," he said.

'*Wow, he's such a prick!*' I thought to myself.

He continued. "I have, for many years now, accepted Jesus Christ as my personal Lord and Savior." I winced. "And the Bible says 'I am the Lord Thy God, thall shalt have no other gods before me. As we all know, these were temples of other gods. Our God is a Vengeful One."

Darren was just incredulous. "Are you saying that God did this in vengeance against the Greeks for having built temples to other gods?"

"That's exactly what I'm saying," The Reverend said,

nonchalantly. "This day and age, with all of the 'gangsta' rap and the liberal 'lifestyle', God needed to remind us of His Wrath."

'Gangsta?' That just did not sound right comin' out of Biggs's mouth.

Darren, ever vigilant, asked, "With all due respect, Reverend, the casualty figures for these *two* quakes, one of which, incidentally, occurred in northern Italy," he turned ever so slightly to the side as he said that last part. "…are estimated to be over two hundred thousand. Many of those feared dead are Christians. How do you feel about that?"

The Reverend slouched, seeming slightly agitated. "If you've accepted the Lord Jesus Christ into your heart as *I* have." - I laughed out loud as he said those words. - "then you will be in the Lord's Kingdom, and if you don't accept the Lord Jesus Christ as your Lord and Savior, then you will be standing outside the Gates. When the Lord has you in His sights, you'd better hope you're on the right side."

"So, you don't feel sorry for the families of the victims?" Darren asked.

"Oh, I feel sorry for the families of the Christians who lost their lives," he replied, and he looked like he was back-peddling a little. "The Righteous Brigade has collected funds and has donated an amount of one hundred thousand dollars to the families of our Christian brothers and sisters."

Darren looked at him for just a second longer than usual. He was probably still stunned by such an incredible buffoon. He went to say something, and Professor Rubin cut in.

"To address the, if any, *point* of Reverend Biggs's argument; the New Testament was written in Greek. There were places hit by this quake that were important to the early Christian church," the professor said.

And again, the Reverend Biggs spoke. "When the Lord comes down to bring salvation to the *true* believers, he will rebuild those parts with fine gold."

"I'm just incredulous about the arguments being put forth by the Reverend Biggs," the professor said to Darren.

The Reverend continued. "Soon we will be able to

experience the Peace that is the Lord Jesus Christ on Earth, and those who doubt now will come face-to-face with their folly."

Sensing that Biggs was tugging the leash loose, Darren acted. "That's about all the time I have for the two of you. Thank you both, gentlemen."

They both said their good-byes, and Darren brought the show to commercial.

I couldn't believe how people could follow that guy. Poor elderly people gave him a portion of their Social Security checks. It was insane. It frustrated the hell out of me.

I went to the kitchen, and prepared my banquet; Ramen noodles. The best food no-money can buy. When I was grabbing the saucepan, I noticed that my tattoo had distorted even further. It no longer even resembled a cross. It scared me, I have to be honest. Cancer was all I could think of. My mother had it. My grandmother had it. This seemed like something that could be a symptom of abnormal cell growth. I'd had a doctor's appointment two days before that I'd missed. I didn't feel sick, so I figured it could wait. I'd have to re-schedule.

After I satisfied the nutritional requirements, I hopped on the computer and noticed that the Zygote icon was back on the desktop. 'I know I threw that away,' I thought to myself.

I went to re-chuck it, and thought about it for a second. Instead I turned the program on. The garbled black and white screen appeared; the customary opening to the program. I remembered Jonesy saying that you could create a virus with it. He said the only problem with it was that the virus attacked CAV applications only, so it wasn't too good for getting a doctored photograph of the First Lady in a teddy on the White House website. (I like to aim high, what can I say?) In light of that, I hadn't seen the useful benefit of a CAV virus. It dawned on me then that, if the HIPPO thing took off, maybe the little germ *could* prove useful.

Jonesy gave me the virus on a piece of paper as a series of rules and 'maps' (screen displays) to be copied, and injected into other rules. Some were stock rules; others were algorithmic rules manually entered, and copied to bit-planes (I kept it because a hot girl I met at a club a week later gave me her number, which I wrote on the other side.) So after retrieving the formula, I plugged away, and upon the final sequence, the screen went blank. The zygote screen, that is. Nothing. I couldn't close it out, either.

Eventually I had to control-alt-delete to turn it off with the Task Manager. Funny thing, too, 'cause when I did, the Zygote icon was gone from the desktop. I clicked on my Recycle Bin, to see if it was in the trash. Nope. That didn't make sense. I went to the 'All Programs' list to see if it was still there. Gone. I even went as far as to search for it, no results. It was as if the program had never been on my hard drive. Couldn't understand it; I figured I'd have to ask Jonesy about it sometime. Maybe *that* was what the virus did. I didn't know, so I plugged in the internet cable and hopped on-line to *The Mug*; Anno Luce's favorite blog-site.

The Mug was a political blog, mostly about local government and politics. 'King Java', the moderator, was a good chap, or lady; no one really knew which, such is the beauty of anonymity. For the most part, the bloggers who visited were intelligent, well spoken, and it had been seen as a 'back-channel' of sorts for political people, usually lower to mid-level, political aids, activists and so on. Today the first story was, surprisingly, about HIPPO.

I read the story, which basically said everything that the Rev. Johns had talked about in Church. Chucky, one of the regular bloggers, commented about the whole 'mark of the beast' issue. *Che Guevara*, another, more radical blogger (could ya' guess by the name?) wrote a nice post on how the government was going to use the HIPPO to 'control the masses.' One of the few times I agreed with Che', I might add. The most interesting post was from Arius, who I'd not seen post before. I knew most of the people who posted on that site.

Arius said this project was being underwritten by the 'Purity from the Release of Drugs.' *PRD?* I'd heard of them, who hadn't? They were the source of many anti-drug commercials, and subsequently many jokes from wayward adolescents.

'*Why would they underwrite this?*' I asked myself.

It also went on to say that; '*As we all know who's behind that!*' I didn't. Really. Felt stupid, I usually knew the conspiracy stuff. I made a mental note to find out.

There wasn't, in the posts, any central argument though. It all seemed hodge-podge. I'd seen that on The Mug occasionally. It usually meant that the issue was over the gang's collective heads. I have to admit that, at that time, it was still over mine.

I scanned over the other issues. A few rants about Council people, including Teymon. Nothing truly inspired on that count, though. I managed to break the eye-lock on my PC to retire it for the evening.

I abandoned CNN that night, opting to read. I was reading a book about Irish Independence, by Leon Uris, called *Trinity*. It was a good book. Joe McGee gave it to me. The central character was a Roman Catholic. Joe said it was his favorite. With that I called it a night.

Chapter Four

A blast of *KALR* greeted my ride to the Mission that morning, as the Anno Luce skyline beamed solid gold reflections off tinted panes of glass, floating in a sea of architectural would-be monoliths.
I got off the ramp to Barker, and drove by the many shops and bodegas rolling the gratings off their windows to start yet another business day. I could hear bass pumping through someone's system, even at that hour. I wondered if I'd actually see somebody throw something down at him from the upper floors.
Nah; if it happened, I missed it.

Things were relatively quiet on the Mount. At that hour, that being eight-thirty, it was usually quiet. But I'd noticed that we were seeing a lull in the page nine stuff; murders, robberies, rapes and other despicable crimes. I mean, there was always tension in the air, and plus the thing with Yashua being attacked, but aside from all that, we were in a definite calm.

I pulled up in my 'reserved' parking spot. It was so reserved through a sign that read; 'Parking for Sex Offenders Only.' I'm not kidding. Looked like a real sign too, but it came off the post easily, so I'd take it off when I got there. It worked. Only one time my space was taken, and that guy actually *was* a sex offender. I had to give it to him.

I had the sign made up after being frustrated by not finding a parking spot close to the Mission. We had a parking lot, but there was only one spot I could fit the Econoline into. And I always had to park a block away, only to have to re-park it when whoever it was that was in my spot finished their business.
After I put in the sign, nobody parked there. Well, almost nobody. Me, and the occasional sex offender.

I walked in the door and saw Alejandro sitting at the front desk, looking generally bored.

"Hey Ale'," I said, and grabbed the clipboard - that being the roll call of who was in residence in the Mission at that moment. Just a force of habit; I didn't really want to know.

"Hey my man!" he said, and nailed me with silly string.

I looked around quickly. No witnesses. *Damn.* You see, you can only 'hit' someone when there are no witnesses. He got me.

"Bastard!" I said. "And I left my piece in the office!"

"Sucka got SMOKED!" he said, pointing his two fingers like a gun at me.

"Damn," I said. "I had a streak too."

"I know," he said.

"Damn," I said again.

Yashua walked out of the Community Room, and looked at the silly string, bits of which were still clinging to my shirt. He laughed.

"I'm guessing you two were in on this one?" I said.

"No, you were off your guard," Yashua said. "Don't pin it on me."

"Yeah, yeah, so I'm dead now. I wonder what dead people do?"

"Depends on what they were doing when they died,"

Yashua said.

"Sounds scary," I said. "Hope I die on a week-day…"

I went into the community room. I saw Joe Krantz and Charlie Havens playing chess. *Chess?* Didn't think they knew how to play.

Anne Marie, an older woman (she hated to be called *elderly,*) was watching TV in the easy chair. She was watching the *Hour of Hope* show, with the Reverend Roy Jones. She usually watched the *Righteous Battle*, which was Biggs' show. Reverend Jones was a televangelist, but he wasn't like Biggs, he was actually decent. If I was to start watching televangelists (wasn't planning on it,) I would've watched him. Maybe Yashua talked her into it. I knew Yashua didn't like Biggs, and Anne Marie just loved Yashua, so it was possible. I wasn't complaining, though.

"Brothers and sisters," he said, clasping his hands together. "We are in an age where we are divided house against house, fathers against sons, and brothers against sisters. We fight and hate in the name of the One who came to this Earth to preach love, and fellowship, mercy and mutual respect, and the peace and the Light of God which unifies us all. This fight must end, and the start, and conclusion of this battle is in our own hearts." He clutched his chest with his hands.

'*Amen, Reverend,*' I thought.

"When He who has come before reveals Himself again, we will expect Him to hate, as we hate, and He will not. So we will not recognize Him. He will embody us, and when He Leaves, He will take us to our day of Final Judgment."

I couldn't exactly figure out what he meant by that, but it sounded good.

"And we will find the spirit of Satan embodied as well," Jones continued, "and it will seek our Lord out, but by itself, it cannot kill Him."

I was still lost, and quite honestly I was starting to drift over to Joe and Charlie's chess game when I heard a high-pitched, shrieking scream, coming from the main lobby. '*Oh shit!*' My standard thought when hearing a shriek or scream at the mission. This one was a little different, though. It penetrated the walls of the community room. I'd heard many loud screams from the lobby when I was in the community room before, and the thickness of the walls always muffled it. I heard this like there was no wall at all.

All of these thoughts like blips ran through my head while in motion, of course. In a second and a half, I was through the community room door, and witnessed a situation that would never leave me.

The scream came from a woman, standing two feet before the front doors in the main lobby. Disheveled would not have been the correct word. *Ragged*. She looked strung out, her eyes sunk into her head, shaking and nervous. But some things just weren't right. For starters, her body didn't show the 'strung-outness', for lack of a better term, that her face showed. Usually people strung out from drugs come from a life of drugs, and hard living, and every part of them shows it. Emaciation, loss of muscle tone, their stoop and gait, basically their bodies go through the wrecker.

This woman didn't show that. She had muscle-tone, she seemed almost athletic. She stood tall, and her 'bearing', if you could call it that, didn't indicate that hard life.

The other striking thing was that her clothes matched. She was actually dressed very nicely, if not for the fact that her clothes were in such horrible shape. Tears, wear, dirt and grime, I couldn't describe how bad they were, but they obviously weren't clothes she had acquired through multiple sources, as most homeless people do. She reminded me more like a survivor of some plane crash than a drug addict, or someone otherwise on the street.

She was staring at Yashua, who was standing about six feet away from her, very calm, and still. 'Oh no, not again,' I thought, and went to get in the way. Yashua held up his hand, as if to keep me back. He seemed serious. I laid off, but I was prepared to jump in if I had to.

She looked at Yashua, with a shifting uncertainty. It reminded me of a video I saw where these people were trying to get a dog to cross a busy median as it hit a lull. The dog didn't know whether they were trying to help it or hurt it. She had that look, back and forth. She looked to lunge towards him, which made me tighten up, but then it was like something was keeping her from it.

She began to shout something, it sounded like gibberish.
And the vocal quality was something I'd not heard before. She had
a pitch that changed, yet there didn't seem to be any points at
which I could determine an emphasis being placed. It just didn't
seem human. You don't truly realize the importance of emphasis in
speech until you hear speech utterly devoid of it. Even computer
'speech' at least *attempts* emphasis. There was none here. She was
wide eyed, and I could see her pupils widening and closing, almost
rhythmically. I couldn't process it, and I was uneasy with the
whole situation.

When she concluded her shouting, Yashua answered in the
same gibberish. At this time, of course, I realized that it must be a
language, and by the other day's experience, my guess was
Aramaic. She shouted back quickly, but Yashua cut her off. He had
a fire in his eyes, and a conviction in the unknown speech I had not
seen in him up to that point. He didn't seem angry with her,
however. When he'd finished, he was once again calm.

She walked towards him, slowly, scared as all shit from the
look of her, and stopped. Her look changed back to mistrusting,
but Yashua said something to her in a soothing voice, and she
stepped forward again. Yashua held out his hand, and said another
thing in Aramaic. She was one step away from arm's reach, and
she turned angry and started to shout again. Yashua then grabbed
a folding mirror from the lobby desk and unfolded it. The look of
her own reflection must have confused her, because it broke her
rage, and her concentration. She then took that last step, and
grabbed Yashua's free arm. As she did, I saw the back of her shirt
and dress flap back, as if caught in a breeze. I knew of no source in
the building that could've done that. It was momentary, but I saw
it. Alejandro did too. As did everyone else, who by that time had
gathered around.

The woman collapsed in Yashua's arms. He continued to
speak with her in Aramaic, softly. I looked at Alejandro, who gave
me the best 'baffled' look I'd seen on him yet. I'd seen my share of
those looks from him. I'm sure he saw my best one too that day.

Yashua looked up at me and Alejandro and said, "I need

water, and a washcloth."

I ran to the bathroom and grabbed a washcloth and a dixie-cup full of water. I came back and handed them to Yashua.

"Is that enough water?" I asked.

"Yes, this will be fine," he said.

He dabbed the washcloth in the water and dabbed the woman's forehead. However, he didn't seem to be doing it to wipe her forehead. He was making shapes with the washcloth, I couldn't see close enough to make out what the shapes were, but he seemed to be doing it on purpose.

Of course, at that point he could've been painting the Last Supper on her forehead, and it would've made just as much sense. I had many, many questions of Yashua right then. I'm sure I wasn't alone.

They would have to wait though. We had the matter of an unconscious young woman on our floor to deal with.

She revived a bit, and we were able to get her up on the couch in the lobby.

"Alejandro ... Did you call the paramedics yet?"

"Not yet," Alejandro said, "I'll…"

"Don't," Yashua said, "she'll be fine here. You just need to give her time."

"All they'll do is check her out."

"If she goes there, she'll die," Yashua said.

"What are you talking about?" I asked.

"That ... *thing*," Yashua said, pointing to the mirror, "will come back. And stronger, ten-fold."

"So, what do we do with her here?" I asked. I was beyond asking him how he knew that the *thing* would return, or why she was in so much danger.

"I'll tend to her. She will be in danger from dusk 'till dawn, and after that she'll be stable," he explained.

Alejandro thought about it. He looked at me, and I just shrugged. I'd been in over my head since it all started.

"Okay," Alejandro said. "But if she gets worse, or starts doin' that freaky shit again, we're calling the paramedics."

"Agreed," Yashua said.

I walked over to him. "If you want to keep us from goin' nuts, you do realize you're going to have some explaining to do?"

"In due time, my friend," he touched the woman's forehead again, "in due time."

It took a few hours, but the woman finally became coherent. Her name was Katherine. She could not tell us her last name at first, but we found out it was Willis.
Later on she was coherent enough to speak. She was hazy on certain points, but the story she told us was as follows:

Katherine was a student at USC, psychology major, and was in Anno Luce to attend a conference on psychology-related computer programs. She remembered stopping at the Ruiz (a bar in the downtown) for a few drinks on the first night of the conference. She remembered nothing after that until she said she felt this 'brilliant energy' and described in vivid detail the feeling of this bliss that had overtaken her. I'd heard that kind of talk before from crack-heads, but she obviously wasn't one.

She next remembered being cut off from it, and she freaked out. She got violently ill, and couldn't stop thinking about getting that feeling back. She was packed into a van, and driven to an abandoned lot somewhere before being tossed out.
She didn't know where she was. She couldn't eat or sleep, she just kept thinking about how wonderful it would be to get that feeling again. She said that eventually she went mad, and started losing control. She said she had felt a new 'presence move in.' She said it wasn't good. It promised her the feeling of bliss again, but it consumed her thoughts with the murder of some homeless man that she didn't even know. Who, of course, turned out to be Yashua.

This 'thing' as both she and Yashua called it, led her to the Mission. Then what she said confused me even more.

"And then I saw The Lord, and knew Him to be who He was. I resisted the voice telling me to attack Him. He was still able to shout curses, but He silenced them, and slowly I drew the courage from somewhere to go to Him. Then, when I was almost there, the thing got a hold of me once more, and began to curse Him. It was when The Lord showed the demon its true face that it could no longer hold me."

'Okay,' I thought, 'this is Book of Revelations shit.' I couldn't tell you the number of questions I had, and I didn't even know how to ask any of them. She was speaking about Yashua as if he was Jesus or something. Was she nuts? Was he nuts too? And the all important question; was I nuts?

She said she saw a circle with two diamonds in front of it, but she couldn't be sure. I knew what that was. That was the logo for ArcEpic.

"So now, this 'bliss'," I said, "was it like some type of machine?"

"No," she said. "It was like something on my head, and I could feel warmth coming from there and from my wrist," she said, and she rubbed her wrist, apparently reminiscing. Then she drifted back out.

I looked at Yashua, and said, "HIPPO?"

"Yes, that's what it is," he said. "Believe it."

Alejandro was looking at us, lost, "What the hell are you guys talking about?"

We explained HIPPO to him, and that she was likely some kind of 'test subject.' I can say that he was, at least, functionally satisfied with this explanation.

"So wait a minute," Alejandro started, "why would they use somebody who would be missed? There are plenty of people around here that wouldn't be."

I thought about the fact that I had not seen Katherine in the news as missing. She was fairly pretty, her current condition notwithstanding, and I knew that the media bias in reporting missing persons tended to favor pretty, young, white women. I couldn't figure out why I hadn't heard her name in the news.

"Her disappearance was in the news, ten years ago," Yashua said.

"Waitaminit! All that happened ... ten years ago?"

Yashua put his finger to his lips. "She needs to relax right now. She'll figure it out soon enough."

"So no one's been looking for her ..." I said, and gave her a blanket, as she was shivering slightly.

"It still doesn't make sense," Alejandro said. "Why would they even take that risk? There are three thousand homeless people in Anno Luce."

"They needed her," Yashua said, now actually wiping her forehead. "She has the mind to evaluate. They couldn't find a homeless person with the same mind. Katherine was just unlucky enough to present them the opportunity."

Katherine yawned, opening her eyes as if waking up in the morning. *Strange.*

"Katherine ... I mean, do you remember being asked any questions about it?" I asked her. "By the people who ran the... whatever."

"Not that I remember, but I don't remember much anyway," she replied.

"They didn't need to," Yashua said. "They had her thoughts when she was plugged in. They had what they wanted."

Nobody said anything for a while. Then I - of course it would be me - piped up with the obvious.

"We gotta tell somebody!" I said.

"It won't do any good," Yashua said.

"Are you kidding?" I said. "What journalist wouldn't love to blow a story like this?"

"Any person who wants to keep their job," Yashua said. "The owner of Paradigm Corp., controls 99% of the U.S. and world media sources."

"Impossible! They're not that big."

"Paradigm is not. But Synermedia, who controls Paradigm *is* that big," Yashua said. "Shells within shells. They'll print the story, but only to discredit it."

I thought about what I'd heard on *The Mug*. That post from Arius.

"What about the Purity from Release of Drugs?" I asked. "I heard they were a part of this."

"Biggs's thing?" Alejandro asked.

"Biggs?"

"Yeah, Biggs," he said. "PRD is funded by the Trinity Foundation. And that's Biggs' little playground."

"I thought the PRD was a government thing?"

"Joseph is only one head of this beast," Yashua said. " ... And there are many."

"But if Biggs is involved, why underwrite this with PRD?" I asked. "I mean, this thing is like some kind of addictive drug, so why underwrite it with an anti-drug organization?"

Yashua got up. He walked to the window, and without looking at anything, or anyone in particular, he said, "This false God will be touted as the 'healthy' (he used the hand-quotes) alternative to drugs. That's how many will be deceived. And the *underwriting* is on paper only. "

"People are gonna figure out how addictive it is pretty quickly."

"The devices can be turned down to draw people in. It'll at first seem non-addictive. But that can be changed with the flip of a switch. Biggs has seventy million viewers, and his aligned organizations account for at least another thirty million," Yashua said. "And that's just Biggs."

We sat silent for a while. Katherine was in and out of consciousness, and Yashua tended to her. Alejandro motioned me to walk outside with him.

We went out to the wooden gazebo on the side of the Mission. We could see inside from there. Alejandro, looking very confused, said, "What the fuck is going on here, Barney?"

"Well, Ale' ..." I started to explain the HIPPO thing again, but he cut me off.

"I'm not talking about that!" he returned, through gritted teeth. "That's a whole other 'what the fuck!?!' I'm talking about Yashua. I mean, the Aramaic, the crazy people coming after him, and some of the people here are noticing things too."

"What do you mean? What 'things'?" I asked.

"Dude, he doesn't sleep ... ever. And that's just the beginning of it," Alejandro said. "I mean, don't get me wrong, most of the strange things are good things, but they're *strange*."

He went on; "No-one here has failed a breathalyzer since he

started with us. And none of them are showing signs of any other drug use."

"You know damn well it's a miracle if you can turn one of these guys around," he said. "But *all of them?* There's something going on here. Yashua's not telling us something."

"Probably a few things," I said. We were silent for a little while. Then I added, "I imagine we're going to have to talk to him. Wanna leave Zee out of it?"

"Definitely," he said, and we went back in.

I went to where Yashua was, tending to Katherine.

"How is she?" I asked.

"She is still in the grip of it, but she will pass through," he answered, calmly.

She looked peaceful lying there, with a pink woolly blanket tucked up to her chin. She was sweating, but just beads, nothing trickling.

"What exactly is wrong with her?" I asked.

"She's..." Yashua said, and paused, as if looking for the right words. "Picture what Satan must have gone through when he was first separated from the Presence of God."

"She's taking it remarkably well!" I said. I wasn't trying to be sarcastic, it's just I couldn't think of anything else to say.

"She suffers. It's just too deep to form facial expression and body language," he said, and began to pray for her, probably in Aramaic, in a soft voice. I put my hand on his shoulder, and then walked away.

It was well past seven at night, and I was about ready to go home. Alejandro and I set aside half an hour the next day to talk with Yashua, although I had a feeling it would take far longer to get anything from him approximating sense. I left with a sense of what can best be termed 'overload'.

That night I had a drink.

And drink I did, though not to excess. I had to work the next day, and it promised to be a doozy.

I sat on the couch, trying to read *Trinity* but unable to. That usually happened when I drank. So I went to something requiring a lesser mentality - the ol' tube. As always, CNN was on. This time it was Peter Fricks and Angela Wyler, the co-hosts of the aptly named; 'Fricks & Wyler' segment.

The topic of that evening's broadcast was 'freedom versus security', a perennial favorite ever since 9/11.
Fricks was a liberal, I mean real left, and Wyler was a conservative, about as far right. I actually liked the show.

"If you ask me," Wyler said, "a secure America is a strong America."

"And an America without civil liberties is *not* America," Fricks retorted. "America is more than a geographic boundary. It is a way of life that is threatened in the name of its own preservation."

"We are living in a very dangerous world," Wyler said. "Everyday there are people, at home and abroad, who plot incessantly to destroy us. And the most successful tools they have in their arsenal are the very civil liberties that liberals like you keep open for them."

To which Fricks countered, "When you live in a free nation, you have to face the possibility that your freedoms will sometimes aid those trying to harm you. But to destroy those freedoms is to do more harm to this country than all the WMD in any terrorist's arsenal."

"All the Patriot Act III does is this; It gives law enforcement the tools they need to prevent terrorism at home," Wyler said, referring to the recent passage of the Patriot Act III bill before Congress, the third installment of crap legislation in a long line of crap legislation.

"The Patriot Act III allows law enforcement to arrest, book, and fingerprint anyone stopped for even a minor traffic violation! Meanwhile, our Mexican border is not coordinated electronically, our ports have not installed neutrino analysis, and our airports have yet to install it wide scale. Are we sure we're giving out the right 'tools'?"

Wyler started looking flustered. "I just want to say, in reference to bookings on traffic violations, that suspects are booked only when an officer suspects a serious crime to have taken place. This has not been used for routine traffic stops."

Fricks returned with two points. "We can't prove whether or not an officer 'suspects' a serious crime, or a simple drug arrest, or anything at all. Even if this is true, abuse can, and most likely will, occur, and when it does, it will be difficult to stop."

"But this is absurd, what you're saying," Wyler said. "A majority of Americans are law-abiding citizens, who wouldn't put themselves in a position to have the Patriot Act III apply to them. We're talking about criminals here."

"What will define a criminal act in 50 years?" Fricks asked. "We may not be alive, but our children will be. What happens when one day our grandchildren wake up in a country where disagreeing with the administration is considered subversion, and punishable by imprisonment? Will this be America in anything but name only?"

"Anyone who is a patriotic American, would be willing to sacrifice a small aspect of their civil liberties to protect this nation. Anyone who looks to that flag with pride," Wyler said.

"If you love those stars and stripes, but not the principals that they were sewn upon," Frick countered, "you're showing nationalism, not patriotism."

"So, do you propose we just welcome these terrorists in and help them blow up the Capitol?" Wyler asked.

"You say 'welcome them in' even though most terrorist acts in America have been committed *by* Americans. But no, I don't say help them. I say let's stop spending money making rich people richer in this country, and start putting money into *physically securing* the United States."

"Work smarter, not harder," Wyler said. "By giving law enforcement the tools they need, we can cut them off before they even get to the 'action' stage," she said.

"How about you *think* a little harder?" Fricks said. *That pissed her off.* "Terrorists, many of them, come from repressive countries. Their own governments have unrestricted law enforcement. They adapt to it, and operate in it far easier than we Americans do. But state of the art security at our critical areas is slightly harder to adapt to."

At this point it went to commercial. I was getting drowsy by then anyway, so I turned the TV off. I nuked some noodles and chowed down before hittin' the sack.

Pitch black surrounded me; I could hear words in monotone, and feel the icy chill of fog prickling my bare limbs. I couldn't tell where I was, or anything around me, as the blackness and fog formed an impenetrable prison. I felt nauseous, and feverish, and I could hear what sounded like piano notes, but their pitch dropped off in an unnerving way. I could hear, in the background, machinery, though I couldn't make out what exactly comprised the machine.

The fog cleared. I was at the front gate of some type of prison. There was a sign in front, but I could not understand the language; it resembled a mix of Arabic and Hebrew. A stone carving on the front face of the prison was also in that language.

The gate was shut. I remember saying something, I can't recall it, and the gate evaporated. The remaining fence melted as I watched. I then heard a cry from within. I walked, almost floated, from the gate to the door of the prison. I looked down to see a stone with the date on it. Only the date was moving, the numbers changing continually.

I looked at the door, massive and imposing. But I pushed it open as though it was paper, and my hand went through it. I continued to hear the cry, and I saw before me inmates, lined along the corridor, upright, blank-faced. They had fire reflecting in their eyes and the inmate numbers on their jumpsuits were changing continually. I was afraid of them. Then a narrow beam appeared, from my footsteps, down the corridor to the main staircase, and up the stairs. I followed the narrow path, toe-to-toe, as if it were a tightrope.

I don't remember making conscious choices. I felt as though I was watching it from without. I reached the staircase and ascended. As I did, the earth seemed to erupt. As I continued to ascend to the second tier, all else had fallen into a dark pit. Looking around, I saw what I can only describe as 'nothingness' enveloping all that had fallen off.

I looked upon the plateau, the only apparent thing left, and I saw a figure, composed of every color of light, on the ground. The light was pulsating, though brilliant when the pulse was strong. And I saw a figure above the one on the ground. His light was dark. But it was near as brilliant as the multi-colored light. And his eyes were pitch black, and radiated this blackness. There were inmates all around the two, appearing the same as those on the first floor. The second figure looked at me, and smiled, showing teeth more like war-heads fused to its gums, and raised up a spear in his hand to kill the multi-color figure, and as he thrust down his hand he screamed and the numbers stopped and...

I woke up in a cold sweat, bewildered as all hell. I don't usually dream, and if I do, I don't remember them. So that was surprising. Maybe all the weird shit that had been going on in the past few weeks was finally catching up to my dreams. I figured I may as well have some coffee. I sure as hell wasn't getting back to sleep.

I went to the kitchen and checked the clock on the microwave. It was 5:30 a.m., so I cranked KALR at full blast. My neighbors weren't near me on this street, and the bottom apartment was empty. Don't ask me why I did it. Just felt like the right thing to do. They were playin' Jimi' though. *Stone Free*. I was singin' along, of course.

I looked out the kitchen window as I waited for my coffee to boil. It was early enough that dawn had yet to hail an approach. The blues and purples still dominated the pre-dawn sky. I knew right then it was cool enough for an enjoyable walk. Though I fashioned being rather lazy, on that particular morning I decided that some foot-action would be the perfect remedy for what ailed me.

I had my cup of coffee, taking sips between getting dressed and throwing on my shoes. I gave a third of my coffee to the earth (dumped it outside,) and took off to the path behind my house.

Anno Luce was an oasis of about twenty-five square miles. There were cold springs that irrigated the area. It was these springs that allowed anyone to settle on the barren landscape. Behind my house, there were about twenty acres of forested area. Great place to walk.

I thought about Yashua. Here was a man that, if I were viewing his words and actions not knowing him, would think he was completely nuts. But knowing him, I had a respect, and a trust of him, and the things he said, for their incredulity, made sense. But who was he? Was he a priest, or an exorcist? I'd seen things that I could only say were miraculous, and I felt that without reading into it. Actually reading into it, I had to come to the realization that Yashua was not an ordinary human being.

But again, who was he? What little I could gain was non-specific. And I wanted so desperately to ask him who he was ... who he really was, but I knew he'd tell me something vague. And Yashua was too nice to press on the issue, so, I was truly in a quandary.

I had a feeling that Alejandro would be asking him questions, though. I just wasn't sure, even then, if we'd get answers that actually answered something.

I was walking up a ridge, where the view was pretty good, when I noticed a white dove. It definitely looked out of place, surrounded by palm trees, scrub brush and cacti. It was perched on a shrub about ten yards away. It looked at me, and cooed, so I cooed back. Then it came straight at me, stopping in mid-air, hovering gently, gliding off of a breeze that didn't seem to be there. Then it took off over my head. And then I got pooped on. Oh yeah - my left shoulder. I just laughed. What else was I going to do?

So with that I trekked back to my pad, cleaned off my lucky charm, hopped in my van and cruised onward to the psychiatric playground known as Jefferson Highway morning traffic.

I wasn't due into the Mission for another couple of hours, and I wasn't in a hurry to get there, so I went to the Anno Luce Public Library on Pueblo Street.

It was a very spacious and well-attired library. The outside was stone, and it almost had the appearance of a castle in London. It was very unique to the surrounding architecture, mostly 'Mock-Spanish' buildings. It was one of the better libraries in California, with a vast collection of books, magazines, and videos.

I wandered the aisles. That's what I'd do at least fifty percent of the time I was in a library. Then I'd end up running my peepers over a title that looked like a good time, and I'd get it.

That day the book to cross my sights almost knocked me off

my feet. The title? *Yashua.*

The thought did cross my mind at first that I was hallucinating. After all, I had been thinking about the situation with Yashua, I was in the library somewhat to avoid him, and there I saw this book, *Yashua.*

So after ascertaining that the book was indeed real, I pulled it from the shelf and parked on the nearest comfortable chair. The book was old, and there was a layer of dust on the clear-plastic jacket. It was written by a group; *Community of Worship to YHVH.* I knew those letters represented the name of God in Hebrew.

I began to read. Apparently, the Hebrew name of Jesus was Yashua, and other similar spellings. It then began to give something of a biography of Jesus. I didn't get much farther than that in the library.

Though I felt like I had just started reading, two hours had passed by, and I needed to get to work. I put the book back and got the van rolling towards the Mission.

I'd like to take this time to say that I had not yet, at that point, realized who Yashua *truly* was. The thought was popping into my head, but it hung in the irrational background, with the thoughts of how you plan to spend the lottery money you have a one-in-please chance of winning. I was, at that point, certain that Yashua was not just another homeless man. That was all I was certain about.

I showed up at the Mission at eight-thirty. I was about a half hour early. I saw Yashua and Katherine sitting in the lobby. Katherine looked markedly different. She'd had a shower, and changed her clothes. But more than that, she looked vital, alive. Color had returned to her face; yesterday she looked gaunt and pale.

She waved 'hi' and smiled. Yashua also smiled, and said, "I told you she'd be fine, Barnabas."

"You're name's Barnabas?" Katherine asked me.

"That's the shape of the ink on my birth certificate," I said. "But everyone calls me 'Barney'"

"Oh," she said. "Why did your parents name you

'Barnabas'?"

"They wanted to give me a Biblical name, but not one that was common, so they chose Barnabas," I replied.

I then went to the staff lounge for some caffeine, and Alejandro was sitting in there, reading the paper.

"How's it been today? Any more possessions?" I asked.

"Don't even joke, yo'!" Ale' said. "Oh yeah, and we're goin' to have a change of plans with our meeting, with Yashua."

"Why, what's up?" I asked.

"Zee's got 'execs' from one of our supporting foundations coming. They'll be here all day. In fact, it would probably be a good idea to get Yashua out of here today. Katherine too." He pointed to me. "So that's your job, little brother."

"Good idea," I said. "Maybe I'll take them up to the Precipice. They'd enjoy the view."

"Your ride," Alejandro said, "your dime."

"When are we out?" I said.

"In about half an hour," he said, looking up at the clock.

"Sounds like a mish'," I said, and walked into my office. I sat down for a second. I thought of turning on the CD player, but I didn't. I didn't want to get into a good song and have to leave. I looked at an African proverb I had on the wall. It had a painted image of an African mother holding a baby up in her arms. It read;

"Let the mothers be mothers, and let the fathers be fathers."

I looked at it in contemplation, not of it per se, but of what I was going to say to Yashua on the excursion.

"In that culture, all women in the village are mothers, and all men fathers," Yashua said as he poked his head through the open door.

"So it *does* take a village to raise a child," I said, looking at the poster.

"More than a village," Yashua said. "So, we are traveling today?" he asked.

"Yeah, we're getting kicked out," I said. "We have to let the executives infest our abode, so we get a road trip."

"Perhaps for the best," he said.

"Yeah, besides, I'll take you guys to the precipice; it's this rock formation a few miles east. It's got a good view of Anno Luce. It'll be hot, but there's shade. It's a nice place."

"Sounds pleasant," he said. "I'll prepare Katherine." He went to get her ready.

I found a few sports bottles, and filled them with water from my water cooler. Yeah, I had a water cooler - good one, too. Damn Skippy. I got the water from a local service. Anno Luce's water was from a natural spring, as I said, but it was the city's pipes I didn't trust. They'd had problems before, let's just put it that way.

I got that, and an umbrella (in case we wanted to stray around on top of the formation for a while) and met Yashua and Katherine out in the lobby. I signed them out, and we hopped in the Econoline. I was fortunate to have air-conditioning, as it was perhaps the only amenity that still worked. Oh, I had everything; power everything, tilt, cruise control. But it all crapped the bed. The A/C kicked in grand though.

We headed down Baker Street, and took a right on to Bolivar Street. It took us out of Anno Luce and went east as it became County Route 4, at which point it was just a ribbon of concrete separating oceans of sand. The precipice could be seen easily from Anno Luce, and as we drove up County Route 4, it loomed ahead.

This is not to say that the precipice was of an extreme elevation. Its rise was about two hundred feet at most. But the greater Anno Luce area was as flat as a week old Coke, so a two hundred foot elevation seemed like a mountain to us.

The top of the precipice was set up as a lookout site, and there was a shelter there that you could sit, or stand in, and see everything. I still brought an umbrella.
There was an access road that shot off of County Route 4, and we took a right onto it.

On the way up the back slope, I was nervous. I knew I was going to have to ask Yashua hard questions, and I knew even then that there weren't gonna be any simplistic, *alrighty then* answers. I liked Yashua a lot, and I didn't want to confront him, or even come off as being confrontational. But I needed to know.

We got out of the van. Katherine was in wonder, and she took off towards the lookout. I was going to tell her to be careful, but Yashua motioned that it wouldn't be necessary. He and I walked.

"Yashua ..."

"You have questions, I know," he said. "And the curious mind asks."

"Well, do you have answers for these questions?" I asked.

"I do," Yashua said. "Unfortunately, none of them would have us leave here without you thinking I'm mad."

"Now look, Yashua," I said in a hushed voice, "I have pretty much figured out that you're a bit different than an ordinary person. You have something; a 'gift' or what have you. And from everything I've seen, you have been nothing but selfless in your time at the Mission. So I know that what you have is, so to speak, 'of God.' But, I feel like I'm missing a gigantic link in this whole chain of events surrounding you."

I looked to see Katherine standing right beside Yashua, and I didn't even realize she was there, or for how long. She was smiling at me, bemused by my questions.

She looked at Yashua. "He doesn't know?" she asked, astounded. By now I was frankly getting frustrated.

"What?" I said. "What don't I know?"

"Yashua...*Jesus*..." she said, rocking subtly on the balls of her feet.

"*Jesus?*" I asked.

"Yes. Jesus," she said.

"Okay, you're nuts!" I said.

"No one else could have had the power to save me from that, *thing*," she said.

I looked at Yashua. He didn't look to deny it.

"I told you you'd think I was nuts," Yashua said.

"No, it's not that. And it actually explains some things. It's just," I searched for a word. Finding none, I said, "fucked up."

Yashua laughed at that one. "Good choice," he said, putting his hand on my shoulder.

"You have not Seen Me to this moment," he said. "Nor will you right now, for it is not the proper time. Katherine has Seen Me because it was her proper time."

"Yeah, b-but," I stuttered a little, "I read the Book of Revelations, it said you're coming down with an army of angels, and it's going to be the end of the world, and…"

Yashua shushed me, and said, "Prophesy must be interpreted, so that those who seek its truth with an open mind, so to seek wisdom, will understand it."

He continued after a brief pause. "However, prophesy must not be altered if it is to remain true, and after thousands of years, things become lost, or assumed to mean one thing when it meant something else in a different context. The heart of Revelations is true. I have come to bring humankind to its final age. But God chooses to form events as He Wills. No book, no entity in existence can deny Him that."

"If you're Jesus, how come you got cut and had to get stitches?" I asked. I felt real bad about asking him that, but he didn't seem to mind. He had a look on his face, like he felt bad for me too.

"Barnabas, I will explain that to you, and more, but in time. You're just processing this. There are things that need to be done right now. Help us, and I promise you, when the hour comes that God determines it, you will See."

I was silent for a good long while. Yashua let me be. I was seriously weighing what I had seen in him already, and how this explanation fit almost all the evidence. The sheer impossibility of Jesus being a homeless man confounded me. But it occurred to me that Jesus had no home ever mentioned in the Bible past his childhood. So would it have been unreasonable to assume that he wouldn't have a home now?

Plus, he was more or less healing people at the Mission. But he wasn't preaching the Word of God. Don't get me wrong, he taught people, but general things, ways to do things, stuff like that. He was teaching one of our residents how to read. But he wasn't speaking to the whole group of residents about God.

I didn't want to think any the worse of Yashua if it turned out he was crazy. He was becoming someone I'd lay it on the line for. But, at that point, I wasn't accepting that he was Jesus internally. I had made it a mental point not to mention any of it to anyone.

Yashua and Katherine were standing by the lookout point, talking. I felt a gentle breeze, and I began to think about Anna. I had taken her up there when she was alive. I thought of her looking down, as if to ask her if she knew who Yashua really was, if he was Jesus, or someone who was 'not all-together there'. I wanted to believe him, but at the same time it felt much safer not to believe.

I went over to them, and joined them in gazing out at Anno Luce. We sat silent for a while, and then Yashua said, without breaking his gaze, "We have to go."

I looked at my watch. "We can't be back there for another two hours, at least," I said.

"I don't mean that," he said. "I mean overall, there is work to be done that cannot be done here."

I looked at him. "Are you leaving the Mission?"

"No, *We* are leaving," Yashua said, and then looked at me.

"Yashua, I'd love to go with you, anywhere, but I have bills to pay. I have commitments at the Mission," I said.

"Oh, Barnabas," Yashua said. "You so thirst for adventure and life, and as it calls you out, you hear it not."

"Look, I mean, how am I gonna support myself to go anywhere without a job, and I don't even know where you're going," I said.

"The journey begins in Africa; Ethiopia, to be precise."

"Oh, and how do you expect us to get there?" I said, then thought about it. "Waitaminit! That endowment we got, you had something to do with that, didn't you?"

"So many questions," Yashua answered. "You will have to trust me on many things, this being only one of them."

I sat there for a while and thought about it. I didn't know what was crazier, the proposition of going to Ethiopia with someone who might be nuts, or that I was entertaining the notion in the first place.

I was silent all the way back. I wasn't being rude or anything, just thinking. Upon heading back to the beginning of Bolivar Street, I asked Yashua when he would leave. He said in three days. I asked if we'd be coming back, and he said we would. I continued to think about it, not promising anything. I dropped them off at the Mission, and took off pretty soon after. It was quittin' time, and I'd had a remarkably draining day.

I stopped at Joe's Coffeehouse on the way home. It was frustrating that I couldn't say anything about it to Joe. Not that he'd think I was nuts. He already knew that to be true. But I would just feel nuts saying something like that to him.
I wanted to talk to him anyways. Joe was, of course, an Irish Catholic. He grew up in Belfast, which meant he got beat up about his religion. I knew he went to Church every Sunday, and he did a lot of stuff with the Church.

"Hey Joe," I said, as I pulled up to the counter.

"Hey Barney," he said. "You look like shit. Y'arright, kid?"

"Yeah, just a wringer today," I said. "How's it on your end?"

"Ya' believe in miracles?" he asked me.

'Can I get a break?!' I thought, then asked, "Whattaya' got?"

He said, "Well, you know I got that ulcer and all…"

"Yeah," I said.

"I went to the doctor's a couple days ago," he said, "and they ran tests. They called me today, so I went back this morning. He said that they couldn't find it."

"So it like ... healed up or something?"

"No, they couldn't even find scar tissue or anything. Like I never had one," he said.

"Yeah, but that thing's been killin' ya for years," I said. "So, you haven't felt it or anything?"

"Not since, jeez, not since the day you were here last," he said.

"Thursday?"

"Yeah, Thursday. It was goin' pretty bad when I seen you, and it went away later, and hasn't been back!" he said, smiling.

"Well good for you Joe, that's cool,"

"Yeah, I better get me arse in Church Sunday."

"I thought you went every Sunday?" I asked.

"Not as much with the ulcer," he said. "I'm goin' this week, tho'"

"Joe, let me ask you something," I said.

"Shoot."

"When Jesus comes back, he's supposed to be all-powerful right?" I asked.

"Well, every way you look at it, he's bringing it all down, so yeah."

"But I mean, is he coming down from the sky? Millions of Angels, ya' know, that whole sort of thing?"

"Well, no one really knows that one. Only God knows," he replied.

"So, do you think it's possible that Jesus is here on Earth, right now?" I asked.

"Possible." He looked around, then said, "Hell, *probable*."

"How would you know it was Him and not someone pretending to be Him?" I said.

"Ya know, I bet the disciples probably asked those same questions back then. I guess it's easier to tell who's *not* Jesus than it is to tell who *is*."

"Amen," I said, and sipped my cup of Kenyan.

"Your friends were in that day, did they ever catch up to you?" Joe asked.

'*Alejandro and Yashua.*' "Yeah, I caught up with them."

"A shame about what happened to that guy, Yashua, was it? The guy that was with Alejandro?" he said. "Cryin' shame. Helluva nice guy. God don't make people like that no more."

"You ain't kiddin,'" I replied. "He wants me to go to Ethiopia with him."

"Go, lad. See the world."

"Well yeah, with what money? How am I gonna live?"

"If he's going, hasn't he figured out the money?" Joe asked.

"I don't know."

"Go if you can, but don't sell the pisser."

I laughed. "I hear ya' Joe," I said, and took off from there.

Chapter Five

I arrived home about seven-thirty. I wasn't planning on staying up late, just enough to check the news. I did that nightly, and I was looking to be in bed in an hour and a half.

I scheduled in an appointment with Juan Valdez, and hit the couch with tornado-like speed. I turned on the tele', and was greeted by CNN. The announcer, Kim Groves, was a refuge from *The Opposition*, a cable news show that was canceled, probably for being a little too truthful in its story selection. Kim was the trade-off, I guess.

"Tonight's top story, a '100%-healthy recreational drug'? That's what Paradigm, a tech company in southern California, is saying about a device they unveiled today. The device, called HIPPO, is designed to stimulate the pleasure center naturally, without the need for chemical substances. In a press release earlier, Paradigm spokesperson Kay Marwill said; "The HIPPO system has applications everywhere, from alleviating depression, to the treatment of substance abuse."

Groves went on, "Furthermore, Marwill said that 'The HIPPO systems can be used in group therapy, as users can be networked to share the experience.'"

The screen flashed to a familiar scene; the front of the Paradigm Building. I saw five scientists in white coats surrounding a short, brawny man in a charcoal gray suit, with gray-streaked, slicked back hair. I recognized him as J. D. Fisher, the president and C.E.O. of Paradigm Corp. I didn't know who the rest of them were.

Fisher spoke into the microphone. "Today," he said, "Today we stand on the boundary of total freedom from the burdens we endure in the name of feeling good. What once took anti-depressants, crack cocaine, and heroin, now can be experienced without the physical by-products, the sheer toll these drugs take, not only on the body, but on society as well. Within one month, it is our ambitious plan that these be in the home of every American."

Clapping and cheering issued forth from the crowd. I was personally disgusted. More than that, I was scared. Yashua was right. And I returned to the question that had been on the front burner for long enough to burn its shadow on the range-top. '*Who was Yashua?*'

I didn't know if I even wanted to believe he was Jesus. So much of my life I'd seen people like Jim Jones, David Koresh, that guy Marshall Applewhite. All these people who said they were Jesus, or the "One who had Come", that kind of thing. And people blindly believed it, going right to their graves for someone who was lying to them, probably lying to themselves too.

Yashua was an anomaly by this line of thought, however. Yashua had even to that point not said that he was the Son of God. He had not indoctrinated, or even proselytized. And there had been miracles since he'd arrived. A miracle allowed him to even stay at the Mission.

I also couldn't figure out how we were going to get the money to go to Ethiopia. I hoped that Yashua wasn't thinking of asking the Mission for it. Not that the Mission couldn't afford it in light of the endowment. But there was no way in or out of hell that Zee, or anyone on the Board of Directors, would agree to it. So Yashua would have to have an alternate source of cash.

And another thing; I didn't have a passport. Those things took forever to get. Yashua was talking about leaving in three days, and I didn't think that he understood the grass-growing pace of our bureaucracy.

I began to realize that my current line of thought had me going to Ethiopia. Of course I had to rationalize it. And I did this by using an either - or. Either Yashua was Jesus, and I should go with him for reasons self-evident, or Yashua was a gifted and good-hearted lunatic, and may need my help staying out of the nut-hatches of Ethiopia. I could live with that.

I went to my computer to do a little research on the arid African nation, only nothing pulled up.

I tried another search engine. Nothing. It was 'Ethiopia', I wasn't misspelling it or anything. But nothing. All the search engines (and I know thirty.) pulled up nada. I tried 'Africa', then 'Ethiopian,' even 'starvation', nothing. Zip. I actually went as far as to restart my computer and try again, which was effective in wasting about five minutes. No help on the search though.

Bewildered, I searched for 'Anno Luce', just to test. I got hits for that. Mostly about the HIPPO announcement. I looked through them quickly, and saw a heading 'HIPPO: Secret Test Subjects Found.' I clicked the link, and The Port website pulled up.

I knew The Port. The website was so named for "…a port in the storm." They were a 'zine, or internet magazine, that specialized in stories that fell below the mainstream. They weren't all conspiracy theory either. They actually did a good job in terms of relevant content.

The article was about a Phoenix man who claimed to have been abducted by Paradigm, and tested with HIPPO. They showed a picture of him, and I knew right away that the story was true. The look in his eyes had been familiar to me. Katherine had the same look.

The man, Edward Pines, was twenty three, and he was in seminary, studying to become a priest. He had been attending a retreat in the Arizona desert, and the bus carrying the would-be priests broke down. He claimed to remember a van pulled over to give them a ride (there were two of them going for help.) The rest of his story followed the one Katherine told Yashua, Alejandro and myself.

As I read it, the reality of the situation was becoming more and more apparent. I stopped reading, book-marked the article, and walked to the kitchen. I opened the cabinet at the far end and pulled out a pack of cigarettes I had kept, but carefully avoided, for almost a year. I fumbled nervously with the cellophane, and pulling out an obviously stale cigarette, lit it from the stove and inhaled deeply.

I walked into the living room, hacking out a lung as I picked up the picture of Anna from the bookcase. I took a drag from the cigarette, looked into her hi-gloss paper eyes and wished, if anything, that she could tell me her take on all of it. I walked out on my back porch. In the moonlight I prayed.

I woke up to an answering machine message. I could sleep through them pretty good but the message was from Jeannie - my ex, Jeannie.

Now granted, I hated her. I thought she was a basket case. She broke my heart. But, she still was my ex-girlfriend, and she dumped me, so I couldn't slumber through.

I didn't pick up, of course. I wasn't being slick. I was just half-awake and would've never made it to the phone in time.

"Hey, Barney, it's Jeannie. I was just seein' what you were up to. I hadn't heard from you in a while. So, hey, give me a call." She gave me her new number, and continued, "I miss talking to you. I know we had our differences, but give me a call, so we can talk okay? Bye."

This message of course turned my *what-the-fuck* meter from red to purple. 'We had our differences'? Yeah, she wanted a guy who was *totally different* from me. She must've been thinking we had some sort of philosophical differences or something. And our not talking didn't have anything to do with me either.

But, I called her. Oh yeah, you know it, baby. I wasn't entertaining any notion of getting back with her. I just needed to know how shitty her life must have been at that moment ... if she was actually calling *me.*

I, of course, ate breakfast first. General Tso's chicken, the breakfast of the Gastric Legends. With a side of coffee - can't forget that. I took my sweet time eating. She always used to put me on hold when I called her, so now, I was putting *her* on hold.

Eventually I called the number.

"Hello?" she said. I knew it was her. You hear a voice nag you enough, you can pick it out of anywhere.

"Hey, Jeannie, how are you?"

"Oh, Barney, I'm so glad you called!" Jeannie said enthusiastically. "I didn't wake you, did I?"

"No," I lied. "I have to be at work in a little while anyways."

"Good," she said. "Listen, Barney, I just want to know that

I'm so sorry for the whole Brett thing."

So suddenly Brett was a *thing?* But to continue...

"And I should've called you since then," she said. "I've missed you, Barney. I missed the way we used to talk, I miss everything."

"Jeannie ..." I said, "you cheated on me."

"I know that," she said, "but I'm sorry. I made a mistake. Can't you forgive me?"

"Jeannie, I forgive you. I forgave you back then. But..."

I thought about it. I knew what I wanted to say, that I wouldn't go back to her even if she *hadn't* cheated on me. But I really didn't feel like saying that at the moment. So I stalled the motor of the conversation.

"Look, Jeannie, I have somewhere I have to be. Can you call me later on tonight?"

"What time?" she asked, and it was apparent that she didn't buy my poorly-contrived scheduling restraint.

"How about nine o'clock?" I said. "Or thereabouts?"

"Okay," she said. "You're going to be home, right?"

"Yes," I lied again, "by then, definitely."

"Okay, then I'll talk to you tonight around nine."

"It's a plan," I said, only half-lying there. It was a plan. Just not one I had any intention of carrying out.

"Alright, bye," she said. I said likewise, and we hung up.

I hung around the house for a few hours, playing on my computer, listening to music. I didn't have to be in until one o'clock, so I had time. I needed it. I was still processing the Yashua situation, and all that entailed the *Yashua situation.* Now Jeannie was calling me out of nowhere too. Couldn't catch a break. But to tell you the truth, Jeannie calling was nothing but a minor complication trying to latch on to a much larger complication. Of course, I would try hard to avoid her call that night. I owed myself that.

So, with that in mind, I went to Joe's for a cup, and then Luella's for a steak-and-eggs. I went from there to work with the full expectation of being shocked, confused, bewildered and amazed, in no particular order.

Everything was quiet. Alejandro was up front, reading the sports section of the L.A. Times. Gene and Alma, two of our guests, were in the community room. They were both in their seventies, and they were sweethearts. It was great to see love even in the survival of the streets.

I didn't see Yashua or Katherine anywhere. I went over to Alejandro, and asked him where they were.

"In the garden," he said.

The *garden* was one in name only. It was really a patch of shrubs and grass. We had planted all kinds of stuff there. Unfortunately, none of it grew. We also had a few wooden benches out there for our guests. By that time it looked more like a *cigarette garden*.

I thanked Alejandro, and walked down the hall to the back door. I looked out, and saw Yashua and Katherine. It looked like they were praying. I also noticed that the garden suddenly resembled one. We had flowers, and some of them looked like ones we had attempted to bring up, which at that point just seemed obvious. Not surprising in the least. It's amazing how relative the concept of *weirdness* truly is. What would've knocked my hat off about a month before was just, by then, eliciting a simple 'oh' response.

I walked into the garden, careful to be quiet. I didn't want to disturb them.

Yashua and Katherine looked at me, and both smiled.

"It's great that you'll be going with Yashua," Katherine said.

"Hold on a second," I said, "I haven't made up my mind yet."

"You've made up your heart," Yashua said. "And you, *generally*, follow your heart. So I foresee you following it to Ethiopia."

"Well, I guess you would know, being that you're, well," I said, unsure of what to actually say there.

"Barnabas," he said. "To you, I am Yashua, your colleague; your friend. That is all I need to be right now. Whether you choose to come with me or not must be based on me as your friend."

"So, you won't be offended if I don't call you Jesus?" I asked.

"I'd rather you not," he said. "It wasn't my name then. It's not now."

"What was your name back then? Was it really Yashua?" I asked, remembering the book I'd glanced at in the library the other day.

"Indeed," he said.

"What about your last name?" I asked.

"Your idea of last names is not the same as in millennia past. It wouldn't necessarily apply."

"So, back then you were Yashua."

"Yes," he said. "The English name 'Jesus' comes from the Latin *Iesus*, which comes from the Greek *Ihsous*. It was introduced after my time."

"So why hasn't any church stopped calling you Jesus? I mean, I read about this in a book. So people must know this?" I asked.

"Stubbornness," Yashua said. "Also, at times, intent. Throughout the years, it's been a useful practice by the religious authorities to keep the flock at arms length from me." He walked over to one of the newly-established flower beds.

"Does it make you mad?" I asked.

Yashua laughed, and I realized that was a stupid question.

"Oh no," Yashua said, "from those who love me, and love God, I consider it a nick-name."

Then I laughed. "As long as it's you they're thinkin' of, right?" I joked.

"Correct," replied Yashua as he rubbed his chin, his thumb and index finger forming a *V*. It looked almost comical in a way, like he was exaggerating it. Yashua was hilarious sometimes.

"The flock cannot be immune from politics, nor can they be immune to their own background culture," he continued. "All religions are influenced by those who practice them, and a culture influences the person within it. The first *Canon* of the New Testament was transcribed into Latin, and the first mass distribution was in English. So I became Jesus."

"I get it," I said. I absorbed that all pretty well, if I do say. I walked over to one of the other flower beds.

"Your handiwork?" I asked, pointing to the flowers.

"I've always fancied myself a 'green-thumb,'" Yashua said, and smiled.

"Touché," I said.

I thought about the trip to Africa. "Hey Yashua ... about Ethiopia."

"You're wondering how we'll pay for it?"

I didn't know if he read my mind or just took an educated guess.

"Yes," I said. "I mean, Yashua, it's gonna take a lot of money to get the three of us there and back."

"Today, we will be taken care of."

"What do you mean?" I asked.

"We will need to meet with someone who will secure our passage," he replied.

"Who's that, if I may ask?"

"Patience," Yashua said. "You'll meet him shortly."

"What, today?" I said. "I can't really leave here today."

"You'll find the time favorable," he said.

He and Katherine walked up to the door, and Yashua put his hand on my shoulder as he went inside. "Barnabas, it will make sense soon," he said, and smiled.

I sat outside on one of the benches. Noticing a cigarette butt, I retrieved the pack of stale cigarettes which had magically found their way into my shirt pocket (yeah, right, 'magic', whatever.) I lit one of them and took a drag.

I smoked half of a cigarette and walked back in. Alejandro smelled me, looked at me with that *look*. An on-and-off-the-wagon smoker knows that look. He didn't care as in being offended at it. He smoked. He knew that I was doing real well, on-the-wagon for so long. He probably didn't blame me. He was smoking more right then too, I'd noticed.

As I went towards my office, Alejandro said, "Oh, hey, Barney,"

"What's up?" I turned around.

"Any way you can take another, uh, 'field trip' today?" he said.

"Why, what's goin on?" I asked.

"KPCZ is coming here to do a story on the Mission, because of that whole endowment thing. Like a special interest story. I just want to make sure, ya know ..." He motioned to the dining room, where Yashua and Katherine were.

"Uh, yeah, sure," I said. "Yashua said he wanted to go somewhere today anyways. I'm gonna need some gas money, tho'."

Alejandro reached in the petty cash box and pulled out a twenty. He handed it to me, and said, "That gonna be good?"

"Yeah, that's good."

I tooled around my office for an hour or so. KPCZ was coming at noon, so I got Yashua and Katherine on the road just shy of eleven-thirty. I asked Yashua where we were going.

"Los Angeles," he said.

I laughed out loud. "Yashua, I have twenty dollars for gas. There's no way we can make it to L.A. from here on twenty, and no way at all to make it back once we get there."

"Leave that to me," he said.

"Yeah, well what if we break down on the highway? It's mostly desert," I said.

"We wont," he said. Then he looked at me. "Barnabas, that night after we went to church, you drove the route later, and scribbled away in your notebook, measures and formulas. What did you determine?"

"That it was impossible for us to have walked there in the time we did," I answered.

"Then we are now about to do one more impossible thing," he said, and grinned.

I thought about it. If we made it to L.A. and back on twenty in gas, it wouldn't be any more surprising than anything else that was happening. So, in the end the thought 'Why not?' won out. We headed for the gas station to fill up.

I asked Yashua many questions on the ride. I felt I had a pretty good chance with a couple hundred miles of nothing but conversation.

"So how come you're only half-Jewish?" I asked.

Yashua laughed. "All things have their reasons. Like every atom has its specific place in a compound," he said. "But, basically, to show that race matters not to God, for He made all humans from dust. Your compassion and your character are not dust, and they matter most."

"So God really sees the body as dust?" I asked.

"Of course," Yashua said. "You cannot control the division of cells, or the methods by which the body ages. You cannot fight M.S. with your mind, or heal a cut with thought. The natural processes of your body are not influenced by your projection of Will. Your heart, in the spiritual sense, is."

"I see," I said. "So does that mean the sins of the body don't count as much?" I asked.

Yashua laughed before taking a breath. "God can damn you for every, and any, sin you commit," he said. "But He has Infinite Mercy. And He also has Omnipresence, which means that every factor in your human life is Known, and Seen at once."

Seeing confusion on my face, he continued, "In the system of law, judges have what's known as discretion. This is because we all know that no set of laws will be perfect, and a judge needs the ability to know when, say, the recommended sentence for a particular crime would not be in the interest of overall justice. Where do you think that came from?"

"But isn't God perfect?" I asked. "Why would he need discretion?"

"It's humanity, not God, that's imperfect here," Yashua said, "and the reason for that is nothing you would truly comprehend."

"Why not?" I asked.

"Because you weren't there…in Eden," Yashua replied, smiling.

I was silent for a second. "Getting back to what you were saying before," I said. "God has discretion?"

"God has everything," Yashua said.

"How do you know what sins he would choose to use discretion on?" I asked.

"You don't."

I was silent, thinking, and he said, "Don't worry so. When someone loves you, and you know it, then they tend to receive your mercy. God is no different. So love God with all of your heart."

"I dunno," I said. "I guess I'm just skeptical, not of God or anything, but of the fact that the Bible has been translated so many times, it's hard to know what's even accurate any more."

"Barnabas," Yashua said, and looked over at me, "the one thing in the Bible that hasn't been obscured is the root of Truth. That is the Word, and it can't be obscured. It is so obvious that it is inevitably overlooked."

We passed a small horse-hitch gas station on the side of the highway. Yashua pointed to it and said, "See that gas station there?"

"Yeah," I said.

"The man who owns it gets so many people who come here desperate, with no money, in need of gas," he said. "He lets them slide so many times that he's just scraping by himself. He does it because he knows what it's like, and he has a heart."

He continued. "He drinks beer every night, and smokes two packs of cigarettes a day, but do you think he's living by the Word?"

"Yeah, of course," I said.

"He read the Bible when he was a kid, and once in a great while he still looks at it. But the Truth, the Word, is in him."

I thought about it. "So, how does that relate to what I was saying?" I said.

"If twenty percent of the Bible is wrong, then that means eighty percent is right. And eighty percent is a lot easier to find than twenty percent."

I must still have had a confused look on my face, because Yashua continued. "You've read the Bible yourself, sporadically, what do you feel my message was?"

"Well," I started, "love one another, treat people equally, and with respect, and forgive people when they sin against you."

"Then it looks like the Word has found you as well," he said. "That wasn't so hard, was it?"

"Yeah, but what about like, gay people, and people who don't believe in, well, You?" I asked.

Yashua laughed. "There are people in this world who see the power that 'righteous anger' has to sway large groups of people. Faith gives you strength, but religion gives you power. And many take advantage of this, for many different reasons."

Yashua continued. "As I said before, all sins, from the smallest lie to the murder of thousands, can be a damnable sin to God. But to say that a person who's gay, or who doesn't believe that I was the Son of God, is condemned to hell, regardless of the life they led, is to say that God has no choice but to do that. To say that is to say that there is a limit to God's Mercy. And anything that puts a limit on God's Mercy is wrong."

"Okay, but take homosexuality, for example. Isn't homosexuality supposedly a sin against God, an *abomination*?"

"Ah, Leviticus..." Yashua replied. "A most holy book; I presume you're referring to Chapter 18, Verse 22?"

"Uh, actually I was referring to Biggs when he goes off on a rant," I said. "He says that's in the Bible."

"You'd be well not to listen to him," Yashua said. "The biggest lie cannot compare to even the smallest *half-truth*."

I pondered what he was saying. No I didn't; I was clueless. He sensed it, too.

"Leviticus 18:22 says that ...*thou shalt not lie with mankind as with womankind; it is abomination*."

"So he was...right?"

"Half-truth, Barnabas. Not the full truth," Yashua explained. "Leviticus 11:10, to paraphrase, decrees that anything in the ocean without fins or scales is an abomination. How much are you willing to bet Joseph Biggs enjoys his lobster dinners?"

I laughed. "I'd bet the farm!"

"You shouldn't gamble," Yashua said. Then he chuckled. "You'd win, though..."

"Barnabas, the point is; there are many *abominations* in Leviticus that are not followed or preached against today. Selectively following the Law of God … That's perhaps the greatest abomination."

Yashua continued. "Far better be your sins only committed against God than against your fellow brothers and sisters. When you sin against another human being, you make them feel worthless. God is perfect, there is nothing you can do or conceive of doing that will make God feel worthless. God created existence, and all that is done in this world is done within it. God is beyond existence."

Yashua continued, as Katherine started waking up. "God experiences these feelings through the hearts and minds of living things. So God only feels that kind of hurt when a living thing feels it. There was a reason I said that whatsoever you do unto the least of God's people; that you do to God. He is within them; within you and all people, as God created all people."

"I dreamt of him again," Katherine said, as I saw her rubbing her eyes from my rear-view mirror. "He knows where we are."

"Who?" I asked.

"The Beast" she said, quite calmly, as if she was telling me what time it was.

"Oh, Jesus," I said.

"Yes?" Yashua answered. He patted me on the shoulder and laughed. "Always wanted to do that," he said.

"Sorry," I said, laughing pretty good myself. "Are you talking about the Beast as in Book of Revelations?"

Yashua all of the sudden had a weary look on his face.

"Barnabas," Yashua said as he rubbed his stubbly chin with his palm, (he was just starting to grow facial hair, I'd noticed).

"What you will see from here on in will be *nothing* like that book."

"So now you're gonna' tell me *that's* not real?"
Yashua laughed. "All will be explained."

"Can ya' explain just *some* right now, so I don't lose my marbles?"

Yashua took a slow, deep breath.

"Many times in those days, politics and strategy were seen as an active part of the newly developing faith," he explained. "As a result, regional political matters were represented religiously. The Book of Revelations dealt mainly with the conditions at the time. It was in no way a game plan for the end-times. God has sovereignty above all else."

"So the Book of Revelations isn't true?" I asked him, very confused at this point.

"It's quite true," Yashua said, "when viewed through the right context."

"And what context would that be?" I said. "I'd sure like to know..."

"It's complicated, but here goes." Yashua smiled, clasped his hands together, thumbs tucked under his chin. "An apocalyptic story," he said, "is an effective way to portray current events, back then or right now. Contemplation of the end causes one to reflect on their current state."

"So, Revelation was talking about their time period?" I asked.

"For the most part," replied Yashua. "It is the Word of God, make no mistake. But it must be seen for what it was; a communication to the many outposts of early Christianity. The author, John of Patmos, was being persecuted for his beliefs. God speaks through the persecuted. But he spoke mostly for the Christians of his own time."

"Okay," I said, "so why are we up against 'The Beast?'" I asked. "I heard once that it was a code for the emperor Nero or something ...?"

"Sort of," replied Yashua. "The beast Katherine's referring to is not a personal, physical being, or thing."

"It's some kind of demon?"

"Not exactly," Yashua said. "Angelic and Demonic forces are bound to Divine Law. Even Satan cannot act independently of his purpose in existence. The beast is more like a manifestation of the energies of human free will; it follows its own course."

"So, is free will is a bad thing?" I asked. "I mean, if it creates a beast and all..."

"To all things, light and darkness," Yashua said, "good manifests as well."

"So ... there's a good, uh, 'beast'?" I asked.

"Yes," Yashua said. "Me."

"You ... right, just what was I thinking," I said.

"Me, Moses, Muhammad," Yashua continued, "And others, like Martin Luther, who spoke against corruption in the church. And centuries on, your own George Washington, who gave up power for the survival of a representative government. Abraham Lincoln, who made a decision in the name of justice that cost him his life. Men like Martin Luther King Jr. and Mahatma Gandhi, who sacrificed their lives to promote peace, and equality. None perfect, none without flaw, and millions the number I haven't mentioned. But all, at one time or another, brought the Truth, and the Word. Be it only a brief spark in the darkness of their lives, but it instilled a course which has brought us to an age where we can recognize the rights, the humanity of all people."

"So I take it the beast has the same thing going, millions of smaller 'beasts'?" I asked.

"Yes," Yashua said. "The beast is something that all humans have a connection with."

"So this beast, does it have a single being, with a personality, like you do?" I asked.

Yashua chuckled a bit. "It has a personality, but not yet a single being; not like me, or for that matter you, or anyone."

"What do you mean?" I asked.

"The beast was not created by God in the sense that it was not given a soul," Yashua said, as he looked in the side view mirror. "God allowed it to be created by the Spirit of Man. Sentient life would not have been possible without it. Without it, there would be no measure of human spiritual success."

His gaze went out the window, and I just tried to absorb everything.

"The Truth, the Word, the 'Divine Essence', it taps into the natural Power of God. The Beast needs to feed on the energy of humans."

He went on as we drove down I-5 on a gas gauge that seemed glued to 'F'. "It will kill many hosts that attempt to directly channel it. So it spreads itself out among a small number and draws everything it can into itself. Eventually, it finds a channel pure enough to manifest, and he becomes what you would know as an," he thought about the next word. "Antichrist."

"I don't get it," I said. "Yashua, I'm really tryin'."

"You're doing well," he said. "It's complicated."

He thought for a second, his finger to his lips. "Okay," Yashua said, "you've always been bothered by the fact that the top one percent of families in America now control eighty percent of the country's wealth, correct?"

"Yeah," I said, "definitely."

"Money has a spiritual significance to some people. It causes them to generate spiritual energy. Bad spiritual energy, the kind that the beast feeds off of. It latches on, and draws that significant object, *money*, to its host."

"The rich people are the Beast?" I asked.

"Not rich people," Yashua said. "It's about a mindset, not an amount of wealth. There are rich people who have helped humanity and those who've harmed it. In fact the future 'antichrist', right now, is poor."

He leaned over ever so slightly, just to emphasize what he was about to say.

"God created no 'groups'. He does not recognize the 'old-boy network', the 'elite', or the 'powerful few.' He recognizes not a race, or a national identity. God also does not recognize a 'Catholic' or a 'Protestant', or a 'Muslim' or a 'Jew', a 'Buddhist' or an 'Atheist'. He recognizes an individual human being, that He created; one He's known *very* well."

We stayed silent for a little while after that. I-5 loomed on ahead, with desert and the occasional brush and tumbleweed peppering the scenic monolith. We'd been on I-5 since we started, and I didn't even remember passing through San Diego. Now we were past Anaheim, where Route 101 split off.

"It's after you, isn't it?" I asked after a long pause.

"Yes," Yashua said. "And with me, the entire world."

We continued in silence down I-5 'till we approached the sprawling suburbs, and gridlock, of L.A. I had many more questions to ask, but I was sure that Yashua had many answers, all of which would just create more questions. There's only so much of it you can comprehend at any one time. There's only so much of it you can comprehend *period.*

Up until that point, it only took a topic as deep as the growing popularity of acid-pop to throw me into 'WTF' mode. Suddenly, I understood acid-pop. At least I could clear that off the burners.

I looked at the gas gauge for the fourth time the whole trip. I was paranoid about running out of gas *normally,* so you can imagine how I was feeling.

The tank was full.

Chapter Six

I had never liked L.A. I had, in my life, only been there twice. Both times I was on business. I didn't like the whole *Hollywood* thing, but more than that, I was perversely proud that no one could touch our ghetto, the Mount.

L.A. reminded me of how ridiculous that was. Seeing places like Compton, Watts, Long Beach, and Norwalk, and a dozen or so other neighborhoods in L.A., nothing really compared. It was like entering another country.

It was as if the lack of resources - and society's indifference had an affair, and those neighborhoods were the bastard children.

The kids growing up on those streets had gangs taking the place of political parties, labor unions, and social clubs. No wonder they had a stranglehold. It was tragic that the kids had more representation in the CRIP's than they did in the Congress.

It took us a good hour to get to the RoseCrans Ave. West exit off of I-5. Yashua had appeared to nod off, which, oddly enough, was shocking. That left just me and Katherine. We talked about L.A., and who we were going to meet. Katherine was by that time wide awake, and she proved to be an expert on L.A. At first, she seemed sort of naïve, but I was beginning to see that she was extremely sharp. It wasn't naivety; it was innocence. Yashua had returned her innocence to her, in battling the effects of HIPPO. She had lost the cynicism that we often mistake for intelligence.

As it turned out, she was a high-watt bulb. She talked at length about the different areas of L.A., and she knew the city politics, too. I asked her what she knew about the Mayor; Jenkins, his name was.
I had heard he was an old machine boss. I didn't know much, I was just trying to keep up a conversation.

"Well, for starters," she said, "he makes most local businesses interact with the city more than they need to. If you want any little thing done here, you have to go through City Hall, and Jenkins. And it has nothing to do with him controlling businesses in L.A. either. It's more like, will you support a challenger if you knew that your business was at the mercy of the incumbent?"

"Yeah, but don't they have a City Council?" I asked, "I mean, they have to be saying something about it, right?"

"They have no power, and little publicity," Katherine said. "They talk about it, but Jenkins has the natural advantage of having the spotlight whenever he wants it. Which, incidentally, is always."

"Can't they push for some kind of reform in the city charter?" I asked, remembering when Anno Luce revised its own charter. "Like equal power or something? Wouldn't the public back them?"

"They tried that ten years ago. It was grassroots. They got the signatures, but Jenkins found a loophole in the California elections law and got the signatures tossed. End of story."

"Didn't the people who signed it get pissed?" I asked.

"They did, but a lot of them were also working full-time jobs and raising families. It's easier to get someone to sign something than it is to get a time commitment. Protest takes time."

"Ya know, I never thought about it that way," I said.

We were getting near the turn off, and I looked over at Yashua, who was sound asleep. I had the address, 1033 RoseCrans West, so I'd just wake him up when we got there.

We eventually made it to the exit, and followed the ramp off onto RoseCrans. The street was mostly commercial. I saw a few restaurants and assorted eateries. It was an eclectic mix of local commercial enterprise.

Of course, in the general neighborhood, 'enterprise' would be reaching.

I had managed to gleam some background, though not much, from Yashua, about where we were going and why; The Parrhesia Institute.

From what I was able to figure out, it was an umbrella organization; kind of shadowy, but for all the good groups, like Amnesty International, Greenpeace, Salvation Army, Red Cross, Doctors without Borders. More than twenty thousand groups around the world had contacts with the Parrhesia Institute. Other than that I was in the dark.

When we pulled up to 1033 RoseCrans, I was *really* in the dark, because it was just a beat up, two-story brick building, with what looked like a storefront and a small addition in the back. It had an assortment of antennas and satellite dishes on the roof, all of which looked pretty beat up. 'You've got to be kidding me,' I thought to myself.

I pulled into the small parking lot on the side, and went to wake Yashua up, but he was already awake. Katherine hopped out quickly to stretch.

"Sure we got the right place?" I asked.

"As sure as I was when I walked into Mt. Calvary," he said, and smiled.

Yashua and I got out and joined Katherine at the door. Katherine rang the bell, which sent off a symphony in chimes across the front hall, visible through the decorative window-panes in the door. A tall, older man, dressed in jeans, a black t-shirt, and a leather coat answered the door. He recognized Katherine and Yashua immediately.

"Katherine!" he said warmly. "How are you?"

I recognized him. *Hernando DeSantis.* He ran for L.A. Mayor when I was in college. No wonder Katherine knew about the Jenkins machine.

"I'm well, in a manner of speaking," she replied.

"Yashua," he said, and shook Yashua's hand using both of his. "It's been a while. How are you? What happened to you?" he pointed to Yashua's arm.

"I'm well. Survival is a wonderful thing," he said.

DeSantis looked at me. "I'm sorry, we haven't been introduced."

Yashua said, "Hernando, this is Barnabas Sheehan. Barnabas, this is Hernando DeSantis."

"Pleased to meet you," Hernando said as he extended his hand, and again, shook mine with both of his.

"Pleased to meet you too," I said. "It's funny; Katherine and I were just talking about L.A. politics on the way here. I didn't know we were coming to meet with *you.*"

"Yes, Katherine was a trooper when we worked together," he said, and smiled at Katherine.

"My condolences about the election," I said.

Hernando laughed. "Yeah, well, sometimes you learn more from defeats than you do from successes."

He motioned us inside. "Come in, please," he said, "We have all manner of caffeinated refreshments. You guys must be tired from the drive, with the exception of Yashua." He looked over at him. "…who doesn't sleep."

"He slept in the car," I said.

"I was meditating," he said, "not sleeping."

"Suuure…" I said, jokingly.

"If the people who fought to get the Charter changed had worked for Hernando's campaign instead, he'd have won, and they'd have gotten the changes they wanted," Yashua said. "Katherine thinks that, though she didn't tell you."

He got me. "Okay," I said to Hernando, "he was meditating. But I'm tired, so I'll grab some 'Joe.'"

"Katherine, I have orange spice tea," Hernando said.

"My favorite," she said. "I'm glad you remembered."

"I bought it by the barrel during the campaign. I should hope so," he said, and jabbed Katherine in the arm playfully.

We made our way into the kitchen. It was plain, but tasteful. Everything in the place that I had seen so far was very simple. It wasn't what I'd expected of the institute that was described to me. The kitchen looked like it could've been mine. Well, not mine. It was clean, and I guessed that the food in its fridge had an expiration date newer than his mayoral campaign. I couldn't say that about my kitchen.

The coffee was great, and they spent a good hour catching up on old times. Though I was out of the loop, I didn't at all feel excluded. Between the three of them, the background information was thoroughly explained.

As I had known from the car ride, Katherine worked on Hernando's campaign. Yashua had a more interesting connection to Hernando, and the Parrhesia Institute.
Yashua had met Hernando when Hernando was thirteen. Yashua was a young man. And Yashua had to come to him years later to find out something about himself, his *bond*; I didn't know what it meant. Hernando then had to find out who his old friend *really* was.

"I agonized over the conclusion," Hernando said. "I'm a strict Catholic, and the Bible says that you're not to believe in false prophets. So concluding that Yashua was the Messiah returned was not an ... easy thing for me to accept."

"I didn't have that problem," Katherine said cheerfully. "I Saw Him right away."

"But when we discovered the *bond*, it was just as hard for *him* to accept." Hernando nodded towards Yashua.

"What '*bond*'?" I asked.

"In time," Yashua said.

"It wasn't until a week after the primary that I saw Yashua

for who he really was," Hernando continued. "Everyone was calling me to offer their condolences, tell me how pissed they were, all that. I kept up the demeanor, but I was dead inside. After every phone call I ended, I slumped back into this pit of hopelessness and negativity." He sipped his coffee, which I must say he made a great cup of. "Katherine stopped by many times to cheer me up, but every time I told her I was fine, shooed her out, and I'd sit in my living room alone; no TV, no music, nothing. Then a knock at my door."

Hernando put his cup down gently. "I almost didn't answer it. It's easier to put up a 'game face' when it's not your face that someone's actually seeing. Having to hide what you're feeling when you're looking at somebody in the eye is tough. But I did open the door, and it was Yashua," he said. "I mean, I knew it was Yashua, but he looked different. *Radiant*. Not human. I know this will sound strange to you, Barnabas, but I saw many colors flashing through Him. I wasn't imagining either. I saw it visually."

I remembered the dream I had about the prison. The conversation was starting to unnerve me.

"I had, for many years, been trying to come to terms with knowing who Yashua really was, and at that moment, everything I had known came together. I could see within him Abraham, and Moses, and Elijah and Muhammad. And I realized that he was the Messiah."

"Okay, now you've both mentioned Muhammad, but aren't Muslims anti-Christian?" I asked.

They all laughed. "No," Yashua said, "Muslims believe I was one of the Great Prophets, along with the Patriarchs, Moses and Muhammad. Christians believe I was the Son of God, and equal to God. In fact, many of the early converts to Islam were Unitarian, or Judeo-Christians. The difference is they don't believe that there's more than one God."

"Well, isn't that right?" I asked.

"Yes, indeed," Yashua said.

"So then you're not the 'Son of God?'" I asked.

Hernando gave Yashua a knowing look. "Barnabas," Yashua said, "my soul, my *human* soul, is the embodiment of the Word. It is the Word that is the Son of God. Do you understand?"

I was confused. Sensing this (apparently,) Yashua put his hand on my arm and said, "Humans have always had a problem with understanding *status*. If I begin my mission with my Divine status, no one will be able to move on from it to what is most important, which is the substance and message of the Word. When the time is right, the real Truth will be known. But when the time is right, humanity, and you yourself," he squeezed my arm slightly, "will be ready to understand it."

To which that moment's segment of *The Divine Status of Yashua* concluded, and the conversation shifted to a more practical topic, that being, why we drove to lovely RoseCrans Ave West in the first place.

Hernando motioned us to a hallway off the kitchen, to give us a guided tour of the facility. I had anticipated this to be about as long as the guided tour of the apartment. I was in for a shocker there.

We walked into the hall, which had nothing in it but a long table. To the left the hallway went to the back door, (which had three deadbolts, and was wired to a security system) and to the right was a doorway with another security system. Hernando punched in the password, and opened it to reveal a stairwell, leading down to the basement.

As we descended the stairwell, I noticed that the stairwell was rather industrial, not a typical basement stairwell. Like everything else, it was simple, but it was obvious that we weren't going to a root cellar.

The stairwell ended in a door, again with deadbolts, and a security system.

"This is the Control Room, for lack of a better term," Hernando said, as he unlocked the deadbolts. "From the inside, one button opens all these, and deactivates the security system," he added. "But getting in takes a second."

He finished with the deadbolts and pushed his thumb onto a dark-plate. A bright-green flash zipped down as a line, registering his fingerprint. *Biometrics*, I'd seen my share of them. He then punched numbers in to deactivate the alarm. He opened the door to what appeared to be a pretty large area, much of which was obscured by Hernando's size.

When we walked in, it was enormous. Instantly I could tell it was much bigger than the size of the building above-ground. The Mission, in its entirety, was 4,800 square feet, and the Control Center, in more or less open expanse, was probably just as big.

There didn't seem to be any rooms; no doors on any of the walls to indicate that. There were quite a few cubicle areas, spacious from where I was looking. At the opposite end of the room stood what looked like a crazy Buck-Rogers kind of control area, with a huge screen; a flat panel the size of a projection screen. There were four sub-screens on either side of it, all with different images. Blurs, really, from where we were standing. There were other pieces of equipment that I couldn't name. Not because it was a secret; I just didn't know what they were. Cables went from the far end up into the ceiling, which, from the floor, looked to be over twenty feet high.

When we walked in, we were standing on a grating, and the ceiling was as high to us as the kitchen ceiling was. So we were looking down and out over everything. I counted about ten people, but there could've been more. Some parts of the layout were obscured from view by equipment, or dividers, some of which were as high as ten feet. There were clocks for different time-zones, just like a newsroom. People were scurrying from area to area with papers or printouts on old computer-paper rolls. Two people were at the main control area.

"This is where it all happens," Hernando said, and walked down the stairway to the left of us. We followed; Yashua first, then Katherine, then me. Katherine was looking around, probably for people she knew.

We walked over to a row of cubicles, and looking in they each had a computer, a TV, and a phone/fax machine. They looked pretty comfortable. A young guy in his early twenties was working in one of them, looking up something on the internet.

"This is where we gather all incoming data from our contacts," he said. "We get thousands of pieces a day; most of it is automatically collected and pre-sorted. The majority of what's done here is field research; making calls, getting faxes, that sort of thing."

"How many people work here?" I asked.

"On any given day, about twenty," he said as we continued down towards the far end, "but our total listed staff is thirty-six."

"Do they work for the other groups too?" I asked.

"No, our staff is centered here," Hernando said. "We don't directly involve ourselves, or share workers, with any of our affiliated groups. It gives us more objectivity and neutrality."

We walked on further, and we came to an area that was loaded with equipment. It looked to me like a bunch of CB and ham-radios, with two computers showing panels of different waveforms. It must have been live, or playing, because the forms were changing and moving.

"This is our audio-signal processing area. Mainly we use this to monitor what's being broadcast, and to analyze signals received when the need arises."

"To see where it comes from, you mean?" I asked.

"Or to see if it's been doctored," he replied.

"Nice," I said. "That's cool."

"Unfortunately, we have to do it when someone's trying to screw people. We never get to do it for fun," Hernando smiled.

We continued walking, and along the way, we saw unopened boxes of equipment, filing cabinets, both metal and cardboard, and loops of cabling tied together with twist-ties. An older gentleman with a trim red-and-gray beard walked by, and shot a 'thumbs-up' to Hernando. He reminded me of Joe.

We made our way towards the center of the far end, where the screens were.

"This is the control desk," Hernando said. "This is where everything incoming goes to, and everything outgoing comes from."

Two women sat at the control desk; one was young, mine and Katherine's age, and the other older, probably near Hernando's age. They had a map on the screen. It showed a shore, and the writing on it looked like Arabic. There was English subtext, kind of like closed-captioning on the bottom of the large screen. There were circles, squares, and triangles of all different colors dotting the map, with lines connecting points that would occasionally highlight, or change colors. At the top right was a satellite image, most likely the area of the map, and in the lower left corner there was a video shot of an urban area in a desert. There was an Arabic Title, and a caption in English, but I only glanced at it. I didn't remember it three seconds after we left it. The screens on either side showed newscasts; many in different languages, and all of them had subtitles.

"We use a combination of GPS and Geographic Information Systems software to tie sets of all the information coming in to geographical reference points, and this acts as the intermediary between us and the groups we assist," Hernando told us as we moved on to the other side.

To the right of the screens we approached a row of cubicles, almost, more like 'divided areas.' These were where the ten-foot dividers were. Looking inside, they were filled with computer equipment, main-frame, server type stuff. Things I won't embarrass myself trying to name.

"This is what runs the show," Hernando said. "This is our central processing station."

The area was alive with the frenetic flash of LEDs of yellow, red, and green, and the whirling and whooshing of rivers of ones and zeros. Hernando added, "All of this has been customized. The only thing 'factory' in half of this equipment is the casing."

"What about the satellite dishes and antennas on the roof?" I asked. "That stuff seemed pretty beat up."

"Artificially distressed," Hernando answered. "That's all cutting edge equipment. But everyone outside can see that, so we distressed it to keep a low profile."

"Oh," I said, and we kept walking.

Further down, back towards the stairwell, we saw cubicles. They were larger than the ones on the other side, but not with the dividers so high. They had larger doorways, and inside I saw a bunch of VCRs, tape storage spaces, a computer, and a TV. The screen was divided into twelve panels, each showing a different channel.

"This is where we collect satellite video feeds that are relevant to what we do. For the most part, computers control this, but we have people who can manually do it, if need be," Hernando said.

One room was empty, and one had a young guy working on the computer with a pair of big, cushioned headphones on. He was clicking on panels of the computer screen, and the monitor would go to that one channel, until he called up another channel. Again, subtitles appeared where the language wasn't English.

At the far end, directly right of the stairwell, was a lounge area. There was a table with comfortable office chairs and a kitchenette. There was also a TV and an electronic dartboard, its red LEDs all a' glo', circling out the magic 'triple zeros.'

"This, of course, is the lounge area, or as we call it, 'the ICU'," Hernando said with a chuckle. It was where we retired to after the tour, as Hernando said the upstairs was really just living quarters for him and his wife, Cecile.

"So," Hernando said to Yashua, "now's the time."

"It is."

Hernando opened a drawer next to the sink and pulled out a manila envelope.

"There's thirty-thousand dollars on the card, and two passports," he said, holding it up between his thumb and index finger. "The passports will work, but the committee can't allocate any more money without drawing attention."

"It will be enough, Hernando," Yashua said. "We will be able to travel on this."

"And we will need your assistance while there, though not with money," Yashua added.

"Of course, friend," Hernando said. "Anything in particular, may I ask?"

"Paradigm," Yashua said.

"Yes, that's a problem indeed." Hernando scratched his chin. "We've been monitoring them. There's a storm brewing, even among our own groups, over HIPPO." Hernando cast his gaze towards the control desk, "In fact," he said as he got up, "follow me."

We walked down to the control desk, as he explained to us the progress Paradigm was making with the HIPPO system.

"They don't have approval of any sort, but they announced its release already," Hernando said, "which is illegal, but when you own the world's media like Fisher, illegal is just a formality."

We got to the screens. "Juanita," Hernando said, and the older lady turned her head, "can you pull up the HIPPO file we've been working on?"

"One sec..." she said, and she started to close down what she was doing.

"Juanita Tierrez, aside from being my cousin, runs the control desk here," he said.

A map of the U.S. popped up, with circles, triangles and squares of different colors dotting the states. It looked like the other map I had seen, except that the satellite map and the video shot looked familiar. More the video shot. *Anno Luce*. The Paradigm Building, to be exact.

"This is the penetration map of HIPPO system use, so far," Hernando said, pointing to the map.

"The circles are suspected recruiting sites for test subjects," he explained. There were about twenty or so that I could see. They seemed to be in urban areas. I saw one in L.A., Chicago, New York, DC, Miami, and other places, probably big cities.

Hernando pulled out a small laser pointer from his pocket and pointed to one of the squares. "These are the confirmed testing sites," he said. "Note that they're all set slightly apart from recruiting sites."

He then pointed to the triangles. There were four of them. One was Anno Luce.

"These triangles are confirmed sightings of test 'victims', for lack of a better word," Hernando said.

"Waitaminit," I said. "There's only one in Anno Luce. What about Guy Francis?"

"That *is* Guy Francis," Hernando said. "How did you know about him?"

"Well what about…" I began to say it, and then stopped. 'He doesn't know yet,' I thought.

"What about what?" Hernando asked.

I hesitated. I didn't want to tell him. I mean, it wasn't my place to tell him. Thankfully the decision was taken out of my hands by Yashua.

"Hernando," he said, in a calm voice. "Katherine was abducted."

Hernando at first looked like he didn't get the joke. Then apparently he got the joke, realized it wasn't a joke, and looked at Katherine.

"When, Katherine?" he asked.

"Shortly after the primary."

"Wait a minute," Hernando said, "that was *ten years ago!*"

Katherine ran her fingers through her hair. "I don't remember it, Hernando. I got away a few weeks ago. Or they let me go; I don't know which."

"Why didn't you tell me?" he asked, sounding almost hurt.

"This has all happened so very fast, and we knew we were going to tell you here anyways." She reached out to grab his hand, which was slumped at his side. "I'm fine. I found Yashua."

He looked at Yashua, who smiled. He seemed to settle. He trusted Yashua immensely, I could tell. But I could see he was angry, of course not at us. It was strange, because by my estimation, he was a kindly, gentle person. But it was obvious that he saw Katherine as a kind of daughter figure.

He turned to Yashua, and asked, in a lower voice (though we could both still hear him,) "Is she gonna be okay?"

"Yes, fine," Yashua said. "She's been divided of the Longing."

Hernando stood silent for a while, deep in thought. He looked at the screen. "Juanita, dear," he said. "We need to create another data set."

"I'm working on it right now," she said, and she was.

"Katherine," Hernando said, this time reaching to grab her hand. "Are you going with them?"

Katherine looked at Yashua.

"You will need to stay here," Yashua said. "Hernando needs your help to monitor the world situation. We will not be able to."

"Yeah, we'll need to keep an eye on you," she said smiling.

I was disappointed. Katherine was really starting to grow on me. It was only during the car ride, even, that I'd realized how much I had underestimated her. I have to admit I was getting kinda sweet on her, and I had been looking forward to getting to know her better on the trip.

Yashua spoke next. "I will need to prepare you, Katherine, to fight the beast when I'm not here."

"Do you need a chapel or something?" Hernando said. "We have a prayer room upstairs."

"Yes, that would be good," Yashua said, and we headed for the stairwell. Hernando directed Yashua and Katherine to the prayer room, and, after they went in, Hernando and I sat in the kitchen and had more tea.

During our tea I told Hernando more about myself, where I worked, and how I'd met Yashua and Katherine. He told me he could've used someone like me on the campaign. He also told me more about the Parrhesia Institute, and what it specifically did.

The Parrhesia Institute was created by a group of seven billionaires. They were all in Forbes and such, but they weren't high-profile for their wealth. They were, however, interested in doing what was right in the world. So they created the Parrhesia Institute as a way to coordinate the activities of as many 'good groups' as possible, which by then numbered over fourteen-thousand. Parrhesia provided free, real-time information gathering, analysis, and distribution, without having a specified agenda of its own. Though it had regular contact with every group, its rules of separation were very clear.

The institute itself was designed by a group of activist scientists, and everything in the place was customized, optimized, hybridized, or whatever other '-ized' you wanted to throw in there. When we were talking, I made a joke about them having more information than the NSA.

"The NSA has more information," Hernando replied, "but

we have more useable intelligence."

Hernando had been Director of the Institute since 1993. Hernando himself had an impressive résumé. He started his life, so-to-speak, when he met Yashua on Dr. King's march from Selma to Montgomery. He had been a runaway before. Yashua taught him the importance of education, and service. Hernando got into a high-school, and graduated four years later. He was a voracious reader, and all the years without formal schooling didn't hinder him. After he graduated, with great heaviness of heart, he served in Vietnam. He'd been drafted. He could've gone to college, and avoided the draft, but he knew someone else would have to take his place.

He fought with valor, and won medals that he never felt he deserved. He said war always claimed the lives of the most deserving.

After he got out, he did go to college, and got three degrees; English, Russian and Economics. He taught English for a while, always in the poorest neighborhoods, and he looked back on those times as his best.

Eventually he got into the news business. He bought a small paper, *The L.A. Source,* and it grew from a circulation of a few hundred to one of two-hundred-and-twenty thousand. That is, until it was shut down for writing one too many embarrassing facts about state and local government officials. Hernando took the paper underground, and he attracted the investors of *Parrhesia.* They made him the Executive Director of the Institute, and hadn't been bothered by his run for the Mayor's Office. He stayed on after the election, and had remained there since.

"Couldn't you have gotten the word out despite the media?" I said, and pointed to the basement, "I mean ... you've got the means."

Hernando smiled, "I couldn't do that. This place is too important to jeopardize."

"Yeah, that's true," I said. We continued our tea talking about Mahavishnu. He was also a fan. Small world.

Yashua and Katherine came out of the room after about

twenty minutes. Katherine had what looked like ash-marks in a strange design on her arm. I added that to the stack of things I would need to ask Yashua about on the way home. We said our goodbyes to Katherine, and to Hernando. I pulled Katherine into the foyer.

"Katherine, I gotta admit to you, I underestimated you before. And, I feel bad about it. I mean, you know your stuff, and I saw how happy you've been, and I thought you were just, I don't know, naïve, and I'm sorry, and…"

Katherine reached over and kissed me on the cheek. "I'll see you when you return. We'll talk then. And don't worry about it." She smiled and my heart melted for the two minutes we were still there.

When I got in the car, somewhat adrenalized, I turned on the engine, and, not to any of my surprise at this point, the tank was still full.

We talked on the way back, as we always did, and Yashua told me a great many things. But I won't comment on them here. Not that I would want to hide anything. It's just a matter of time.

I now see why so much of Yashua's life was not written down in the Gospels. In the early history of Christianity, there were over one thousand accounts of Yashua's life, or testimonials, or to shorten that, Testaments. From talking with Yashua for even a little time as I have, I've come to realize that even if we still had all of those testaments, we'd know only a small sliver. So I'll keep you updated on the relevant stuff, but, for brevity, I'll have to skip a lot.

We arrived in Anno Luce in the late evening. Some call it morning, but how are you gonna call it morning when it's dark out? I never figured that one. As we drove up Barker Street, and I looked around, I was amazed that, in light of where we just were, the Mount actually seemed pleasant.

I dropped Yashua off at the Mission, and noticed the gas tank was still full, a freebie. No questions asked.

"Tomorrow, we have to make our reservations to Addis Ababa," Yashua said. "You may want to tie up your loose ends."

"Addis *wha?*"

"Addis Ababa," Yashua repeated. "The capital of Ethiopia."

"Oh," I said. *Of course.*

"I don't know what I'm gonna say to Zee," I said, thinking about possible explanations.

"You needn't worry about that," Yashua said. "Tell Zee you're going to Jerusalem with me to show gratitude for recent...generosities."

"Isn't that lying?" I said, shocked somewhat that Yashua would say that.

"Not at all," Yashua said, and smiled. "You will be."

I drove up Jefferson Highway on the way home, KALR blasting, as usual. I was surprised that after driving for as many hours as I had that day, I wasn't the least bit tired. With so much to think about, I guess sleep went on vacay' for the night. As I drove on, the lights of Anno Luce shone like crushed diamonds in my rear-view mirror.

Zee wasn't altogether happy to hear about our plans to travel to "Jerusalem", but there wasn't much he could do about it short of firing me, and he knew that. He was more upset to be losing both me and Yashua at the same time, rather than seeing just me go. Somehow, I think he understood. Well, he understood something. And as much as he enjoyed having Yashua work there, he realized that Yashua's presence was causing some ruckus. Alejandro was a different story. Me and Ale' were close. I went into the office, about a half-hour after talking to Zee. I could see it on Ale's face. Not anger, but a confused, disappointed look.

"You heard, I take it?" I said, tossing some papers on the back desk.

"Oh, yeah," Alejandro said, flipping his pencil through his fingers. "Should I ask you if you're outta your fuckin' mind now, or at the airport?"

"Ale', I know," I started, but he cut me off.

"You've only known Yashua for three weeks, and this has been one mind-fucking three-week period!"

He leaned closer and his voice softened.

"Look Barney," he said, "I know your heart's in the right place. And I know that whatever Yashua's got goin' on, it's genuine. But just make sure you know what you're getting into. I mean, you're goin' overseas with someone, however cool, that you didn't know a month ago. A homeless man."

I started to protest, but Alejandro put his hand up.

"Don't even try an' play me like that, I know what you're thinkin'," Alejandro said. "It doesn't mean shit that he's homeless, I know that. But not bein' judgmental about a fact isn't the same as not seein' it at all. I mean, how much do you know about him?" Alejandro said.

"As much as you do," I said. "Maybe I little bit more."

"And how do you know he can even get the money he says he can?" Alejandro asked. "It isn't cheap, especially if you're staying there for any length of time."

"We went to see Hernando DeSantis yesterday," I told him.

"Hernando DeSantis?" he asked, surprised. He had done a little grassroots for DeSantis, back during the mayoral campaign. "How do you know him?"

"I don't," I replied. "But Yashua does. Katherine too. She used to volunteer for him. I'm surprised you didn't know her. "

"I only volunteered a couple of days," he said, "but you're changing the subject."

"DeSantis is giving Yashua the money," I said. "You should've seen the place, man."

"I have," Alejandro said.

"He's working behind the scenes," I said, and added. "You should go see him." *Maybe Katherine and Hernando could explain it better.*

"Maybe I will," he said. "But I'm still skeptical, just so you know."

"Well," I said jokingly, "we here at Calvary always go the extra mile."

Alejandro laughed. "In this case, twelve thousand of 'em."
I laughed. "Yeah."

"Take care of yo'self, son," he said as I walked out.

Yashua was in the main activity room, sitting on the couch, staring out the window. He looked pensive, more so than usual. Whatever we were about to do was important to him. *'Perhaps to us all,'* I thought to myself.

"Yashua," I said.

"All has been prepared." He smiled.

"Okay," I said, "as crazy as this all is."

Yashua got up and walked over. He put his hand on my shoulder and said, "Barnabas, you must know that this is your decision. Though I know what you'll decide, it is because I know you. But you must be doing this of your own volition."

"I know," I said, "and I'm in this all on my own."

"No, not on your own," he said.

Chapter Seven

I asked Zee if I could take Friday off to go and take care of any loose ends. I told him I didn't know how long we'd be, but I knew there'd be a chance that we'd be on an extended ... business trip. We had agreed to leave Friday, so as to give Zee a week to make preparations. I recommended Jeanne Stanwix to replace me. Jeanne knew the field, and had been trying to get a job. Yashua, quite honestly, would be irreplaceable.

Driving down Carter Street, on the west side of the Mount, I felt a sense of intimacy with the place; perhaps because I thought I might never see it again.

I hopped on Jefferson Highway and drove to the post office to have my mail held. Again I chose radio silence. It was weird because I used to have a big problem with silent driving. My radio broke once, and I went nuts. Suddenly I preferred it.

I arrived at the post office, a tiny building for our postal area, and walked in. I was waiting in line, and, like everyone vigilant (or bored) enough to do so, I took my try at memorizing the top-ten most wanted list adorning the side wall. Among the bearded, beady-eyed bandits, I came upon one who immediately caught my attention.

He had that *look*. The same look as Katherine had when she came to us, but not exactly the same. Probably how Guy Francis would have looked had I seen him the day he'd attacked Yashua. But even that didn't describe it. I'd *seen* him before, but I couldn't for the life of me remember where.

Victor Ray Tanner, his name was.

Victor was wanted for multiple murders, kidnapping, armed robbery, assaults, rape and escape from a correctional facility in Georgia.

I had an uneasy feeling. I just *knew* I'd see him again.

I had the post office hold my mail, as fast as bureaucratically possible, and left, driving just a little faster.

I went to Joe's. I owed him a goodbye. I walked in and there was old Joe; newspaper in hand, coffee at his side, good ole' Irish cheer on his face.

"Joe, the toast of the town!" I said. "What's good today?"

"Everything's been good, Barn'," Joe replied. "Maybe not in the world, but, here it's all heaven."

"That's good." I looked around, hesitating. I knew he'd be the hardest one to tell. Before I had a chance to say anything, Joe said, "You're going to Africa with Yashua, I know already."

"How'd you know?" I asked.

"Yashua and I talked about it," Joe said. "Plus, I know you."

He put the paper down. He leaned in and said, "Now, I don't know who or maybe even *what* Yashua is. But he is something. And I know that whatever he is, God's with him."

"Joe, I wish I was as calm about this as you are," I said. "I mean, do you think I'm doin' the right thing here?"

"Aye'," Joe said. "And it's okay to fear goin' overseas, some of it for good reason."

"But if you don't take a chance, you don't live, you don't

grow," he said. "Ya' know, ya get caught in ruts, stuck in your ways. Ya' end up shuttin' yourself outta' the world around ya'." He spiced his coffee with some pencil lead. "You just have to remember your path, even if fate diverts you from it here and there."

Joe's wisdom always astounded me. An old windbag like him, too. Who would've guessed?

I drove up Route 30. The road only goes north, but I might as well have been driving aimlessly. I couldn't think of anywhere to go, but I had to go somewhere. I mean, I had things I had to take care of, but not many. My life was pretty simple.

So, without anywhere else to go, I arrived at the apartment. I had a bit of arranging to do; figure out what to pack. I went into the fridge, to see if there was anything I needed to eat quickly. Turned out there were things I needed to eat *last month*. They were promptly and unceremoniously thrown out.

As custom, on went the rule of life; TV. The BBC came on. *Huh?* I always watch MSNBC, or CNN. How did it get on BBC? '*Was someone here?*' I wondered, but I couldn't figure out why anyone would have a reason to break into my house to watch the BBC.

The anchors, a British man and woman, were reporting on a story about Ethiopia.

"The President, in a fiery speech today, issued a warning to the Ethiopian government, stating; 'We will not sit idle while terrorists are allowed to have safe harbor in any nation.' This was in response to the terrorist incident in Berlin, the masterminds of which are alleged to be in Ethiopia. The Ethiopian authorities deny this, and claim that this is merely an excuse for the U.S. to establish a military presence in Ethiopia. Ethiopian President Moso Obonye said in a press conference; 'The U.S. is determined to secure its economic grip on the world, and this is an excuse for pre-emptive military invasion. We harbor no one. This is the beginning of a justification.'"

I kept trying to think about what value Ethiopia had to the United States. I also thought that Yashua would have something to say about it.

The rest of the news passed by me; mostly drivel. I rearranged some of my stuff, but mostly I just sat there smoking the cigarettes I guiltily bought from the corner A&M EZE-GO, lost in a maze of notions.

I revolved around the gravity of belief and the open invitation to skepticism and doubt. And I didn't want to doubt. But what you need controls you, not what you want. Maybe I needed the skepticism. I mean, would I have been able to accept all the things I'd been through in the past week, if not for the ability to say it wasn't what I thought it was?

So, I sat, alone, in the dark, with slits of purple twilight forming razors across the empty wall. I felt completely aloof from what appeared as life. But I also felt, for the first time, connected to something. Even if it was bullshit, wasn't it worth it?

I sat in the dark for hours that night; thinking, rethinking, and asking many questions of God. Of course the problem was always that the questions I asked most were the questions I knew the answers to.

The rest of the week went surprisingly still. A quiet had pervaded in the Mission. It was like a monastery, I'm not kidding, and to be honest with you, I wasn't complaining. I didn't interact too much with Yashua. He seemed to be spending a lot of time 'off'; not absent, but dissociated. I understood, and felt a little 'off' myself. So, in a daydream trance, I wandered through a row of the calendar, ending at the night before we were to leave.

That night I sat, uneventfully. I cut myself off from caffeine at six o'clock; cigarettes at ten minutes before lying down. That night I had another dream.

I was in an open expanse of tall grass, stretching far beyond that which a human being could see. A bright, synaptic pulse energized the fields; waves were coming from nowhere, extending infinitely. Many beings had assembled at the center of the field. Though they were a half-mile in the distance by the look of it, I could see them clearly, in full detail. Some had the appearance of death; others life, and there were larger beings too. Some of these large beings had faces. Some had many faces in constant revolution.

They lined up in rows facing each other as battle lines were drawn, and energies swirled about the center ranks of each. The colors of both energies changed in opposition to each other; light hues to dark hues, purples contrasted by yellows, reds by greens.

The largest figures on each side set out dual thunder in a language that I couldn't understand, barely did it sound human. But it was answered all across both sides, in many languages. At times, I could recognize human languages, even English.

Then the colors on both sides began to swirl, and grow. The front lines charged, and battle ensued. The energy began to swirl faster, and it began drawing in the energy of those who fell in battle.

The swirling energies on both sides began to influence each other, drawing them to swirl together like a hurricane of turbulent light. The speed of the battle, and of the energies surrounding it, reached a fever pitch. It then abruptly shot up into the air, forming a globe like the cap of a mushroom cloud.

The globe was turbulent, but translucent. Within it I could see a panorama of what looked like civilizations; of stone, from simple stone villages to Chinese and Egyptian cities, to Roman and European type civilizations. I saw events, wars, and speeches, inventions and artwork, written words and pictures.

It eventually turned into American cities, some of which I recognized. It flashed through; the flash of urban and rural landscapes becoming break-neck. Then the perspective rose above a desert, and then it began to zoom in. Eventually it approached a city; I recognized it by the Paradigm building. Anno Luce. It continued to zoom, faster now, and the energies became lighter, less turbulent, more radiating and more familiar.

I remembered them from my last dream. Surprising, as it itself was a dream. I'd seen those colors in the one who'd been slain. The zoom slowed, and the energies became turbulent again. The lighter energies I had known were suddenly competing with the darker energies from before. The zoom went over highways, lights, trees, and it became clear that I knew where it was going. I was in a daze as the zoom approached my street, phasing into my apartment through the roof and to a sleeping me about to be woken up. My open eye caught the orb above the field and I saw myself. But the look in my eye wasn't my own. It was that of the man in the post office bulletin; Victor Ray Tanner.

At that point I woke up, and damn near fell off the bed. I looked at the alarm clock; *6:45 a.m.* At least I was only up a half-hour earlier than I wanted to be. I was thankful for it; not the dream, but the wake-up call. I would have much to discuss with Yashua.

I took off with only the bare essentials; toothpaste, toothbrush, washcloth, towel, three changes of clothes, and a book for the flights.

I met Yashua at the airport. He brought nothing but a brown leather sack, like an attaché case. Other than that, nothing.

Our flight left from the San Diego airport, so we had to drive there. On the way, I told Yashua about Victor Ray Tanner, and the dream I'd had.

"You're getting closer to the Source," Yashua said. "You're being slowly let in on the true nature of existence. Expect to have more dreams like that."

"As regards to Victor Ray Tanner," Yashua said, "we will indeed see him. He was a murderous criminal before Paradigm got him. They used him as a 'worst case scenario' in their product testing. He will become the Beast's purest channel."

"The antichr ...," I corrected myself, "anti, well, *you.*"

Yashua laughed. "Yes," he said. "The anti-*me.*"

We arrived at the airport at about eleven o'clock. We had a noon flight. After going through the exquisite hassle of security checkpoints, courtesy of 9/11, we took off and diverted for the remaining forty minutes. Yashua went to one of the airport chapels, and I went to my own shameful chapel; the airport smoking room. I can't even tell you how many cigs I chained. About thirty minutes worth. I didn't enjoy flying; I made it an infrequent occurrence. But eventually we hit the moment of truth, as they called flight 480 to Chicago (our first flight). From there we would be going non-stop to Heathrow in London, then on to Addis Ababa. From there I would be flying by Yashua's lead. Not that I wasn't doing that already.

As they called our zone, Yashua put his hand on my

shoulder and smiled. "Peace, child," he said, and at once I felt it. My stomach stopped tightening in knots, and the stranglehold my muscles had on my clenched, grinding teeth let go.

We entered the long tunnel to the cabin, and I looked back, almost like I was looking back on my old life, but all I saw were other passengers trundling down the long tube.

We entered the cabin, and took our seats. After the customary pre-flight safety instructions, I looked out the window. It was cloudy out, and that made me nervous earlier, but the clouds were passing over. I looked at Yashua as the sun began to shine, and gestured towards it.

"Your work?" I kidded.

"There have to be some perks to the job," Yashua said.

I laughed aloud as the grind of the engines became the shielded roar that signaled our leaving the solid world. Yashua closed his eyes and went to sleep. Or what passed for it with him.

I spent some time scanning the microscopic landscape as we reached cruising altitude. I could never get over the fact that up there, you could see the curvature of the earth. Probably the *only* cool thing about flying.

We hit a spot of turbulence, a nasty one. Yashua was 'sleeping' and I thought to wake him up for a second. Then I thought of Peter and that boat in a storm, so I thought against it. I swear, at that moment, Yashua smiled a little.

O'Hare Airport was the busy mess that I guessed it to be. As we went to our gate, which was of course after I stopped in the neighborhood smoking lounge, I couldn't believe how comfortable Yashua was with the whole buzz of the airport. Yashua, as complex as he was, was a simple man. I would've expected to see him uncomfortable in such a hectic setting. But I didn't see that.

I felt bad, too, because when I went in the smoking box, I had to ask him to wait out in the hallway. He didn't, of course. He came right in. So I felt even worse about giving Yashua a dose of second-hand smoke.

He was practically a celebrity in there. He had all kinds of people talking to him. He took all their stories in with that generosity and good cheer I had come to know him for. Seeing him with everybody, I realized that I would indeed take a bullet for him, if one was coming. In light of what we were about to embark upon, that thought unnerved me just a bit.

We eventually found our gate, and waited patiently (well, Yashua waited patiently) for our flight to be called. We showed our tickets and our passports, as we would be leaving the country on that flight. We then boarded Flight 1440 for London.

After we hit cruising altitude (that was still a grip-the-seat and grit-the-teeth moment, though not as bad), I asked Yashua to explain the dreams that I'd had.

"There is much to those dreams that I cannot explain," he told me. "I have the explanations, of course, but if I was supposed to tell you those things, you would not have had those dreams. Much of it is for you to discover. But I can tell you about some of the second dream."

He paused, and put his finger to his lips, which I'd come to signify as his 'How am I gonna put this easy' thoughts. "Bear in mind that this explanation is only given to prophets, and in ordinary times you would not be privy to them," Yashua said, as he stretched out a little. "In the beginning, and I do not refer to the biblical "In the Beginning," for God is timeless; *this*," he said, gesturing to all around, "is in its way timeless. I refer to the beginning of the process. These are events; not days, hours or seconds. There is no measure of time to God, through which all suns and laws of physics derive their meaning."

At that point I was trying to keep myself from saying 'huh?'

"A chain of events on the ethereal plane preceded physical creation," Yashua said. "A war, a battle the likes of which humanity alone could never fathom."

"The battle in my dream?" I said, taken aback by the gravity of what he was saying, plus a little turbulence.

"Yes, that was it," Yashua said. "It's been written that *there was war in heaven*, and that was true in a sense."

"But there wasn't yet heaven." The stewardess smiled as she walked by, oblivious to our discussion. Yashua continued. "*Heaven* is a human existence. Apart from God in Its Eternal, there existed only the ethereal plains, and the beings God had given Existence to. What you would call 'angels' or 'demons', and even the Spirit of Man was present then; the 'soul' of Adam and Eve, if you'd call it that. In reality they were energies of different orientations."

I didn't think Stephen Hawking would've understood Yashua's explanation. I sure didn't.

"Physical creation requires two forces, both of which are separate entities; love and conflict," Yashua continued. "The first to occur was love. This was the lineage of God's energy that all of the created beings were composed of. But being separated from God, who is Perfect, the energies could not perpetuate perfection. The only thing that could result was some level of degradation from the Source. This created conflict, which caused the First War, and the conditions necessary for the dynamic physical existence we're in right now."

"So ... the story in the Bible is bunk, then?" I asked.

"Not at all," he said, and smiled. "God created your world, and this whole universe, and all that came before it, and all that will come after it. But he had to have this occur before ethereal Essence was ready for physical Existence. This always occurs. The story of Genesis was how God revealed the product of such a process to a Semitic farmer in exile, named Moses."

"I'm not even gonna' say I understand, but I somewhat do," I said.

"You understand more than you think. What you saw was the ethereal plains. You witnessed the first battle."

"Yeah, but it was only like five minutes, if that," I replied. "What kind of battle was that?"

"As I said, the ethereal plains are without time," Yashua answered patiently. "What you saw was the prime battle. You saw it in five minutes, but it may have taken five million years."

"Do you remember seeing their faces?" Yashua asked me.

"Yeah," I said. "It was weird, because I felt like I was a half-mile away, at least."

"That's because the ethereal plains are also without space," Yashua said. "A half-mile is about as meaningless as five minutes there."

"So ..." I said, and quite honestly couldn't think of where I wanted to go with it, until something popped in my head. "Do the ethereal plains still exist? Are there still angels and demons there?"

"Yes," Yashua said. "Well, yes and no. Physical existence polarized all beings created prior. The ethereal plains were once a place of harmony. The Great War caused a rift in that harmony. God had to set up a Throne, by necessity really, whereas prior God needed none. The Purest Spirits assumed functions at the Throne, and the most Degraded Spirits assumed function in the created existence, namely the universe, and of course, the Earth."

"So why did God create a place like this," and this time I motioned all-around, "to be filled with the bad forces?"

"Well, many have asked that question of God and only half of them seriously," Yashua answered. "And I don't know if I can give you an answer you'd accept, even if it be true."

He moved about in his seat to cross one leg over his knee, and continued. "The created world is a proving ground for God. Our substance was created by, and is composed of, God's Divine Essence. Living in an uncertain world, with so many obstacles ... finding the peace, love, tranquility and grace that is your birthright requires you to grow in strength. Only a few are able to surpass the many obstacles. And that spirit, being created, returns to God. That which had followed the path of material substance will be consumed by it. You must have enough goodness in you to appreciate Heaven; if you don't, you're soul will go its way."

"But you can save people?"

"I can save those who truly seek it," Yashua said. "You have to find your own inner light before I can be of any help."

"Okay, what about Katherine?" I asked.

"She called to me," Yashua said. "The path to your own inner light is humility. Katherine knew she was in the pit, she wasn't strong enough to beat it and she admitted that to me. She honestly called out for my help."

"Many call to me in mockery and delusion, and use a twisted form of my words as a crutch, and then a shield to protect them from the tragedies and hypocrisies of life."

"But is it wrong for your words to be a shield?" I asked.

"My words have been many things; a crutch, a shield, a sword, a blanket, a walking stick, even," he continued. "But if you use them rather than listen to them and try to understand them, then no matter what thing you're using them for, it's not acceptable."

"Yeah," I said, just pondering all that he had said.

What always surprised me was the clarity and lucidity with which Yashua spoke of such things. I've heard many people talk about angels and demons, and Yashua didn't resemble any of them. He spoke matter-of-factly, yet he would pause when he knew I wasn't going to believe something. And he never asked me to believe anything he said unless it was a 'life-lesson' thing. He would go at length and with such detail about historical events and people he knew in his life, and I just *in-my-heart* knew he wasn't making it up. I started to feel real guilty about causing Yashua to have to go in a smokers' room. I know, such a small thing, but the example is only one of many.

I conked out for a while; something I didn't normally do on flights, but we were going to London. I awoke as the plane was seconds away from touching down at Heathrow Airport in London.

We had a layover in Heathrow for about four hours. Nothing noteworthy happened. Just the same ritual, but we got some food. That was about it. I sat around the gate mostly, and kept reading *Trinity*, which I had brought. One of the security people at Heathrow looked at it suspiciously. I hadn't realized when I was packing that they might look at me funny because I was reading *Trinity* in London. Oh well. I had no bombs, not much luggage, and I wasn't a terrorist. So without any event, we finally got on our final flight to Addis Ababa.

Chapter Eight

As we boarded the plane, I could hear the flight attendant saying 'hello' in a cheery voice to the people in front of us. As I got to her, I noticed that she had a look in her eyes. She had energy; more than vital; more than alive.

I felt good about that, comforted a little bit too. I was able to relax, and flying didn't seem to concern me too much. The engine roared up, and the plane went to taxi. I wasn't even queasy when it left the ground. First time that had happened.

When we were in the air, we talked about what we were going to do in Ethiopia. We talked quietly, mindful of anyone who may have been listening.

"We must retrieve the Ark of the Covenant," Yashua said. "It is required."

"I'm just going to assume you're being serious," I said. "But why are we going to Ethiopia?"

"The Ethiopian people are unique," Yashua replied. "It is believed that the human race started in the Nile valley, but the human race began in Ethiopia and spread first to the Nile Valley. From there it spread onward to cover the globe."

"The Ark has been in their care when it was seen that it could no longer be kept pure elsewhere. With them it has remained all this time," he explained as he opened the window-flap.

"And they will give it to you, without a problem?" I said.

"Certainly," Yashua said. "They have been waiting for this moment for a long time. It is their birthright."

"So Ethiopia's gonna be light?"

"Getting the Ark *will* be. Getting it out will be harder."

"But not the Ethiopians," I said.

"No," Yashua said. "Before we leave Ethiopia," he paused as the stewardess walked by, "America will take military action *by proxy*."

"By *proxy?*"

"Yes," Yashua said, "a private military contractor, to hide their hand."

I remembered the news report I'd seen.

"So we'll have to transport it out, umm, *under the radar?*" I said.

"Yes, and we have to be with it. If we are not within a distance of it when it travels," Yashua said, and his voice trailed off. "We need to be by its side, let's just say that."

"I won't ask."

"We will be arriving in Addis Ababa," he said. "We will stay there for one day, and then we'll depart for the Ark."

"Okay," I said.

Yashua and I talked more about the Ark, and how it wound up in Ethiopia.

The Ark was constructed during the exodus, and was a dwelling place for the Spirit of God. Where it was, God was. I asked Yashua why God would need it.

"God didn't," Yashua said. "The Israelites did."

"I don't get it."

"There are to be no idols unto God, no statue of His likeness, for his Likeness is the universe, and it can never thus be represented," Yashua said.

"Yet the Israelites could not understand having a God in whose physical presence they could not be. So they created a golden calf in the desert, I'm sure you remember reading that."

"Yeah," I said. "And Moses broke the original Ten Commandments."

"The tablets had to be broken, as the First commandment had just been broken," he said, and continued. "Though God was upset with them, He knew that they would have to have some part of His Essence amongst them, for they could not yet comprehend faith."

Yashua sipped his soda. "And so God designed the Ark, not as an idol, but as a vessel for the smallest portion of His Divine Self."

"So you mean God Himself, or a part of Himself, is

physically in the Ark?" I asked.

"Yes; well not exactly *in* the Ark, but amongst it," he said, wiping his mouth with a napkin.

"Now wait a minute," I said. "I know about the Ark from things I've read, and I've read that only the High Priest of Jerusalem could go where it was, just one day a year, for an offering or something."

"Correct," Yashua said. "And that holds true to this day."

"So how am *I* gonna be able to spend days with it?" I asked.

"It won't be easy," Yashua said. "But you'll manage." He smiled.

I laughed and sat back in my seat to meditate, or sleep. Whatever you'd call it. We landed a few hours later at Addis Ababa.

Addis Ababa was everything I would expect of an African city. The buildings had the look of what I always used to think of as a modern adaptation of our '70s style. There was a large boulevard that we started on; I don't know the name of it. The city was disorienting, and later Yashua told me that was how Africa affected most Westerners when they first got there. He said I'd orientate by the time we left. I laughed.

We drove down the boulevard, amidst shop-keepers and donkey trains sharing the roadway with us. I felt happy. It was comfortable being there.

We had been met by a short, frail-looking Ethiopian man. He was elderly, his face was well worn, and he had salt-and-pepper stubble for hair. His name was Mihret Goto. He was kindly, and he spoke English fluently. His accent reflected a London University education.

Mihret explained to us that tensions had been high, and frustrations growing against Americans there, as a result of the U.S. ultimatums and declarations. He told us not to worry, as we had friends there. That was comforting.

We were brought to the *Mercato*, the largest open market in Africa, and Yashua bought us lunch. He also bought a few other things. We sat in the open air and enjoyed the cuisine; kitfo, which was basically a steak strip and tartar, but hot. Yashua ate something called Dulet. I'm not sure what was in it.

I had begun to see more in the people as they walked by; eyes, energies, lacks thereof. It made me uneasy to drive down the bustle of urbanization and catch the gaze of children, no more than six or seven years old. Some of them would have a vacuous stare piercing through their eyes, searching for a way to escape. It reminded me of the look of HIPPO addicts.

Just then I heard thunder in the background, and the sun started to disappear beneath the approaching clouds. We were driving in a convertible, and Mihret flipped a button after telling us to get our arms in. The collapsed vinyl roof came up and slowly sealed the car from the rain that by then was washing dirt-streaks from the windshield.

We arrived at our hotel, if you could call it that. It was a high-rise building, about eight floors, and it looked unsafe. I glanced over at Yashua, who looked at me and smiled. Then he shook his head, like 'You should know better, Barnabas.'

Satisfied that we wouldn't get buried in eight floors of masonry, I took my bag from Mihret and proceeded to the counter.

Mihret had made the reservations, and he spoke in a language I didn't know. But the woman at the counter smiled, and went to the board behind her to retrieve two keys. Yashua and I were each handed one.

"The rooms adjoin," Mihret said.

"Thank you, Mihret," Yashua said.

"I'm happy as always to help you, Yashua," he said, and then he shook my hand.

"Welcome to Ethiopia," he said.

"Thank you," I replied before Mihret walked out the front door and to his car, which was still running.

"Mihret has taken great risk to pick us up," Yashua said. "You'll not see him again."

"Should I ask why?" I asked.

"You wouldn't like the answer," Yashua replied.

"Oh," I said. I probably wouldn't.

Yashua and I went to our rooms. My room had two large windows, full-length, with a small iron patio outside of each, no bigger than they would need to be to stand on. The condition of the room wasn't great, but I'd stayed in dingier places in 'Cali'.

I didn't have anything to unpack, so I sat there on the bed for a while. Eventually I made my way to the window, and pried it gently open. The smell of the air in Addis was something I wasn't used to. I could smell diesel, but that was in any city. The spices and other odors present mixed with the diesel, and made it bearable, almost desirable. I can't explain it in a sufficient way, except to say that the smell of magic was in the air.

I wanted to go outside and walk around, but I didn't know if it would be safe. I went to Yashua's room and knocked. He opened the door, and I asked him if it was safe to check out Addis Ababa. He said yes, and referred me to the University, where he said I would find some interesting museum exhibits.

I thanked him, and took the stairs down the five floors to the lobby (I wasn't taking chances.) I had to walk a few blocks to get to the University, but the rain had let up by then.

The Addis Ababa University campus had a unique looking entrance; a stone arch with two lions at the top, facing each other. I walked through and found the Gallery of Historical Ethiopian Art, which Yashua had recommended.
There were great artifacts on display, and I noticed that many of them were embellished with Christian or Hebrew symbols. It seemed strange, being in Africa. Granted, the Ark was there. It was still a curious juxtaposition.

I got to the main exhibit, and recognized it without having to read the multi-lingual description.

It was Lucy. The oldest human ever found. 'Lucy' was over three million years old. I looked at the ancient bones, feeling the need to contemplate our humble beginnings, and a realization struck me physically.

'*This is what Yashua was talking about,*' I thought. Our race was born here. What I was seeing was not 'Lucy' ...
It was Eve.

I felt a small quake rumble through the room, but it shook nothing except me. I became disoriented and backed away from the skeleton, whoever it was. I turned to look at something else to regain my composure, and I looked at a sword on display. It was polished silver, carved with symbols.

And the symbols were glowing.

Red at first; then red became yellow, became green, and I turned my head to the floor, as I couldn't look at it anymore. I looked forward enough to trace the hallway. I began walking as fast as I could to get out of there. I wasn't ready for it.

I eventually found my way out, and after taking a breath of fresh air, I calmed down a bit. I wasn't about to go back, but I was able to check out more of the city.

I always found the slums when traveling in a strange city, back home anyway. I felt that the character of a city's downtrodden was the true character of the city. So the monuments and 'touristy' things never appealed to me as much as the sprawling neighborhoods on the civic peripheral. And in Addis, I went there.

I saw poverty. I knew I would. Ethiopia's one of the poorest countries in the world but I saw perseverance in the eyes of the people I came across, and I saw a great many 'good-lights' in them. Yes, I saw the 'bad look' as well, but it was well balanced in the cramped streets. That surprised me, slightly.

I saw a little girl, playing near the edge of the street, and she started to climb up a ladder that was braced precariously on the wall of the building behind. There was a drop off the other end; I didn't know how deep.

"Somebody get that girl!" I shouted. "The ladder won't hold."

An older woman ran over and grabbed the girl who, by then, had climbed up about five feet, just before the ladder slipped its hold. It fell towards the drop-off.

"Thank you!" the woman said, and she clutched her child close to her.

"No problem," I said, and I kept walking. Then it occurred

to me that I didn't know the language that I'd just spoken. That's a freaky thing, let me tell you.

At about that point, dusk had begun its approach, and I returned to the hotel. I got there as the final sliver of daylight had been consumed. I got to my room, and went to Yashua's to ask him about the two experiences I'd just had. Also just to hang out, as I was pretty bored.

The door was ajar. Yashua was on the phone; each room had one. I was surprised it worked. He motioned me in as he glanced back.

"Oh dear," he said, after about a minute of silence. "We must make haste then."

"What?" I said. I couldn't help it.

Yashua put his hand up as the caller kept talking. "I feared that may happen. I should let you talk to Barnabas." He handed the phone to me. "It's Katherine."

"Katherine?" I said.

"Barnabas!" Katherine said. "How are you?"

"I'm okay," I said. "We just got here, but it's been interesting." Katherine chuckled on the other end. "How have you been?"

"Okay, or what passes for it. We miss you," she said.

"I miss you too," I said, "and, I mean, Hernando and Juanita too, ya' know,"

"I know what you mean, silly. *I* miss you too." She laughed, and so did I, but mine was a bit more nervous.

"Listen, Barnabas," Katherine said, "things are going on here. I have to tell you about something that your not gonna' like."

My stomach churned. I knew it wasn't going to be good.

"Are you sitting?" she asked.

I wasn't, but I grabbed a chair pretty quick.

"There was a fire," she said. "Mt. Calvary's gone."

I froze.

"What? When? Who did it? Was anybody hurt?" I blurted out when I came to my senses.

"Calm down," Katherine said. "We'll do one at a time."

"Okay," I said to her, "I'm sorry."

"It happened yesterday morning, sometime around ten a.m., well that time here I mean. I don't know when it would've been there," she said. "A guy got in, and doused the maintenance room in gasoline."

"That's in the middle of the building," I said, blankly.

"No one was seriously hurt, Barnabas, and everybody thanks God for that," she said.

That gave me some relief, allowing me to regain my composure, but my thoughts turned to Katherine, and I was suddenly very fearful for her safety.

"Katherine, they're gonna come after you too," I said with my voice trembling slightly.

"I know," Katherine said. "I haven't left Parrhesia since the Mission burned. And I don't plan on it any time soon."

"They'll attack you there too; that's what I'm worried about," I said.

"We're prepared for a whole lot, believe me."

"I hope so," I said, and paused for a second. "Katherine, there's something I gotta tell you,"

"Barnabas," she said, "I know, and we'll talk about it when you come back here."

"Okay."

"Do what you need to do," Katherine said. "I'll be praying for you," she paused slightly, "and thinking of you."

"Same here," I said, and I was glad she couldn't see the flush of Irish red in my face.

"Be careful," she said.

"I will. I'll see you soon."

"Okay," she said. "Bye, Barney."

"Bye, Katherine," I said, and we both hung up.

I thought of the mission, and snapped back to reality. I looked at Yashua, and he appeared suddenly worn, tired. He looked at me, and I knew he felt responsible for it. He *was* responsible, though it was not anything he had any control over.

"I knew this would happen," he said. "I'm sorry, Barnabas."

"Yashua, you didn't do this," I said. "But, if for any reason you know who did, I have to know." I was pissed.

"Tanner," he said. "He's trying to attack us from there because he can't get to us here."

"Tanner?" I said, "The guy on the Wanted poster...the one in that dream."

"Yes," Yashua said. "...the Beast's purest channel."

"The Antichrist..." I said. Yashua nodded silently.

"I'm worried about Katherine," I said as I stared out of the window.

"She'll be fine, Barnabas, I can assure you," Yashua said. "But when we get back, she will be a part of this, and then she'll be in danger, as will you and I."

"I really like her, Yashua."

"You love her," he said.

"Yeah, actually. I think I do."

"She loves you too," Yashua said. "I know."

"Really?" I said. "Because you know what she's thinking?"

"The first thing she said to me after 'Hello' was 'How's Barney?' I don't have to be, well, *me* to know what that means," Yashua said, smiling.

I laughed, feeling a charge inside, some extra energy.

"I can't wait to see her again," I said.

"You will," Yashua said. "I can promise you that."

The hotel had a dinner prepared, and after we ate, we talked about my travels earlier in the day.

"Your assumption about 'Lucy' was correct. It is the remains of 'Eve'," Yashua said when I asked him about it.

"How could they find her?" I said. "Of all the skeletons they could have found, they just *happened* to uncover Eve?"

"God revealed Eve to them," Yashua said, "for she needed to be revealed in this age."

"And then everything went crazy in there! What was that about?"

"You had a realization," Yashua said. "An *epiphany*. When you have these, existence reacts. This has happened every time you've ever had an epiphany. It happens when anyone has such a thing. You're just seeing it now," he said, again with a smile on his face.

"And I spoke in a language today that I didn't know. Ethiopian, it must've been. But I don't know Ethiopian."

Yashua laughed. "Barnabas," he said, "you know every language that has ever existed, exists, or ever will exist. Everyone does. You called out to that woman with your heart, not your mind ... and your heart found her language."

He poured a cup of water from the mini-fridge in his room. "I don't want to sound like a broken record, but, again, *the Source...*"

"Will I be able to do that all the time?" I asked.

"Only if you always speak with your heart," Yashua said. "And that's not easy to do. So don't count on landing a job translating for the U.N. when this is done."

We sat and talked a while, and we played card-games with a deck that Yashua had packed. Yashua knew 'em all. The surprises never ceased.

As we were playing a game of Gin, I asked him how it was gonna be for him to stand before the Ark. I sometimes looked to Yashua as not a human, but as an invincible, flawless figure, even though I knew that not to be the case. Yashua had told me as much. So I wanted to know what anxieties might be going through his mind.

"It affects me, Barnabas," he said, and his expression changed. Right then he looked fragile; I hadn't seen that in him before.

"When I was here last, I did not approach Him," he said. "I came close, and could feel His Spirit close to me. And I became angry at the disrespect given to His temple."

"The money changers?"

"Yes," he said, and lowered his head.

"Did God make you angry?" I asked, as I discarded.

"No," Yashua said, "my anger was my own."

"Did God disapprove?" I asked.

"No," Yashua said. "He understood. But it saddened Him. He was disappointed; not in me, but that the world could cause in me such an outburst."

"Yeah," I said, "you're a pretty mellow guy most times."

Yashua laughed, and put down his hand; three aces and a 9-10-J-Q straight flush.

"Gin," he said and we set up for another game.

We played cards for a few hours, and talked about a great many things. Not mystical, paranormal stuff; just personal stuff. He reassured me that Anna was in Heaven, and Katherine would be okay. The night ended with an even amount of wins on both sides, and I made my exit. We had to get up at 6:30 a.m. to begin our new adventure. I didn't know where we were going, and Yashua wouldn't tell me.

I woke up to the sound of a rooster crowing. It was loud. Then I remembered that we were on the fifth floor. I woke up fully, and noticed that the rooster was on the dresser, pacing back and forth. Then it let out another crow and I nearly jumped out of bed.

I got up, and opened the window, expecting it to fly away. But chickens don't fly. So I opened the door, grabbed a newspaper that was on the nightstand, and shooed it out the door. It took a minute, and the rooster departed, leaving the room full of feathers.

Yashua was up, and had already washed. I washed up quickly, and we went down to the dining area for breakfast. A television was on, showing the BBC. There was a story on about the U.S. and Ethiopia again. It was just wrapping up, so I couldn't follow the gist.

The anchor wrapped up and a picture came up that I recognized immediately; the HIPPO device.

"The Paradigm Corporation in America has just started an advertising campaign to push the global distribution of its newly unveiled HIPPO device. HIPPO is a device that can produce a natural, drug-free state of well-being. It is not physically addictive, and these experiences can be shared socially through an 'UP-LINK' feature."

He went on, as the picture changed to a skyline shot of the Paradigm building.

"This is a big move for Paradigm, as the devices only went on the market a few days ago, but HIPPO's key sponsor, billionaire media mogul J.D. Fisher, has decided to speed up global distribution due to 'the unexpected popularity of the device, and the need the world has for it.'"

The screen cut to a podium, and once again there was the man behind the black-magic; J.D. Fisher.

"We are on the precipice of being able to heal ourselves of anything that ills us; physically, mentally, spiritually. We believe the HIPPO device offers that, and we wish that all nations, rich and poor, have the opportunity to share in it."

The picture shot back to the anchor, and he said; "Paradigm Corp has ambitiously set a date for distribution in select European markets to be Tuesday."

'*Tomorrow,*' I thought.

I almost shit myself. I looked at Yashua, and his brow furrowed. I had a feeling he already knew, but knowing what was going to happen must not have meant it didn't affect him. I felt bad for him.

"What does that mean to us?" I asked.

"It means we must hurry," Yashua said simply, and sipped up the last of his tea.

He went into the serving area to get more tea. As he reached for the teakettle the announcer came on again and said;

"In other news today, police in the Midwest of America have been engaged in a multi-state manhunt for Victor Ray Tanner, an escaped convict and active serial killer..."

On hearing this Yashua promptly burned himself on the hot kettle. I looked over when he cried out, though he only cried out an '*Aaahh!*'

I felt it sort of wash over me. I could actually feel the burn for a second. His hand was red, and soon a small blister began to form. I fell back on my training at the Mission, dressing his arm in a linen cloth. He didn't flinch, but I could see heaviness in his eyes. It was almost like he was sorry for *getting burnt.* Strange, indeed.

After that we met another man, younger, muscular. He introduced himself to me as Kebede. We would be using his vehicle to get to the Ark.

"You have to hurry," he said to Yashua. "You must reach it before dusk."

"Yes," Yashua said. He looked at me. "Are you ready?"

"Well," I said, "I have no idea what I'm supposed to do, so you tell me."

"You're ready," Yashua said, and we left the city of Addis Ababa for a trek across unnamed dirt roads.

We drove through the foothills of the Entotos Mountains, and at many points a dirt path no bigger than five yards would take us perilously across the edge of one of the cliffs.
I saw all kinds of animals; birds, monkeys, grazing animals and rodents, and they seemed to have no apprehension of us as we approached. Many times we would see a goat or a monkey at the side of the road.
I would get nervous that it would panic, run in front of the car, and we'd hit it, or worse swerve into a nosedive off the cliff-face. But the animals just stayed there, watching us; pensive, but unafraid. I saw birds in the air, and they appeared to be circling. But they'd keep the same distance from us, like they were following our journey.

We drove for what seemed like four hours, probably longer. The fantastic, picturesque views out the window kept me busy, and I couldn't believe I was seeing such beauty in Ethiopia.

Eventually, the last dirt road we were on emptied out into a small clearing, and through the trees I could see a large field. It was abounded on all sides by water, and a rocky cliff surrounded the water's outer edge. There was about a hundred yards of water between the edge of the field and the cliffs.

"This is it?" I asked Yashua.

"Almost," Yashua said. "But we shall walk from hereon."

We got out of the car, and walked across the clearing, to the edge of the trees separating it from the field. I felt the breeze pick up slightly, and it was pleasant, refreshing.

We broke the tree-line and entered the field. We reached the edge of it in no time. Yashua looked out across the water, and then looked at me.

"We need to cross this to enter the Sanctuary," he said.

"How are we gonna do that?" I asked. "How deep is it?"

"It's a body of purification. It is very deep except in one place, where it is only five feet," Yashua said. "We will have to cross there."

He began to walk the edge of the field, and settled on a spot. I looked into the water, nervously.

"We'll be fine," he said, and began to go across the water. He dipped his head below, and proceeded to walk across the submerged ledge.

I followed him closely, not wanting to lose my footing. Then, all of a sudden, the ledge dipped about a foot, and I took a good dunk. I almost fell off it, but I caught my footing and recovered myself. The dip returned to normal, and I kept walking.

"Why did it dip like that?" I asked.

"It's just in case you forget to submerge your head," Yashua said.

"Ya' know ya' could've told me about it!"

"It wouldn't have been any fun that way!" Yashua said. "I have to find humor somehow."

"Yeah, funny…" I said, and we reached the rock cliff.

Yashua paused, and told me to step back. He raised his hands, and light converged into his palms. It rose in the air, forming a large dove in suspended flight before the cliff.

"*I am here as You are needed,*" he said in Aramaic. I could understand him.

The dove opened its wings, and crystal spires of light exploded from the wing-tips. The center of the dove pierced into the rocks of the cliff in a spray of concentric symbolism, composed of light. The rocks glowed with these symbols, *grew* with these symbols, without overtaking us. I could see the cliffs expand, yet they took up no greater space.

I gazed into the rocks of the cliff, at the symbols, and I

became entranced by the inner bliss that was overtaking me. I felt alive, and I felt justice, and love, and freedom, and peace. In a single moment, a blinding flash pierced my body and mind, fusing them, for a moment, into one coherent, living being. Me.

I felt terror. I was afraid, deathly so. My head swelled, and I could not gain my balance. I felt like I was staggering; I moved not an inch.

I felt a presence upon me, one to which I knew I was inferior. And it *knew* me. It knew every little detail; every little asshole-moment I'd had in my life, every lie and every betrayal, no matter how slight. It could see into all the lies I told myself, like *Someday I'll be a famous guitar player,* or that I couldn't have helped Anna, or how it didn't bother me that Jeannie left me for Brett. It also knew that I had doubts about Yashua.
It pierced me, pinned me motionless and still, taking measure, taking me in. I was suspended, my thoughts were in mid-fire, for that brief moment I was trapped within living time, and all I could say over and over in my head was; *"I'm sorry! Dear God, I'm sorry!"*

In the midst of my panic, my eyes opened, and I felt clarity. The presence upon me was no longer measuring me. It was bringing me to my feet, and giving me peace and strength. And love.

Suddenly I was in a field again, but a different one. Yashua was walking over to me.

"Welcome to the club," Yashua said. "You took that well."

"What was that?" I asked him.

"That was the Presence," Yashua said. "You must confront that to complete your purification." We started walking.

"Was that God?"

"Well, a part of Him," Yashua said. "A very small part of Him."

"What does it mean?" I asked. We were already well over more than a mile into the field.

"It means different things to different people," Yashua said. "More generally, it means you've been deemed purified to enter the Sanctuary of the Ark of the Covenant. You share that with ten other people not born within its boundaries."

"So where exactly are we now?" I asked. "Aside from the *Sanctuary?*"

"If you have not been purified, a mountain exists where you stand now."

The environment we were in was alive, like the ethereal plains, but it didn't feel chaotic. It felt orderly, and tranquil. It felt like home, though I'd never been there before.

I saw symbols of white light float periodically from the grass in the field, which was tall, but soft. The symbols were sporadic, but they were all beautiful, and comforting.

We walked, and I looked to my left to see a young gazelle. It looked newborn. I was startled, but it wasn't.

It was following us.

I looked to Yashua, and he extended his hand around. I looked to see a few animals following us. Two monkeys, a few rodents and a bird, hopping from tall blade to tall blade, were keeping pace with us.

We kept walking, and Yashua said, "You should be expecting this sort of thing by now." He smiled.

"Yeah, you would think."

As we were walking, I could see that down the field a mile or so, there was a hill, or a rock-face, I couldn't make it out clearly. There was a gentle breeze, and the smell in the air was great, though I couldn't figure out anything that it resembled.

"What's that up there?" I asked.

"That is our destination. It is a cave, and within it, the Ark, and Its protectors."

"You mentioned that people have been born here," I said. "Were they, *are* they, the protectors?"

"Yes," Yashua said, "protectors, and ministers."

As we walked, I could see people in the distance. I couldn't tell how many. They were all wearing robes, but I couldn't tell the color, and I could see staffs in some of their hands.

"The protectors?" I asked.

"Yes," Yashua answered, as he and I continued to approach.

They formed six columns of twelve men per column, and they were angled three columns to a side, concave away from our direction of travel.

We approached them, and I could see that they were all black; African, that is. Their robes were beige and brown, and they had a sash that went all the way to the ground, decorated with symbols. As the tip of each sash touched the ground, white sparks of energy arced.

As we got to within ten yards, the men bowed down, all six columns collapsing to the ground. I was unnerved, and looked at Yashua. I didn't know if I needed to as well, but Yashua looked at me in a way to indicate that it wasn't necessary.

We walked past the men, and twelve of them rose from the back line, silently forming a new line.

"They will bear the Ark from its resting place out of the Sanctuary," he said. "We must see it from there."

"But how?" I asked. "It'll take twelve of *them*, I mean…"

Yashua laughed, and proceeded to enter the cave. I followed at his heel, more or less, and the protectors walked behind us in their formation.

The tunnel to the cave was long, and as we got deeper, the symbols of light I'd seen earlier lit the cave walls. I felt entranced, without time, and I knew we were walking but I didn't feel it. No one spoke. No one had to. The further in we went, the more intense the light of the symbols, and soon we approached an area that we could see no more of anything, except light. We stood at the edge of it, and I was afraid. Yashua looked at me, grabbed my arm and pulled us both through.

We were in a room of gold; sheets of it that were reflective, and luminous. Patterns of astronomy, symbols, and geometric shapes reflected in the golden sheath. There appeared no light source, yet the room radiated. In the center of the room, upon a three-tiered stone platform, sat the Ark of the Covenant.

I had seen pictures of what the Ark of the Covenant was supposed to look like, but nothing could have been very accurate to describe what I was seeing. I saw a chest, or a container. It had two rails for carrying. At the top were two angels in gold, facing so that the tips of their wings touched. That ends the physical description.

Energy in the space between the Ark and the cherubim wings burned white hot, but I felt no heat. There were ancient symbols all about the Ark, and the symbols I had seen earlier were being spawned from it, disappearing elsewhere in an instant as vapor. At times it was translucent, and the vastness of the universe began to play out on its outer wall. The Ark reflected scenes of whole galaxies bursting forth from cataclysms of primordial force, and it looked so enormous, bountiful and infinite.

At that point, Yashua nudged my shoulder. I looked at him, and he made the gesture that I not look at it directly. Immediately I looked to the ground, ashamed.

The protectors approached the Ark, and bowed before it, in silence, three times. At no time did they look at it, but they walked to it with their heads bowed and assumed positions to carry it. I noticed that they put their palms up when lifting it. Then I noticed I was looking at it again, and quickly looked away.

'I'm sorry, God,' I thought.

Yashua turned back to the gateway and motioned me to follow. We stepped through, and I didn't need assistance this time. We flew through the tunnel and out into the field; I don't remember taking a step, but we'd covered what looked like two miles. We were back in the center of the field.

Yashua finally spoke, the Ark in the open air. It shook, and what sounded like thunder issued from it. The sound washed over all it came across. I could not understand the language Yashua spoke, but I was certain it was not Aramaic.

I couldn't help but catch a glimpse of the Ark, it was difficult not to at that point. I saw within it a mountain scene, almost like the place we were at before we entered here. It became clearer to me, and clearer still, and suddenly a very loud, unrecognizable sound came from the Ark, and the scene within rose through the top. It swirled through the tips of the cherubim feathers, and smothered us both in its environment.

The next moment we were there, within the scene that had last rested in the Ark. The mountains loomed in the distance, and we were once again in the clearing. The field we entered the Sanctuary by was just past the trees, and I could see the water and the rocky cliffs beyond.

The Ark was with us this time, however, and the men who had carried it were gone. I was about to ask Yashua what we were to do now when ...

'*Don't Speak. Think.*'

The thought popped into my head, and I know I wasn't the source. It was Yashua.

'*So what now?*' I thought, not sure if he'd answer.

'*Suitable transportation will arrive shortly,*' Yashua said, or thought, or whatever you'd call it.

'*How will we get it out of the country? And where is it going?*' I thought to Yashua.

'*Very carefully,*' Yashua thought back, '*and Jerusalem.*'

'*Oh, that's gonna be fun,*' I thought.

'*We will have our work cut out for us in Jerusalem,*' Yashua thought.

I looked down the road to see what looked in the distance like one of the donkey trains I had seen in Addis Ababa.

'*That's them,*' he thought.

'*Can't God hear our thoughts?*' I thought to him.

'*Yes,*' he thought back, '*but they're less disrespectful to Him than our words.*'

'*How long do we have to keep doing this?*'

'*As long as the Ark remains outside of the Sanctuary, and off of the Temple grounds,*' he thought back.

'*In Jerusalem?*' I thought, as the donkey train got to within hearing distance.

'*Yes.*'

The mules pulled up to a few yards away, and then they all stopped at once. I looked for the driver, but there wasn't one. The train was empty.

'*So how do we lift it onto the train?*' I thought.

'*You carry one side,*' Yashua's thought came back, '*and I'll carry the other.'*

I didn't question him further on it mentally, though I was uncertain how we would be able to lift such a heavy thing by ourselves. It had taken twelve men to get it there. But I made sure my palms were up, and Yashua and I lifted on a mental count of three.

It rose easily. I could tell it was heavy. It was enormously heavy. But though it was my hands at the side, I did not feel as though I was lifting it. It was lifting itself.

Yashua and I rested it on our shoulders at its center, and it balanced itself. We carried it over to the donkey-train slowly, silently, and we went to set it down. I had my end off just a hair, but as it neared touching the wagon, I felt it pull itself to the center of the wagon-bed. Yashua and I let go of it, and we climbed on the front of the train. The donkeys rose, and began to slowly turn around and head back the way they, and we, had come.

We saw animals on the sides of the path again, but more of them. They formed lines, and in places were more than one creature deep. They did not move and like before, they did not appear afraid.

I had many things to ask Yashua, whether with word or thought, but I kept quiet on both fronts. We spent the remaining four hours of our journey back in silence.

Chapter Nine

Yashua told me (or 'thought' me) that we would be transferring the Ark to a truck properly outfitted to carry it. It was a hydrogen-methanol mix, so it burned no petroleum, and didn't pollute. All plastics and polycarbonates were eliminated, except for those necessary for it to move. The area in which the Ark was to be stored was covered with gold sheath to recreate, in a sense, the Most Holy Place.

We came to the truck, hidden from view behind a grove of trees on the side of the road. It was parked just at the outskirts of Addis Ababa. The donkeys stopped themselves and we got off the wagon. We carefully went to the Ark, and this time I did not look at it directly, only in my peripheral view.

We lifted the Ark off of the wagon, carrying it slowly over to the truck. The back was open, and the gold sheathing inside shone fiercely in the setting sun. We walked over to it, and I wondered how we'd be able to get it over the bed of the truck ... when I felt the ground swelling beneath me.

It swelled right to the edge of the truck bed, and we walked it in without having to rise. I was amazed, but I didn't want to break my concentration. We were inside of the truck, and we slowly set the Ark down. Again it found its own place, magnetically drawn to it.

Yashua and I remained silent in word and thought, and we exited the truck. The door closed behind us and the ground sunk. I turned to look at the donkeys in the train and they were dead, every last one. Their harnesses had let go, but they had not moved from the train. And they were not only dead, they were dust. It looked as if they'd been dead in the desert sun for months.

I looked at Yashua.

'They had to be sacrificed. That was their purpose,' he thought to me.

I made no mental reply, and we hopped in the truck. Yashua gave me directions as thoughts; he did not tell me where we were going exactly, just *turn here,* or *slow down* as we hit a tricky area.

We eventually left Ethiopia, I was told later, about two hours after it became dark, and we entered Eritrea on what probably wasn't a road. This confused me, as it had been the opposite direction that we had gone when we took the donkey-train. We somehow covered an incredible amount of ground in two hours.

Eritrea didn't look much different than Ethiopia, and Yashua informed me that Eritrea was, until recently, a part of Ethiopia.

An hour after entering Eritrea we stopped. It was fully dark by then, and all I could see was pitch black ahead of us. As I got out I smelled the familiar smell of the ocean and heard the breaking of waves on a shore.

'*What are we doing here?*' I thought.

'*Our ride is right in front of us,*' Yashua thought back. And as he thought that, a light blinded me from the shore.

It was a ship; small, it was an old military vessel. SC-710 was faded along the bow. It looked like something out of World War II.

A figure approached, but he stopped about ten yards away. He did not come further. He didn't speak, and I didn't recognize him as the light from the boat illuminated his face. His eyes were darting back and forth with Yashua's; I took it to mean that they were communicating.

Yashua looked at me and thought, '*We have to do this again.*'

He motioned to the Ark, and I took my position at the rail. We lifted, palms-up, and onto our shoulders. The Ark was once again light. We walked it to the beach, where a wide wooden plank was extended out from an open bay, cut into the ship's hull. We placed the Ark; or rather, it placed itself on the board, which quickly retracted into the ship. I knew that no human or machine would have been able to pull it in that fast.

There was a ramp also extending from the ship, and, after our Captain, Yashua and I climbed the ramp. We prepared for a voyage certain only to be unusual.

We stood on the deck of the ship as the crew brought it off of the Eritrean shore. No one said anything, and all was still.

"*Identify yourself, drop your Anchor. We have you surrounded!*" boomed a voice from the water.

We all looked at each other. Suddenly what felt like a hundred spotlights lit up and shone on us. They were coming from every direction, even the shore, from where we just were.

"*Prepare to be boarded!*" another voice said, and one of the spotlights came closer. We ran to the opposite end, but there were spotlights on us there too, so we crossed back.

'*What do we do now?*' I thought to Yashua.

Before he could answer me, the voice boomed, "*Get on the deck or*

we will open fire. We are prepared to shoot you if you do not comply!"
The boarding ship came in view, illuminated by the spotlights behind it. It was a small interceptor from what I could tell; probably the mercenary contractors Yashua spoke about. They were speaking English, anyway.
I watched with the utmost anxiety as the ship began to approach us. It came in slowly, and I looked over to Yashua. I could see his face, with the spotlights playing across his features. His eyes were closed, but he was facing the direction of the boarding ship, which by this point had closed in. It was close enough for its wake to slap our ship when, without any warning at all, it exploded, sending shards of plastic and metal, wood and Plexiglas all around like grapeshot. Then the night erupted in firepower.

We all ducked and attempted to take cover, but bullets were plinking off metal, and we knew it would only be a matter of time before one of us got shot. I tried to get up, but the port-hole above me shattered with a popping sound as a round went through it.
And then the ship's surface got warm. I could see the wooden planks that composed the deck start to effervesce. It became brighter, and with a shudder that felt to me to bend time - and a glittery flash - explosions rocked the night.
I stayed prone on the deck, expecting to be hit. But the only thing to hit me was dead silence.
After two minutes or so, I got up. Yashua was already standing. The boats that tried to board us had been obliterated. Pieces of debris floated on the breakers, collecting on the shore. I could see small fires on the shore as well.
The captain, Yashua and I looked somberly at the scene before us for a short while, and we had a moment of silence, from thought as well, for those who'd just lost their lives. With haste the ship once again took its course.

We traveled north up the Red Sea. We stood on the deck, Yashua and I. The captain was below decks, overseeing the crew. The ship was small, about 100 feet from bow to stern. It was a dull steel gray and its bolts and seams were ringed with rust. It was solid though, and I didn't think an aircraft carrier would fare any better than it would.

We had a crew of twelve, I picked up from Yashua's thoughts.

'What's with the number twelve?' I thought to Yashua as we scanned the Red Sea; quiet, and still. *'Twelve tribes of Israel, twelve disciples, twelve donkeys, twelve crew?'*

'The number twelve,' Yashua thought back, *'is significant to the order of Creation. The explanation beyond that,'* he gazed out across the water, *'you wouldn't understand, and you're not privy to it. I'm sorry.'*

I wasn't angry with Yashua for not explaining it. I realized that I had suddenly become 'privy to' a whole lot of information that I didn't know was out there. I appreciated that I knew as much as I did, and quieted my mind.

I could see lights sporadically on either side of the ship, but they were distant. The night sky was enormously bright, and I spent a while scanning it.

I noticed that there were three stars shining brighter than the rest. They were too bright to stare at directly, but they were triangular in proportion to each other. Perfectly so.

I motioned, mentally to Yashua, to look at the stars. He did so, and closed his eyes for a second.

'They are the guide-light,' Yashua thought to me. *'They will appear before the Ark until it rests.'*

'In the temple?'

'Yes.'

'Can everyone see them?' I thought to him.

'Indeed.'

I knew that people would be talking about this, and I knew we'd see it on the news in Israel when we arrived. I breathed in the sea air and paced the deck, walking to the opposite end of Yashua. I just needed space for a bit. He understood. I know he did. I could tell he knew the difficult things he had asked of me. But I was in it until the end. Ultimately, that was what counted.

I don't know how long it took us to get to the Gulf of Aqaba, which split off east at the north tip of the Red Sea. It was far narrower, and I could not only see lights, but buildings, oil refineries, massive oil tanks and the occasional populated area.

I became very nervous at this. I knew people were after us first hand. But I wasn't as afraid for our safety as I was afraid that the Ark was about to make a big scene again. I can tell you it's not an easy thing to be a part of.

I walked back to where Yashua was standing. He had not moved, and, in the reflected light of the shoreline, I could see that his eyes were still closed. I would have alerted him but I didn't. I knew damn well he was aware of the situation. So I walked up next to him and continued to scan the sea.

I saw a ship in the distance; a small ship, fast. It had lights on the front, and a searchlight suddenly shot out from it, darting to the left of where we were.

'Uh oh,' I thought, as I saw the searchlight swing back in our direction.

The ship was cruising towards us, and I knew they'd see us in the searchlight at that distance.
The light came across, and I expected to catch it in my eyes. But as it swung across, it didn't flash into my eyes as bright as it should have. I saw the searchlight head-on, I knew I did, but it looked no more intense than any of the ship's other lights.
As it hit the ship, the edges of the ship glowed, but the center, where Yashua and I were standing, was dark. Then the light kept moving, as if they had not seen anything. It did not even pause on us as it swung by.

'Einstein formed the hypothesis, proven by experiment, that gravity can bend light, Yashua thought, his eyes still closed. 'God created gravity.' He smiled.

The ship was heading in our direction, though not right at us. As it approached, I noticed that the wake of our ship flattened out. I thought we might have stopped, but I could feel the ship still moving. I walked over to the side railing and looked down at the now silent wake. I ducked when I saw the other ship pass us.
It was painted black. I could see that even in the star-light. It was not as large as our ship, but it looked new, built for speed. It reminded me of one of the Coast Guard's drug-interdiction boats.

There were three men on it that I could see. They were dressed in black uniforms. They were all armed with machine guns. At least one of the guns I noticed was an AK-47. I at least knew what one of *those* looked like.

I was about ten feet higher than them, from their boat to our deck. As the boat passed us the men did not look up at me. I saw one look at the side of the ship, but he didn't seem to notice it.

As the search-ship passed by, its wake didn't seem to touch our ship. It just ended in a standing wave, about a yard from us. I stared at it in amazement as the boat sailed off.

When it had passed I rejoined Yashua on the forward deck.

As we continued to travel up the Gulf of Aqaba, we encountered many such small ships, and low flying airplanes as well. But, as with the first ship, lights could not penetrate our vessel, and it was redirected away.

We passed in silence into the northern tip of the Gulf of Aqaba. We then docked in a port on the shore. It was enormous, and our ship was dwarfed in comparison to the tankers we pulled up against. Those ships traveled the globe with their freight, mainly oil.

'This is Jordan,' Yashua thought to me, and the captain came up to the deck.

'*The Ark is ready for transport,*' he thought to Yashua, and I heard it. '*We'll need to move as soon as we anchor. We haven't a big window here.*'

'*I understand,*' Yashua thought back. He looked at me. '*We must carry the Ark, but be careful. No matter what happens, you must remember what you are carrying.*'

'*Okay,*' I thought, and we went below decks to prepare for going aground.

We would have to pick up the Ark outside, as the same plank that had taken it in would be bringing it back out. I waited in nervous anticipation until I began to feel the sounds of us anchoring.

After what felt like forever, I saw the captain come up to open the door and lower the ramp.

I looked at Yashua, smiled nervously, and we exited the

ship.

There was a large freight area, mechanized, mostly, but I could see a few people here and there; some loading crates from trucks, others operating fork-lifts.

We walked off the ship and waited for the Ark to come out. Then, it was there.

I looked at it, stupidly; the way you look at something you think is lost, only to find that it's right in front of your face. Then I felt heaviness in my head, and I realized I was staring at the Ark. I looked away, and my head cleared up.

Yashua and I walked over to it, and as we had done in times previous, we lifted the Ark in our palms, balancing it on our shoulders. We walked past the captain, as he had taken to a knee and had his head down. I saw a truck at the other end of the dock. I wouldn't have noticed it, except that it was identical to the one in which we had transported the Ark before. I almost thought it was the *same* one.

As we carried the Ark, the people who had been working on the dock turned to look at us. As soon as they would see us, they would fall to the ground, prone. They spoke Arabic, but I knew they were praying.

Occasionally, we would see someone who did not fall to the ground on their own volition, but were felled where they stood; a snap of confusion in their eyes as the life left them. I knew that they had died, the ones who did not fall in prayer, and the power of the Ark shook me. I started to lose my focus. The Ark became heavier in my hand, and it felt as if I would break my grip. Suddenly I heard Yashua.

'*Barnabas, focus!*'

That calmed me, and I felt the Ark become lighter again as we continued to walk to the truck.

The sun peeked up over the cargo boxes, splashing onto the dock. The truck loomed large in the morning shadows. We walked towards the back, and the doors opened up of their own power. (Well, not exactly of their *own* power; you know what I mean.)

As before, the ground, in this case the concrete, swelled up to meet the back gate of the truck, and we were able to get it loaded without problem. And again, as before, the ground returned to its previous condition, flawlessly, as the doors closed behind us.

I drove; Yashua could not. As we pulled out I saw that the people had risen, and were looking about. Out of the corner of my eye I could see that, also, some of them had not.

We drove up a long road in relative isolation as the desert sun rose up through the mountains, miles away on our right. I had a great many questions for Yashua, but I dared not ask them, even *think* them, for they concerned the Ark. They concerned God. I knew they were best left un-thought, but I'd be sure to ask them when I could.

The sun had cleared the mountains, and it bore down on us. I had no water, but I wasn't thirsty, nor did I sweat.
We drove for hours in silence, across blank terrain, with no view save the ragged spikes of mountain that lined our one side.

I was lost in thought - idle thought, nothing specific. Observations of the road and the weather, mostly. Then I began to hear the sound of engines behind us. The sounded was punctuated with thudding beats, and I looked in my side-view mirror, curious as to what was causing it. What I saw in the mirror made me feel like I was about to be one dead cat.

Two armored vehicles were accelerating upon us. One of the vehicles had a gun turret, and I could see what looked like a large-caliber machine gun mounted on it. What scared me more was the thing above the vehicles, kicking around the desert sand; an Apache helicopter.

That's what it looked like, anyways. I don't know if it was an Apache, but it was armed to the teeth. It laid back but flew nose down, as the vehicles sped up.

'Remain driving,' Yashua thought to me, '*at the same speed, with the same ease.*'

That wasn't easy to do. My side-view window exploded in a million pieces when they started firing on us. I could feel the visceral impulse to floor it push through my gut, into my right thigh, and as it reached the calf, I stopped it. I knew I had to remain calm, and I did. I wasn't brave, just panicked into doing whatever would get us out of it in one piece. That, I'd figured out by then, meant listening to Yashua.

I could hear bullets ricocheting off the back of the truck. I couldn't see behind me; they'd shattered my side-view. I looked over to Yashua's side view, and noticed that in the other vehicle, the one without the turret, a man was fiddling with something, and I had a strong hunch I knew what it might be;

'An RPG Launcher!' I thought.

'Don't worry about it,' Yashua answered. 'Just keep driving, and don't let your hands leave the steering wheel.'

I could hear a humming sound coming from the back of our truck, where the Ark was. I looked once more in Yashua's side-view to see the man with the RPG launcher taking aim from his vehicle, when all of the sudden he flipped out of the front, falling under the front tires. Something had stopped the trucks, but I didn't know what. I glanced again to see that the vehicles were sinking. The ground had become too soft to support their weight. The Apache had disappeared too. I couldn't see it above the trucks, and the sand was not being swirled around by it. I looked away from Yashua's side-view to check the road ahead, and I found myself staring straight at the face of a man whose eyes were filled with dark energy. He stared at me from the cockpit of the helicopter as it flew in reverse, just inches from our grill and windshield, keeping pace perfectly. I couldn't freak out about a helicopter being in front of me as I drove, because all I could do was look in the man's eyes. That was about the only thing I could freak out over. He smiled at me, as if he was having a great time, and then he saluted Yashua; a mockery, filled with contempt. He backed up. He nearly clipped us when he pivoted around; I could suddenly feel the spray of the sand and the mad throwing of wind about the road as it rocked the truck. I could, for the first time, hear the loudness my initial shock had made silent. I quickly glanced back again; the trucks were almost completely sunk in the sand, just specks in the road behind us. When I looked forward again, I could see that the chopper was flying away, and had already gotten a good distance on us. It was going the same way we were, and that worried me.

We drove on, without incident. We didn't see the chopper any more. We would occasionally see a camel or two, and a small caravan with people nearby. As we would pass, they fell to the Earth as the dock-workers did, and prayed.

I was thankful that, as we made our way to the West Bank, we did not encounter anyone who refused to pray when the Ark passed by.

As the sun began to set, we hit the Allenby Bridge, which crossed over the Jordan River, separating Jordan from the West Bank. I knew we would have checkpoints, and I had no idea how we'd manage them.

As we were driving over it, I noticed that it was bubbling.

'Why is it bubbling?' I thought to Yashua. 'Is it supposed to do that?'

'Not normally,' Yashua sent back, 'just wait and see...'

We pulled up behind a line of vehicles. Israeli Soldiers were checking identifications, and there were dogs running around cars. One vehicle ahead of us was being searched, and it was holding up the line. I finally felt myself start to sweat, and was trying hard not to.

They finished searching the car, and the traffic moved. When we pulled up, an Israeli soldier came to the window.

"Papers," he said, and although he spoke in Hebrew, I understood him. Yashua handed me his passport, and I handed both to the soldier.

He looked at them, then at us, and then at the truck.

"What's in the truck?" he asked me as he looked inside the cab. I didn't know what to say.

I didn't have to say anything. From the river behind us I heard an awful groan, as loud as a train whistle, and I felt the whole checkpoint shake. I looked out of Yashua's window to see what was happening.

One of the largest whales I had ever seen had beached itself. Out of the Jordan River. Yeah, I know. It literally raised the shores as it came out, seemingly from nowhere. But aside from blowing everything I knew about rivers, it took the attention of every soldier, not to mention everyone else within sight distance.

'*Drive,*' Yashua said, and I got it. We passed right through the checkpoint without any hassle, and I could feel the Presence of the Ark exuding from its transport.

We drove on the main road on which we'd crossed over, as it went into Israel.
Eventually, Yashua motioned me to pull off on what looked more like a trail than anything else, and we continued on that. We took a few turns periodically, though it was hard to tell in the arid landscape what constituted a trail and what constituted just dirt and sand.

We could see a large outcropping of rock in the distance.
'*We will rest here tonight. This is Masada,*' Yashua thought.

I had heard of Masada before. It was where the Jews of the First Century committed mass suicide rather than be conquered by the Romans. It was an odd place for us to rest, especially because right then it was a historical park.

'*What about the tour-guides?*' I thought.

'*They will not cross our path,*' Yashua thought back, and by then we were approaching the base of Masada.

We parked, as dusk crept up around the edges of our sand-blasted skyline.

'*Are we going in?*' I thought as I realized how high up it actually was.

'*No,*' Yashua thought back. '*God's Presence will not reside within it.*'

'*Why?*' I thought. '*Because they killed themselves?*'

'*Partly that, but more because they refused to fight.*'

'*But God doesn't like fighting, right?*' I thought.

'*God doesn't appreciate violence, or hatred, or rage,*' Yashua mentally explained, '*but a fight is an action, devoid of morality. You can be right in fighting or wrong in fighting. They would have had to fight to do what was right then. And they did not. They threw away what God gave them to avoid doing what God had expected of them.*'

'*But if they fought, they would have died?*' I thought.

'*They would have given their lives,*' Yashua answered back, '*not taken them.*'

'*So is this place cursed?*'

'*No,*' Yashua said. '*Just not fit for the presence of God. The proper atonement has not yet been made.*'

'*Is that what you have to do here?*' I thought to him.

He looked at me, and I could see the intensity in his eyes.

'*Yes,*' he answered and looked off into the dry barren desert surrounding us. It was getting very cold.

We went out to collect firewood, which I almost laughed aloud about, it being a desert and all, but as I wandered around, I found small pieces of wood. It looked like driftwood, but very old. I gathered up small sticks, twigs sometimes, and, within a few minutes, we had enough to start a small fire. Enough to keep us warm. The wood lit instantly, and perfectly, burning so evenly, I had never seen such a fire before. We sat on two nearby rocks and talked. Well, *thought*, I should say.

'*You have questions, and are afraid to ask?*' Yashua thought to me.

'*Look, Yashua,*' I answered him, '*I probably know more than I need to already.*'

'*But you have a right to the truth, so long as it is something you can comprehend. And when you have questions, I want you to ask, at the proper time.*' He stirred the sand with a stick. '*Now is the proper time, so ask away.*'

'*Why is the Ark killing people?*' I asked.

'*I can explain, but you'll have to bear with me,*' Yashua answered, and he took a breath.

'*God gave humans free will, and you, we, and they can choose to follow Him or not. But when you're in the Presence of God, you must show reverence, and respect. Falling to the ground, praying, in whatever faith, these things are what show respect to the Presence. If you do not, you pay with your life, or your sanity.*

To put it this way, if you do not respect a bee, you get stung. If you do not respect a snake, you get bit. How much more powerful would the consequences be of not respecting the Presence of God on Earth?

Yashua had a point.

'*So how much will the Ark ...,*' I corrected myself, '*the Presence, protect us? I mean, like, what won't it stop? Bullets?*'

'*If you have faith, not in the Ark, or in the Presence, but in God Himself,*' Yashua answered, '*He will empower you to turn the bullets away yourself.*'

'*Did it always do this when they carried it?*' I thought.

'*Yes, more or less,*' Yashua thought back.

'*That's the reason it was in the Sanctuary, isn't it?*' I thought to Yashua.

'*When Solomon died, the house of Israel was divided, and the ten tribes to the north split from the tribes of Judah and Benjamin, and the priestly tribe of Levi, in the south. The northern kingdom was called Israel, and the southern kingdom, Judah.*

The Presence of the Lord could not be upon the divided kingdom, and the Ark that carries it was transported by the last remaining uncorrupted members of the Levites at that time.

So, this Ark left, traveling to Ethiopia, to a place that God had prepared for it,' Yashua thought as he drew a rectangle in the sand. '*where we just were.*'

The Sanctuary. '*Wait; what do you mean, 'this' Ark?*' I thought.

'*There were two sets of tablets,* Yashua's thoughts said. '*One broken, one intact. Hence there are, were, and always have been, two Arks.*'

'*Where's the other one?*' I questioned.

'*Deep beneath the temple, where it has always been, since the beginning of Its day.*'

'*Well, which one do we have?*' I thought to him, and his laugh filled my head. I knew I wasn't going to get an answer.

We sat around and thought back-and-forth for a while, and I heard a subtle symphony of animal noises in the desert eve. The fire burned all the way through the night, although we shouldn't have had enough wood for that. Shortly before I fell asleep, I saw a scorpion crawl past my leg. I jerked, and it turned toward me. I saw the tail rise, but no sooner did I see that than it caught fire, popping in a spray of dark, wet chunks.

It was nowhere near the fire.

Yashua 'laughed' at my shock, and I took that to mean I owed God yet another one. With that, I found a comfortable spot and fell asleep.

Chapter Ten

I awoke with a snap. I opened my eyes wide, and the sun was just coming up. I got up and turned to look for Yashua. He was nowhere to be found. I looked over at the truck, thinking maybe he was there.

But he wasn't ... and the truck was glowing. The Ark was glowing within it, bright enough to darken the dawn sky. Its power eclipsed that of the coming sun.

I felt myself floating, my head light. I felt Its Presence as before, when we'd entered the Sanctuary. It was horrifying. I hunched over and dropped to the ground. I wanted to be as low as possible before It. Partially out of fear, partially out of awe, I prayed. I rarely said prayers of pure worship in my life. It was usually 'Get me outta this,' or 'God, I'm sorry,' but I found myself praising the Power and Glory of God alone, by Itself. Words formed in my head, phrases, foreign to me but I knew them to be timeless. I praised God for being Himself, and I finally understood that part of praying.

Eventually, I felt the Ark calm down, and the energy retreated back within. I was able to get up, and as I shook it off, I saw Yashua standing there, smiling.

'Perhaps I should have warned you about that?' Yashua thought.

I laughed (inside) as we hopped in the truck, and I went to adjust my side-view. Of course there wasn't one. It had been shot out the day before.

'*Oh, yeah,*' I thought as we pulled away from Masada, plotting a course for Jerusalem.

We spent many hours driving, through mountainous areas with names like Har Ben Ya'ir, Har Namer and Har Harduf. Spectacular scenery, and as we went over a pass that crossed the rift of two mountains, I got a sense for how fast we were actually traveling. I saw a plane hovering in the air between the two mountains, and it did not move at all relative to us. So that's how fast we had to be going. But it didn't feel that we were going any faster than seventy, which is what the speedometer said when I'd glance at it.

Occasionally, we encountered people on the road, but they didn't appear to notice us.

'*Why aren't they bowing?*' I thought to Yashua.

'*The Lord has retreated to Within Himself,*' Yashua thought back. '*They can't feel His Presence.*'

We continued driving. We must have slowed down when we passed people or other cars, but I didn't feel it. We came to pass an area of population, the first we'd seen on the whole drive. It was not what I would have expected. The scenery we now encountered was a synthesis of ancient and near-ancient. I saw houses and buildings that looked thousands of years old next to buildings that could have been built in the twentieth century. We had to pull off the mains and drive the dirt a little to enter the heart of the West Bank. We were able to find a part of the Separation wall that had fallen in disrepair; unguarded. Perfect.

It was within there that I first noticed the military presence in Israel. Armored personnel carriers cruised through the streets occasionally, and soldiers walked by with automatic weapons. I saw many weapons, some in the hands of civilians, some in the hands of young teenagers.

'*Welcome to Bethlehem,*' popped into my head. I looked at Yashua, and he nodded. And I could see the sadness in his face, for he was born here, and he saw the same things I did.

He motioned for me to take a right down a very narrow street. We were surrounded on both sides by tall stone buildings, older looking. We came off of the street we were on, into an open area. There was sporadic flora and plentiful sand. We were driving next to a hill. As we ascended it I saw a large fence and a bunch of dreary, dirty concrete hi-rise buildings contained within. I thought they might be a prison.

'*It's a Palestinian refugee camp.*'

I looked over after hearing Yashua's description to see his eyes locked with it. Disgust poured out of them. I felt it myself, but nowhere near as much as he must have. His gaze seemed to dart between the refugee camp and a section of the Wall, supposedly guarding Rachel's tomb.

'*I remember when this wasn't here,*' Yashua thought, pointing to the Wall.

We continued past the camp, and I could see an armored personnel carrier parked at the front gate. There were two soldiers standing there, automatic rifles in hand, and I could see a guard, or what looked like one, in a booth to the left of the gate. We passed unnoticed down the road.

We drove for about fifteen minutes, Yashua mentally directing me here and there. '*Take a left here,*' and '*Take a right at the monument.*'

Eventually, he directed me to pull the truck into what looked like an old meat-packing plant, and back the end up in front of the door of a loading dock, which I did with unknown finesse.

We got out, and a door opened up to the side. An Arabian looking man came out. He motioned for us to come, and we walked into the building.

It was as I had suspected when I first saw it; a meat-packing plant. I saw Arabic writing on signs all throughout the areas I could see.

Yashua and the man stood together. I was sure that they were communicating. I was also apparently not privy. I kept looking around; I didn't know Arabic, so I couldn't read anything in there. But I did see a wagon, the lower wheels barely visible under the sheet of burlap covering it.

Yashua walked over to me. '*We are ready to rest the Ark for its final journey.*' As he thought this, the back doors of the truck opened up. The Ark was glowing slightly. The other man fell to the ground in worship.

Careful not to stare at it, I went and took my place next to Yashua. We lifted it up, as light as it had ever been, and I felt my feet being raised, leaving the ground. I didn't know what to do; I almost panicked, but before I had a chance we were moving, traveling the main area of the plant until we approached the wagon.

We wound up suspended to either side of the wagon, and in a rush of wind we were both on the ground, with the Ark securely resting in the center of the wagon.

From there we went to speak with the man who greeted us, whose name was Bilal. As we were walking, Yashua informed me that we would have to part ways until the next evening.

'I must accompany the Ark to Haram al-Sharif. It would be best that I do this part alone. We will meet tomorrow evening.'

'Where do I go?' I thought.

'You will go with Bilal. He will introduce you to our friends here,' came the reply.

'We have friends here?'

'We will always have friends,' Yashua thought back, and we joined Bilal.

He shook my hand. *'I am honored to meet you, Barnabas,'* he thought in Arabic, but I now understood it.

I wondered why he'd be honored to meet me, and Yashua looked at me and smiled. I don't think I realized, even at that point, how important what we were doing was. I don't think I ever will.

We talked (thought) outside, as the Ark had not yet begun the journey to Haram al-Sharif. I learned that the meat-packing plant prepared 'Halal' meats for many of the Muslims in Jerusalem. 'Halal' is the Muslim version of 'kosher.' I remembered hearing that animals killed for Halal were killed humanely. I had considered 'going Halal', but it was expensive in 'Cali.'

Bilal owned the plant. He lived in Bethlehem, and we were to go to his home, Bilal and myself. Yashua was to stay with the Ark, and I would not see him until the next night. He informed me we would meet up at the Garden of Gethsemane.

Bilal's house was small. It was much smaller than I would've expected for the owner of a successful meat business. As we walked in, I saw a medallion with an Arabic inscription on it. I assumed it to be a house blessing.

As we entered, I saw Islamic pictures and writing adorning the walls. It wasn't overdone, didn't seem fanatical in any way. I could sense a deep devotion.

He had a small television, and an Arab news channel was on; I wasn't sure which one. They were speaking in Arabic, but I could understand them.

'*This is my kind of guy,*' I thought, in reference to my own constant news-watching.

The anchor was speaking to a field reporter. Behind the reporter was a street coated in thick ash, like a grey snow.

"As you can see, the presence of the eruption was felt here, and we're about fifty miles from the crater."

Fire trucks flashed lights and sirens in the background, and they had oriental script on them. It looked like Japanese, but I was no expert.

"A volcano?" I asked. "Where?"

"Japan," Bilal answered.

"When did this happen?"

"Two days ago," Bilal answered. "Almost three."

I was surprised I hadn't heard about it, but in all the activity of the past few days, I shouldn't have been.

I learned through talking with Bilal (and by the way, what a joy it was to finally be able to use my voice again!) that being Palestinian in Israel was the reason why his house was so small. He didn't seem bitter, but I could sense a weary determination that told me the region's history had left its share of scars.

Bilal was an older man, over ninety. He had been born when the Holy City of Jerusalem was in Palestine, and the nation of Israel did not yet exist. He was a young man during World War Two. He had even helped the Allies skirt Rommel, the 'Desert Fox', in Tunisia.

Back then he lived on ancestral land in Jerusalem that had

been in his family for over three hundred years. When Israel declared its statehood in 1948, Bilal and his family were told that they had to leave their home to make way for Jewish settlers.

Originally his family was promised an amount of money to resettle, but it never materialized, and would not have been enough had it been given. So they were put out, and like many others, were homeless for a while. They were then given housing in a newly established camp for Palestinian refugees.

The conditions were horrible, he said to me. Open sewage ran in man-made streams down the sides of the camp. The housing was inadequate, rarely did the hastily-constructed plumbing work. And there was poor ventilation in the hot desert; many people died from the heat, including children.

Though leaving the camp meant certain harassment and scrutiny, especially after the Arab-Israeli War, they were not able to keep them from doing it.

And so Bilal, his wife and his youngest two sons left, but his daughter and his eldest three sons had to stay. Bilal had sworn to come back for them when he could, and he left the only land he called home. Bilal and those he'd collected of his family went to Jordan.

Bilal had always been a devout Muslim. Not fanatical, but even-tempered, generous, gregarious, and most of all tolerant. He started to prepare Halal in Jordan, and it was here that he had first met Yashua.

He was in the field, rounding up sheep. The radio told him that there was a bad thunderstorm expected that day, and he wanted to gather them in before it hit. He crossed a ridge, and the pasture came to view. He saw a man standing in the middle of the field. Surrounding him were the sheep, forming perfect, concentric circles around him, motionless. Bilal called out. The man looked at him, and smiled.

Bilal walked up to him, and the sheep took off in every direction. The man continued to smile as Bilal approached. I, of course, took that to be Yashua. He likes to smile.

Yashua didn't tell him why he was in the field, but Bilal took him into his home, treating him with the utmost hospitality.

Yashua stayed with him for many days, and over that time it was revealed to Bilal who he was. And, of course, Bilal went through many of the things I'd been going through; the doubts, the uncertainties, the anxieties.

But one day Yashua had to continue on, and he left Bilal. Six months passed, and Bilal noticed that the animals on his farm were reproducing faster than normal. He suddenly found himself with more meat than he had customers. He was finally able to return to Jerusalem, establishing himself in Halal. His business grew to become the preeminent Halal dealer to the Muslim community of Jerusalem. All of the Imams of the mosques and Islamic institutions bought their meat from Bilal's business, including the meat that went to the Imams in *Haram al-Sharif.*

Bilal wasn't bitter, or hateful of the Jews. He had fought Rommel, remember. He said his eyes would fill with tears when he saw pictures of concentration camps, to that day. He knew that the situation would be inevitable, and that those in the higher levels of the Israeli government were to blame for the ugliness, not the Jewish people. He had many Jewish friends.

"Yashua is Jewish," he said smiling.

Bilal asked me if I wanted to go to one of the camps. I asked him if it would be dangerous, and he said not really. He had a way in that wasn't ever patrolled. I did want to go, so we put on our coats and left for the camp.

His house was about two miles from the camp we were going to, and we decided to walk. I was nervous as hell; I'll admit to it. As freaky and uncertain as the after-nether-whatever we'd been waltzing through in the past week was, this was real life; real people, real bullets, real pain, real death. And no Yashua around to save my sorry ass.

We walked a dirt road for a while, and we came to a hill of tall grass. We climbed it and approached a small path surrounded by many trees I couldn't tell you the names of.

The path continued for about a mile, and Bilal told me that the refugees would be nervous around me at first, because I was American. That gave me a boost of confidence, I can assure you.

We approached a fence, and I didn't see any kind of way in. Bilal motioned me off the path, and we walked in to the woods, about ten feet. Bilal stopped, stooped down, and brushed his hand through the arid dirt. He grabbed hold of a square stone slab, and pulled it off. There was a hole, which I presumed led to some sort of tunnel.

He hopped in, shining the pocket flashlight he'd brought. I could see about a seven foot drop, with stone pegs in the side wall so that we could step down, which we did carefully.

I could see a small tunnel ahead of us, wide enough for me to be able to walk straight. Bilal told me that one advantage of being an old Palestinian is an exhaustive knowledge of the land. We walked a hundred yards, at least. Then the tunnel ended. There were Hebrew letters on the tunnel's terminal wall. Bilal told me it was the wall of another structure. But he pointed up to a square covered with wooden boards, about as big as the entrance to the tunnel was. He grabbed a big stick resting in the corner and rapped a disjointed, odd-metered repetition of knocks. A few seconds later the wood came off, and I saw a pair of hands reach for Bilal.

I was helped up as well, and suddenly we were in a cramped room. There were many people there. I wasn't counting, but twenty would've been close. I smiled nervously, and I saw a piercing mistrust in most of their eyes.

"I would like you all to meet a friend of mine, Barnabas," Bilal said. "Barnabas is the companion of Yashua."

The look in everyone's eyes changed instantly. I no longer saw suspicion, but almost a strange wonder. A curiosity, perhaps, but I suddenly felt that I was trusted by them, respected, even.

"You are American?" one man said, in broken English, whose name I later found out was Ibrahiim.

"Yes," I said, in Arabic. "California." That set everyone more at ease.

"Do you know movie stars?" one, younger man asked, and I laughed.

"No," I said, "but I saw Cameron Diaz in L.A. once."

That, of course, went right over their heads. *Shewp!*

"Are you Jewish?" one man asked.

"No," I replied. "Catholic, but I don't really go to church..."

A look of confusion swept across the room. I thought about it for a second, and actually had to put my hand to my mouth to keep from laughing at the absurdity of that fact.

"Barnabas has spent his life in Allah's service," Bilal said. "The Merciful Allah calls His servants as He needs them."

The confusion faded, and they all looked at each other, as if to contemplate their own imperfections.

"What is to come?" one asked me, and he had an earnest pleading look in his eyes. I wished that I could have told him something, and I almost wanted to just make up something about how the world and his situation would be better. But I honestly didn't know the next day, or three hours from that moment. I had to shrug my shoulders and tell him that I didn't know. He was disappointed.

At this point I had some questions of my own.

"Do you all live in this camp?" I asked. They all nodded.

"But you can leave, right?" I asked.

They all looked at each other. A hard-looking man, probably ten years younger than he actually looked, answered. "In your American cities, you have ghettos," he said and took a drag off of his cigarette (a few of them were smoking,) I nodded as he blew the smoke out, and he said, "Why do they not leave?"

"Because ... they have nowhere else to go," I said.

"As it is here," he said and tapped his cigarette in the tin ashtray by his side.

"But why stay in Israel?" I said. "What about Jordan, or Syria, or Saudi Arabia, or some other Arab country?"

Another, older man spoke up. "Many people in the Arab world," he said, "talk about us and say that *their people* suffer, and they're talking about us. But they don't want us. We are treated with contempt and suspicion, as second-class citizens, wherever we go. In Israel, amongst fellow Muslims, even in America, the land of freedom, we are seen as potential terrorists. We are monitored, picked out for searches at airports, denied meaningful employment."

He paused for a minute and said, "Here, we are at least

home."

What he said was powerful, and I was silent for a few minutes. I felt the sadness in his plight, in his eyes, in the despair in his voice. I saw that broken look, the thing that Yashua didn't have, which set him apart for me. And for the first time I truly understood the look. And I felt a swell of moisture in my eyes. For the first time I saw the real face of compassion, and it was the face of that man.

We sat and talked, about the conflict, about the conditions of the refugee camp, and of those of the other camps, in the West Bank, in Bethlehem, and in Jerusalem. I heard stories closer to the hearts of the men there. Stories of lovers lost, of children separated from their parents, of being ridiculed as an ID card, necessary for everything in Israel, was taken without explanation. I had no idea, and was in full absorption.

Just then the door to the building splintered from its frame and four men, all uniformed and armed, stormed into the room.

"Everybody on the ground!" one of them said, and the old man, who had made me feel such compassion, rose up. He wasn't doing it to resist; it looked like he didn't hear the man who'd told everyone to hit the floor. In fact his hands started to go up.

"On the ground now!" the other man said in Hebrew, and he slammed the stock of his gun into the hollow of the man's collarbone. The old man shrieked in an awful way, and I saw the look in his eyes the second before he passed out from pain.

Something welled within me. Anger? You could call it that. Rage? That might fit. But it wasn't that. It was different. I felt the fluid energies, the physical effects of anger and rage, but I wasn't bound to it. What I felt I had never felt before, not to this level, or meaning.

I felt offense.

The room lit up. The edges of every solid thing were sharpened. The colors were intensely saturated, and brighter. I could see the atoms and molecules forming the objects in the room. Emotion became motive, and without any understanding, I reacted. I directed the flow of molecules in a pipe wrench that was lying on the kitchen table, sending them, and with them the wrench, cohesively through the stale air and into the forehead of the one who'd hurt the old man. He was instantly knocked unconscious.

I arose from the ground, and looked about, my gaze dispassionate and true. I saw the three other men with their guns on me, but they were scared. I could see the alterations in their heat signature. I could *see* their heat signature. I could hear their muffled gulps, and smell the odor of their uncontrolled sweat.

"On the ground, or we'll shoot!" one of them said, a young kid. I looked at them, and I knew that there was energy in my eyes. I knew this because I could see it reflected in their own. And then they opened fire.

'*Dust,*' I thought, and long plumes of fine dust came from their guns as they pulled on their triggers.

'*Crumble.*' And the guns came apart in their hands. I could feel the shock that sent endorphins through their bloodstreams. I could *feel* their endorphins, as if they were my own. They all stared at me wide-eyed before taking off.

Not all of them, though. Not the man who I'd hit with the wrench. He sure tried to run out the door, but I yanked him back, slamming him to the floor without touching him. He stared at me with terror in his eyes. He knew there was nothing he could do. He knew that at that moment his life was in my hands. And I was *furious*. The smell of ammonia that suddenly hit the air told me he'd relieved himself. And I had wondered how many people *he'd* done that to in those camps.

My anger grew. I could feel the static pulses of energy dancing across the hairs of my neck, and a kitchen knife flew from the table in the corner, sinking into the floor as it pierced the shoulder of his uniform, pinning him.

"P-p-p-please..." he sniveled. "I will do anything..." He reached into his pocket, or tried to. "I have money."

A low growl collected in my lungs and suddenly every solid object in the room, not nailed down, rose and aimed. I could hear shuffling in the background, as the men in the room must've been taking cover at this point.

I stared at this man on the ground, stared *through* him, and images came into my mind of all whom he had mistreated. How many he had made feel this way, terrified, willing to offer him anything, even the change in their pocket, to get him to stop beating them. The children whom he had ripped out of their mother's arms, joking as families were being destroyed.
I would kill this man where he lay.

Just then I heard Bilal call out my name, and it sounded like Yashua, only I knew it was Bilal. I looked at him, and I saw that same look of fear. Only it was *me* he was afraid of. I scanned the room and saw that everyone had this look.

I turned back to the guard, who at this point was bawling, snot bubbling out of his left nostril. Suddenly I felt ashamed. The objects in the room dropped with a loud clamor, as the energy keeping them on target had evaporated. I lowered my head and let my heart sink.

I felt the hand of Bilal on my shoulder. "You did what was right," he said. "Don't be hard on yourself."

I looked around again. The guard collected himself and ran out the door; the other men had regained their feet, and were standing around, talking fast and nervously. I then realized that I had brought a great deal of attention to them, and that, as a result of my anger, they would be placed in serious danger.
My heart sunk even lower.

Bilal pushed back on my shoulders, and my head rose so that my eyes reached his.

"Now you know why I do not hate the Jews. Anger is within us all." He pointed to the trap door. "We must go now," he said.

I knew we needed to move, so I took a breath and apologized to everyone. No one seemed to hold it against me, but they all knew what they'd face on my account.

We left through the tunnel, and walked quietly down the path, back out on the road to Bilal's house. We did not hear sirens, as I would have expected, but I didn't know whether or not that was a good thing. I thought about the maniacal 'Beast-like' man in the cockpit of the attack chopper. How he just flew away. The look in his eyes. Perhaps, tonight, that guard had seen the same look in *my* eyes.

That night I prayed with Bilal. He did many readings from the Qur'an. I read one myself, in a version that bore the English translation on the opposite side of the Arabic.

"The messenger believes in what was sent down to him from his Lord." I spoke in Arabic, though I was reading the English.

"And the believers; each one believes in Allah and His angels and in His books and His messengers." I continued, "We make no division between any one of His messengers. And they say; we hear and we obey. Oh Lord, grant us Thy forgiveness; unto Thee we return."

It helped. It was just what I needed. I went to sleep sometime before midnight, and dreamt.

Sitting behind the steering wheel of an old car, a Nova, maybe, or a car similarly shaped. I could hear country in the background, slow and twangy'.

A looked over at a bottle of rot-gut whisky on the worn vinyl passenger seat. It looked warm and inviting, and I opened it up and slugged deeply. It went down smoother than liquor ever did for me.

I pulled out a cigarette, and I could hear the guitar in the country song cry out in that raggedy way. But the music didn't move me.

Rage moved me. Everybody was after me. Hadn't fucked in longer than it was comfortable thinking about. I was goin' around doin' shit for an asshole that could care less 'cause he did whatever he wanted. And what did I get for it? Jack shit. A chance to have a little fun. Well, fuck, I could have done that on my own. That bastard was nothing without me, and do ya' think just fucking once I would get a 'thank you?' or he'd teach me something I could use to, I don't know, win some money? Or get laid?

'What a fuckin' waste,' I thought, as I lit up a cigarette, not my normal brand, but I didn't give a fuck. It felt good.

I wanted to explode, man I knew the hunt was on, and I stored the animal-like surges into potential energy, anticipating, tasting the chance I'd have to release.

Then I started feeling weird, like I was detached from myself. I thought it was the whisky. And then I could feel lust activating the nerves in my groin, and I smiled. Soon enough, I thought, and a familiar face popped in my head.

Katherine.

Suddenly something didn't feel right. Her image was in my head, and it didn't look different, but it meant something different. She was an object to me. And my vision blurred; my focus blinked out for a second. When my sight returned to normal, I was still thinking about Katherine. But bad thoughts. Really bad thoughts. I realized right then that they weren't my thoughts. I took control for the first time and turned my head to look in the rear-view mirror.

I saw the face of Victor Ray Tanner.

His face was unshaven, and his hair wild. I – he - looked into the mirror, and smiled, and I felt sick. I wanted out, fast. But I didn't know how I got there in the first place, so I didn't know how to leave. Just then I looked out the window, and I recognized the two-story brick building in front of us.

The Parrhesia Institute. Katherine.

I screamed inside with such force that Victor himself screamed.

I woke up back in Bethlehem, screaming.

I told Bilal of the dream I'd had, and he reassured me that Katherine would be okay, and that the Beast would attempt to sway me this way. I felt better talking to Bilal but it wasn't like talking to Yashua.

After we said morning prayers, I prepared to take a ride with Bilal into Jerusalem. He said we would not be able to visit the tourist sites, as they would be looking for me, but he could show me a few of the Old City's hidden treasures.

On the ride into Jerusalem I thought about Yashua. I was ashamed over what I had done the night before. I was also ashamed of the fact that it took me so long to realize I was seeing through Tanner's eyes in that dream.

Many of the things he was thinking I identified with; I thought I was thinking them. If he hadn't thought of Katherine the way he did, I wondered if I would ever have realized it wasn't me. This weighed heavily on me, and our ride to Jerusalem was quiet.

Jerusalem was the focal point of everything on Earth, it seemed. A giant juxtaposition of architecture, religion, and people greeted us as we drove. It was also, apparently, the focal point of militarism in Israel. I saw more of the military presence there than I'd seen anywhere else in Israel, anywhere else in the *world* aside from an actual military base, or a war zone. I guess it *was* a war zone, however undeclared.

Bilal took me around streets and back-alleys; walking, as we had parked past the city limits. He told me that people rarely drove in Jerusalem.

We came upon an old building; dull gray stone, smoothed out from what looked like a millennia of open air. Bilal told me that the building was from pre-Hellenistic times, and had been in the city, untouched, since the Fifth Century B.C.

We walked in, as the door was open, and we entered a spacious area, with mats spread out across the floor. There were Palestinians praying, and I realized that it was a mosque. I became mindful that I was in a house of God.

Those praying didn't stop as we walked in, but they rose as the prayer was done. They looked at me, an American, and at first I thought they'd be suspicious of me. But I think they understood that, indeed, we were in a house of God, and they were most gracious.

I spoke to them in Arabic, and like the men at the camp, they opened right up. They told us about Americans who had come in about a week before, disrupting their service, asking them questions about the building. Bilal told them that I would like to see something he called the 'lower chamber', and, as he had the men at the camp, he told them I was the companion of Yashua. I received the same look; awe. They very quickly spirited us into an adjacent room, and peeled back a portion of the stonework to reveal a passage that spiraled beneath the building.

We entered with the man, whose name was Ali, down the flight of stairs and into a small room. There was a torch that was beside the landing, and a flash-light hanging by its cord from a peg on the wall. Ali grabbed the flash-light gently, and it shone bright, illuminating the room well.

I could see Hebrew lettering on the walls. Some of it looked as if it was supposed to be there. Some of it looked like scrawl. There was a door at the back wall; plain, old wood and ironwork. It looked very heavy, but Ali pushed it open with little effort.

The room inside was dark, and the light from the flash-light did not reveal all of it as we entered, myself following Ali and Bilal. As we got inside completely, the flash-light did a better job of lighting the room. I saw more Hebrew lettering, and what looked like strange pictograms depicting different things. I ran my hand across one wall, and could feel heat as my fingers traced the lines of the characters. I suddenly pulled my hand back.

There was a low table; circular, almost reminded me of a Japanese restaurant, because it was so low. There were three men sitting in what appeared to be a Lotus position behind the table. Of course, this made absolutely no sense to me.
They were old, and made not a sound. I didn't even know if they were alive, or mummies of some sort. I looked around for anything else distinguishing, and could find nothing, save the symbols and an iron fixture. Whatever the fixture once held had long since broken off of it.

"What is this place?" I asked Bilal. "Who are they?" I pointed to the three men.

"This is where Yashua celebrated the last Passover; what you Christians call, 'The Last Supper,'" Bilal replied as he wiped dust off one corner of the table, for no apparent reason. "The three men have been alive since times past. They are who you would recognize as 'disciples' of Yashua. They began their devotion when He left last, and they've been here since."

"Wow!" I exclaimed. "Do they eat or drink?" I asked him. "What keeps them alive?"

Bilal chuckled as he answered me. "If you've gotten this far, I don't think I need to answer that."

"Oh, gotcha," I said. "God."

I suddenly felt that feeling of being in the Presence that I'd gotten so used to lately.

"But wait a minute," I said. "Wasn't the Last Supper in a second floor place?"

"Back then," Ali said, "this *was* the second floor."

"But there are no windows ... and the door is one floor above us."

"Try to understand," Bilal said, "that the geography here is very dissimilar to what it was then. Elevations have changed as well as buildings. The rear side of this building had a main entrance one floor below this room," Ali said.

"Why aren't there windows?" I said. "*Were* there windows?"

"No," Bilal said. "I imagine that was why Yashua chose it."

"What do you mean?" I asked.

"There was not glass in every window as there is now," he said, "and Jerusalem is, and always has been, a dense city. The possibility of eavesdropping was present."

"Oh okay," I said, and took in the room. I tried to imagine what I had always been told about the Last Supper, about Jesus, *Yashua*, pointing out his betrayer. But it didn't seem the same. For starters, it looked nothing like the painting. It was small, and would have been far more intimate then. Also, I had the feeling that flowing, colorful robes wouldn't have been found here, as all the apostles had in the painting.
The Hebrew symbols would reflect light, scattering it in unpredictable ways. It was strange to look at. We didn't stay too long before returning to the mosque above.

We, Bilal and I, found food in the Old City, and talked about the Holy sites. He had told me that when the Israelis had begun to emigrate (which, according to Bilal, began in the late 19th Century,) displacing Palestinians in the process, they hadn't the best understanding of the Old City; where the true Holy sites were. It was knowledge the Palestinians had, and it was treated with all the sensitivity you would imagine for the one thing that couldn't be taken from you. So, the Palestinians in Jerusalem were almost ranked according to how well they knew the land.

We had gone to a few other places, but most of the places I had asked him about had been lost even to him. Many of the locations that marked the scenes of the Passion, much of which he remarked was inaccurate to begin with, had been lost. He also said that Yashua's presence in Jerusalem was limited to the end of his life. Many of the more memorable events of his life, the Sermon on the Mount, the wedding feast of Cana, and many of the miracles, happened outside of Jerusalem.

"I doubt that time will allow your visit too many of those places," he said to me. I nodded, feeling the gravity that had become familiar to me.

Bilal did take me to the Garden of Gethsemane. This is where Yashua had prayed, and was captured. This was also where I was to meet him in about two hours. I didn't know the time, but the sun was beginning its late-afternoon lean. Bilal knew I wanted to explore Jerusalem for a while, and he had other preparations to make, so he cautioned me about 'standing out' (picking up objects with my mind was a good example.) and we parted ways.

I walked about the Old City, taking in a history that had recently become personal to me. I hadn't noticed before, but the people around me were frenetic. They were calling to each other, and I could sense a ton of anxiety.

"The end is near!" I heard a man say in Hebrew.

I thought he was a nut or something, but when I turned the corner to see him, I saw that he was a rabbi, impeccably adorned in robes. Obviously not psychotic, plus there were people gathered around him.

It made me nervous, because I didn't know how far my little 'incident' had spread. I soon realized that their behavior had nothing to do with me.

"And the Lord has brought forth a Great Life from that which could never hold such a Life," the rabbi said.

I realized that he was talking about the whale. I hadn't really thought about the reaction people would have to that. I was so deep into 'react-mode' when that was going on, that I had forgotten about it until just then.

"The end is near!" the rabbi said. "The day of final reckoning is upon us!"

And I could hear the chatter of others, saying that 'the Lord has cast judgment,' or 'the day of Salvation is at hand!'

Down the streets, through back alleys, from fruit stands,

between armed soldiers talking to each other in whispered tones. This was serious. What kind of attention would we be drawing to ourselves at Haram al-Sharif?

I wandered the streets for the entire two hours, avoiding the spots that I could tell were tourist areas. There was restless energy in the air; intangible, permanent, intense.

As the sun went down I began to head towards Gethsemane, to face an uncomfortable, awkward reunion with Yashua. I knew I'd have some explaining to do.

I wandered the garden of Gethsemane, amidst olive trees whose progenitors had probably stood there during Yashua's time. I could feel the Mount of Olives in the background, although it was too dark to see. And I saw a figure leaning against a stone wall. Though I could only see a silhouette, I knew the silhouette to belong to Yashua.

I walked over towards him, and I could see that he turned to look at me. Though I couldn't see his face, I knew that he was smiling. That was just him. Yet as he greeted me, I could sense his disappointment without being told a thing. Maybe, I thought to myself, I wanted him to be disappointed.

"Barnabas," he said. "It's good to see you friend."

"Same to you," I said, and prepped up for what I knew to be a difficult apology. "Yashua," I said, but then he began talk.

"Barnabas," Yashua said. "You were angry when you saw that man being beaten," Yashua said. "And you let that anger wrestle control from you."

I hung my head in shame. "As a result," he continued, "you have attracted attention to us, at a time when we need as little as possible."

I felt like dirt; lower than I had in the Presence of God, in fact, at the entrance to the Sanctuary ... because I knew I had let Yashua down. And I loved him. I knew I would've died for him.

But then he turned and said to me, "I saw it too."

That made me feel even worse, but he continued, as he looked out over the garden. "I would have felt the same way. I may not have done what you did, but I would have wanted to."

"Barnabas," he added. "The Bible recounts my anger in the Temple over the money-changers, but there were many instances back then where I felt my anger got the best of me."

A breeze picked up, and I could still hear the frenetic buzz of people in the city below. "There were many times when I myself had objects in the air, aimed at someone. And like you, at that last minute, I came to my senses." He looked at me, and I could sense he was smiling, though it was too dark to make out his face.

"The power that lifted those objects was not your own, you should know that by now," he said.

"I was wondering about that," I said.

"You are on land that God has had consecrated since the beginning of your time," Yashua said.

I stood silent for a second. "Is God pissed?" I asked.

He laughed heartily, and I was very glad to hear it.

"No," Yashua said. "Well, yes and no. He's angry that you let it get that far, but He's happy that you stopped yourself," he added. "He's seen it many times before in the people He calls, and He's used to it. The energy that threw the wrench and lifted those things was God's. Not yours. If you defy God, you do so with your own, *human* power. Not His."

"So God threw the wrench?" I asked, confused.

"No," he replied. "*You* threw the wrench. God simply let you."

This time I laughed. "That must have made Him mad, too?" I said, referring to what the guard did.

"Of course," Yashua said. "But unlike you and I," he picked an olive from a low hanging branch and flipped it through his fingers, "God doesn't have to throw wrenches to get His grievances redressed."

We sat there for a while, silent, and I couldn't help but think of how many memories Yashua must have had going through his head. I had always hesitated about directly asking him about his last life. I never wanted to seem like I was pressing him for proof. I knew who he was now. And I still had doubts, in the deepest reaches of my heart. I won't lie. But I *knew*, that on a night like this, two thousand years ago, he sat up on this very spot and prayed.

And was captured.

"Barnabas," he said. "It has been mentioned ... *my bond*, and I told you I would explain, when the time was right."

I nodded as a gentle breeze picked up.

"Now is that time."

"I'm listening," I said.

He paused, rubbing the sides of his arms. It was an uncomfortable pause.

"I am here to herald the end times," he said. "When I leave this Earth, there will not be one living thing remaining, one insect, one flower, one tree, one man or woman."

He paused. "Barnabas, I am a mortal man," he said. "I live, I breathe; I feel pain. I laugh and I cry; and I can be harmed. But my body, my cells, my blood, is bonded with the fate of this planet."

"I'm not following you."

"Do you remember the earthquakes that hit Greece and Italy two weeks ago?" he asked.

"Of course," I said. "Why?"

Yashua pulled up his shirt sleeve, showing the scar from his encounter with Guy Francis.

Then I remembered. The shape of the fault lines, and the aftershocks, they had been strange, and I remembered the fact that Yashua had stitches.

Yashua then held up his hand. He had removed the bandage earlier. "You didn't see the volcano on the news because you were tending to my blistered hand when it became '*Breaking News*'," he said.

"Oh my God!" was all I could think to say.

"Barnabas," Yashua said. "Humanity has been given the final exam. If I'm not killed this time, then man will have my full life-span, which will be a number of years I will not reveal. But, if mankind cannot recognize me in time to avoid killing me, then they will cause the cataclysmic destruction of their existence."

We sat there for a while, Yashua obviously strolling, or staggering, through the past, present and future; me, re-writing all of my own. People passed here and there, but they were blind to us.

Just then a dove flew in from above, and as it landed on an olive branch it began glowing blue-white. I felt a rustling in the trees around us, and I could hear a tearing sound above. I looked up to see olives growing furiously in the tree branches, at a high speed, pushing each other out of the way.

Soon they began to fall, hitting the ground like hailstones.

I looked at Yashua, and he gave me the same look he usually gave me, as if he could tell me what was going on, but I wouldn't understand. It was difficult to avoid the gaze of the dove, as the light was so warm and comfortable, as if somewhere in my make-up there was a *natural* color, and it radiated through the dove from the center.

It was magnificent, brilliant, and was everything that I would call 'perfect.' And I knew its Power, and I knew that in the end, it was His, no matter what. And I felt Joy.

The dove spread its wings, and flew through a spot in the trees. Surrounding the dove and drifting along the wingspan were ethereal symbols.

Yashua picked up two olives from the ground, and ate one. He tossed me the other. I bit into it, (I don't normally like olives,) but it didn't taste like any olives I'd ever had. It was sweet, but not too sweet. And it just had a flavor I can't compare to anything.

The olives on the ground began to dissolve and as they went into the ground, the grasses became taller where the olives had dissolved into them. They dissolved; they didn't decay or decompose.

When it was over the pathway was bare of any residue.

Yashua looked at me. "Mysterious ways," he said.

Yashua told me that I would be going with him to Haram al-Sharif, and helping him perform the Atonement. But he told me I would not see it, as only he alone could be in the Dome of the Rock. He needed me outside.

He told me that we would be attacked, by human and ethereal forces alike. I would have to lead the defense of the Most Noble Sanctuary while the Atonement was being performed. I damn near passed out when he told me that.

"How am I going to do that!?" I asked. "Yashua, I really wish you'd have told me this about, say, a week ago?"

"You would not be prepared now if I'd told you this any earlier than now," Yashua said to me and I understood.

Strangely enough, it made sense. I would've frustrated the hell outta' myself. "But I really don't know what I'm supposed to do," I said.

"All you have to do is remember that there will be powerful forces that you will be against," Yashua said. "But you will be able to see them in their own playing field. And you will know how to play the game. It boils down to you recognizing that you're on the team that always wins, and making sure you *stay* on the team." He smiled.

I laughed and we sat there for a second. Then I felt something change. I can't say it was physical, I can't pick one thing and say it was different, but it was mental, emotional, *spiritual,* and it wasn't just me. Yashua felt it too.
It was not good.

"We must begin," Yashua said. "I know a way to the Sanctuary that will afford us safe passage in."

We started walking and as we descended the slope on our way back into the City, I looked down to see a tall blade of grass. I watched it wilt as I walked past it.

"Remember what we talked about," Yashua said, and we began the journey that would be our last overseas.

Chapter Eleven

We walked to the entrance of a long tunnel. Yashua told me it had formed as a result of building on top of buildings, through the centuries. It was known only to Palestinians, and only a few at that. It didn't exist during his time, but he'd been to Jerusalem often in his current lifetime, and of course he'd find out about it, if anyone would.

There was a shimmer in the air around us as we walked. It had a dark red hue to it, and it felt bloody. I know that may be hard to understand, but that's what it felt like.

"Demonic forces cannot enter the Old City directly," Yashua said. "That is by God's Decree. They can influence humans though, so you will have a battle on your hands."

We found an entrance, in the back-door of a building, but it wasn't a back door as we went through it - it was an alleyway, and you could not tell from the street outside.
The alleyway descended, and I could see the splits of different periods of architecture, cutting jaggedly across each other as we descended into it.

We walked for what seemed like ten minutes, and then we came to a door. It was much like the door to the room of the Last Supper; it appeared simple, yet strong and heavy.
Yashua stood before it, and said something in a language I'd heard him use before, but could not decipher. The door swung open evenly, and with ease.

The inside was a large room, lit, with a group of men and one woman sitting in it. Some of the men I'd recognized from being at the camp. Some I did not recognize. I counted ten. Yashua and I would make twelve.

Bilal was there, as was Ali Muusa, whom I had seen earlier. The old man I felt so sorry for was there too. I was glad to see he was alright. His name was Ishmael Mu'hammed. The other six men were; Rasam Aziz, an Imam who ministers to Haram al-Sharif, Kalik Shiriz, a partner of Bilal's, Hassan, Abyan, and Abdullah Aziz were the sons of Rasam, and all had positions within the Noble Sanctuary ministry. There was one more man in the room, his name was Ibrahiim Hassan.

Yehudith Kavetz was the woman. She was an activist with Gush-Shalom, which I found out was an Israeli group that opposed the occupation of Palestinian lands. I wasn't aware there were such groups.

"You'd be well amazed by what you *don't* hear in your country," she said.

"Well, I'm a news hound in my country, and after some of what I've seen here," I replied, "I think I have a good idea."

"Oh really? And what would that be?"

"…that most Israeli's think the Palestinian land belongs to them." Yehudith laughed, not in a mean way, but I knew an earful was coming.

"Barney; can I call you that?"

"Please! It'll be nice to hear *someone* calling me that!" I looked at Yashua. "No offense." He put his hands up in the *none taken* gesture.

"Barney," Yehudith continued, "most Israeli's live in *Israel*. They don't enjoy not knowing whether their next bus ride will end in an explosion. Most Israeli's look with distaste upon the occupation. In my group, we deal with public opinion, and public opinion is critical of it."

"So why do you; I mean, *people*, still occupy the land?"

"You've got two types, generally," she said. "For one, you've got the people who believe that everywhere the Bible mentions belongs to the Jews forever. Those people get backing from your American fundamentalist Christians."

She went on. "The other type is poor people or working-class; the Israeli government gives them loans to build houses in the occupied territories. If they live there ten years, they don't have to pay the loans back."

"Our countries are much alike," she told me. "Some of our people seek peace; others seek gain." She smiled and so did I. Oddly, I felt much better hearing her say that. I was glad to have her 'on the team'.

I had heard about Ibrahiim Hassan because he was the leader of a group of Palestinians in Jerusalem; *Freedom and Justice in the Holy Land* is what it would translate to. I'd heard them described in America as a terrorist group, and I asked him about it.

"Terrorists kill innocent people," he said. "We fight terrorist groups, but America doesn't care to separate groups. We're all terrorists in their eyes."

The group had a reputation for taking out bad apples in the region, something people in America didn't hear about.

He would be directing his people, who were surrounding the sanctuary, keeping a low profile. Yehudith had her people as well, working with Ibrahiim's team outside the Sanctuary.

"Every group that has a reason for sustaining the status quo will be here tonight," Yashua said as we went through a ritual purification.

As always, I wondered how much he really knew. Enough, I hoped. I knew what happened that night would pass my current range of experience and kick dust in its face. Oddly, I smiled at that.

After we were all purified and relieved of any gold or silver we might have been carrying, Yashua approached the front of the table, where an old parchment map of the Most Noble Sanctuary sat.

"At midnight, the atonement will begin," Yashua said. "A minute later, expect all hell to break loose, *pardon the expression.*"

He leaned over the map, as if inspecting it. "I will need forty-five minutes to complete the Atonement. Once it is completed, you'll know it. All of Jerusalem and Israel will feel it, and within twenty-four hours, the entire world will know about it, and feel it. You need to keep me safe for those forty-five minutes," he said. "After that, the people after us may be a bit distracted."

I looked around the room, and I saw a look on the faces of the people in it. There was grit, and determination. There was dedication, and sacrifice, and I knew in my heart that some of those people would die that night. I also knew that they considered it their destiny.

As for myself, I did not know what I was going to do. I was told by Yashua that I was to stay within the Dome of the Chain, which marked the exact center of the Sanctuary. He said from there I could get the best sense of what was going on. Bilal and Ali would take station in Al Aqsa mosque, which was at the edge of the southern wall, as it was expected to be a breach point.

I asked them how the Most Noble Sanctuary would be cleared of pilgrims, it being one of the most Holy Sites.

"We've prepared for this night for many years," Hassan

said, "and there are many here now."

"What do you mean?" I asked.

"There are one hundred and forty-four people that have chosen to stay," he replied.

"Why? What will they be doing?" I asked.

"Praying," he said.

I didn't question that. I knew we'd need them, but I feared terribly for them.

At eleven o'clock, we prepared to take our positions. Before we went, Yashua pulled me aside, for a pep-talk, if you'd call it that.

"Barnabas, you're main objective is to see that the efforts of our allies hold. God will put His Own Divine Spark in your hand. You're to use it to supply energy where it needs to go." He pulled me closer. "Do not, I repeat, do NOT let yourself get caught in a side-battle. It'll try to draw you into one. Be focused."

"Okay," I said. "Yashua…"

"Yes?" he said.

"Be careful," I said. "And good luck."

He smiled, and then ascended a different staircase. The rest of the men and I followed suit. We left for our positions and our dates with Destiny.

I walked out to the Dome of the Chain, as I had seen it on the map. It was a dome of gold, held up by columns spaced equally throughout. It felt strange standing in there; it was dead quiet. I could feel the cold night, and it felt good. It anchored me to the land, as many parts of me desired to float.

I looked about, and I could see Al Aqsa to the south. I couldn't see Rasam, but I could sense him. That's how it was with the others, too. I could sense them and I could sense others, too. They were scattered about the Sanctuary, in Al Aqsa, in other buildings.

They were Muslims, Jews and Christians; I could feel them as points of energy … wells of hidden strength.

Within a minute of standing in the center of the Shrine I was beginning to feel others still. There were many of ours outside of the Sanctuary; around street corners, in alleyways, under street-lights. They were waiting, watching, preparing.

I could feel our friends, but I could also feel something else; something menacing. Something lurking, like shadows behind flames. It too was waiting, and watching, and preparing.

I wasn't afraid. I could have been, and looking back later I should've been, but I was calm. Not cocky; confident.

The minutes ticked down. I wasn't wearing a watch, but as midnight struck, I could hear church bells going off elsewhere and in seconds I felt the Presence again. Out of instinct, I dropped to one knee. I did not fall prone; I knew I would need to stand, but I had show reverence right then.

●

Victor jumped back, startled. A scream came outta his mouth; he didn't know why but he wasn't the type to dwell on what he couldn't understand.

The woman he'd soon see walking out of the brick building across the street; The Parrhesia Institute. He'd see her, walking to the dumpster to throw something out. He knew she'd been staying there, hiding out from him.

He spent the next ten minutes thinking about Katherine. All the things he could do to her. All the things he *would* do. Lewd things. Dirty things. Violent things.

Vic understood why he felt such animosity towards her. When Fisher assigned him to 'take care of her', Vic grumbled about it being a waste of his talents. But when Fisher showed him a picture of her, it turned his blood steaming hot. He hated her, and he knew why.

Vic took another slug of whiskey, and wiped his mouth with a wide, sweeping motion. It was a no-name brand that came in a plastic jug, but Vic liked it. '*Alcohol don't know no culture,*' he used to say. '*It all gets ya' drunk.*'

Vic pulled out a cigarette, lighting it with a match from a book he'd picked up at a strip club the night before. He drummed a

beat on his steering wheel as he scanned the street. His fiɪ
went along with the country tune blaring out his speakerь, ʋuɩ
much faster; eight beats to its one.

Vic saw two kids in baggy jeans, foolin' around as they
walked down the street. One pushed the other into the road, and
the scene brought Vic back to his childhood.

He was a kid once. He had friends that he fooled around with, and
he pushed a kid into the road too. That kid got hit by a car passing
by, and he died. That's where Victor Tanner's life took the course
that would see him stalking a young woman from his beat-up
Nova.

Vic had a turbulent childhood to begin with; the son of two
people who didn't want to be parents. His father was a
businessman (or so he was told; he never knew him) and his
mother was a teenage girl. The relationship was forbidden in those
days, as it would've been then. She was only fifteen, and he was
her father's boss. He was an upstanding, church-going man, and
she was a scared little girl.

Their first sexual encounter was the story of a young girl
mesmerized by a much older, much smoother, much more
experienced man. Their second encounter, and all that followed it,
was the story of a threat against her father if she didn't submit, or if
she told anybody. And then one morning she got sick in first
period math class, and it kept on until a physician with a sad look
told her that she was six weeks pregnant.

When she told the baby's father, he was enraged. He didn't
beat her, as he knew it would be noticed. But he assaulted her
verbally, belittled and humiliated her, and he told her it was her
fault. But, he was as God-Fearing as he was God-Offending. He
told her that he would pay for her to have the child, but she must
not have an abortion, for it was a mortal sin. He also told her that if
she told her father who had gotten her pregnant, than her father
might 'have an accident at work.'

And so Vic came into life, unwanted and most certainly
neglected. He never saw Dad; and to Mom, he was always a
reminder of Dad. So Vic grew up without love, without care, and
without direction and, since the default direction in life was

downhill, he went that way.

Vic started out small, beating up the neighborhood kids, shop-lifting and defacing property. One day, his mother bought him a hamster, perhaps one of four days in her life where she actually thought of him as something other than a problem. And he loved the thing. He took it everywhere.

Then, one day, the hamster bit him. Enraged, he threw it against the wall with all of his force and he stood over it as it twitched. He had hurt it bad, internally, and it was near death. He stood there and as he watched the little thing die, he found it to be peaceful, powerful, and gratifying. He felt no guilt, only a rush of adrenaline that pricked the tops of his ears. He knew, right then, that he'd found his calling.

The day he pushed that kid off the sidewalk into the on-coming truck, he didn't plan on it. It wasn't his intention to cause the kid to get hit. Not originally. But, as he saw the truck coming down the road, and his friend playing around on the curb, joking like he was gonna fall, a young Vic wondered how it would actually feel to kill another human being, to watch them die in the middle of the street.

Three minutes later he stood over his friend's broken, quivering frame, and it was then that he remembered pushing him. The driver had gotten out of the car and was looking at him, flabbergasted. He was screaming, but Vic only heard 'blah, blah, blah…' He was mesmerized, nearly catatonic. Electricity coursed through his veins, making every hair stand straight. He felt the thunder, and for a moment he was God.

When he was sitting in the back of the police cruiser on the way to the station, he came to, and the gravity of what he'd done was brought fully into focus. He thought he should cry, or say he was sorry but, as he looked at his reflection in the back window, he didn't do any of those things. He smiled and laughed instead.

He spent three years in a juvenile home, and two years in an actual prison. He was released when he was twenty-one, wizened by the amount of time he'd spent absorbing criminality.

He was smooth after his release. He didn't get caught. He'd

learned how forensic evidence could be used against him. When they sent him from juvee' to prison, the guards thought they'd teach him a lesson by throwing him in general population. He was taught many lessons, but not the kind the guards liked. When three of the prison's gang leaders were all found dead on the same day, their throats sliced to their stomachs, all the rumors and accusations landed at young Vic's cell door.

Nothing ever stuck. Nothing could be proven. He was working on his PhD in murder by then, and there was no trace of him at any of the scenes. He lovingly referred to them as his 'dissertation'.

On his twenty-first birthday he was released into the world like an institutional virus.

He readjusted well, got a job in an electronics factory in Anno Luce, showed up on time and worked hard. He made friends, and found women irresistibly drawn to him. Perhaps it was the confidence he'd had from deciding life and death for other humans; maybe it was the fact that he saw women as objects, and had no concern for them as human beings, just sources of sex. Many women were attracted to him by the misguided notion that he could be changed, or 'tamed.' Many went to their deaths fully believing that they had succeeded. In reality Vic faked it to see the surprise on their faces when they realized how horribly wrong they'd been.

Vic's 'blank', as he called it, happened about a month ago. He'd been at a strip-club, of course. Vic liked to conduct business in strip clubs. The girls' eyes were on the money, and the guys' eyes were on the honey. Perfect for 'quiet' dealings.

Some guy wanted his wife whacked, and he wanted Vic to frame someone else for it. Vic had had a bit too much to drink, but not in the club. It was full-nude, and they didn't serve alcohol. Of course, that's what he was drinking in there, but he didn't get it at the club.

He didn't remember anything coherent until a week later, just random images of machinery, and feelings of terror.

'I must've been abducted by aliens or something,' he would tell himself, though he didn't believe it. It was the only thing that made sense, because after he woke up, things started getting crazy.

He was stronger. He was 'built' ever since prison, but he was much stronger, all of the sudden, than he should've been. That past week, he went to collect a debt that was owed him, and the guy tried to run, eventually hiding behind a car. Vic shoved the car aside and killed him with a single punch.

Vic's instincts had grown, too. He could always tell when someone was lying to him. Now he could feel the subtle rise in their temperature. He could smell their sweat before it became the beads on their brow. He could hear their heart beat faster, the up-tempo of their breaths. And the killing became magnificent.

Vic looked at the clock on the dashboard; *8:30 p.m.* He knew in fifteen minutes the current object of his lust would be taking out the trash. It was the only time she ever left the building, he'd discovered, in the five days he'd spent stalking her, parked in various locations and vehicles around the Institute.

He licked his lips, checked himself in the mirror. He didn't need to; it wasn't his appeal he wished to impress upon her that night. He just did it to be an asshole. He opened the door slowly (he'd broken a few, lately) and stepped out into air spiked with the day's smog.

●

Two explosions rocked Jerusalem, and the night erupted into gunfire. I was swayed by shockwaves, but stood firm. I felt a jolt of energy course through me, and it was difficult at first to be coherent. Then the feeling subsided and I understood its purpose. I could see the players, the field and the game, just as Yashua had said. I was everywhere at once, mentally, in the streets of Jerusalem. I could sense our friends as they held back our attackers, and I realized that there were many on our side, more than I had imagined. I could feel their energy, and the intensity of it. When they would take fire, I felt their energy diminished, personally, and I would direct energy to them, to restore theirs. The pitch of this was astounding, for there was warfare on all sides, and I could hear the sound of helicopters and aircraft coming from different directions. I could hear people calling out the names of Yahweh, Allah, Jesus or Isa (the Muslim name of Yashua.)

I could feel the opposition too, and they challenged me as we challenged them, trying to draw me into a fight but I didn't allow it. I stayed focused, interchanging energies, holding firm the line of battle.

I could see the Dome of the Rock, and I could see a strange, luminescent smoke pouring from it. It didn't leave the shrine, but swirled about it, spiraling up the walls in strips of uniform length.

I looked up to see a helicopter heading straight at me. It wasn't like seeing the chopper on the road in Jordan. I could see this helicopter, and all of its components, wires and gears, and they were infused with a dark red glow. The energy welled up underneath it, in two places, and I knew that they were missiles, even before the trails of their exhaust followed the clinking sound of their release.

They came at me, but I wasn't afraid. I looked at them and they fell apart in the air; small pieces of metal, wires and dust cascaded down to fall outside of the Most Noble Sanctuary.

The scene on the ground in Jerusalem was intense, and though I wasn't there physically, my mind *was*. We were fighting Arabs and Israelis, foreigners and Americans. They fought us together, though they hadn't realized it, and they were strong. I was somewhere in the Old City, my mind anyways, and I saw one of our men get struck by a van. It hit him as it landed, thrown by an Arab man whose eyes were filled with Beast-red.

I suddenly heard a blood-curdling scream coming from one of the buildings within the Sanctuary. I scanned it, and I could see one of our men had become infected with the Beast, and he was screaming. I felt him move through the other rooms after the people praying inside. I felt their life forces snuffed out as he began to kill whomever he came across. Though they made not a sound at the moment of their death, I felt it stab into me. It made me queasy, and I begin to lose my hold of the battle outside.

I could feel the surge of the Beast pounding against my consciousness. It had found a chink in our armor, and it had every intention of exploiting it.

I began to lose my breath, and it became harder to keep my focus. I could feel the men protecting us in the city dying, and it was my own death, every time.

Suddenly, my arm began to burn, where my tattoo had been shifting for the past month. I grabbed my forearm in pain, but then I felt my palm burning, and I pulled it back quickly. I stared at my arm, and what I saw amazed me.

The tattoo had reformed. It now took the shape of a dove. That's a simple way of putting it.

It was ethereal, symbols that composed the outline of a dove. There was energy that swirled within it, as I had seen in so many of the ethereal symbols. That was what was causing the burning ... but it was beautiful. I could've spent hours staring into it without seeing the same energy pattern twice.

The reality at that time was that I'd already stared at it too long. The burning feeling anchored me, brought me back into the reality of that intense moment, and I turned my direction to the man in the Sanctuary.

He had killed several of the men praying, more than a dozen. I could sense the rooms they'd met their deaths in, and I could see strips of blood on the walls of those rooms, pools of it soaking the mats on the floors. I could sense him preparing to enter another section of the building, where a large group of men were praying. I knew he couldn't be allowed to kill them. I would have to kill him first.

Just then I realized that he was one of us, and this was not my fight. Yashua had told me not to get into side battles. Killing the possessed man would do that. So, in a move that I didn't know I was capable of until then, I blessed him. At once the Beast could not stay, and the man fell to the ground, unconscious.

I returned to the battle outside, and infused my newly found energy into it. Just in the knick of time, too, because our men were not faring well. Many had died, and many were wounded. Those wounded were instantly healed by the infusion of new energy. They rose, took again to their weapons, and returned fire. I knew that they could not last forever. I could use the power given to me to heal, but not to raise the dead. We had lost a dozen men within the Sanctuary, and the energy that they were adding was no longer available.

My mind was by the Beautiful Gate, which in Yashua's time past had been called the East Gate. I was adding energy to those who were defending that area. They were up against three groups of soldiers, armored personnel carriers, and an assault vehicle. Fire was being exchanged heavily, and we were taking casualties. I scanned the opposition, and saw one young man with the Beast glowing in his eyes. And I could see something else in his eyes that horrified me.

I saw Victor Tanner peeking out from behind a dumpster, and a woman opening the lid to throw a bag in, unaware of the vicious man hiding just three feet from her. And I could tell by the hair tie, green with pink stripes, that it was Katherine.

I was enraged, and those soldiers tasted a full measure of the energy that was coursing through me. But then I realized that the Beast was pressing deeper everywhere else. It had distracted me, and I scrambled to maintain my 'center'.

'*Yashua, please hurry,*' I prayed, and faced an uncertain fight.

●

Katherine hummed a song that had been in her head all day; *I Love You More Than You'll Ever Know,* the Donnie Hathaway version. She always liked the song, and Hernando had a CD with it on there. She was just feeling it that day.

Her thoughts were on Barnabas. She wondered how he was, what he was doing right then. She knew they'd see each other again, and that they'd talk, and she was nervous. The feelings she had for him were, in her opinion, disproportionate to the amount of time that she'd known him.

Katherine wasn't a prude, in her own estimation. Of course all of her friends called her that. She never 'hooked up' with a guy she'd met at a bar the same night, though many a night she'd had to crank the TV to avoid hearing her roommates hooking up. She didn't judge them; in fact, she sometimes wished that she could be like that, but she couldn't.

Katherine was always a smart girl. She was able to count to one-hundred, and do basic addition and subtraction by the age of four. By the age of ten, she had the reading level of a college sophomore. Her parents had enrolled her in advanced classes throughout school, and they were frequently approached with suggestions that Katherine be moved up grades. Katherine didn't care, but her parents felt that it was important to keep her among students her own age. So they encouraged her to go to the library and study independently.

She did just that. She studied all that interested her. One week it was ancient civilizations; she found three different books for that week. She'd cross the spectrum, from world religions to art, history and philosophy, politics and government to ghosts and the occult. She absorbed anything that interested her feverish young mind, everything from introductory books to topic-specific, post-graduate level books. She would spend hours at night reading, with a Webster's Dictionary by her side to look up the words she didn't know.

Katherine was pretty straight-laced in high school. She didn't party like everyone else, yet she'd gone to most of those parties. She was cool with everyone in her school, and they all knew that she didn't drink or do drugs. No one ever pressured her to do anything. She was just a fun person to be around.

But she never fit in, at least not in her mind. She had many friends, and she knew they'd do anything for her. She'd do anything for them too, but she was different. The things that interested her weren't the same as the things that interested her friends. Often she couldn't tell people what was on her mind. Not because she didn't think they'd understand them, but because they wouldn't care.

She was always passionate about causes. She felt them to be the only worthy pursuits. When she was in her senior year of high school, she informed her parents that she would join the Peace Corps after graduation. Her parents counter-informed her that she *would* be going to college. They weren't being hard on her, though. They told her that after she went to college for at least two years, they'd support her joining the Peace Corps. They were humanitarians themselves, and her biggest role-models. They were proud of her, but they also wanted her to have an education. And so Katherine applied, and was accepted to USC with a full scholarship.

When her mother and father died in a bus accident two months after her starting USC, she was destroyed. They were her best friends. They were the only ones who truly understood her. Their deaths made her empty. To stave off despair, she forced herself into her studies.

She majored in Psychology. She thought of being a psychologist at the time she had to decide; that's how she usually made her decisions; on the moment, at the time. She fit in well, and on campus she met Hernando DeSantis.

He was speaking at the University Park Campus, during his Mayoral race. He was speaking about the conditions in the poor neighborhoods in South Central, and the conviction in his voice, the ability he had to bring her right into the lives of those people, touched her. After he spoke she approached him and signed up to volunteer. It, and Hernando, changed her life.

During the campaign she did everything; phone-banking, canvassing, writing, checking petition signatures. And she saw first-hand the results of poverty, and neglect. She met many people who had no hope, no way out of the life they were in, no way that they could see, anyways. She learned that even though there was always an answer, it seldom answered the right question.

She learned about the seedy side of politics. She learned how the right questions can be drowned in a media blitz when the opposition has the money. She learned that the news media is, first and foremost, a business, and they made more money from their advertisers than their viewers or readers.

And she learned about Hernando, and his life. All the people he had known in his life, and all that he had been through, things that she'd read about in books. But what impressed her about Hernando was his willingness, and even eagerness to listen to people. And a person knew, when talking to him, that he was paying attention. He had a heart that he didn't wear on his sleeve;

it was too big to fit.

Katherine was crushed when he lost; more so, perhaps, than Hernando himself. And he was pretty crushed, but they stayed in contact, daily at first, and eventually it was on occasion. She had in fact called him to say hi about two weeks before she was abducted by Paradigm. She had even asked him to send her a copy of that Donnie Hathaway song.

The very same song was now rolling its howling melody through her head as she gathered up the trash bag in the kitchen. She knew it wasn't safe to take the trash out, but she had to get out. Parrhesia was a big place, but she had a serious case of cabin fever. Besides, it was only a few feet from the dumpster to the door. If anyone approached her, she could run back in quickly enough.

She wandered down the hallway, nervous about Barnabas and Yashua, and restless. She'd not been able to do anything except watch the news, and it wasn't good. There was unrest in Ethiopia; speculation was a U.S. invasion *by proxy.* She knew Yashua and Barnabas had gotten out in time, because what was all over the news right then was Jerusalem.

Every eye of every media outlet was on Jerusalem. Two days ago, a large whale beached itself on the west bank of the Jordan River, only yards from a key bridge connecting Jordan and Israel. She knew this had something to do with Yashua, and it was causing uproar in Jerusalem. She'd been glued to the set for the past fifteen minutes, watching reporters talk into microphones that were picking up the sounds of combat. They were covering a terrorist attack on the Dome of the Rock.

That didn't make sense to Katherine. She knew that no true Muslim would dare to attack that Holy site. And then she saw a soldier on the side attacking the dome, and she saw him dressed in a black uniform that looked familiar. The camera zoomed in on him, and she could see the insignia on his chest. Surrounded by Arabic letters, she saw the Paradigm logo.

It made her sick; she needed air. She took out the garbage every night at 8:45, like clockwork. Hernando was always upstairs by then; he was an early riser. As she drifted down the back hallway she was lost in thoughts so deep even *her* mind couldn't penetrate them.

She opened the door to the fragrant smell of industry and commerce, garnished with the odor of trash in the almost-filled dumpster. She walked over, glancing both ways, mindful that there probably *was* someone after her. She opened the lid and threw in the one full bag she was able to find. As she shut the door she was carried in a whirlwind, ending on the ground with a strange man on top of her, his one hand over her mouth, a knife in his other. It was glistening in the distant street-lamps, and she could see that it was stained.

The man leaned in towards her face and sat there, hovering, his face inches over his hand, and she could smell the noxious odor of alcohol on his breath, steaming from his pores.

"Hello there, Katherine," he said, as he brought the knife to her throat. "Remember me?"

Chapter Twelve

The battle had intensified as we passed the first half-hour of the Atonement. The energies swirling around the Dome were becoming brighter, more powerful, and I could see ethereal symbols swirling through it with an uncanny luminosity.

But the opposition was becoming more powerful too and they were sending heavier and heavier equipment. Whereas the initial fighting was being done hand-to-hand, I heard more explosions ... and tanks were rolling.

The walls of the sanctuary were taking fire, but they held. My mind was furiously about Jerusalem, supporting the men and women that were helping us. I knew we couldn't hold our adversaries off forever, so I prayed for Yashua to be successful. And I prayed for myself to remain standing, no matter what.

I began to feel connected to the entire battle. Before I was switching my attention between different groups; now I could see our side all as one. We were all in it together, and where I once knew that figuratively, I was then feeling it personally. I felt the bullets when they hit anyone. Though the pain didn't fell me, it hurt like blazes.

The minutes ticked on, and I couldn't tell how many had gone by, but I knew it was close. I could tell by the Dome. I could feel it.

Just then an explosion rocked Al Aqsa, fire flew from every opening. A wave of pain exploded over me; I couldn't feel anything for a second, from the dual shock of the explosion, plus the deaths of those inside, but I regained. I had to. There was no option *not* to. The outer wall had not been breached. It took a second to figure out, but someone was able to sneak in with an IED, and they'd run into the Mosque. I couldn't go there now; I knew it but I had the urge to nonetheless.

I recouped, and felt the battle once more. Though the Beast had pressed in with force after the explosion, we held him back. But it was tenuous. There were many of his vassals upon us, and I felt it, even in our fighters, that we were on our last leg.

•

"I don't know why Fisher's got it in for you," the man said as he traced the blade of the knife gently across Katherine's throat, leaving a red mark, "but I got something for you myself. It won't hurt too much," he said, and smiled, a row of misshapen teeth peeking out of his mouth. "Won't hurt me, that is."

Katherine tried to scream, but no sound could escape her clamped mouth. His hand was suffocating her, his breath was suffocating her; his very *presence* was taking the air from her lungs.

"You don't remember me, do you?" he said, and all she could do was whimper 'no,' shaking her head.

"You were too good for me at the club that night, weren't ya'?" he said, and Katherine could feel him pin her down with violent force. "Little bitch!" he said, and he pulled her hair tie out hard enough to bring tears to her eyes.

"That's alright," he growled as he unbuttoned the top two

buttons of her blouse, oblivious to her attempts to wriggle free. He slammed her down again with the same force as before. "I made Dawn pay dearly for your refusal."

Then Katherine knew who he was. *Victor Ray Tanner.* She was with a few of her friends, Dawn being one of them, at a club in LA one night. It was Katherine's twenty-first birthday. They were at the bar, and a very crude, younger-looking version of the man came up to her, hit on her. She tried to be polite in telling him she wasn't interested. Then he'd grabbed her arm.

Dawn, the out-spoken, 'loud-mouth drunk' of the group came up to him, and ripped him apart. He was mad, and he tried to go after her. At that point, two of her male friends, Marines, came up and told Vic to get the fuck out of there. He did just that, but she could remember the creepy smile he flashed before he did so.

Dawn was raped that night. She told Katherine the day after, a sobbing wreck. She didn't want to talk about the details; it fucked her up mentally. She'd found out his name from Hernando, and was warned against going after him. But over the years since it happened, Katherine had lost touch with Dawn, and she had all but forgotten about that weekend.

Until just then.

It all came back right at that moment. And as she looked at Vic, a madman, who had destroyed one of the best friends she'd ever had and was about to destroy her, she replaced her fear with rage.

Vic slammed her down again. Well, he tried to. It didn't move her; not an inch. Vic didn't have time to think *'What the fuck?'* before he felt his head cracking into the dumpster.

Katherine got up. She wanted to beat him into a sobbing wreck, but instead she found herself running back into Parrhesia, locking the deadbolt behind her just as Vic pounded on the door. She ran downstairs into the institute's main control room.

She didn't want to put Hernando in danger, and she hoped he wasn't down there. Behind her the door tore open with the scream of tearing metal. He was a lot stronger than a normal human being, and she knew it, but she was feeling stronger herself.

Katherine realized that she wasn't running away from him. She was drawing him to a place where he couldn't hurt anyone. She had some payback in mind.

She entered the Control Center, and she knew right then it'd be empty. Hernando would have woken up to the sound of the door, and that worried her. She didn't want him down here. She ran down the central corridor, and stopped at a spot in the dead center of the room. She could see clearly from there, and if he had a gun, there was a row of servers she could duck behind.

Tanner came barreling through the doorway to the control room. He looked at her and smiled. But he had lost just a touch of his previous cocky 'charm'.

"Come here ya' little bitch!" he screamed, and he ran down the stairs.

Katherine didn't move. She didn't know why. Every ounce of her normal, common sense told her to keep moving, but she stood still.

Tanner walked down the hall in 'mock-stroll', all six-foot, three inches of him, and stopped about ten feet from Katherine. He licked the blade of his knife at the same time as he twisted his right nipple in his fingers through his stained 'wife-beater'.

"Oh, you're not scared now, is that it?" he said, over-animating his movements. "Been there, done that. I'll have just as good a time killing a whore that's not scared of me as I would have killing one that is."

"You had no right to touch Dawn!" Katherine said, and she stared into Tanner's eyes dispassionately. She truly felt him to be nothing. Flesh wrapping bone.

"I have all the right. But I'll have you know I pretended it was you," he said in a fake sweet voice.

"I don't get with losers," she replied, and added, "besides, Dawn said you had a small dick." She usually wouldn't say such a thing; it wasn't like her, but she knew it would burn him ... and it did.

He flew into a rage, picked up a full rack of electronics as though it was made of paper and launched it at Katherine. She didn't duck. That's because instead of hitting her it all changed course in mid-air, spinning around to crash down on the floor at Vic's feet.

Vic was stunned, his jaw slack for a moment. Katherine remained expressionless, motionless, but her shock was far more powerful than his. She knew she had just done that. She didn't know how. She just imagined it being thrown at Vic's feet, and as she pictured it, it happened.

"You don't scare me with your 'hoodoo shit!" Vic said, but she could tell he was scared, even though he was still dangerous. To prove her point, five box-cutters flew at her from across the room. She didn't even see them move. She redirected three of them mentally, as she had done with the rack. Two found a mark. Neither was any more than superficial.
One put a slice across her left arm, and the other nicked her right shoulder. Blood seeped out of both wounds, and Katherine decided to move. The area she was in was too open.

Just then she heard Hernando coming down the stairs. She knew Victor would use him, so she caused the dead-bolt to be thrown on the inside, locking him out.

She needed to be on the offensive. Tanner would try to get to Hernando anyways, and a dead-bolt wouldn't stop *him*. Plus, she had a score to settle with the rotten bastard.

She waited at the edge of a row of servers. She could feel where he was in the room, and she knew he was about to walk by. She had something for him. As he walked by and she could see his bloodshot eyes, she smiled. Every server on the racks launched into him with explosive speed. He was hit in the face by every single one. He flew back, and Katherine thought she'd killed him.

He lay motionless on the floor, and after five minutes of deadly silence, she walked up to him.

He looked dead. She kicked him; timidly at first, then she hauled off. Nothing. She bent down to get his pulse, and she felt his hand grab her wrist. In a fluid motion she was pinned beneath him again. His face was bloody, torn up. He was enraged; humiliated, and Katherine felt fear again.

•

The battle raged on in Jerusalem. I was worn, weary, and mostly on autopilot. I couldn't give up; I knew that. I would die standing, if that was what it took. I wasn't being a hero. I was being any one of the men and women outside of the gates; suffering, sacrificing, shedding their blood, and their lives, along the ancient, legendary streets. They all walked into that night knowing they might, and probably would, die standing.

As I felt their pain, I felt their strength, but I felt their strength waning too.

We'd lost too many and the Beast seemed to have an inexhaustible supply of carriers, filled with ungodly power, from an unseen source. They lifted and threw cars and smashed through doors with their fists.

Objects flew about the battleground, wiping out whole groups of our people at once. Those people were constantly trying to draw me into a battle of wills, to divert my attention from the rest.

I could feel my own strength waning and it seemed as if it was being taken from me. The fighting intensified, and I could feel the wall of the Beast's energy pressing in deeper. I prayed and tried with everything I had left in my shaking form, but I couldn't stop it. The energy was sucked out of my body, and I saw men with guns running in towards me. They opened fire.

And then it happened.

The sky opened up, and the moon grew bright enough to illuminate the entire sanctuary, as if it were day.

The Dome erupted.

Not physically, for it remained intact. But all of the symbols and energies that had swirled around it grew to a critical mass, and I felt it rumble before reality disappeared.

I can't tell you what the one minute of my unconsciousness was like. I can't tell myself. The images and sights, sounds and smells, are grafted indelibly into the area of my brain that doesn't know words. It was splendid, perfect and magnificent, but that's a blank, lifeless way of describing it. It was as if for the first time in my life, I could be comfortable with my failures. I knew I'd just failed, and they'd gotten through, but it was okay. I knew that God loved me, and that he'd forgiven me. I felt restored, and I felt true peace.

And then I awoke on the ground beneath the Dome of the Chain. The gunfire had ceased. I could still hear explosions, and fires now raged far deeper into Jerusalem, into the New City, but silence surrounded the Old City as a shroud.

I looked around. The soldiers who'd come in were gone, but I could see outlines of white where they had been before everything went crazy. It reminded me of pictures I'd seen of the shadows of people in Hiroshima that had been burned into the ground by the intense energy of the detonation.

Al Aqsa stood still, and I realized that the walls of the Sanctuary had never been breached. I began to see men come out of the buildings they were in, men who had stayed to give prayer. Yashua had told us all to gather at Al Aqsa when it was done, anyone who'd survived.

As I began to walk towards the mosque, I found that I could still scan the battlefield. I could scan what was left of it, anyway. I saw the bodies of the fallen, ours and theirs. And I saw people getting up, men attending to women, and women attending to men, our friends, what few were left, stood about in utter confusion.

All of those who had opposed us; soldiers, terrorists, lay dead. I got to Al Aqsa, and went inside. The building itself had been untouched by the IED's explosion. There were, however, flash-burned images of men. But these imprints were glowing in the color of a pale blue flame.

As I waited for the others to arrive, men came pouring in. They were shouting, many of them.

"Praise Allah!" they shouted. "Allah is Great!", "Allah the Merciful!" And I felt the same way. I even said it, and I don't think God cared that I called Him Allah. But, I was worried about Yashua.

I stepped outside and, as I looked to the Dome of the Rock, I saw Yashua. He was walking toward the mosque, and I could tell, even from afar, that he looked very different. He came up to me, and stood there silent for a second. Then he smiled. As he stood in front of me I could see how truly different he looked.

His hair had grown, and it hung at the shoulder exactly. His eyes were translucent. Well, not really; I guess that's one way you could put it. He had the eye structure; iris, pupil, what have you. But when I looked into them, even as he approached, I could see more, like there was a scene playing out in them, between the corneal layers.

His skin glowed, not noticeably, but subtly, I had a feeling that it was one of those things that only a few us on Earth had the ability to see. The glow was multi-colored, like the one in my dream, who'd been slain. And though I knew that Yashua was Jesus, and the Messiah, I had always held a tiny grain of doubt. All throughout this journey I had to come to grips with it and on many occasions, it was the source of a failing. But at that moment it was undeniable.

I fell to the ground. I did it purposefully, but I don't know why. I just felt the need to. Perhaps it was guilt from not truly believing for so long. But I fell down, and I prayed.

"Rise, Barnabas, for we've not the time right now," he said, and I rose to my feet.

"You've done well," Yashua said. "Thank you."

"But ... I failed you," I said.

He pointed to the Dome. "The Atonement has been finished and the Sanctuary is still here. You stood firm, and held them back."

"But I couldn't hold on to my energy," I said. "It left me, and they were about to take the Dome."

"You couldn't hold on to *your* energy because it wasn't *your* energy," he said. "It was God's. And at that moment He withdrew it into Himself. Those soldiers would never have reached the Dome. Come," he said, and began walking. He was faster, even his normal walking pace.

"What about the men in Al Aqsa?" I asked, scrambling to catch up. "Aren't we supposed to meet up with them?"

"They have no need of us right now," Yashua said. "That regrouping point was designated for them, not us. We have elsewhere to be."

We approached the East Gate of the sanctuary.

•

Tanner pounded Katherine in the face with his fist.

"Bitch!" he screamed, and Katherine was facing a string of shocks. She would pass out from the pain, only to be snapped back in by further pain.

"I'm gonna make you pay for this!" he said, and he grabbed for a box-cutter that was lying on the floor.
Katherine could hear Hernando pounding on the door. She was terrified that Tanner would go after him, but right then he was more occupied with her.

He grabbed her hand, and she clenched it into a tight fist. "I wonder how long it'll take you to bleed out?" he said. "When I start cutting each of your fingers off." A joyless laugh bellowed out of him.

Blood was dripping from his face, and some of it had landed on Katherine's lip. She was nauseous, and crying.

Suddenly the main screen in the front of the building came on. It was showing the BBC.

"We will be returning to Jerusalem, a scene of utter chaos tonight," the anchor said. "A pitched battle has been waging for hours in Jerusalem's 'Old City', and we are receiving reports of a possible radiological attack on the Dome of the Rock, called *The Temple Mount* by Jews and Christians, and one of the holiest shrines in all three religions."

Tanner and Katherine were both transfixed by the screen. The city was erupting, and plumes of fires billowed up in many places. But it was the Dome that they couldn't take their eyes off of.

It was glowing, in wisps of what looked like smoke. She could see strange shapes going in, and coming out of the smoke.

She couldn't make anything out, but she saw angles, and uniform curves. She knew it wasn't radiation. She also knew that Yashua was in there. She could *feel* his presence amidst that violent panorama. She knew Barnabas was there too. She could feel that also, but for different reasons.

The scene's hold over Tanner was quickly broken. He wasn't shocked by violence; he got off on it. He didn't care about the Dome. He turned back to Katherine, and looked at her breasts, her blouse covered in the mingled blood of them both.

"This time," he said up close to her, smiling, "I won't have to pretend."

And at that moment an explosion came from the TV screen, and Katherine burned white hot beneath Tanner's grip. He jumped off her, and shrieked out in pain.

Katherine rose, as if not entirely by her own power. She was filled with something she'd never known before, a force of pure life. She looked at Tanner, who was backing up, engaged in a confused growl. She smiled and raised her hand, her index finger pointing up. She looked at him, and, still smiling, shook her head. Then she brought her finger to point at him. A burst of white energy, like lightning in its intensity, shot out and connected with Victor's chest.

It didn't knock him off his feet. It held on to him, carrying him through the air. Katherine waved her arm around, and she crashed him viciously into pieces of equipment strewn about the room; she seemed to find everything that would hurt the most. Katherine didn't know what was happening, but she knew she wanted him as far away as possible. After bashing him wholesale, she directed the energy that he was impaled upon out of the building. He was thrown out of the Control room door, and up the hallway, before being rocketed out of the back door of the Parrhesia Institute, the one he'd not too long ago ripped open.

Katherine was shaking. She didn't fear him coming back. She didn't know if he was still alive after the pounding he'd taken, but she was a wreck. She felt her face, expecting a wave of pain as she brushed her hands over her lacerations, yet she felt none. She didn't even feel any swelling, though she could feel it just three minutes before.

Her clothes were a mess, torn and blood-soaked, but she had no lasting physical damage.

That didn't stop her from falling to the ground, sobbing. She could hear Hernando pounding on that door, and at about that time she saw four LAPD officers in SWAT gear come running in. She did one final mind-trick as she threw open the bolt, letting Hernando in.

•

Yashua and I stood before the gate, and paused. He looked to me. "You'll want to back up about ten yards," he said, and I did so.

Something happened. I can't say what exactly but the bricks that had sealed the East Gate suddenly shattered, exploding outward in a barrage of brick pieces and dust.

But, Yashua didn't do it. It didn't feel like he did it when I saw it happen. It was almost like he *became* the action; his form melding with the gate, and the space between was irrelevant.

He looked at me and said, "Come. We have to continue."

We walked out of the gate, and I felt all kinds of internal strangeness as that happened. I won't describe it here, as I'd lose you, but as soon as we passed through, Jerusalem became much darker. I realized it was due to the moon returning to normal brightness.

As we walked, I could see a very thin, translucent, bluish haze clinging to the fabric of the landscape. There were many bodies, on both sides, and they were covered by the haze. As I looked out across my field of view, I saw at least a hundred dead. That number rose as we covered more ground.

We had attracted a great deal of attention, and amidst the symphony of sirens and flames, I knew they would be coming to where we were. I didn't know what to expect when they arrived ... which they did, within minutes.

A tank, a row of armored personnel carriers, and soldiers carrying automatic weapons were heading our way, and we could see them in the distance. I didn't sense the Beast, as before. Just a bunch of confused people wondering what the fuck had just happened.

'*Oh shit!*' I thought.

"They won't bother us," Yashua said, and a profound sense of shock gripped me as I looked around. The dead were rising from where they had fallen. As they got up, I could tell they weren't themselves. Many had broken bones, and they rose as though they had nothing wrong with them. Many of them fell back down when those broken bones could not support them. Others had lost limbs, or had been cut in half by things that had been thrown at them. They wriggled on the ground, and pulled themselves along by grasping at whatever they could.

They weren't alive; that was plain to see. They were animated, that was about it. They just wandered around aimlessly, bumping into things, falling down and getting back up to do the same thing. There wasn't any kind of agenda. They weren't trying to come at us, or each other. They were just wandering around.

"They'll not cross our path," Yashua said to me as we continued to walk. They didn't either. They would come close, but then seemed to change direction, before getting too close.

Ahead of us, the soldiers opened fire. Not on us, but on the dead. I could hear screaming. I didn't have to sense their fear to know they had it. I had it myself. You're not supposed to see dead people get up and start walking around. It causes an internal paradox.

"They've been reanimated as a result of God's energy," Yashua told me as we approached the soldiers, who were completely oblivious to us as we side-stepped them on the road.

We could have gotten shot, but it would've been a ricochet.

"The effect is temporary, until dawn," he said. "And it is only affecting Jerusalem."

"The Old City?" I asked.

"Yes," Yashua said.

"What about the New City?" I asked. "Why are there fires? What's going on there now?"

"The New City has been destroyed," Yashua said. "You'll be hearing all about it when we get back to America."

"So, we're going home?" I asked.

"Yes."

"So this is over?" I asked, knowing the answer already.

"No," Yashua said. "But first things first, we need to leave Israel."

We walked through the streets of the Old City, using a route he must have known for ages. The dead were everywhere, wandering, and I was surprised to find myself familiar with the fact. We walked, Yashua humming a song, and me pondering one pretty heavy situation.

As we walked through the Old City, I had many questions of Yashua, but the first one was Katherine.

"I saw Katherine," I said, "...and Tanner." I felt suddenly very sad. "Tell me she's okay."

"Oh yes," Yashua said. "She's fine."

"But Tanner?" I said.

"Tanner was soundly defeated," he said.

"How?"

"You shouldn't underestimate young Katherine. She has an inner strength."

I felt good right then, about Katherine, anyways, but I felt utter devastation as we entered the New City. We reached it by climbing over a pile of shattered stone and concrete. I suddenly realized that it used to be a part of the Wall.

"What about the Wall?"

Yashua shook his head, let out a laugh. He pointed to the rubble.

Occasionally I'd expect an explanation, and Yashua wouldn't give it. This was, apparently, one of those times. I just kept my mouth shut and focused on the wreckage into which we were carving our path.

Most of the buildings had collapsed, and twisted iron beams, crumpled concrete bits and glass created a story of Wrath penned by God Himself. The bluish haze ended with the Old City. Here we walked, and we could see the dead, but they were not animated. They were just dead. Fires raged, some small, and one fire, off in the distance, was engulfing an acre or more. The smell of gas and burning diesel was in the air, as well as the smoke from the fires. I looked to Yashua and I could see the same things I saw before. It was more subtle, and I didn't think anyone else was able to see it.

"Where is the Beast right now?" I asked. "That energy, I mean."

"It has scattered to regroup," Yashua said.

"It was real strong for a while there," I said.

"The HIPPO system is feeding it energy," Yashua said. "The Beast wasn't created by God, and therefore must be fed energy. It cannot generate its own."

"How many people are connected to that thing now?" I asked.

"One hundred and eighty million in the U.S.," he replied. "Elsewhere, it's growing. The Pacific Rim now has over seven hundred and fifty million."

"The Pacific Rim?" I asked incredulously. "How?"

"It was launched there with more of a marketing push than it was in America," Yashua replied.

"But that means more than half of America is plugged into that thing, doesn't it?" I asked.

"Yes," Yashua said. "Most non-essential citizens, and almost all children."

"But ... how can they get away with that?" I asked.

"It was made affordable, and was marketed to all the demographics. It was also set with an internal timer. It took a few days to reach full field-strength. Now they can't disconnect."

"What about the *essential* citizens?" I asked. "What must they be thinking about all this?"

"They've had marketing targeted at them as well. They've been convinced that this is all simple addiction; that the people who are in could disconnect if they wanted to," Yashua explained, as we were approaching a less densely populated area. I was thankful for a break, however minor, from the extreme.

"So, they don't plug in as a matter of keeping themselves 'straight'. They have been directed away from Paradigm by having the issue refocused to one of personal morality," he said.

"Biggs?"

"Not yet," he replied. "He's still deluding himself into thinking that it's a Godly thing. There are others, more localized influences."

We walked through the streets. They were in better shape; better only being a relative term. The area was still shattered. Whatever hit the New City had laid indiscriminate destruction upon it.

"We have a big poop stew waiting for us in the states, don't we?" I asked.

"A gumbo."

We were walking, getting ever closer to Jerusalem's city limits. I heard a child crying. I knew we had to leave, that eventually they'd be on us. I also knew there'd be many like this little child, crying in the streets of the New City, but it didn't matter. I turned to Yashua to ask if we could help, and he had disappeared. I went off after the sound, knowing Yashua would be able to find me.

It turned out I'd found him, along with a group of men, pulling up the demolished framework as another man had a hold of a grateful, scared, tiny hand. With a heave from the group, the framework came up, and the girl flew out into the arms of her rescuer, screaming her head off. She was okay, just scared.

I rejoined Yashua and smiled at him. That was just how he was. Not as the Messiah, but as a decent guy. We kept on walking, and we approached the city limits. We saw the Israeli military going by constantly, but they were headed into the city.

We walked a lonely road that led from the chaotic scene, and I realized that we were suddenly surrounded by an eerie calm. Nothing at all was going on where we were walking. It was then that I fully appreciated the magnitude of what we'd just been through. We had just been a part of World History. Perhaps we'd just heralded its end.

We climbed a small hill, and it leveled out into a grove of olive trees. We walked right up to, and I actually bumped into, the truck. It was the same truck - three times now. Well, it wasn't the same, but it looked identical to the trucks we'd carried the Ark in, but I did not feel the Presence this time.

We stood there for a moment, reflective as we gazed into what remained of Jerusalem. Then we hopped in the truck and I twisted the set of keys in the ignition, as I got in. The engine roared to life, a sound muted out by the other roaring of the evening.

Chapter Thirteen

We drove through desolate quiet, surrounded by the calm proceeding from perhaps the greatest storm. Yashua told me that we would depart from Meggido Airport, and we would be on the road for a few hours. He couldn't shorten travel, for that would put us on the Beast's radar. Though it had been scattered, it was still strong, and would still be a problem. So, for the first time in the past few days, we spent a few uneventful hours on the road.

We talked, as we always did.

"Where are we landing in? New York?" I asked.

"New Orleans International."

"Any particular reason?"

"It has to be," he said. "It began there."

I didn't think he was talking about Katrina. That was only ten or so years ago, and even though Yashua looked to be in his forties, I knew he was double that.

"What do you mean?" I asked. "Katrina?"

"No," Yashua said. "Well, yes and no..."

"Go on..."

"The development of HIPPO was expensive," he said, "and it had to be kept a secret. It was always a private-public partnership, although you'll never hear that."

We passed a woman and her young child guiding a donkey-cart beside us in the street.

"The government needed to draw money that could in no way be traced to the project. Money was redirected to HIPPO that should've gone to other projects."

"The levees?"

"Correct," Yashua said. "It was covered up by donations made to the campaigns of Levee Board members who wouldn't complain about the lack of money coming in."

"Unfortunately," he continued, "the members, many of them anyways, managed to squander what little money was coming in from city levee taxes. So the levees fell into disrepair."

"So hurricane Katrina was really the bad luck of the draw?"

"No," Yashua replied. "It was an act of God."

"Yeah, but why would God do that?" I asked. "See, that's what I don't understand sometimes..."

"During that time, when the streets were flooding and people were kept in," he replied as we drove, "the Presence of God was With them, as you have yourself felt it."

"You mean like when we were with the Ark?" I asked. "And, by the way, what happened to the Ark, or Arks, I should say?"

"Okay," Yashua said. "Both questions. Yes, and they have rejoined. They now lie in preparation for the outcome of all this."

We drove in silence for a moment. It was a clear night, and we'd long since passed the sounds coming from Jerusalem.

"I was there," Yashua said.

"Where? The Dome of the Rock?" I said, still thinking of the Ark. "I was there with ya', ya' know..."

"No," he said, with a thousand yard stare. In him that was eerie. "In New Orleans. During Katrina."

"Wow!" I said. "Were you trapped?" I asked.

"No," he said. "Well, yes and no." He looked off at the night sky.

"Did you know it was going to happen?" I asked as we drove up a hill on what was little more than a dirt road.

"Yes, I knew."

"Could you do anything to stop it?" I asked.

"No," Yashua said. "God had to."

I paused for a moment, uncertain whether or not to ask him this.

"Did you want to?" I asked.

"Barnabas, I love everyone. Of course I did." He was almost angry when he said it.

"I'm sorry, Yashua. I didn't mean..."

"I know," he said. "I'm not mad. God needed to do it, and I knew He needed to, and I never questioned it. But I didn't *want* them to suffer any more than He did. It wasn't their fault."

"So why were you there?" I asked.

"To help Him attend to the victims," Yashua replied.

"What was it like?" I asked. Yashua then told me of his experience with New Orleans.

"I was living at a shelter at the time. It was about a month prior that I had arrived. I was volunteering there, as how I met you. I was in charge of cooking meals, and I was able to serve dishes with ingredients that would help bolster the immunities of people coming in. It was a small thing, but it helped. I told everyone who asked me to leave when the storm was first announced. Many did as a result of talking to me but I could never have reached enough people. Not nearly enough," he began.

"When the storm hit, I was running through the lower Ninth Ward, screaming at everyone to get on their roofs. I knew the people who didn't have axes; I told those people not to go into their homes. I did everything I could, running up and down the streets in the shadow of the Industrial Canal, desperately trying to get people on their roofs. I was with three others, one of whom you know; Hernando."

"Wow!" I said.

"And when I knew it was time, we went to a flat-roofed garage where we had a small powerboat ready, gassed up and propped on cinder-blocks," Yashua continued. "I knew its owner would be able to get out of town; I knew the owner, actually."

Yashua pressed his hand to his forehead, "We untied it, got on board and waited, nervously, for the Industrial Canal levee to breach, which it did, with ferocious force."

"As the first rush of water became steadier, it wasn't long before it was up high enough for us to launch the boat. We spent hours getting people onto roofs. But there were so many, and we could not help them all, not even me."

"Eventually, there were other places in the city that we needed to be but, by that time, most of the city had taken on water. We gunned the engine to leave, and as I looked out, I saw desperate looks on faces, lives in danger, confusion as to why we were leaving. And the weight of my heart could have sunk our boat at that moment."

I was suddenly seeing a different side of Yashua.

"We needed to be at the Superdome," he said as he looked out. "We couldn't cross the Industrial Canal with the boat, but we crossed over the bridge on North Claiborne, where I'd had another boat secured, that time on the roof of a bakery. The bakery's roof was high; we needed ropes to lower that one. We had to rappel down, too!" He smiled weakly. "But not to digress; It took us well over an hour to get to the Superdome. There were areas where the waters were too shallow to cross, and there were areas where debris was submerged, dangerous to the boat's propellers. We had to zigzag across the upper Ninth, and eventually Midtown."

I drove along, lost in Yashua's tale.

"When we reached the Superdome, we had picked up about fifteen people, as many as the boat could hold with my help. I 'docked' it; I guess you could say, a block away from the main entrance. We all had to walk in the water for the remaining block. There were a few thousand people there at the time, and new people were pouring in relentlessly. I gave my boat to a man I knew from the shelter. I told him where I'd tied it, and to go and bring people back, and not to worry about the gas. He took off and I went inside."

Yashua paused for a second at this point. "You've seen a battle similar to what I saw in there. In Jerusalem," he said. "The Beast was clinging to the dark corners; in the corridors, in darkened areas. In men who saw sick opportunities in the tragedy. In child molesters, rapists and murderers. The Beast was seething, waiting for a flash-point to ignite the room, but it couldn't. In the midst of a human hell, the Spirit of God was there. In the men who had made sure the elderly and the sick got their rations first. In younger men who, never having respected the law before in their lives, then felt compelled to enforce it in its utter absence. The Spirit of God was there, as you have seen it; in the Sanctuary at Ethiopia, and in Jerusalem. But the Beast was kept in check, for it cannot best God."

We drove through a mountain pass, and a signpost. I couldn't read the name. Yashua sat silent for a little while. This was obviously bringing up memories. I think he needed to say it, though.

"There was much suffering," he went on. "There was violence, and there was death. There was an odor in the air that burned straight into the brain, lodging in the spot where the concept of 'misery' forms. There was sickness, and emergency in the pleas, to God, to myself, for relief. God was there, as was I and I healed as many as I could. I couldn't be seen doing it; else I would have been mobbed. So I had to let many go."

He again paused, and he wiped his fingers across his lower eyelid. "And one in particular, Josephine," he said. "For the first time, this time around, she made me realize my humanity."

"Josephine?" I asked.

"She was in her late nineties, a retiree living New Orleans East." His voice changed slightly. "She was hurt pretty bad, and they had brought her in, one of the few emergencies to come in at that point. A great many would follow. She wasn't crying or screaming or anything, but I could tell she was in pain and ... I knew she was dying," he continued. "She had a deep wound on her side, and her shirt was soaked in blood. She saw me, and she smiled, but I could tell it hurt her to do so."

Yashua was remembering a lot, and I asked him if it was too hard to talk about, but he said no.

"I knelt by her side, and put my hand to her head. I knew that I could not heal her wound without revealing myself, but I could ease her pain, and I did. Her face suddenly became easy, and she looked at me."

'Thank you,' she said. 'Please don't leave me.'

"I told her I wouldn't, and I never did. It was then that I had noticed the mark on her wrist," Yashua said with visible pain. "The intensity of the Superdome made me unable to sense her as a Holocaust survivor. Normally I sense them. Even in more peaceful situations, the pain of holocaust survivors is difficult for me to bear; for the Holocaust was done in my name."

"Yes, but Yashua," I said, and reached out to him, "it was against your intent, correct?"

"Were I on the Earth then to stop it," Yashua said bitterly, "I would have. But there's more to this story."

"What?" I asked. "I mean, if you're okay tellin' me..."

"Yes, Barnabas," he said, and he paused for what seemed like forever. "My mother had that mark on her wrist. One of the first memories I had of her, was her..."

This time I stopped him. "Yashua don't," I said, reaching out to him. "I know, you don't have to say it."

"Thanks," he said, and he stared off for a moment.

I was shocked. I had never even thought about his mother, Jewish in 1945, being a Holocaust survivor.

Yashua continued as we drove. "We talked; the old woman and me," he said. "Until the moment of her death, we talked. Of many things, but the last thing she was talking about, it left me broken."

Yashua hesitated; it was hard for him. He eventually continued.

'I could have left,' Josephine had said. 'But there are a lot of us old folks in my neighborhood, and I didn't want my neighbors to be unable to call someone if the power went out. I had a cellphone and most of 'em didn't, so I figured I'd just brave it out and check on them after the storm.'

"She died shortly after that," Yashua said, again with the thousand-yard stare, "and I had to find somewhere to be alone. I found a utility room, chain-bolted and locked. I made the chains and the lock fall apart; I don't think anyone noticed me. In that room, for the first time in both lives, I yelled at God. I had never before felt that, but I did. I questioned, and I pleaded in a way I'd never before. I felt destroyed; miserable. For a good long while, I sat amidst the pipes and machinery, sobbing. Outside, as I sat there, the power went out. At once I felt sorry, and ashamed that I'd 'went off' as you would say, on God. He understood why though. He let me rant; He didn't blame me. I went out and continued to heal people, silently, subtly, and I would look across the Superdome and see the Spirit of God giving comfort to a woman with epilepsy, who kept having seizures. God's Spirit filled a young man who attended to her, who kept her from succumbing to them. And I saw God giving a moment's peace to the frightened child of a frantic mother, but tensions rose as conditions degraded."

We passed through a small town, I hardly noticed.

"And I was beginning to attract some attention. I had to leave, and that meant entering the water again. Which I did. It hurt me physically, as it would another. I had two rashes afterwards. That touched off another two hurricanes."

"Rita and Wilma," I said, in reference to the two hurricanes that came shortly after Katrina, in about the same place.

"Yes," he said. "And I knew something would happen when I stepped in that toxic stew. But I did. I had to. I wandered through the streets, towards the Convention Center."

"That's where the government had lost track of thousands of people. Kinda' abandoned 'em for a few days, right?" I said.

"Yes," Yashua said. "It was a bit more complicated, but that was what it amounted to. Hernando had gone there when I went to the Superdome."

"What did you see in the Convention Center?" I asked.

"The same thing I saw in the Superdome, nothing different," Yashua said. "Pain, confusion, violence. More of it, really. I could tell you many stories of things I had witnessed in New Orleans those weeks, and the time I spent bringing comfort to the men and women who had to enter it after it was drained."

He did too. He told me about a few of the people he had met, the stories of hope and grief, miracles both small and great, and unsung heroes.

Before I had realized it, I could see the shining spotlights, tracing beams through the air. We were nearing Meggido Airport.

Yashua had told me earlier that Meggido Airport only accepted domestic flights. He had arranged for a pilot to fly us out, and Yashua apparently had a plan for us not getting shot out of the sky. I asked him how a small plane was going to get us to a major airport outside of Israel, and he told me we were going to America directly. Of course, I asked him how exactly we'd be able to do that.

"It's amazing how far you can travel when you're not worried about gas."

At that point I just accepted it.

Meggido Airport was all lights. Well, to be fair, there were hangars, and a control tower, but it was small. So far, I'd seen the biggest airports, so it paled. It was smaller than Addis Ababa airport, I can tell you that much.

We drove up, and I noticed that there were guards with dogs up ahead. They were stopping and checking cars. I was nervous, and I asked about it. Yashua told me they would not recognize us.

We got up, and the guard shined the light in. I looked over to Yashua, who suddenly appeared as a very old man. His facial features were different. He looked like many of the Jews I'd seen at the Wailing Wall, praying.

I turned back to the guard, and as I did my eyes swept across the rear-view, and I noticed that I too looked like an old man. I was even wearing a black Yamaca, though I didn't feel it on my head.

The guard waved us through, and when we had driven off, out of earshot, I laughed pretty hard. Yashua laughed too. It felt good to laugh, after the heaviness of the previous conversation.

Yashua directed me to a hangar; it was in a row of them. It looked like they had been built in the fifties.
We pulled in and a man was standing there, scanning the scene, his arms folded. I recognized him as a man from the Palestinian camp, in Bethlehem.

When we got out of the truck, he walked up. He waved to me and smiled. He looked at Yashua, and as we approached, he took a knee and reached out for Yashua's hand. He kissed the back of it.

"I am honored that you would have me be a part of this journey," he said, and I was glad to see him.

I trusted his flying skills, as Yashua said he used to fly fighters in WWII. We went into the hangar, and I saw the plane that would cross the Mediterranean and the Atlantic, without getting caught.

When I saw it, I almost thought he'd kept the same plane he was flying in WWII. It was from that period, anyways. It wasn't a fighter, but a transport. It was beat up, for sure, but oddly I wasn't as nervous as I could've been. Remember that I'd been afraid to fly, once upon a time.

We got into the plane, and the man from the camp (Aziz was his name, Aziz Malek) started her up. The cockpit instrumentation came to life; it shone through the doorway.
I could also feel something about the plane; in the fuselage, the bolts, coursing through it. I'd, by that time, come to know what it was. It was God holding the piece of crap together.

The engine roared, I prayed, and in a minute we were airborne, on to an eerie homecoming.

Our ocean journey took about twenty-four hours total. Yashua, Aziz and I talked for many hours about everything; sometimes about nothing really. Twenty-four hour flights will have that effect on you.

We did discuss the game plan, somewhat. Yashua didn't really say anything about what he had to do; he simply said he would have to do his part alone, and I would know when we arrived. I, on the other hand, would have plenty to do.

I told Yashua about the Zygote program that I'd got from Jonesy, back home. He told me that we would need Jonesy; he would be able to help organize an attack on HIPPO from its CAV components. I was to get back to LA from New Orleans, and meet up with Katherine, Hernando and Juanita. We would all come back to Louisiana.

We approached America at the dusk of an evening like any other. Or so I hoped. Quite frankly, I didn't know what to expect. I expected us to get hailed once we entered American airspace, but nothing of the sort happened. We flew low, and it took some extra time. We didn't want to cross over Florida, so we circumnavigated.

As we had approached the first landfall in over a day, I could see strings of street-lamps marking the narrow strips of land emanating from the southern Louisiana coast. I thought about how that must have once looked. Louisiana officially re-drew the map by an act of Congress, after Katrina. They never wanted to, because they lost federal money due to the loss of land.

We flew up over West Black Bay, low, and flew parallel to a roadway, not much more than that. Yashua told me it was Route 23, and that many had died in the areas we were flying over. There were whole towns and tight-knit communities that were wiped out, and no one would ever know about them.

Eventually, I could see the lights from the metropolis of refineries that composed modern New Orleans. I knew a kid named Samuel Loutre, who came from New Orleans. His mother ran a successful T-shirt and souvenir shop in the French Quarter, on Decatur Street, and they lived in an apartment above. He used to call it 'New Oilans', sarcastically.

"It's not oil they refine there," Yashua said as we passed over it. "Paradigm owns the plant."

"What do they use it for then?"

"They store energy," he said. "The city thinks it's a refinery."

We approached New Orleans International airport, and I was still in fear of being shot down, yet we landed without incident. Before we landed, Yashua handed me what looked like an M-80 without a wick. There was Hebrew lettering on it.

"You'll know when the time's right to use this," Yashua said.

"What do I do with it?" I asked.

"Throw it to the ground," he said, and he leaned closer.

"Barnabas," he said. "No matter what happens to me, you

have your task. You must go, no matter what."

"Uh oh!" I said. "You don't even have to tell me. You're going to get arrested down there, aren't you?" Yashua nodded.

"Yashua, I'm not going to just sit there and let them throw you in jail," I said. "No!"

"Barnabas," he said as he put his hand on my shoulder. The plane was taxiing and I could suddenly see cars approaching. They were all black, with tinted windows. "When Peter said he'd not leave me, I told him the cock would crow when he would deny me three times. And it did, as he did. I had also told Peter, that he was the rock upon which my church would be built," Yashua continued. "So, I was telling him what God needed him to do. If Peter had died along my side, you would have never heard of me. Barnabas, now it's your turn. Peter never denied me in his heart," he said as the plane came to a stop. "Nor will you, but you must get out of here."

As Aziz prepared to open the hatch (scared shitless, I'm sure), Yashua gave me the final prep.

"Avoid all military vehicles and law enforcement. They're not necessarily bad, but they'll think you're looting the homes of people plugged into HIPPO. You'll find someone who can help you get to LA," he said.

"Okay," I said.

"Barnabas, be careful. And remember that God is with you."

"I will."

The hatch opened to a group of federal agents, all armed. Funny thing is, I thought of sayin' 'What, no cake?' but I was too busy mentally shitting myself.

"All of you turn around, and put your hands up!" one of the men said from a loudspeaker in one of the cars.

I looked at Yashua, and he said, "Go."

I looked at the M-80 thing. I had it clenched in my hand since we'd gotten off the plane. I went like I was gonna put my hands up, and as I did I threw the thing to the ground with as much force as I could have, without causing them to shoot at me.

The thing exploded forcefully on the ground, and brilliant lights escaped from the casing. They floated over to the men, encircling them. I don't mean 'floated' in any kind of a slow sense. They moved incredibly fast at times, and then they would come to near stop, before spiraling about crazily. The movement was fluid. They were like a swarm of lights of many colors, disorienting to me as I saw it from a distance.

'Go.'

The thought popped in my head, and I knew it was from Yashua. I looked over before I took off. I saw him, and his face looked sunken a little. It drove home to me how much I cared about him.

But he needed me to do this, so I thought, 'Goodbye Yashua. God be with you,' and I took off running in the opposite direction.

I ran, and ran. I wasn't thinking of directions; I didn't even know New Orleans. I just ran as fast as I could towards the fence surrounding the airport. I could see the reflections of the lights in objects as I passed them by. I turned to look, and the men were still encircled. They hadn't been able to move, mesmerized by the spectacle they were witnessing. I saw that Aziz was gone, apparently fled. I could see Yashua, just standing there. It put a dull tension in the pit of my stomach. I reached the fence running break-neck; I had to slow down as I approached it to keep from bouncing right off it.

The fence was torn in one spot, and I hopped through it. I found an access road, and carefully skirted along the side of it, until I could find a way out.

The area around the airport was called Metairie. I had seen that on a road sign, that's the only way I knew. I went through side streets, avoiding any roads that had traffic. I only crossed main roads after looking around for a while.

Metairie itself was *dead*. I didn't see people leaving for work as the sun had just come up. I expected it to be quiet, as it was 'wealthier residential.' But it was just dead. I saw that every house had lights on, and then I sensed it.

The Beast.

I could sense the people within, connected to HIPPO, their energy fed into a cable that left each house. I hadn't even noticed it at first. It was subtle. When I looked closely at one of the cables, I could see it. That kind of energy was familiar to me at this point.

Military and law enforcement vehicles predominated the main roads, and many times, I had to duck in someone's driveway to avoid being seen.

I was getting close to the Lakeview "Refinery". It was massive, and I didn't want to get too close. I knew they'd have security, and a fence, so I followed Clearview Parkway. I saw a sign for the Mississippi, and I followed it. I knew reaching the Mississippi would give me a relative bearing for a destination, as yet unknown.

I was clueless as to how I'd get out of the city. I knew I needed a car, vehicle; some means of transportation. If Metairie was any indication, getting to LA wouldn't be easy.

Chapter Fourteen

I went south, keeping close to Canal A. Formerly known as the 'Seventeenth Street Canal', it had breached as a result of Katrina. It flooded much of the city, and left the Lakeview area in six feet of mud and debris when the city was drained.

The area of Lakeview, like so many others, was toxic after the flood, and of course it was hushed up. As a result, people who had returned started getting sick within a few years. After a slew of lawsuits, the area, like so many others in New Orleans, was deemed uninhabitable by the EPA.

Those who had returned and rebuilt were unceremoniously bought out, and not for the original value of their homes, either, I might add. That was crap, in my opinion. It could've been cleaned up. No one wanted to spend the money.

They built a series of parks that they called the Crescent Gardens, in 2012, but little would grow in them, and the grass always died. In the end PetroUSA took over everything a mile south of Lake Ponchartrain; a wide swath starting at the eastern edge of the former Lakeview area and ending at the east edge of what once was called the lower ninth ward. They created a mini-city in the Big Easy, with lights strung up the pipes over a hundred feet tall. You'd almost think it was a bunch of high-rises. Apparently all a front, including PetroUSA.

I made my way south, and eventually found myself on a side street off of St. Charles Ave. I was getting nervous. I was pretty much on the edge of the Central Business District. I was worried about patrols, which I could already see more frequently. I found an obscure place to gather my thoughts. I thought of Yashua, and I couldn't sense him. They must have taken him out of New Orleans. I thought of Aziz, and I *could* sense him. He was close. Just then I heard a van coming down the street. I was hidden, but I sensed Aziz in the passenger seat. I could sense the driver; a stranger, but he didn't feel hostile. I stepped out into the street after looking around. The van, a white Econoline with the words 'New Orleans Department of Public Works' emblazoned upon the side, pulled up. I saw Aziz smiling brightly.

He reached back and popped the side door. It slid back, and I hopped in.

"I am so glad you are alright," he said, and he shook my hand profusely.

"Barnabas, this is my cousin, Rahiim."

Rahiim smiled and extended his right hand, his left clutching the steering wheel.

"Pleased to meet you, Rahiim," I said, and then I said to Aziz, "I didn't know you had family here. How come you didn't tell me?"

"I have not talked to Rahiim in five years," Aziz said as we drove down St. Charles. "I did not know he had moved here."

"I saw him trying to flee the airport," Rahiim said. "I was working there; I work DPW in the daytime."

"So you knew it was him?" I asked.

"Once I got a close look," he said. "I could never forget the face of my cousin." He smiled broadly.

We were heading to the French Quarter, where Rahiim had

an apartment. I was surprised at how much it cost him when he'd told me. He said it was normally expensive, but it was cheaper for him because he was a city employee. He said that the labor shortage from HIPPO junkies had rapidly changed the city dynamic. Within a week property was available to him in the French Quarter that he never would have gotten just the month before. He told us he had just moved in.

We drove down St. Charles, and that took us around Lee Circle, which consisted of a statue of Confederate General Robert E. Lee.
Rahiim told us that he'd heard that the statue was oriented so that General Lee's back was to the north. I saw an old military Humvee driving in the outer lane. They didn't seem to notice us.

We took the circle to Andrew Higgins Drive, and in the buildings, many of the lights appeared dim. But all of the buildings' lights were equally dim. 'Weird,' I thought.

We took a left onto Magazine Street, and we passed by the D-Day Memorial. As we drove towards the French Quarter, Rahiim brought me up to date on what had happened in the past week.

The day we'd left, HIPPO, was unleashed upon the world, with an advertising assault that included ridiculous coupons mailed to poor families. He remembered seeing his neighbor get a coupon that would have made his device cost only twenty-five dollars. It was advertised at over five hundred.

What Rahiim thought was weird was that his other neighbor, who was a little better off financially, got a coupon that would have made his seventy dollars. Rahiim took that to mean that they were going by income with the promotions.

The coupon they sent him would have made his seventy-five, if he ever would have bought one. Islam forbade drinking, and some, more devout Muslims in America, had rejected the device. Some reacted angrily. They disappeared, either through detainment, expatriation or through going into seclusion.

The rest, like Rahiim, were given jobs in the newly-incapacitated America, and, over the past three days, Rahiim noticed it had become very quiet in New Orleans.

"Did only Muslims revolt against it?" I asked.

"Oh, no," Rahiim said, "devout people of all religions have rejected it. But many are forced to hide out."

Rahiim had also said that what happened in Jerusalem had kept anyone in America, not connected, glued to the TV every day. He said that the day before, Reverend Biggs announced that he'd be seeking the Presidency. It was obvious that Rahiim wasn't happy about that. After all, he was one of the 'hell-bound' souls that formed the gravel of the path through Biggs's fevered imagination.

"Good God," I said.

"Allah will not allow this," he said.

"I don't think He will, either," I said, and Magazine Street turned into Decatur. We had arrived in the French Quarter.

I'd seen pictures of the French Quarter, and videos of Mardi Gras. They still held it every year. It was one of the few success stories to come from New Orleans in the years since Katrina. Mardi Gras had always been a beautiful blend of cultures. A marvelous procession, down streets as old as the tides of the Mississippi that had greeted French, Cajun, African and Creole settlers ages ago, when they first laid the bricks and crafted the ironwork masterpieces lining the upper balconies of so many of the streets and avenues. All of the tradition and regalia, the meal for every sense, the culture cooking in a unique American melting pot that had been simmering slowly for centuries.

The one promise upheld by politicians, in the wake of Katrina, was the establishment of a community of New Orleans-born artists, musicians and other cultural icons. This had less to do with their commitment to New Orleans culture, and more to do with public pressure, back when that was a non-zero number. So, Mardi Gras survived, and it was the part of the city that never died. As a result, a lot of the commercialism that the celebration had gone into, before Katrina, evaporated two years later, and the focus shifted to preserving the traditional celebration.

Mardi Gras became ten times as spectacular, and was known more for music, food, floats and costumes than for young drunk college girls showing their tits to strangers for beads. *And* it kept the New Orleans economy alive. Well, until PetroUSA sort of 'acquired' most of the city. The full facility was finished in 2015. They'd spent about three years building it; it was massive, but Mardi Gras kept going strong, despite the new intruder. In fact the festivities became much brighter as a rebellion against the building of the Lakeview Refinery. Unfortunately, the paraders, musicians, float-drivers and costume-makers had little say against PetroUSA or Paradigm.

As we drove Decatur past Jackson Square, I noticed that I didn't see any military presence.

"They stay out of the French Quarter," Rahiim said, as we turned left on Dumaine Street, across a row of shops. "They only patrol the areas where the HIPPO junkies live, so that no one loots their homes. We are the worker bees here. I don't think they want to frighten us."

We drove down Dumaine, a very small, narrow street, and there were balconies above the sidewalks. I marveled at the fact that it all looked so delicate, but at the same time solid and strong.

We crossed Chartres Street, and pulled over. Rahiim lived in the second floor of an antique shop. It was a beautiful building, like all I'd seen, and we entered in through a gated door that was all intricately carved iron.

Rahiim's house was amazing, though he had very little in the way of furniture. Like Bilal, he had many Islamic writings on the wall, but the architecture of the rooms was impressive. It felt pleasant and comfortable; safe.

Rahiim had a small TV that he turned on. The BBC popped up, and I really wasn't surprised. A reporter was talking into a microphone. Behind him was rubble, everywhere. Wisps of smoke wafted past occasionally, and I could see emergency vehicles driving down the road. I didn't need to see the lettering on the sides of the vehicles to know they were in Jerusalem.

"Jeanne, there is still a great deal of confusion in the city, even though it's been over a day since the earthquakes," the reporter said.

I asked Rahiim what they meant by 'earthquakes.' He said

that the day before yesterday, four large quakes rocked Jerusalem at the same time. Most of the greater Jerusalem area was demolished, but it hadn't touched the Old City.

He went on to say that the quakes followed an intense battle that had been fought in the Old City, where terrorists had tried to destroy the Dome of the Rock. He also said that there were reports and video-footage of the dead rising in the Old City, and a whale had come up out of the Jordan River.

Of course, I knew these things first-hand. I told him of my involvement, as he knew of Yashua, and that he was taking a great risk in harboring us. I owed him that. But there was also much that I couldn't explain. He understood, and I didn't detect any skepticism in him. I think it would've been easier to be skeptical when the BBC wasn't covering the end of the world.

The correspondent continued. "The government of Israel has, as of this morning, closed all of its borders and declared a national State of Emergency."

That didn't surprise me one bit.

"The U.N., for the first time since its inception, declared the greater Jerusalem area to be under an international quarantine," he continued, and I saw a small plume of flame in the distance. It looked like the sun would be coming up over there soon.

"Peter," Jeanne said, as the image of Peter became a box at the top right of the screen. "We've been kept in the dark somewhat about the attack on the Dome. Do authorities know whether the attack and..." she paused, "well, let's just say light-show, at the shrine on Friday evening, was radiological in origin?"

"Well Jeanne, I haven't heard any official comment from the authorities in Jerusalem," he replied. "But I can tell you that the emergency crews have stopped wearing protective suits."

"So maybe they know something we don't?" she commented.

"Maybe," he said. "But I do know that there is a great deal of suffering, and an overwhelming sense of confusion. It'll take decades to rebuild, and we may never truly understand."

He looked back behind him as a helicopter flew low overhead. "And from this," he said, "Jerusalem, and the whole world, has been forever changed."

"Thank you, Peter," Jeanne said. "Peter Montgomery, reporting live from Jerusalem. It is a scene of utter pandemonium this evening; a scene that has the whole world asking many, unanswerable, questions."

James Godfrey, Jeanne's co-anchor, took the floor.

"In related news, in America and around the world, the number of HIPPO addicts has grown exponentially overnight. As a result, the global infrastructure is now being crippled by a lack of workforce. Within a week, the social dynamic of the world has had to undergo a radical change. Here to report on the ramifications of these changes is our guest correspondent, Dr. Richard Seiner, a Professor of Social Anthropology at Cambridge University, in a segment titled; 'The HIPPO's Bite.'"

The segment was informative, Aziz and I watched in silence, as this was catch-up for us. Rahiim gave us background when we had questions. I was surprised at how knowledgeable he was about the topics that were being discussed on the BBC.

Rahiim was a scholar, aside from a DPW employee. Books were more prevalent in the apartment than furniture. The books looked like they cost him more than everything else he owned.

Apparently the reduction in the workforce was causing a great deal of talk about implementing mechanization; talk had been met before with stiff opposition, on the grounds that it put people out of work. These mechanizations were meant to just 'pick up the slack' caused by the labor reduction, and help to take care of the close to 3 billion people that were currently connected with HIPPO.

Dr. Seiner went on to talk about the dirty little 'technicals' of the Polymorphic system. When a person became unplugged from HIPPO, they went insane. I'd seen that in Katherine, and Yashua had been attacked by Guy Francis. And, of course, who could forget Vic Tanner.

But when people plugged in, their bodies required less energy, and thus less sustenance. Yet it still required *some* sustenance. People who had no one to feed them were starting to die. In industrialized nations, there seemed to be a contingency plan in place, though officials denied it. In industrial countries, arrangements were made to feed the HIPPO junkies intravenously. They used the nutrient tubes that were designed for the disastrous 'Manned Flight to Mars' the year before. I'll not get into that one.

Countries that didn't have a plan in place for feeding and care were really starting to lose people. Even though the product was not pushed aggressively in places like Africa and Southeast Asia, it *was* pushed. Rahiim said that forty thousand Africans would die, or be yanked out by friends and have to be institutionalized every day. In those countries, institutions were in short supply, and many of the crazy HIPPO junkies were just being shot.

The Organization of American States had plans in place from Canada through to Argentina, but in Central and South America, the planning was poor, and many were dying there as well.

That didn't surprise me. The OAS was really just the US annexing North, Central and South America. I'd heard it was originally just a trade thing, but a government usually starts by regulating trade. Now America was (technically) a whole lot bigger, but the Central and South American Districts always got the shit end of the stick, if you know what I mean.

Use of HIPPO crossed all cultural lines, geographic boundaries, races, languages and religions. Three billion people were not plugged in, however, and that made me feel hopeful. However, many were in hiding. There was a figure in the segment that there were almost five-hundred million people in hiding in the world.

There were about one and a half billion people in the world who were in isolated, rural areas that had no means of being hooked up to the device. The current fear of Dr. Seiner, was that if the full force of mechanization were brought to bear, most of these people would be displaced to urban areas, where they'd have access to the HIPPO devices. This was a conclusion that was being denied by government officials, or anyone having anything to do with HIPPO.

Of course, I wouldn't believe anything any of them said

anyways. All a lying bunch of crooks, they were, and I saw the 'Dishonorable' Reverend Biggs, flashing his dollar-store smile on the screen.

"We are standing upon the gateway to the Kingdom of God on the Earth!" he shouted. "You have seen the signs in Jerusalem. This is the herald to our new age! One free of war, of conflict, of suffering," he said, and he raised his hands.

"A world is coming where we can all simply be, in the Presence of the Almighty God," he preached, animating his movements with all the grace of a Black Mamba.

I wanted to hurl, but Rahiim was a gracious host, and I didn't want to offend his hospitality.

"God gave man the technology to follow the light of the Lord Jesus Christ," he said.

'*Fuck you,*' I thought at him, invoking Yashua, who right then I was worried about.

"We will, someday, all be able to walk in the light of God's Love right here, on this Earth. For this has been the prophecy. But ... it will require that those of us chosen by God, must now reach out to care for those who've gone before us," he said. "But in the months and years to come, we will all be one in Christ."

"Oh, what bullshit!" I said. That surprised both of them, and I apologized. But c'mon, I had to. It was bullshit. Biggs was leading people into this thing, telling them it was 'Heaven on Earth.' And there was still a bunch of people who didn't have TVs, much less the BBC, who'd get sucked into it without a clue about what it was doing to other people around the world. I was mad.

I then understood why the Beast was so powerful. These devices were pumping out the kind of energy it used. I knew that the Beast was timeless; well, as old as man anyways. And I was guessing that Fisher and Biggs weren't bright enough to actually *see* the beast, so they probably had no clue they were feeding it. I also figured they wouldn't have given a fuck about it if they *could* see it.

At this point we turned off the television. It was getting late and I knew I needed to leave New Orleans tomorrow morning. Rahiim had told me that he knew a guy who could get me a ride to

LA for a fee, which Rahiim agreed to cover.
I went to bed. I had another dream.

*I was looking in on a room, about fifteen feet square. There was a
steel table in the center, glinting along its face in the glow of a rusty
fluorescent light overhead. I felt the Beast in the room, as it always was,
seething.*

*I saw Yashua, sitting in a chair with the blank gray wall to his
back. In front of him, a man dressed in a black suit, the cut of which was
almost geometrical. He was holding a folder, and an old VCR tape was on
the table. The man paced about, and I could tell that he was asking him
questions. Yashua appeared silent for the most part. Occasionally I saw
his lips move.*

*But, behind the wall, I could see the viscera of the Beast, pulsing
and twitching, glowing red and oozing black energy. The viscera made a
tunnel from the door, and I could see it as an umbilical cord, shooting
outward. It extended about five hundred feet, before sharply dropping.*

*As my eyes hit that spot where it dropped, I was suddenly rushing
along with it, parallel to it as it dropped down for what seemed like a mile.
Then it straightened out, and it was blowing ahead full steam. I felt its
movement even though I myself was traveling just as fast. It was as if
relativity had been eliminated.*

*I could see buildings in the distance, in a scene that simply
bubbled into existence. I could see square white gun towers as I got closer,
and barbwire fencing. I knew it was a prison; I couldn't tell where. As I
got closer to it I could see a sign in brick at the front gate.*

Louisiana State Penitentiary.
*There were inmates standing in a perfect formation, fifty wide and ten
deep. They all had HIPPO devices on, and I noticed that their eyes were
vacuous points of grayish-white. Occasionally, one would glance in my
direction. Inside the main building a siren sounded off, and the inmates
began to enter in double-file.*

*I saw the face of the Beast, grinning as it devoured the inmates
when they walked through the set of steel doors that it used for a mouth.
In two of the upper windows its eyes glowed like fires raging, and I saw
those strange numbers that I'd seen in my dream before. They flashed in
piercing white, running across the bottom of the building in what looked
like a streaming stock quote; groups of four numbers, each separated by a*

space, the numbers spinning and changing as they ran around the building.

As I looked at the penitentiary, it stared straight at me. I could feel the animosity in its stare, and I could see the building shift as its concrete face formed expression. It smiled, and veins of black energy slithered from the two windows, encircling the building. Larger veins poured out along the grounds. They shot to the guard towers, and tiny fibers of blackness entwined themselves with the fence. It crawled to the edges of the razor wire, causing the metal to glow dark red.

I awoke from that dream more frightened than after any dream prior. I knew now where Yashua was heading.

That morning Aziz told me that Paul Demesser was the friend of Rahiim's who would take me to Los Angeles. Aziz would stay; he said he had spoken with Yashua, and there were things in New Orleans that he had to do. He told me that Paul's religious views were extreme Christian right, and he knew nothing of Yashua, or our mission. He also said that Paul was a decent and loving soul.

I met Paul, and he was indeed a nice guy. We took off early in the morning, in a truck that had a Louisiana DOT marking on it. We got back on Decatur, and went through the central business district, to get on I-10. We passed by the Superdome, and I thought of Yashua. I couldn't sense him in the city, as I'd said; they had arrested him. I didn't know where they had taken him, but I knew it was out of the area.

We made it onto I-10, and took off for points northwest. He told me we'd be able to take I-10 all the way to LA, but that it would take two days. We would need to stop for the night, or take turns driving. I opted for the second. I wanted to get to Katherine as soon as possible.

I saw a PRD sticker on his dashboard, and I asked him about it.

"I got that at a rally the Reverend Biggs organized," he said. "That was before he strayed from God."

I was surprised at that, in light of what Rahiim had told me about him. I would have thought he'd be all about Biggs. I asked him what he was talking about.

"The Reverend Biggs used to have the Lord Jesus Christ in his heart, before he was infected with this whole HIPPO nonsense," he continued. "The rally I got this at, he had the passion and the fire in his voice. He had even healed the demons of a heroin addict that day, just called them out in the name of Christ ... but it was all a sham."

He went on, as I tried to imagine Biggs pulling demons out of a heroin junkie. "He started touting this HIPPO thing, like it was the gateway to heaven on Earth."

"He'd even partially underwritten the project," I said.

"Doesn't surprise me," he said. "I wouldn't put anything past him now. He knows how addictive HIPPO is. He's even playing it up like those of us that aren't connected are performing this great sacrifice for those who are plugged in."

He unrolled his window and spit out. "In reality we're cleaning up their piss and shit, wiping their noses," he said.

"Do you believe, Barnabas?" he asked, suddenly. "I mean, *really* believe?"

"Oooh yeah," I said, without my customary flavoring of sarcasm.

"He's coming," he said.

"Maybe He's already here," I said.

"Perhaps He is, but the signs have been given, so the time is soon."

"Are you talking about Jerusalem?" I asked, trying not to let on anything.

"Yes, Jerusalem," he said. "The Dome of the Rock was not attacked with radiation. It was God."

"I know they're not wearing protective suits anymore," I said, hoping we'd get off the topic soon. Paul was a good guy, and I didn't want to lie to him, unless I had to.

We drove through Baton Rouge on I-10. I could see a giant cross, with smaller crosses around it, off to the right. It looked like they were made of steel, painted white, but they could have been wooden. The big one was at least seventy foot tall, by the looks of it. I suddenly felt Yashua's presence as we drove through the city. I couldn't get any kind of lock on him ... but I knew he was there.

For some reason I thought to look at my arm, where the 'tattoo miracle' happened. The dove was still there, but it wasn't glowing or doing anything funky. It still didn't look like a normal tattoo. The lines were too perfect, holding their proportion even as I twisted my arm. It was almost like the lines moved freely through my skin, undistorted by its movement.

Paul lowered his voice some, for what reason I don't know; we were alone, after all.

"Ya' know, ya' might wanna look into making preparations for the final days," he said. "I have friends near Los Angeles; they can make arrangements for you to ride out the chaos that's gonna come. They have food, weapons, ammunition, generators…"

"I'll be alright," I said, again not wanting to reveal anything.

We drove on in silence for a while. I'm not sure if I offended him, but I was growing weary of the topic, being that I'd been stuck in a living Bible story for the past month. I welcomed the silence, and prayed for Yashua.

●

Agent Phillipson paced the room as he interrogated a suspect that it seemed the whole world wanted.

"Mr. King, we have enough evidence to put you away for the rest of your life!" he said to Yashua. "Is that what you want?"

Yashua was silent. He had long ago asked for a lawyer. Phillipson said one was coming, but there was no guarantee how long it would be before Yashua actually saw him.

"Now, I would be willing to talk to the U.S. Attorney on your behalf. He's a friend of mine," Phillipson said as he flicked a pen in his hand. "That is, of course, if you cooperate."

"You will not find what it is you seek," Yashua said; one of the few times he spoke.

"You better hope that's not true, Mr. King," Phillipson said, and his tone had changed ... a shade harsher. "Or else you will not find another day of freedom in your life."

"Edward," Yashua said, "you've not had your freedom in

ten years."

Agent Phillipson became very angry at that, wheeling around the table and getting right in Yashua's face. A bead of sweat on his brow launched onto Yashua's cheek.

"I don't know how you know my name, asshole!" he said to Yashua, their faces just inches apart. "If you wanna fuck with me, I'll hurt you. I don't care if we're supposed to treat you with kid gloves. I don't care if you're an old man; you look like yer' in your forties." He jabbed his fingers into the small of Yashua's left shoulder. He winced, but said nothing.

"I'll hurt you," Phillipson said. "I can do it without leaving a mark."

At that point the door slammed open, and a Louisiana State Police detective named Solomon Carroll walked in.

"This is our jurisdiction until the arraignment," he told Phillipson. "Get outta here. I'm not gonna tell ya' twice."

Phillipson backed away from Yashua. He looked at Detective Carroll, then back at Yashua.

"We'll talk again," he said to Yashua. "I'm lookin' mighty forward to it."

Phillipson gave Carroll a cold look as he walked by, and he left the detective in the room with Yashua.

"I'm sorry about that, Mr. King," he said, as he sat down next to Yashua, folding his arms in a very easy, non-menacing way.

"Do you mind if I call you Yashua?" he asked.

"No," Yashua said, "please do."

"Look Yashua," he said. "We don't normally get these kind of," he hesitated, "*situations*. I don't profess to know exactly what you're being charged with. We've been swamped since the time you were brought here. They're making us hold you until you can be brought up on charges," he said as he rubbed his arms.

"I'm the Deputy Superintendent of Investigations here. I'll be damned if anyone's gonna' get bullied in our headquarters. We don't run things like that here," he said. "I'd like to know, from you, what you are being accused of."

"I will be charged with attacking the Temple Mount," he said.

"You mean..." he looked in the folder, "The Dome of the Rock, in Jerusalem?"

"They are the same," Yashua said.

"They have a videotape of you leaving the East Gate after it was destroyed. Do you have an explanation?" Solomon asked.

Yashua tried to explain what perhaps was unexplainable. Solomon heard him, every word. But he always paid attention to people's facial expressions when they spoke. He was a good detective. He noticed that Yashua's lips hadn't moved when he gave his explanation. It wasn't like ventriloquism. It sounded like he was talking aloud. Solomon was unsure of what to make of that, but he went on.

"Then, why were you there?" he asked. "I don't understand..."

Yashua paused, and he looked directly at Solomon. His eyes appeared as they had after the Atonement Offering in Jerusalem, as translucent scenes sunk beneath the pupils.

"I am He who has Come," he said, and Solomon immediately saw scenes. They were depicted in the fluids of Yashua's eye, with uncanny brightness. Flashing, very quickly, were scenes of Israel, and Jerusalem, snapshots of a man preaching on a hilltop, of a boat in a stormy sea and of a garden, and a crucifixion.

Solomon Carroll had always believed in Jesus as a child, and to that day, he still did. He got into police work to protect the victims of crime, and he was always an honest cop - not neurotically 'by-the-books,' but he always worked in the interest of justice.

Suddenly, he sat in front of a man who was claiming, in a round about way, to being Jesus Christ returned. And, judging by the look in this man's eyes, and the miraculous events that had transpired in the past couple of days, Solomon, for a moment, found the admission almost plausible.

But he was a detective, so he knew that he had to be skeptical, and keep paying attention. Yet, in his heart, he felt he needed to be careful.

He looked back at the mirror, mindful that Agent Phillipson was probably listening back there. Then he realized that Yashua's lips still had not moved. Solomon's gut, so relied upon in the course of his work, was spinning in circles.

"You're saying that you are Jesus?" he said.

"My name is Yashua," Yashua said. "But yes. I walked this very Earth, two millennia ago, and I am returned."

Solomon sat back for a moment, unsure of how to proceed. He had to be skeptical. He had to question it. Not as a detective, but as a human being he had to question it.

Two weeks before, had he talked to Yashua, he would've gotten a kick out of the notion. But right then, the revelation of his suspect just plain kicked him.

"Look, Yashua," he said, as he leaned in closer. "They're looking to nail you to the wall on this. From what you've said to me, you yourself have confessed to at least being at the scene of the attack. Plus the video…"

He thought for a second, then continued. "Yashua, I've been a Christian my whole life. I regularly attend church, and I help out at a local city mission. I believe."

He paused for another second. "What you've told me, I would laugh at most people who'd say that to me. I'd think they were nuts," he said. "But, I don't think you're nuts. I don't know if I'm ready to believe that you're the Son of God, but I have a hunch that whatever you are, whatever the situation is here, God's a part of it."

Solomon then told him, not sounding as a detective, more as a concerned friend; "They'll imprison you, Yashua. They'll send you to Angola."

"Solomon, I know what they will do to me," Yashua said, and a somber look filled his eyes. "I am ready for it."

"Yashua," Solomon said, and he put his hand on Yashua's shoulder. "I won't let them mistreat you. You're in my custody until arraignment, and I have a reputation for bein' a pit-bull around here."

"Thank you, Solomon."

"If they set bail, do you have anyone that can pay it?"

Solomon asked.

"They won't release me," Yashua said.

"Probably not," Solomon said. "And if they did, I imagine Israel would want a crack at you."

"Solomon, you are a good man."

"I wish I could help you out more," he said.

"Things may get," Yashua said as he leaned closer to Solomon, "*complicated*, in the next week. You may be approached by those who come in my name."

"The men that escaped?" Solomon asked.

"You may be more of a help then," Yashua said, and smiled.

It was clear to Solomon that he wasn't getting an answer to that one.

He got up, and asked Yashua if he wanted something to eat or drink, a jacket or fresh clothes. Yashua respectfully and politely declined, saying that he was fine. Solomon told him that he could get him back to his cell in a minute; he had to take care of something real quick, but he'd be back to bring him downstairs. As Solomon went towards the door, Yashua said one more thing to him.

"Gerard Martinez was not insane," Yashua said. "He had ingested a near-lethal dose of PCP, the day that he took Sarah hostage. He had also planned to kill her. He made the plan a week before. He would have killed her regardless."

"How did you know that?" Solomon asked, almost automatically.

"God knows everything," Yashua said. "You used to ask your dad what different words meant, because he knew words that you didn't. Well, when I need to know something, I ask."

Yashua smiled, and Solomon found himself in shock as he returned to the task of filling out the paperwork for the apocalypse in Baton Rouge.

Chapter Fifteen

We drove I-10 in mixed conversation. Paul had let go of the whole 'God' speech. Rahiim was right about him though. Paul was a good guy. He was a truck driver, and occasionally he would do 'odd transports' - like me.

Paul never transported drugs. He was against them, obviously from the PRD sticker on his dash, but he transported people at times, usually people in hiding. He always helped those in need.

Now I've known many fundamentalist Christians in my life. I always walked away with the feeling that what was preached wasn't what was practiced, but Paul, though I didn't agree with his views on who would be saved, practiced Yashua's message. He told me he had helped out Rahiim and gave him a place to stay, until he was able to get the apartment on Dumaine Street. I asked him why he would help Rahiim, because Rahiim was Muslim.

"Rahiim is a human being, and a good man," Paul said. "And, many a night, we talked about our faiths. We have our differences."

"But to be a Christian means that I have to treat Rahiim as I would want to be treated," he continued. "And I would want someone to respect my religious beliefs. So, I respect his, and I treat him with the same kindness and hospitality as I would anyone."

"And he has become a good friend," Paul said. "Though I pray still for his soul."

We drove on and continued to talk. Before we left Louisiana, we got off I-10 and switched vehicles, replacing the DOT truck for a commercial semi-truck. We drove through Texas, which took hours, and went through El Paso, where we grabbed a quick bite. I drove from there to Tucson and we ate dinner at a Mexican restaurant on the outskirts of the city. We also stopped in Phoenix, but just to get out and change drivers. Paul drove from there to LA.

It was a long trip, for both of us, and frequently we'd stop off by the side of the road to stretch our legs, surrounded by desert landscapes of picturesque beauty. We also spent a good deal of it in silence. Half the time one of us was sleeping, and sometimes we just ran out of things to talk about. It happens.

We saw military vehicles occasionally. They didn't seem to pay us any mind. I guess having a truck that says *ZNexus* on the side of it gets you 'off-radar'. We didn't see a whole lot of regular traffic. We saw some, but it was no where near what I-10 *should have* looked like. Even passing through Phoenix, I noticed that the traffic resembled Anno Luce. Phoenix was five times the size of Anno Luce. I was uneasy with it. It was almost my home turf.

I got to know Paul pretty well. He was the son of a Baptist preacher. His dad believed. He wasn't out for people's money, and he taught Paul a good inner path.

Paul went into the Army as a helicopter pilot when he was 18. He served a tour in Iraq, back when that war had just started. He came back and became a preacher himself for a few years. But he was disgusted with what he called 'the snakes'; preachers who fleeced the flock, so he got away from it. Paul never lost the path, he just saw it veering from where many that said they believed, followed. He left to do charity work.

He started his life anew by joining the Coast Guard, volunteering his spare time in a homeless shelter. When Hurricane Katrina hit, he went to New Orleans immediately to help with the rescue effort. He piloted one of the helicopters, and in one week he'd helped to save hundreds. He was exposed to anguish, and confusion, and heartbreaking decisions.

He was himself traumatized by what he'd seen. The people on roofs he'd helped load into helicopters had stories they had to tell, not to deal with them, but to inform the crew of what they were up against. He'd heard stories of alligators swimming in the streets, eating people. He also heard that rescue workers were being shot at. He was also one of the few to realize that most of the shooters on the roofs weren't shooting *at* them, but *in the air*, to get their attention. He wasn't distracted by the fire as a result, and his crew was able to get to more people.

Paul developed what's known as "Helper Syndrome." This is common to people who do any sort of rescue, or disaster response work. The immediacy of the need and the raw emotion makes it very difficult for the helpers to disconnect from the situation, when they're no longer needed. Paul never left. He stayed long after he'd landed his helicopter for the last time.

Paul was on one of the first wave of search teams that went into the devastated city, when the water had been drained. What he saw redefined the landscape of Hell that his imagination held since childhood. Bodies, mostly bloated, some partial. Debris in arcane configurations lay indiscriminately about, covered in a slimy residue that the sweltering sun had begun to put an outer skin on.

Paul could smell it, even through the face-mask. Ever-present was the sweltering heat, soaking everything within his protective suit with sweat. Add to that the dead quiet, absolute stillness that surrounded the team as they went down the street, having to navigate through twisted car wrecks, shattered frames of structures, and shards of broken, slimy glass, sticking up everywhere Paul turned.

They were all careful about the glass; that could rip the suits, and expose them to whatever nightmare pathogens and irritants were in the slime. His team was one of the few to actually *wear* protective suits. They went to houses, two per house, according to a grid they mapped out, in conjunction with three other search teams in the area.

They were, for the most part, flying by the seat of their pants. Almost everyone was. There was very little direction coming from the top, and, in the beginning, a day would go by and they didn't run across anyone representing the federal government.

Paul wasn't alone with helper syndrome, however. There were other guys like him, chopper rescue guys that had stayed to search on the ground and they'd just finished having to grid the city out from the air, again, 'off-the-cuff'. So, for the first couple of days, they worked closely with all the other emergency groups and volunteers who came down. And in the first few days they made it up as they went along on every level.

Paul found many people in New Orleans. As many as he'd rescued in the air, he'd found dead in the second floors of their homes. He would see scratches in the ceiling planks. He saw that one man had almost managed to break through the roof with his bare hands, but fell just short. His fingers were still gripped in the roof, as if in death he was still trying to tear away that last final plank. The sight made Paul collapse, sobbing uncontrollably. He almost ripped his suit. His breakdown only preceded that of his partner by five minutes, who collapsed on the porch outside after spray-painting '1-found' and the group tag on the wall.

Paul told me as we were crossing into California that there were angels there as well.

"There were angels there to comfort us, many from faith-based groups," he said. "They really took charge with the human issues of all of this."

He went on to describe one man in particular, who he'd spoke to during the first couple of days after the city was drained.

"I'll never forget him," said Paul. "When you hear stories like this, you react. It affects you mentally."

"But this guy was different," he continued. "He didn't shock. He didn't look at me different, didn't seem to judge me for having witnessed it. But he seemed to know perfectly what I was going through, and it made me feel stronger, more solid. It was then that I saw the rash on his legs. I'd seen it before, in people who'd been trapped. And even though this guy had been trapped himself, he was there to comfort me."

I knew Paul was talking about Yashua. I didn't know it as fact, but I just *knew* by the way he'd described him.

I didn't say anything, of course. Not because I didn't trust Paul; my initial hesitation had long since turned to admiration, but because I knew he'd think I was nuts.

We got to California, and a strange knot in my stomach developed. I didn't know if it was something I should've been alarmed about, like some kind of precognitive thing. But then I realized that I was nervous about meeting up with Katherine after so long. I laughed aloud that in the midst of what may have been the end of the world, I was being rocked by the butterflies of love. Amazing.

•

Solomon drove 'sans radio' down Perkins Ave in Baton Rouge, past a big strip mall set back in from the road.
Down the street he could see the tall signs advertising check cashing and bail bonds. There were two strip clubs on the block; Solomon remembered when there were none.

He pulled into a CC's for some coffee. CC's was a chain of coffee-shops in Louisiana where they served Community Coffee, which Solomon liked. He frequently stopped to get a cup and read, or work on his computer.

He was plainclothes to begin with, but he never went there as a detective. None of the people who worked there knew he was LSP. In fact few people that Solomon was acquainted with realized he was a cop. Only those close to him. He appreciated the idea of being low-key.

Solomon had always been low-key. He attributed that to his time in the NYPD. Solomon wasn't originally from Louisiana. He left New York in 2002, after the September 11th attacks. He needed to get away. Of the army of demons that Solomon battled in his life, the leader had risen from the pulverized concrete of the World Trade Center.

He sat out that day. It was a nice day, the sun was just starting to go down, and it was about seventy degrees, unusually dry. He sipped his coffee, and his gaze went off in the distance.

Baton Rouge had changed in the ten years since Katrina. It was a state capital that had penis envy. That's why it had the tallest capital building, courtesy of Huey P. Long; former Governor.

Solomon liked Huey Long. He did a lot for Louisiana; helping blacks and poor whites become a part of the civic process. He built over a thousand miles of roads, and made sure students in every county had textbooks. Of course, he made enemies too. He was a true populist at a time when that was dangerous and

Solomon felt his untimely death was proof of that.

But what surrounded Huey P. Long's monument to Louisiana, its capital, had changed rapidly. Baton Rouge had become a major city. With major headaches.

The city doubled in population within the first two weeks of Katrina. It held steady for about four years, then it got real bad. Many were left high and dry within the first year, as they were knocked out of receiving assistance by paperwork errors, signing the wrong line ... trivial stuff like that. Solomon thought it was awful the way the evacuees had been treated.

Then the population dropped off for about six months, due to a massive relocation effort. Then the Louisiana Reintegration Act was passed by Congress in 2012 to counter the migration. A big, fat NIMBY left hundreds of thousands of American refugees. The Reintegration Act forced previous evacuees who'd received federal assistance to return to Louisiana unless they owned property in their host state. Most didn't.

Baton Rouge quadrupled in size, as people displaced to other states were forced to return to Louisiana. Baton Rouge grew to have a population of about one million. It had not been a welcome sight for people born and raised there.

Solomon didn't gripe about it, like a lot of his fellow troopers and friends had done. He griped about little hassles, but he understood that it wasn't the fault of people who'd been more or less *corralled* by America into cities like Baton Rouge, Shreveport, Lafayette, Lake Charles (which itself had been nearly wiped out by Hurricane Rita.) It was just a lousy situation to begin with. But right then the bustle of the nascent "shanty-metropolis" didn't bother Solomon. It wasn't there.

The sounds he'd so recently in his life had to acclimate to were gone, replaced by an eerie silence. Solomon felt like he was in a Twilight Zone episode he'd seen where the guy was running around a neighborhood, but there was no one there. Nothing was real.

Ever since HIPPO was introduced, the city had a sense of calm about it that it didn't have pre-Katrina ... but not a pleasant calm. It wasn't a break from tension; rather, the calm that preceded it all snapping loose. Solomon knew that HIPPO was sinister business. He didn't trust J.D. Fisher or the Reverend Biggs one bit; 'snakes', both, his gut told him. Just the way the guys carried themselves.

He felt as trapped as the people in their houses. Their minds were locked into a "drug-free consciousness-raiser" that knocked them out and hopelessly addicted them. He saw what it could do to people who got cut off. It drove them nuts. And Biggs was on TV smiling, talking about how great it was.

'*Liar*,' Solomon thought to himself, as he peered at the brilliant reds and oranges playing on the dusk sky. It was then that Yashua came into his head. Solomon was ashamed that after 'liar' came 'Yashua'.

The truth was that he believed Yashua. He had plenty of doubts, and he'd never just taken a person's word for anything. But he saw things in that interrogation room, like Yashua talking without moving his lips. When Yashua told him who he was, his eyes were telling a story. Solomon saw it. He didn't understand it, but he knew it was well beyond what could be considered ordinary.

He kept milling it over in his mind as he sipped down to the dregs of his coffee. In a completely uncharacteristic move, he went in and ordered another. He saw no one inside except those who worked there. That had become commonplace over the past week.

Solomon went back outside and drank his coffee, deep in thought. He knew that Yashua would receive poor counsel if left on his own. He knew a defense lawyer, a good one. Every detective worth his salt knew a good defense attorney, and Solomon was worth his salt. He would have to call Dan Champere that night. Dan believed in what he did.
Solomon just hoped that he was prepared to believe just a little bit more.

•

As we arrived in LA, I was apprehensive, but eager to see

Katherine. I needed to know she was alright, and I so desperately wanted to tell her what we'd been through overseas. But I also had something else I needed to tell her.

I hardly knew her. If this whole thing hadn't happened, if I had met her at a bar, I'd probably be on a second date but this whole thing had just ... happened, and I knew she'd be the only one who could understand me. I just hoped she did.

As we drove I-10, entering the city, I was miraculously introduced to fresh air. Well, relatively fresh. It wasn't a blanket of smog like it usually was. I realized that traffic had cut to a trickle thanks to HIPPO, and there was hardly any exhaust in the air. I chalked that up to being the one, and only one good thing to come from HIPPO.

Paul told me he'd be heading back to New Orleans, and that he was very glad to have had a chance to talk with me.

We made our way to RoseCrans Ave, and as we drove down I could see Parrhesia in the distance. All of a sudden it dawned on me that, even though I'd had to learn so much about myself, so much about the world, the universe and existence in the past week, there I was, feeling high noon about having to tell a girl how I felt about her. It made no sense whatsoever.

We pulled up in front of the building. Paul and I said our goodbyes as I got out. I walked around towards the back, and I noticed that there was a lot of equipment outside. Beat up, smashed electronics, all piled by the dumpster. As I started to turn the corner, I could see that there was plywood over the back door. That worried me.

Then I saw Katherine, and when she saw me, the smile on her face energized me. She ran up to me, almost knocking me over as she wrapped her arms around me. It was the greatest hug I ever got. And then she kissed me. Well I should say we kissed, because I was no passive participant.

"Welcome back," she said as I held her in my arms, stroking her hair. "I missed you so much." She gripped me tight.

"I missed you too," I said, kissing her again. "I thought about you all the time."

"I thought about you too," Katherine said.

"Are you okay?"

"Never been better," she said, smiling.

"What happened here?" I said, pointing to the door.

"Victor Ray Tanner happened," she said. And his name made my blood boil.

"Did he hurt you?"

"He tried to," Katherine said. "But I tore him up."

I laughed. "Really? How?"

"Barney, I don't know," she said. "But I'm sure it had something to with Yashua."

"When did this happen?" I asked, though I had a hunch already.

"The night you were in Jerusalem," Katherine said, and then she fell limp in my arms.

"Barney, I don't know what's happening to me," she said through sobs. "I did things, moved things with my mind. I don't know how, but I threw Tanner around with some kind of lightning bolt when the Dome of the Rock exploded! Barney, what's going on here?"

"Don't quote me Katherine," I said as I stroked the side of her arm gently, "but I think it's the end of the world."

•

Victor drove down I-10, licking his wounds with sandpaper.

"Bitch!" he screamed to no one. He got beat by a bitch. *A filthy slut. A whore.* Victor Ray Tanner didn't get beat by whores. He beat whores.

'*But you got beat by this one,*' said a voice in his muddled brain, '*'cause you ain't shit but a punk.*'

That's what Victor's step-dad of seven years used to say about him. Every time he could. Until he caught the death Vic pitched him. Victor was proud of that one, but the .303 fast-ball only sent his step-dad's voice into his head from the grave. And now it taunted him.

'*Maybe you should cut yer' dick off, and get yourself a nice fancy dress, Victoria.*'

Vic pounded what little whiskey was left in the bottle he'd stolen, in an unsuccessful attempt to drown out the voice of old Drunken Tom.

'*See, you'll never be nothin'*,' the voice said. '*Ya can't even do a good job killin' a whore!*'

Victor screamed and he slammed on the accelerator. He reached 130 mph before the engine started protesting, and he brought it back down.

He wanted to go back, and give that little bitch as many hours of agonizing suffering as stitches she'd made him give himself. But he couldn't, and he couldn't bear to admit that she really had beaten him.

'*She had help.*' The thought popped into his head but it wasn't Drunken Tom. This was someone, something, different.

"Yeah, fuckin' a' right!" Vic said aloud. "Ain't no way that bitch beat me fair and square!"

'*God helped her,*' the voice said.

"Fuck God!" Vic shouted as he slammed the empty whiskey bottle against the passenger window. It broke into glass-shards and whiskey mist.

"Where was He when I was gettin' whooped by my step-dad all those years? Huh? Where was He!?"

He stopped for a second, and his vision blurred a shade darker. He became trance-like.

"Where is He?" Vic said quietly, and the voice answered.

'*You can never get to God,*' the voice replied. '*But His Messiah is here.*'

"Where?" Vic asked, quite aware he was talking to no one, and not caring.

'*He will be on the news tonight,*' the voice said. '*Watch it, any channel.*'

Vic looked at the clock on the dashboard. He saw a few clocks, in fact, but he picked the one in the middle ... it said 5:30. He needed to find a TV soon.

•

I never wanted to leave Katherine's embrace, but we both knew we had to play catch up. I turned around finally to see Hernando and Juanita there, smiling.

"Congratulations!" Hernando said. "Welcome back."

I hugged Hernando, and said thanks. I hugged Juanita, and I told them that I'd missed them both. We went in through the front door, and Hernando took the one bag I had, which Rahiim had prepared for me.

I was dumbfounded when I saw what had happened to the control room. It was utterly destroyed. Most of the power cables lining the walls had been shredded, jutting out awkwardly. All across the room equipment was in various manners of destruction. I heard what sounded like a radio, but I saw no operable television screens.

"What did he do to you?" I asked Katherine. "Katherine, be honest with me."

"Barnabas, my dear," she said jokingly, and she put her arm around me in an animated, 'old-chum' manner. "Almost everything you see here was from me giving Victor his 'what-for'."

I laughed. "For real?"

"I'm not kidding," she said. "I really don't know what happened, but I'd like to."

"Yeah, me too," I said. "We'll have a whole bunch of stories for each other in the next few days. But I have to tell you guys something."

"Okay, what is it?" asked Katherine.

"Yashua told you that I'd be coming here alone. That he had something else to do," I said. "But what he didn't tell you was that the thing he had to do ... was to get arrested."

They were shocked, of course. I expected they would be.

"Is he okay?" Hernando asked.

"I hope so," I said. "If the planet blows up, we'll know otherwise."

"What are you talking about?" asked Katherine.

Then I told them about Yashua's connection to the Earth, and about the quakes in Greece and Italy, and the volcano in Japan. They took it with the incredulity I did when I learned it. Except Hernando; he already knew.

"So what happens if they kill him?" Juanita asked.

"We all die," I said, "the whole world; *kablooee*."

"But, he's in jail now. Who's gonna' look over him?" Katherine asked, "Barnabas, I'm worried…"

"He'll be okay for a while. Don't ask me how I know, but I do. God has His ways," I said.

"We need to get there," Hernando said. "I can have us out of here tonight."

"Not yet. We have things we have to do in Anno Luce," I said.

"We have to go after Paradigm," Hernando said.

"Yes. We'll be going from there to wherever Yashua is, and we'll need to assemble a separate team to attack Paradigm. I got someone in mind."

"Better hope he's not plugged in," Hernando said, "or in hiding. Much of the country is one or the other right now."

"He'd die before plugging into this," I said. "And if he's hiding, I know where to find him."

We agreed that we would leave for Anno Luce in the morning. That night we spent catching up, informing each other of what had happened in Jerusalem, and America.

I was joyous, being around friends, around Katherine, having a moment not to have to react to the unexpected. My heart felt unburdened, my spirit lifted, and everything I'd been through was worth it for five minutes of that time.

At the end of the night, Hernando pulled out a TV. It had cable, probably the only TV in there that did. BBC came on, and Jeanne was anchoring. I liked Jeanne, but I didn't like what she had to say that evening.

"In world news, American authorities have arrested a man they claimed was responsible for the recent attack on the Dome of the Rock, in Jerusalem."

"Oh, that's bullshit!" I said, even though technically it was true.

"Furthermore," Jeanne said, "The man, identified as Yashua King, is an American with dual citizenship in Ethiopia. Authorities in America are holding Mr. King in Baton Rouge, Louisiana." She went on. "Formal charges are expected to be brought against him later today."

I tried to figure out what time it might be. I was still plugged into the time-zones overseas, and I realized that they would bring charges against him probably in the morning. I knew we couldn't try to bail him out. I doubted that they'd even give him bail, and I was still on the run.

"We'll be there, Yashua," Katherine said. "Just sit tight…"

●

"Just sit tight in your little cell," Vic said as he turned off the TV in the motel lobby. "I'll be comin' for ya' soon."

Vic could tell just by looking at him, when they'd shown him being brought down a hallway in cuffs. He was the Messiah, the Son of God. Jesus.
He laughed to himself. *'You're in my playground now.'*

He smiled and turned to look at the owner of the motel whose lobby he had walked into. His wife was clinging to life; shot in the stomach by the .38 Special Vic kept close to his heart.

He didn't think he'd need it that night with the *bitch*. He was wrong. He regretted not being able to drop her. But life was *full* of victims.
He was staring at one, his hands up, tears running down his cheeks. Vic raised the gun, and lowered it at the sobbing owner.

"Please, no!" the owner said. "I won't tell anyone what you look like."

"Ya' know, I wasn't even thinking of that," Vic said. "But now that you mention it, you *do* know what I look like, don't you."

"Oh please, God, Jesus…" the man sobbed.

Vic stopped. Not his usual par, but he thought of something.
"Jesus died for your sins," he said. "And he's about to do it

again."

Vic walked out the door, hopped into his car and sped off, leaving the old man behind to tend to his dying wife. Vic laughed maniacally at his decision not to kill the owner.

He drove through New Mexico. He was probably eight hours from Baton Rouge.
As the desert grew cold in the night, Vic grew hot by the bottle of Vodka he'd stolen from the motel lobby. Vodka wasn't really his thing; he got too mean on Vodka, but a mean drunk was just what he wanted right then.

'*Soon enough, God,*' he thought, "soon enough, Jesus Christ!"

Vic realized, as he floored the accelerator, that he had never felt more powerful than at that moment. He looked in the rear-view mirror and he could swear his eyes had an angry red glow in them. He wasn't surprised - he was impressed.

Chapter Sixteen

I awoke at five-thirty the next morning. The sun had just begun to come up, and as I sat outside, pondering our situation, I realized how seldom I ever saw that hour. Well, before recent days.

"Penny for your thoughts," Katherine sat down next to me.

"You can have 'em for free," I said. Katherine leaned over, putting her head on my shoulder.

"Katherine, I love you," I blurted out. So much for subtlety.

"I know," Katherine said, and paused.

"I love you too, Barney," she said, finally, and we kissed again.

"I don't know what we're gonna do," I said to her. "So far, this whole thing has been Yashua telling me the answers will present themselves when the time was right."

"So, they will here," Katherine said.

"Yeah, I know," I said, "but it still helps to have Yashua around. I miss him, Kat."

"I know." Katherine ran her hand through my hair. "Me too."

"I'm worried about him," I said.

"He'll have help," Katherine said. "He's got a friend in the Highest Place, after all…"

I laughed. "True." We watched the city of Los Angeles come to what passed for life in the new 'HIPPO-adjusted' America.

Shortly afterwards, we went back inside. Hernando and Juanita were up, and Hernando was cooking breakfast. I could smell steak and eggs, my favorite breakfast food. I could smell the coffee brewing, awakening my nostrils to the start of the day. Even though I'd been up for about an hour at that point, until I smell the coffee, the day hasn't started.

As I thought about the coffee, Joe McGee came into my head. I hadn't heard anything from him, or about him. I asked Katherine, but she said she didn't know him.

I called Joe's. I had to look the number up in a phone-book; I'd never called before, never had to. Joe didn't answer. I knew I'd have to check in with him when we got to Anno Luce.

●

Patrolman Ernie Helser got the call at 6:30 a.m.

"Attention all units, we have reports of gunfire near the Riverboat District," the dispatcher said. "Calls are coming in from witnesses. There may be a hostage situation. Be advised to proceed with caution. Do not approach the subject alone."

'Another one of those fucking HIPPO-addict nut-jobs,' Ernie thought to himself. 'Hell, I'm closer than anyone else.'

He took the call. He put on his lights and sped west on Florida Ave, towards the River Road. He didn't know why he bothered putting on his lights or sirens. There wasn't anyone on the roads to notice.

Patrolman Helser arrived at the location the dispatcher had

relayed. He pulled the car up over the tracks, and turned it hard left. If he was gonna get shot at, he wanted as much of the car between him and the bullets as possible, also hoping it would obstruct the view of the shooter.

He got out of the car, and ducked down. He had his police-issue Glock 9mm out, hands wrapped around it in a firing grip. He moved over to the side of the patrol car, and carefully looked around the edge of the grill.

He saw a man, standing in the middle of the river's bank. A little girl was in his grip, and there was blood streaking his shirt in all manner of odd angles. The girl squirmed; Ernie could hear the sea-shell gravel crunching beneath her feet. The man didn't lose his hold.

"Drop your weapon!" Ernie shouted. He could hear the sirens of his back-up approaching.

"Drop yours!" the man said, taunting him.

"Please," Ernie said, "before anyone gets hurt."

"Oh, it's well too late for that," the man said, and he pointed the gun behind him. It was then that Ernie saw the seriousness of the situation. Behind the man were two lumps. Ernie didn't have to be a cop to know they were bodies. The shells around them were stained blood-red.

"Take it easy, mister," Ernie said, suddenly aware of how much danger the little girl was in. "It doesn't have to end this way."

Behind him he heard two cruisers pulling up.

"Of course not," the man said.

"We can talk about this," Ernie said.

"Of course we can," the man replied, and it unnerved Ernie.

This guy was too clear-speaking to be a HIPPO addict. That made Ernie more nervous, rather than less.

"Do you have any demands?" he asked as Price Loyo, a fellow patrolman, crouched down beside him.

"Is he an addict?" he asked, making sure his gun was loaded.

"I don't think so," Ernie said to him. "Either way, he's already killed two people down there."

"If you two are done chatting, I have one demand."

"Let's hear it!" Ernie shouted.

"WBRZ News 2 Louisiana," the man said. "They got a chopper, right?"

"Yeah," Ernie said to him, "yeah they do."

"Call 'em! There's something they'll want to report."

"You don't have to hurt the little girl," Ernie said, and out of the corner of his eye, he caught the small outline of a sniper taking position on the roof of the RiverCenter.

"If he shoots me, she dies," the man said, and he held the trigger as tight as he could without it going off.

"Shit, we can't risk it," Ernie said to Patrolman Loyo, and he put the call out to the sniper to hold his fire.

"Nobody's gonna' shoot you," Ernie said. "I just called him off."

"Smart. Now, as I was saying; WBRZ has a news chopper. I want it up in the air around here, taking beauty shots o' me."

"Will you let the girl go if we do that?" Ernie asked.

"Yeah," the man said. "I'll let her go, *if* I see the bird flyin'."

"Anything else?" Ernie asked.

The man didn't answer right away. Ernie put the call out to get WBRZ News 2 on the scene.

"One more thing," the man said.

"What is it?" Ernie asked.

"Tell 'em they're gonna be getting an exclusive!"

"What's that?" Ernie asked.

"The surrender of Victor Ray Tanner," the man said, and he smiled a broken grin.

•

We gathered up our things after breakfast, and Hernando and I carried everything to his van. He had a white van that the Institute used to bring people around. Big long van; an Econoline, bigger than the one I left parked in front of the mission in Anno Luce. It probably could've held about twenty people.

We went back in to the institute, to fish for some last minute supplies. The TV in the control room was on, as usual tuned to the BBC. A different anchor was on; I didn't recognize her.

"Authorities in Baton Rouge have arrested a man they believe is responsible for a crime wave that has torn through many parts of America, leaving families and communities shattered."

"Yashua?" asked Katherine as we watched.

"Can't be," I said. "I know what he's gonna' get charged with. This has to be someone else."

We started to turn away, mindful that we were on a time limit, until we heard something that stopped us cold.

"Victor Ray Tanner, the man in the footage you're seeing, has claimed first place on the F.B.I.'s Top Ten Most Wanted List, for the past five years."

We saw Tanner with a little girl in his arm. He looked up at the camera, and threw the girl out in front of him. He then dropped the gun and raised his hands in the air. As soon as the girl was out of harms way, the police swarmed him.

"Tanner apparently turned himself in," the anchor continued, "but an official with the Baton Rouge Police Department has informed us that before police were called to the scene, he'd already killed the parents of the little girl he was holding hostage."

We looked in horror at the face of Tanner, who was smiling at us. We knew that he was staring right at us, taunting us as the cops walked him up the slope of the shore, into a waiting police cruiser.

"Tanner will be taken to the Elayn Hunt Correctional Center, in St. Gabriel, where he will be held until his arraignment for two counts of first degree murder and kidnapping. It is likely that if Louisiana doesn't seek the death penalty, Tanner will be extradited to a state that will seek it. Tanner is wanted for first degree murder in twelve states."

As the cops dipped his head into the car, the news chopper still had him in their sights. I saw Tanner's hands, wrapped up in cuffs, with his middle finger jutting out prominently like a badge.

"Isn't that cute?" Katherine said with contempt.

"He knows what he's doing," Hernando said. "He knows

who Yashua is."

"Most likely," I said, scratching my chin, and we sat there silent for a few seconds.

"Come on, we gotta go," I said. "We can't waste any more time."

And with that, we left beautiful, sunny, brain-dead Los Angeles, getting on I-5 South to San Diego and going over the game plan. As we got on the on-ramp, I felt the thing on my arm tingle. As I looked at it, it was glowing, pulsating. It was dim, but Katherine noticed it. She was sitting right next to me, though. I knew Hernando and Juanita couldn't see it.

Katherine touched it, and the weirdest sensation shot through my body. It felt good. Katherine and I looked in to each others' eyes, and I knew right then if we did manage to save Yashua, I would spend the rest of my life with her. However long that would be.

●

Dan Champere walked into the Louisiana State Police headquarters, where his client awaited arraignment. He had never met the man, was not called by him, and his client had no money. But Solomon said he was in need, and Dan would never see another case like this, so, he was intrigued.

Dan always had a soft spot in his heart for poor defendants. He got into Law School with the dream of defending the poor with the best counsel he could. Then he became a D.A. Go figure.

When Dan had chosen to 'work the other-side', as he called it then, he had not intended to. A defense lawyer who specialized in helping people unable to pay also specialized in macaroni-n-cheese, beans-and-franks and thrift stores. He needed to get paid, and he didn't want to go the corporate way. Hell no.

And then one day he had to defend a client against a rape victim. He knew his guy did it, but the cops mishandled the evidence, and he had to use that to get the case dismissed. He later found out that the victim killed herself shortly after the trial. Dan decided to change direction.

He knew his ability to win cases came largely from shoddy police-work and incompetent A.D.A.s. So, he submitted his resume to the East Baton Rouge DA's Office. He was accepted eagerly, and became an A.D.A. in Baton Rouge.

He was good; the DA didn't like going up against him in court when he was on the defense, but he loved him as an A.D.A. Dan was indeed good at his job, and though he was always fair with defendants, he was focused, and he won a great many convictions. Unfortunately for the DA, he also saw corruption in his boss's office.

Dan decided to challenge him one year, and was promptly fired. It was difficult for Dan to feel shut out like that, snubbed suddenly by people who used to be friends, but it gave him that much more resolve. He fought it, and his boss, in the November D.A.'s race.

Dan found a small group of grass-roots political organizers, or they found him, rather. They'd seen his work as an A.D.A. and his work as an advocate for the poor, into which he'd poured equal amounts of his dedication. They gave him support, and helped him to set up his campaign.

He won the primary by a landslide. The general election in Baton Rouge tended to follow the primary, and that too he won. But, in the end, that didn't make him happy either. He had a mess to clean up after the previous DA, and he had naturally racked up enemies during his campaign, who took every opportunity they could to make him look bad.

He eventually cleaned up the office, and he was a successful DA. He even won re-election once but he didn't run twice. When he was an A.D.A. he began to invest what he could, here and there. At the end of his second term, he returned to defending poor people. He didn't have to go back to mac 'n' cheese and he was able to pay the bills, and, for the first time in a while, he was happy.

But today, he didn't know what to expect. He had the charges; he had the details of the alleged incident but he couldn't really make one bit of sense out of it. Yashua King was his client's name, and the jurisdiction issues seemed like a nightmare.

"Fucking amazing," he said, as the guard buzzed him in.

He walked down a row of holding cells, mostly empty. It didn't seem like anybody was around to commit crime; everyone was jacked into HIPPO. A man sat in the third cell down, his legs crossed Indian-style on his bunk, his hands folded in his lap. He seemed to be praying, meditating perhaps.

"Mr. King, you have a visitor," the guard said as he rapped on the bars. Yashua opened his eyes, and looked at Dan. He smiled. The guard opened the door and Dan went in to meet his client.

"Yashua," he said. "Is that it?"

"Yes, that's right," Yashua said. "You're my lawyer?"

"Correct," Dan said. "Dan Champere." They shook hands. "How are they treating you?"

"Fine," Yashua said. "Solomon has seen to that."

"Solomon's one-of-a-kind," Dan said.

"Indeed," Yashua said. "As are you, I'm told."

"Well," Dan said, "we'll see after this one."

"You won't win," Yashua said.

"Well, let's look at the case first," Dan said, but Yashua stopped him.

"Daniel, you are not supposed to win this one," Yashua said, and Daniel saw something strange in his eyes, but he couldn't quite say what it was.

"Yashua," Daniel said, "there are jurisdictional issues, evidence issues, really all they have on you is that you were on the property, and…"

"Daniel," Yashua said. "There are men with far more resources than you who will see me into Angola in five days time."

"Who, Israelis?" Dan said. "Palestinians? And even if you were convicted, a trial would take longer than a week!"

"I will be formally charged tomorrow," Yashua said. "My trial will begin two days from then, will last two days, and a verdict will be returned the next day."

Dan realized that Yashua was right about the sped-up trial process. In the week since HIPPO came out, the courts had become less burdened. This did speed up the time between arraignment and trial, but two days? Dan knew himself, there was no way he'd have his case rested in that time, much less the prosecution too.

"Daniel, I do not want you to defend me in any way, other than as I tell you," Yashua said. "Yes, I know you could stretch the case out, but you mustn't. You really don't understand."

"Understand what, that I have a client who doesn't want adequate counsel?" Dan said, flustered.

"You don't understand," Yashua said patiently, "that they're not after me for what I did, but for who I am."

"And, who exactly are you?" Dan asked. Yashua reached over the table, putting his hand on Dan's shoulder.

And then he saw it. In Yashua's eyes. There was a scene depicting itself in the corneal fluid. Instantly Dan was sucked into it.

It was a court scene, or it looked like one but it was in the past. It had to be; everyone was dressed in tunics, with bands of different colors.
Dan could see writing; it looked like Hebrew letters. A man was seated, being questioned harshly by almost all in the room, except for one man, who was defending him. The man being questioned looked like his client. There was a rather large man that seemed to be the main accuser, and he spoke, somehow.

"Answerst thou nothing? What is it which these witness against thee?" the man's main accuser said angrily as he pounded on the table, inches from where the man was seated.

The accused sat quiet, and his defender put a hand on his shoulder as he whispered to him. It was obvious he was a friend.

"Nicodemus," the main accuser said, motioning the defender away. "Please…"

Nicodemus backed up, and the main accuser went on. "I adjure thee by the living God," he said, "that thou tell us whether thou be the Christ, the Son of God!"

The man being questioned spoke up, in a very clear and commanding voice. Dan recognized that it sounded like the man into whose eyes he was now seeing all this. His client. Yashua.

"Thou hast said," Yashua answered as he rose to his feet. "Nevertheless I say unto you, hereafter shall ye see the Son of man sitting on the right hand of power, and coming in the clouds of heaven!"

The main accuser shrieked out, and was only a second ahead of the congregation of men that Dan now realized was the Sanhedrin. The man then tore apart his shirt, and as he ripped the cloth it flashed across Yashua's eyes, causing them to return to normal, ejecting Daniel back into reality.

Dan sat there utterly confused. He knew what he'd just seen, but he couldn't possibly believe the implications of it. He believed in Jesus, went to church on Christmas and Easter, ate fish on Fridays, the whole lapsed-Catholic package. But, there was no way, in a logical universe, that he could be sitting there in front of Jesus Christ, the Son of God, being asked most graciously by Him not to put up a defense. Dan sunk his head into his hands.

"You will have doubts about who I am, but so did my disciples," Yashua said. "And I didn't hold it against them."

"I'm sorry to doubt, but you gotta understand," Dan said, and never finished the thought.

"You have to choose to believe in me or not. I do not, and can not, demand it of anyone. Choice is the gift of free will, but it comes tied with a burden, that of doubt," Yashua said. "God created an uncertain world." He smiled at Dan, and Dan laughed.

"I have to give you a defense," he said. "If there's even a chance you're tellin' the truth, about the, uhh, you know."

"I know," Yashua said, still smiling.

"Then I'll go to Hell if I don't give 'em my best!" Dan said.

"God will guide your case. Only He can defend me. You need only open your ears to Him when He wishes to speak."

Dan looked like he was turning twenty Rubik's Cubes in his head. "How am I gonna' know when that is?"

"He'll let you know," Yashua smiled, "*mysterious ways...*"

Dan laughed, and they talked for a few more minutes before the arraignment. Yashua was arraigned for Conspiracy to Commit an Act of International Terrorism. Though Dan tried to fight for bail, it was denied.

Yashua's trial date was set for, as Yashua had predicted, two days later. He was brought from the courtroom to his cell in handcuffs connected to leg irons, with six armed Sheriffs. Dan thought that strange, but it was claimed that the crime required it. He argued it with the judge, who turned a deaf ear. Yashua was brought from the arraignment to Elayn Hunt Correctional Center in St. Gabriel, a few miles outside of Baton Rouge.

As Dan walked out of the courthouse, he dialed Solomon's number, but he didn't get an answer. Solomon didn't always have his personal cell on, so Dan left a message. He drove down South Acadia parkway, turning left onto Hundred Oaks Drive, where he lived in a small house that looked more like a cottage. He pulled in beneath the arching bough of a live oak that stood as the centerpiece of his lawn. He had some homework to do.

Chapter Seventeen

Solomon Carroll drove his unmarked LSP vehicle into the parking lot of the Christian Community Outreach. He was hoping that Selma Blanforte hadn't left. Selma was a woman he'd had many meetings with; their lines of work brought them into regular contact.

Selma was in her thirties, which made her about thirty years Solomon's junior, yet he always found himself at her door when he needed a sounding board for issues beyond the norm. The two had had many talks about God, life, love, joy, grief, sorrow - and so many other realities typified in abstract.

He noticed her light was on as he pulled in to park, but that was no guarantee. Selma sometimes forgot to turn it off. She could be a bit forgetful about things like that. He walked over to the front door, ringing the buzzer in four quick bursts, which Selma knew was *his* ring. He waited there for a long moment, thinking she might have left already, but just as he was about to turn around, he saw her shadow walking across the lobby. She unlocked the door and let him in.

"Hey Sol," Selma said. "How's the silent jungle?" (They had joked the other day about HIPPO turning Baton Rouge into a "silent jungle".)

"Okay," he said, but Selma must've sensed something was troubling him. She put her hand on his arm with the gentleness of a mother.

"Something's wrong," she said.

"Selma," Solomon said, "I need to talk with you about something ... something you might not believe."

"Okay, sure," she said. "Let's go into my office."

They went into Selma's office. It was cluttered with papers strewn about. The funny thing was, Solomon knew she could find any paper in that heap, if she needed to.

"Please excuse the mess," she said, sweeping papers off a chair. "I slept through spring cleaning."

Solomon laughed. "That's okay, Selma," he said, "I'm used to it by now."

"So," she said as she sat down in the computer chair behind her desk. "What's on your mind, Sol?"

Solomon paused for a moment. He really didn't know how to say it. Even though Selma wouldn't think he was crazy, Solomon was afraid, strangely enough, that she would think Yashua *was*. She would think Solomon was just gullible.

"Selma, we've had conversations about what it would be like if Jesus returned, haven't we?" he asked.

"Yeah, like the one where he'd miraculously teleport the evidence of the Reintegration Act payoff to the NY Times newsroom?" she said, jokingly.

Solomon was silent, still pondering how to lay it on the table.

"I was just kidding," she said.

"He's here."

"What do you mean?" she asked. "*Who's* here?"

"Jesus," Solomon said, and Selma gave him the look he'd

been dreading. But she didn't keep the expression.

"I don't understand," she said.

"His name is Yashua King. You've seen him on the news."

"Wait, you mean the guy behind the Jerusalem attack?" Selma asked.

"Yeah, Selma," he said, "that's him."

"You can't be serious? What, did he tell you this?"

"Yes, but that's not why I believe him," Solomon said. "Things happened, Selma, things that I can't explain ... And he knew things about me, things inside of me that I've never even talked to *you* about."

"But, Solomon ..." Selma said. "Think of how absurd that sounds."

"I know, Selma, but I believe him. I can't explain it. I can't make sense of it, but it's true."

They sat there quietly for a second. Neither of them was looking at the other; neither of them was looking at anything, really. They were just filling their eyes with scenery while the gears ground about in their heads.

"What are you gonna do about him?" Selma asked. "Try to break him out?"

"No," Solomon said. "Not even if I could. I know he wouldn't have it."

"What's going to happen to him?" she said after a pause.

"They'll have him in Angola within a week. The courts put in an expressway since HIPPO cleared 'em up. Plus the feds are all over him."

"Waitaminit," Selma said. "Why Angola?" She picked a pencil up off her desk and spun it in her fingers. "I mean, if the feds are on him, wouldn't they be putting him in a federal prison? Angola's not federal," she said.

"That's the part I don't get," Solomon said. "I overheard two FBI agents talking about how Yashua was gonna' enjoy Angola. It didn't make sense to me at the time either."

"So what *are* you gonna do?" Selma asked.

"I don't know," Solomon said, letting out a sigh reflective of a heavy burden. "I guess all I can do right now is just to make sure he's treated right, while he's around here."

"After that," he added, "I don't know."

They sat there for a while, quiet. Then Selma put her hand on Solomon's.

"If Jesus, or 'Yashua', as you say, *has* returned, then for this part of his journey, I know he has an angel in his corner." She smiled, and Solomon did as well.

"Well, a miracle or two would be nice," he said, and they continued to talk about the deeper aspects of Yashua's presence. Solomon left as the night had officially established itself, feeling a little better, though no less confused.

•

As we drove down I-5, we went over a general plan of action. We would find Jonesy, and enlist him in getting a hack-team together. Jonesy had more hacker friends than he had non-hacker friends. I was one of the few people he hung out with who wasn't a hacker.

I knew Jonesy, on and off for over a decade. I knew he hated Paradigm, ZNexus - and the rest - with a passion. He knew a lot of stuff about the HIPPO program from having worked there. He told me he never had clearance, just good sharp ears, and he'd overheard a whole lot more than anyone there realized.

I'm sure he knew about the addiction rate being 100%, and about the block they'd put in to fool people about it. I'm also sure he knew what would happen to people who were forcibly disconnected; how it drove them insane. That's probably why he quit.

Jonesy became a major conspiracy theorist after he left there. Only he wasn't paranoid-nutso about it. He knew the real conspiracies. He'd always told me that the day it all went down, he'd be in hiding. One night at 3 a.m., when he was at my door thoroughly trashed, he even told me where. And to think; at the time I was pissed about him puking on my windshield.

'I got something useful out of the whole deal after all,' I thought to myself as we drove down the nearly empty highway.

We saw a black limo drive past us. It was truckin', by the look of it. Not that there was anyone on the road to slow it down. As I looked at the tinted windows, I wondered, as I always did when I saw a limo in California, which famous person might be inside.

●

J.D. Fisher pressed 'End-Call' on his cellphone impatiently. He was irritated with Biggs, and he took out his frustrations on the bottle of fine malt scotch that he pulled from the mini fridge in his limo. He looked out the tinted window as he passed a white Econoline van. It reminded him of the workhorses Biggs used to drive disabled children to their photo-ops.

Reverend Biggs had a deal with Fisher. He was supposed to use his PR Company, *The Righteous Brigade*, to push HIPPO. Then he was supposed to go all teary-eyed in front of his flock, which at that point should've been all essential personnel, and say that he'd been tricked, that he was wrong, that HIPPO was a bad thing.

Fisher didn't care if everyone who was left hated HIPPO. It was a necessary evil by now. No one was going to deactivate the hub. No one wanted the blood of three billion people on their hands.

America was done, in Fisher's opinion. He needed to concentrate on corralling rural areas elsewhere. America could no longer offer him anything. He needed to move on.

But that bastard Biggs didn't hold up his end. He was still pushing HIPPO's salvation. Fisher didn't want people performing their essential tasks, thinking that it would only be temporary, until everything was mechanized, and then they could plug in. Biggs was fucking up his game plan, and his run for the Presidency was going too far. Fisher was stirring his drink with a swizzle stick, drawing the conclusion that Biggs had forgotten his place in the food chain.

Fisher had precious little tolerance for people. He wasn't a 'people-person.' He saw people as unsuspecting opportunities, suckers waiting to be fleeced. He didn't understand emotion.

Where others saw love, he saw sex. Where others saw friendship, he saw mutual use. Where others saw charity, he saw waste, and what other people found to be true and noble, he found to be naïve and stupid.

He told the driver to speed up. They were already doing 90. He needed to be in Anno Luce yesterday. He'd been waiting for five years to see the finished ISIS.

ISIS was a project developed in conjunction with HIPPO. Originally it was intended to make the experience more real, by using a target human genome as a template for the integration of HIPPO's sensory features. They found out during the test trials however, that HIPPO didn't need to be any more integrated. It served its purpose perfectly fine by itself.

The ISIS Project would have been shelved, but then Fisher found another purpose for it, in the half-educated rantings of Reverend Biggs.

Biggs had babbled on when they first met, about the signs. 'I've seen them, Mr. Fisher,' he'd told him over drinks the evening they'd met.

He suspected that Biggs did this to everyone he met, but Fisher humored him. At the time, it made good business sense. He needed Biggs's flock.

But Biggs took him deep into his delusional world, and Fisher, neither a religious nor a spiritual man, discovered that despite his new sucker's obvious insanity, he'd done his homework. Fisher was intrigued. Not by the coming of Jesus, per se. He didn't believe in Jesus but he did know that many of the *people* believed. And, if the people were given this man, and given the proof, he could harness from them more power than he could fathom.

All he needed was a way to take advantage of the situation. It was then that the ISIS Project manager called him to confirm its closing and Fisher saw that as his own 'sign'. He had his opportunity. He told the Project Manager not to shut down; the project would continue.

He didn't believe that the man Biggs was trying to track was the Son of God. But he did his *own* homework, garnering a bit of the man's blood. From what he'd discovered, he knew that the man's DNA was unique, could be used in the ISIS to be revealed to all those within its web. Spiritual energy was far more powerful than ecstatic energy, but it couldn't be extracted without introducing the Divine element. 'Or the appearance of it,' Fisher thought.

But Fisher himself didn't grasp the full reality of it, until a few days prior, when he saw the reports coming from Israel. The whale coming out of the Jordan. The attack on Jerusalem; the way the Dome of the Rock glowed. The earthquakes. All exactly as Biggs had predicted.

As they flew down the highway, Fisher dialed a number on his cell, and wiped sweat from his upper lip. If the partition window to the driver's compartment wasn't tinted jet black, he would've seen the San Diego skyline off in the distance.

●

Dan Champere sat in the LSU Law Library, studying the changes in state law that had taken place since the Louisiana Reintegration Act. Many of them, he realized, were more the result of the implementation of the Patriot Act III, but tailored towards the problems the Reintegration Act caused in Louisiana.

As a result of problems created originally by the population re-shift; Louisiana had become the state with this highest level of 'P3 Implementation' when it was passed. Before this whole HIPPO mess, P3 had been the buzzword among civil-liberty types such as himself.

The original Patriot Act was passed by Congress in 2001, after the terrorist attacks on September eleventh, in New York and Washington. Many thought, even then, that the Patriot Act dangerously expanded the power of the executive branch. A second Patriot Act was passed in 2003, formally called the Domestic Enhancement Security Act. It was done in the relative secrecy that had marked the Executive branch at the time.

The president that signed the original Patriot Act went down as the worst president in U.S. history. Many people blamed the subsequent collapse of the dollar on his economic policies.

And in the outrage (and riots) that followed, the Congress was given every reason to leave the Patriot Act on the books, so the Act and its protégé were kept on; expanded, even. Americans hardly noticed, as the provisions in these acts were always carried out in secret. Not that Americans were looking too hard.

It wasn't until the Omnibus Patriot Bill became the Omnibus Patriot Act, Patriot Act 3, P3, or, Dan's favorite, the "Ominous Patriot Act" that Americans started waking up to the fact that the constitution was one inch past the brink of irreparable harm. Use of the P3 provisions drew America into a totalitarian oligarchy of rich corporate CEO's and elected puppets.

Implementation of P3 varied among states, but the resettlement caused Louisiana to take the lead. Federal agencies within Louisiana used the provisions indiscriminately. State and local law enforcement used them as well, but less so. Perhaps the most significant aspect of P3 was the reversal of *Posse Comitatus,* a law passed in 1878 that restricted the military from acting on domestic soil. Daniel knew that a great degree of resentment had been building between state and local law enforcement, the feds and the military. Now, with HIPPO turning America into a national echo chamber, everybody was confused, even the feds and the military.

Dan knew a few federal agents. He was a DA before, after all. And he knew that it wasn't them either. Half of them were using provisions that they were ordered to use and they knew enough about the P3 not to want to be on the receiving end of it. Yeah, there were a few assholes that got off on the power, but they were the few. The federal agents Dan knew had family and friends that weren't in law enforcement. They didn't like it any more than those they had to target. But then, they were just as *plugged in* as anyone.

As Dan looked through the P3 provisions, he realized that Yashua was right. He couldn't win. He couldn't keep Yashua from going to prison. The laws of evidence were relaxed in P3, and much of the case, uncorroborated hear-say, would be usable in court.

Dan sunk into the chair he was sitting in, and took a deep

breath. He always had an answer. He always had a way out. He prided himself on this. But there he was, being called upon to defend a client, in what might be the trial to end all trials, and he knew that in three days time, his client would be convicted. There was no way out; no answer. He could find no solution.

Daniel left the library when it closed and drove home.

As he sat in his living room, wisps of cigarette smoke slithered about in the air as smooth New Orleans jazz danced a second line through tweed covered speakers. A gin and tonic held position in his left hand, a Bible in his right.

He scanned the New Testament for the trial of Jesus, and he read every one until he got to Matthew. What he saw in Yashua's eyes that day he read verbatim in Matthew's account. He wasn't a Bible quoter, so he didn't have any of it memorized except for the parts he heard everyday, like 'love one another', 'turn the other cheek', and so on.

Dan would never have been able to make up a delusion like that verbatim.

And the reality of it; he didn't have the imagination to conjure that up. He'd heard the men speak in a language that he couldn't understand, yet he knew exactly what they were saying. He felt the accuser's tunic rip as though it were being torn from a garment he himself was wearing.

Dan fell asleep with the Bible open in his lap, the alcohol consumed, and the cigarette burnt out in the ashtray. When he awoke the next morning, the Bible was open to the Book of Job. Dan couldn't remember reading it.

•

I was getting antsy by the time we approached the exit ramp that would take us off I-8 and onto Jefferson Highway. I wish I could say it was good to be home, but I was pretty ambivalent about it. Truth is, if I could have avoided being there, I would have.

They say that when you become famous, you can never go

home again. I think that anytime you go through life-changing events or periods, you can never go home again.

Working at the Mission, I'd heard rape victims tell me that they had to leave the town they'd lived in before the rape. Not because places or people in the town gave them problems, or brought back memories of the rape; that was a factor for many. But a few told me they left because the town didn't feel the same anymore; it wasn't 'home' anymore.

Not that what I'd been through in the past week was in any way like a rape, mind you. Not at all. But I'd been through experiences that made Anno Luce lose the sense of overbearing uniqueness that had previously kept me from moving to L.A.

As we drove down Jefferson, Anno Luce glowed in the setting sun. The Paradigm building was, as always, the most prominent thorn in the Anno Luce skyline. I did notice that it was glowing brighter than the other buildings.

"It must be storing energy," Hernando said.

"Probably," I said. "In New Orleans, I noticed the dimming of the building lights. Which I couldn't figure out, because this thing's supposed to be taking human energy, not electricity."

"Why not take both?" Juanita asked. "No one's around to notice."

"She's got a point," Katherine said.

"Have you talked to Alejandro or Zee?" I asked Katherine.

"Hernando and I talked to Alejandro after the mission was burned down," Katherine said.

"And I called him this morning to let him know we were coming," Hernando said as he drove.

I had Juanita turn on KALR as we neared Anno Luce city proper. Easy listening greeted my ears. 'WTF?'

"They've changed the format of a lot of radio stations recently," Katherine said to me. "Sorry Barney!" She playfully jabbed me in the side.

"How am I gonna' get my Clapton fix?" I said.

"Umm?" Katherine said. "Save the world?"

I laughed. "I can't save the world without Clapton!"

"You don't need Clapton," Katherine snuggled up close.

"You got me."

"Oh yeah, that's right," I said, gripping her tightly. "But I'm gonna have to teach you how to play the blues."

"Maybe I already know." She smiled mysteriously.

"You can play?"

"I taught myself to play guitar when I was ten," she said.

"Did you get lessons?" I asked.

"Sure," she said. "Piano lessons."

"So, how did you learn guitar?"

"Piano and guitar are a lot alike. Once you learn basic theory on a piano, it's not too tough to apply it to guitar."

"Oh," I said. Katherine really was the *shit*.

"Here's Barker Street," Hernando noted, and we turned off Jefferson Highway.

I had never seen 'The Mount' look so dead. It was just like Metairie had been. Everyone at home; everyone plugged into HIPPO, the streets dead of the shouts and bass-thumps that were the neighborhood theme music. Gone were the sounds of the African drummers I knew; their playing spot was conspicuously deserted.

I didn't hear the kids shouting, or the adults shouting for that matter. I saw city vehicles, maintenance, public works and ALPD, but that was about it. We were one of the few non-city vehicles driving around, and that made me nervous.

We went up Baker St., which ran up the ridge parallel to Barker St. It always used to confuse people who weren't from there, the street names being so close. Barker was a main road, though and Baker was a small residential street. We were trying to stay low, so we avoided Anno Luce's highways and main roads.

As we neared Mt. Calvary, I could smell the remnants of burnt wood, plastic, and a hundred-and-fifty other materials that a week ago composed the Mission. The smell preceded my vision by about five seconds, and my seeing it preceded my heartbreak by about zero seconds. I couldn't believe what I saw.

Mt. Calvary had indeed been burnt to the ground. Sure, there was some semblance of structure. Part of the Mission was brick, and it still stood, though I could see the black smears of soot that streaked out from every shattered window. I could see construction supplies, and for a second I thought they were for rebuilding. Then I realized that the supplies were there before the fire. The stuff was probably there for the renovation they were planning when Yashua and I left.

As I got closer I could see that the construction materials were covered in soot too, validating the conclusion I had just drawn. They would be able to rebuild from this, with the money they got from the endowment, but from the look of the vacant streets, I thought, 'They may not have to.'

I saw a figure standing out front, looking into the pile of rubble, motionless. I didn't have to guess that it was Alejandro. I knew that profile from any angle. His dreads were a dead giveaway. I always used to joke about his "baby dreads." He had the hardest time growing his hair; it took him ten years just to get them to come down past his jaw-line. I was happy to see those baby-dreads that day though.

We pulled up, and Alejandro turned around. When he saw Hernando in the driver's seat, he walked over. Hernando motioned to him that we were gonna park in the back lot. He nodded his head and we parked. I didn't need my 'Parking for Sex Offenders' sign this time. Parking spaces at this point were irrelevant.

When we got out I gave Alejandro a big ole' bear hug, but I was careful not to crush his ribs. I didn't know what my strength was in Anno Luce, and I didn't want to take chances. I made a joke about how I leave for a week, and he manages to burn down the building. It may have sounded in poor taste, but ya' gotta know Alejandro to understand how it wasn't. He laughed, and called me an asshole.

It was good to be back home.

Alejandro told us that we shouldn't sit out there too long. He'd seen his share of ALPD, and he'd even seen a couple black cars drive by with tinted windows. He didn't know if they were feds, but he knew the trouble that Yashua was in. He'd seen it on the news the night before. He told us to follow him to his mother's house, where he'd been staying since the fire.

Alejandro's mother lived in Mercado; a suburb of Anno

Luce, about five miles north of Silverton. It was nice; a bit wealthier than Silverton. Alejandro's father had been an engineer, and had worked on many of the projects in the fifties and sixties that made Anno Luce an actual city. So, Rosita, Ale's mom, was well off. Well off enough to live in Mercado, anyways.

Rosita frequently gave to the Mission. Many times it kept us afloat. So she was always *persona grata* when she came to visit Mt. Calvary. But she was *persona grata* with me just because she was real cool. I, like many of Alejandro's friends, was 'adopted' by her long ago. I was quite looking forward to seeing her.

Rosita had not been sucked into the HIPPO thing. She wasn't the kind of woman to go for any fad, and Ale' told her not to trust the thing, so she didn't. No one messed with her in Anno Luce, especially not Paradigm. That's because she had made considerable investments in Paradigm stock when the company had its IPO.

She had about ten percent share in the company, though she never bothered with it. Limiting her interaction with Paradigm to cashing dividend checks suited her just fine. And I'm sure that was fine in Paradigm's eyes as well. Aside from that, there was no law at this point that required anyone to plug in; just enormous amounts of public pressure and advertising.

We pulled up to the Ortiz house. It was very elegant, Spanish style, stucco walls formed with great care, foliage dotting the lawn in an intricate bouquet of tropical flowers, stone statues and assorted ironwork. The house wasn't huge, but it was a little bigger than the other houses on her street.

We pulled into the circular driveway, and stopped near the front door. We all piled out, and Alejandro went up to ring the bell. Kindly Rosita answered, beaming a smile Scotty would've been proud of.

"Barney!" she said exuberantly. "You've returned from your little jaunt across the world. How are you?"

"Fine ma'," I said. "How've you been?"

"Oh I manage," she said. "Though I don't know how much longer any of this is gonna' last..." She motioned all around.

"You mean 'cause of HIPPO?" Katherine asked.

"Oh, ma', this is Katherine," I said, introducing her. "Katherine, this is Rosita, Alejandro's mother."

"Pleased to meet you, Rosita," Katherine said, extending her hand.

"Please, call me 'ma'," Rosita said. "Everyone else does."

"Hello Rosita," Hernando said. "How have you been, dear?"

"Hernando DeSantis," she said. "I didn't recognize you by the look but I'll never forget that voice." She gave him a look that embarrassed the hell outta' Alejandro.

"Nice to see you too, ma'," Ale' said.

"Oh, you know you're my favorite!" she said, and gave him a peck on the cheek. She was introduced to Juanita, and we proceeded to go inside. I walked in knowing this would probably be the only homecoming that I'd enjoy.

●

Dan went to see Yashua the next day. He always hated going to meet a client when he knew he couldn't win the case. He never knew how they'd react, but he knew he'd have to tell them, if he was to do his job correctly. Defendants and their lawyers needed to have an honest relationship; dishonesty on either side could destroy the defense.

But Dan already knew how Yashua would react. He wouldn't be angry. Yashua himself had told Dan he couldn't win. But for some strange reason this would be the toughest time Dan would ever have to say it.

He went to EHCC, and a guard let him into the room he'd meet Yashua in. He saw Yashua as the guards let him in. He smiled when he saw Dan, and the guard secured his leg irons to the table before he undid his handcuffs. Dan was dreading this pre-trial consultation, if he could call it that. He felt like a doctor confirming cancer.

"Yashua, how are they treating you?" he asked.

"Fine," he said. "The guards have been gracious hosts, however unwilling."

"Any problems with other inmates?"

"No," Yashua said. "They are held back. How is Solomon?"

"He's good," Dan said. He'd talked to Solomon the night before to let him know Yashua's legal situation. "He can't come here to see you, but he's been keeping an eye on you."

"I know," Yashua said. "I can feel it."

"Look, Yashua," Dan started, but Yashua cut him off.

"You've realized we won't win," Yashua said. "I know."

"Well, if you are who I think you are," Dan said, "you probably know a whole lot."

"I know a few things," Yashua said, and smiled.

"Yeah." Dan let out a long breath. He loosened up for a moment. "So, how do I defend the Messiah?"

"As I said," Yashua answered. "At the trial, free your mind. Allow God to speak through you."

"I have to prepare in some way though," Dan said. "I'm not going to have anything that way."

"Daniel," Yashua said. "Tomorrow morning, put about a hundred sheets of blank typing paper, in your briefcase."

"And do what?" Dan asked.

"Don't open your briefcase until ten minutes before the start of each day of the trial," Yashua replied.

"That's it?"

"You don't need evidence in this trial, nor testimony, nor experts. If you had bounty in all three, it would still do no good. You need only faith."

"Just faith?" Dan said.

"There's never *just* faith," Yashua said. "Faith carries with it truth and love, hope and strength. If you have one, you have all."

Daniel sat quiet for a while, contemplating any legal moves he could think of. Contemplating the trial. Contemplating faith.

"You won't exonerate me," Yashua said. "It is God's Will that I be incarcerated. If you fight this beyond what God expects of you, you fight God."

"Why me?" he asked.

"I've asked that question of *myself* a few times," Yashua said smiling. "God chose you for a reason that not even I know. Trust His judgment, and do what He wants of you."

"I don't even go to church anymore," Dan said.

"Well, I only went to temple during times of obligation in my previous lifetime. God measures you by the size of your heart, not by the stack of mass bulletins you rack up."

"Besides," Yashua continued, "many of the masses I've been to are little more than rote rituals, with the original significances and meanings separated from those who participate in them. You'd be amazed what some people think about when they're in church."

Daniel laughed. "You read their minds?"

"I have to. Thoughts like those are rather loud to me," Yashua said.

Dan thought for a moment.

"Yes Daniel, I can read your thoughts too," Yashua said. "But, don't worry about it. I've heard it all, and I don't take any offense. Most of the time I just tune you all out."

Dan laughed. "Okay," he said. "Well then, you know what's really on my mind here."

"Yes, Daniel. Who I am will be a part of your defense."

Dan let out a breath. "Oooh boy!" he said.

"You'll be fine."

"They'll never let me into a courtroom again, that's for sure," Dan said, folding his arms. "I'll probably get laughed right off the bar."

"They won't have very long to laugh, Daniel."

"Are you saying what I think you are?" Daniel asked. "Is this the end?"

"One way or another,"

Dan sunk back into his chair, overwhelmed.

"Daniel, you mustn't fear. You have been handed a direct assignment from God. Few are the number God Calls. Fewer still those who answer that call. But those who do, those like you, are cherished by Him. Rejoice."

"Rejoice," Dan said, blankly.

"Yes. Rejoice," Yashua said. "I used that word often back then; to have joy, to be happy. How many people in this world go about their day, living a life of drudgery, bitter at the world, and yet they go to church on Sunday and say 'Rejoice!' Daniel, rejoice. Be joyous. In the midst of what will be your own greatest trial, rejoice."

Dan looked around, and thought about what Yashua said.

'*Fuck it*,' he thought. '*Rejoice.*'

Yashua laughed. Dan apologized before laughing himself.

"I guess I won't need to pad my resume after this trial," Dan said.

"You won't need a resume after this trial," Yashua replied.

●

Solomon walked into the East Baton Rouge Parish Sheriff's Office, apprehensive about the guy he was being called to interview. A real piece of work, from what he was told by the deputy who'd called him.

Victor Ray Tanner. Solomon had heard about him, of course. Tanner was on the FBI's Most Wanted List, Number One, for five years; serial killer, spree killer, armed robber, kidnapper, rapist. All of the above the guy was.

Solomon had interviewed killers before, plenty of them. Robbers and rapists too. He'd even had to interview a serial killer before, back in 2009. Larry Gents was his name. But Tanner was as bad as they came. Gents had killed ten women. Tanner killed beyond the law's ability to count.

Serial killers, in Solomon's opinion, fell into two general categories. There were those that wanted to get caught, and those that didn't want to get caught. Tanner was the type that didn't want to get caught. He didn't leave evidence. He didn't leave notes. He didn't leave witnesses.

Except, of course, this time. A motel owner survived an encounter with him without a scratch, and was able to identify him. Tanner killed indiscriminately; men, women and children. They suspected that he may have killed as many as ten children under the age of fourteen. He didn't molest them, either. That was the usual situation with child-killers. Tanner just killed them. And he let a little girl go after killing her parents, so that he could give himself up and get his face on the six o'clock news? It didn't make sense. Something wasn't right there.

He walked into the briefing room. Sheriff Laverne was there, as well as Deputy Williams, Deputy Robinson and two other men that he didn't know. They were feds, but not the same feds who'd barged into his headquarters. The men were standing around a map of North America on the wall, peppered with push-pins of different colors, scattered everywhere from Canada to Mexico. Laverne was pointing to Louisiana.

"Sol," Sheriff Laverne said, "good to see ya'."

"Henry," Solomon replied, tipping his hat.

"Sol, meet agents Dave Barnes and Mike Chenko from the FBI Washington field office. Agents Barnes and Chenko, meet Solomon Carroll, Deputy Superintendent of Investigations, Louisiana State Police."

The men shook hands with Solomon, and they began to brief him on the situation with Tanner, and more specifically, why they wanted him to interview the guy.

"Victor Tanner told us that he'll only speak to you," Agent Barnes said.

"That's insane," Solomon said. "I don't even know the guy!"

"He asked for you by name, Sol," Henry said.

"How?"

"We were hoping you knew," Agent Chenko said.

"As I said, I don't know the guy," Solomon said. "Other than that he's on the FBI List."

"Sol, we'll be monitoring the interview," Sheriff Laverne said, "but we really don't have the time to brief you properly. You're gonna have to play it by ear."

Sheriff Laverne and the FBI agents went over what Solomon roughly needed to know; little more than a briefing about what happened the previous morning in the Riverboat District. Then, with a 'good luck' from Laverne, Sol walked into the interrogation room. Everyone else went in the observation room, where they peered anxiously from behind the mirror.

"Good afternoon, Mister Tanner," Solomon said as he sat

down, "I'm ..."

"Solomon Carroll," Tanner answered him. "Deputy Superintendent of Investigations, Louisiana State Police," he said, and flashed a grin sure to make even the most iron of stomachs turn.

"I see you've done your homework," Solomon said.

"And I see you haven't," Tanner said, again with that smile. "It's okay though. I'm the one that's gonna do all the talking."

"Very well," Solomon said. "What do you want to talk about?"

"Death," was his reply.

And then, without another word from Solomon, Tanner began to do just that. He began with his first kill, a friend he'd pushed in front of the on-coming truck. Then he went on to talk about his 'dissertation' in the jail he was sent to for that crime. Then he talked about his first kill after he got out. And on and on he went, explaining in graphic detail every one of the murders he'd committed. He examined every detail; every scream, every squeal, every plea spoken out in desperation by people who, up until the end, thought that they'd be spared.

He talked about the mind games he would play on his victims, about pretending he was in need, and, when they offered to help, they were really offering him their lives. He talked about his methodologies; about ways that he could prolong agony, and boost his own ecstasy when the vitality finally had to release its grip from his victims. He spared no detail, and every time he felt Solomon react to what he'd said, he'd push the topic further.

He didn't admit to raping anyone, saying it wasn't his style. But Solomon knew he was lying and that was perhaps the only time Tanner wasn't in total control of the conversation. But he changed it pretty quick.

"I killed that fag Timothy Silver. Remember him, Sol?" Tanner said.

That definitely pushed Solomon's buttons. The Silver case had plagued him for ten years. He found the killer, a right-wing neo-Nazi high-school kid, named Pete Carerra. Solomon had forensic evidence, eyewitnesses that saw Carerra calling Silver a faggot, days before he'd turned up dead. Silver's body had a swastika cut into the chest. Solomon had a photograph of it sent to the FBI Crime Lab in Quantico, to compare with samples of other swastikas Carerra had drawn in his notebooks. They matched. But the case had always bothered him, because the crime scene looked too clean to be the work of a punk kid like Carerra.

But the DA in East Baton Rouge at the time, Dan's former boss, had enough evidence to roll with, and the case was out of Solomon's hands before he could say a word. Other cases came in, so Solomon just had to hope he was wrong about the crime scene.

Now he knew he was right. Tanner did it, and he'd set Carerra up. Now Carerra was sitting in Angola for a crime he didn't commit. Now he understood why Tanner knew his name. Solomon was furious, half at Tanner, and half at himself. Tanner laughed, knowing he'd touched a nerve.

"Yeah, that was me," he said. "Never did like fags. Or Nazis. They're both pussies in my book. You should've seen the look on Carrera's face when the gavel hit." Tanner imitated a judge banging a gavel. "Oh yeah, you *did*." He started laughing.

It was everything Solomon could do to keep from reaching across that table and ripping the laugh right out of Tanner's throat ... he didn't though. He'd been up against guys like Tanner before, who'd do whatever they could to get you to hit 'em. Solomon never bit, and he wasn't going to bite then.

Tanner was surprised, by the look on his face. He continued on for another five minutes or so, ending on the parents of the little girl in Baton Rouge, which had brought him here.

"So, why did you do that?" Solomon said. "The motel owner, the little girl, you let them live. I don't get it."

"The motel owner ..." Tanner said. "That was just a fluke; havin' fun really. And the little girl..." He clasped his hands together, touching his chin with his outstretched index fingers. "If I killed her, your buddies in the Baton Rouge PD woulda' blown me clear across the mighty Mississip'."

"I'm here on business," he added, "and I can't rightly do business if I'm dead." He guffawed, like it was the funniest thing he ever said.

"And what would that be?" Solomon asked.

"If I told you," Tanner said, "it would be because I wanted you to know. Which I don't."

"Well, I don't see what kind of business you're gonna do in Angola," Solomon said in an attempt to get him to slip.

Tanner laughed. "You're a top dog these days," he said. "The two biggest cases in America, and you're on 'em both!"

Solomon thought to ask Tanner how he knew he was involved with Yashua's case, but he'd been in the game far too long to slip up like that. Yet, he did want to know. He knew Tanner was trying to pump him for information. He didn't underestimate his current adversary. Tanner was pathological; nothing he did was arbitrary. Solomon decided to play it cool, and reverse the direction of the pump. '*Let's see what Tanner knows,*' he thought.

"What case would that be?" Solomon asked.

"You know what case, Sol."

Solomon could hear the impatience creeping into his voice.

"Baton Rouge is a big city," Sol said. "I got a lot of big cases. You'll have to be more specific."

"Okay," Tanner said. "The terrorist. What was his name…?"

Solomon had no intention of answering him.

"Yashua King," Tanner said finally. "Yeah, that's it."

"What makes you think that's *my* case?"

"I saw it on the news."

"They never said who was handling that case on television," Solomon said. "So, you're lying to me."

Tanner smiled, affirming that he had made that up.

"What can I say?" he said, leaning back in his seat. If his arms hadn't been secured to the table, Solomon was sure that Tanner would've raised them up and held the back of his head in his interlaced fingers. "I think we've established the fact that I'm no … angel."

"How did you evade us for so long?" Solomon asked. "Bein' such an awful liar?"

"Now, now," Tanner said, rolling his head around in fake dramatic gesture. "A magician never reveals his tricks."

"Someone on the inside?" Solomon pressed, not wanting an answer really, just wanting to have Tanner on the ropes for a little while. Maybe he had a mole with the feds. Barnes and Chenko *were* here, after all.

Tanner was silent, but still smiling awful. Solomon decided to change course.

"Tell me about Martha Smith," he said. Martha Smith was the only rape charge they had evidence for, somewhere in California.

"I didn't rape that bitch!" he said, coldly.

"Well, Mr. Tanner," Solomon continued, "it appears that you left evidence at the scene; DNA, even." He leaned in closer. "Did Houdini forget to wear his top-hat that day?"

Tanner lunged at Solomon, and the shackles and leg irons were not able to withstand it. Tanner was stronger than any man Solomon had ever seen. They had three sets of restraints on him, and two of them ripped apart. The third set held, but barely.

Tanner didn't hit Solomon when he lunged. He didn't scare him either, but that's probably what he was going for. Solomon had done enough interrogations to know how far you lean into someone before saying something you know will get their goat. He'd been lunged at before. But he had definitely underestimated Tanner's strength.

Tanner sat back down and relaxed. He shook his hands as the three sheriffs and the two agents came in to subdue him. Tanner didn't fight back. He just smiled. Solomon knew right then that none of those people would stop him with anything short of a bullet.

They got Tanner to his feet. He had a spot of blood on his lip, courtesy of agent Barnes. He looked at Solomon, and chuckled disjointedly.

•

"Well, Solomon Carroll," Vic said, as they paused before taking him back to his cell. "I guess this concludes our little lecture. I hope I've given you sufficient material to fry my God-forsaken ass."

"Be assured of it," Carroll said, and the agents grabbed a tighter hold on him. They rushed him through the door, down the hallway, and into his cell.

Vic could've iced those guys in a blink. He only had one restraint on him, and those assholes were stupid enough to have their guns at their sides. But Vic had business, and taking out a couple of peons wasn't worth sacrificing the big fish.

Vic sat in his cell, pondering life. Although to Vic, 'pondering' meant mental rants, free of introspection.

Vic longed for the days when law enforcement posed a challenge for him. When he started out in criminal activity, after the first kill (which was just the start of his apprenticeship,) he felt that every criminal act had to be planned out, formed with the highest degree of precision. The only random element was the target. Everything else was methodological, meticulous and predetermined. It was all a game; his mind against theirs, his anonymity against their resources, his darkest fantasies against the sanities of their profilers.

But, as he got better, killed more people, learned more about criminal justice, the rules of evidence and the judicial system, he realized that they couldn't catch him unless he intentionally screwed up. That was never a part of his game. It started to lose its fun after awhile. He even stopped killing people a few years back. The killings he did recently, up to and including the parents of that little girl, all happened since he'd had his blackout. He chalked it off on the 'new groove' he'd been feeling. But now he had one and only one target in his head. Yashua King.

The One Vic's asshole father prayed to when he knocked up his ma'. The guy his daddy always had money to pay every Sunday, when Vic's ma' screamed at him on the phone every time she could; '*You promised me money to support OUR child, you son of a bitch!*'

This Son of God, who 'pops' probably prayed to the night Vic's granddad got killed on the job. He probably used Holy water to short out the electrical system that caused the explosion. Vic's whole life he wanted to fuck his father's 'God' up. He'd finally found a way.

He paced his cell, around and around; he was anxious to be arraigned the next day for the 'shore-job', as he referred to it. He knew he'd be sent back to Elayn Hunt temporarily. He also knew that King was there, but he wouldn't try anything. He knew where he'd strike. Angola.

He'd done his research before leaving California. He wasn't stupid, just sadistic. J.D. Fisher owned SecureCorp, the private firm that ran some of Louisiana's prisons. *Some.* Elayn Hunt wasn't one of 'em. But Angola was transferred to their ownership in 2010. Fisher owned it, and Fisher owed him.

Vic would never get to Yashua in Elayn Hunt. They'd have him in isolation, and Yashua ... probably protective custody. He could rip through the bars without a problem at this point. Tazers and tear gas wouldn't work; they never worked, even before all the craziness started happening with him. But he couldn't stop bullets. If he could, he would've killed the little girl. He had to be careful, and wait for an opportunity. Like Angola.

He could make sure Fisher had both of them 'accidentally' placed in general population. He had stuff on Fisher; they went way back. And, he didn't think Fisher would give a rat's ass about anything other than saving a few dollars not having to house an extra inmate. They couldn't connect prisoners to HIPPO directly. Vic knew that because he knew people on the inside - of jails, that was. And he knew Fisher.

Fisher, if he could, would've killed 'em all; Vic knew that. Maybe when everyone was connected to HIPPO, Fisher'd get that chance.

Sheriff Laverne and a Deputy walked by. They looked into his cell with a mix of disgust and fear. Vic smiled, breathed in their emotions like a fragrance. He continued to pace, whistling a tune that nobody knew except, well; not even he knew it.

Across from his cell there was a digital clock, the time spelled out in large LEDs. As he looked at it, the numbers began changing. They changed slowly at first, sometimes it would be an actual time, like 05:30, sometimes it would be a number, like 99:99.

Vic stared at it in amazement. He wasn't causing it, and he couldn't explain it. '*Fuckin' a' right,*' he thought, as he sat on his bunk and slept.

Chapter Eighteen

J.D. Fisher walked into the Lobby of the Paradigm Building on Friday night, shortly after seven in the evening. He was the king of his castle, surrounded by a moat of indifference. The secretary didn't say '*Hello, Mr. Fisher. How are you today?*'

The last one who did was promptly fired. Fisher didn't want to talk to the lower end of the food-chain. He rarely enjoyed talking to the upper end.

He went to the central elevator, and pressed the third floor button.

He got off and walked down a small hallway to the other elevator, one with a full biometric scanner. He rested his chin on the plastic rest and relaxed his eye. The green bar passed over it and the elevator opened when the scanner confirmed his identity. He entered and pressed a button labeled simply 'A'. It rose slowly, pneumatically. Beyond the third floor, there was no use of electricity. Everything was powered by Essence, pneumatic, or mechanical means. They had phased out electricity as the system came on-line, because it was dangerous. Now a portion of the Essence coming in was siphoned off for running the facility.

The walls, from the outside, appeared to contain office windows, lights, and if you looked closely, the silhouettes of people moving around. That was all a generated façade. For the next 500 feet up was hollow, and it housed the mechanism that ran the world at the moment; the hub.

The building was conical, and going into the ground seventy feet from the base of the structure was a sub-basement consisting of four floors. On these floors, collected Essence was stored in large devices that acted as capacitors, to put it in terms of electricity. The units were tall and thin, wafer-like in appearance - and there were many of them. Twenty thousand to be exact. Fisher knew every little detail of the things his money was invested in, with the exception of those details requiring a PhD to understand. He never let his investments out of his sight, or out of his mind.

There was a stairway that went down from the elevator entrance along the back wall, and Fisher walked down it to join his business partner, Pierce Wayland, from Houston. Pierce owned ArcEpic, which functioned as Paradigm's human testing laboratory. Pre-release trials were all outsourced to ArcEpic.

They reached the floor of the hub. Dr. Spici was at the collection unit, taking readings and holding them against each other. A new piece of equipment was near the auditory generator. Fisher knew what it was; the ISIS unit.

"Tell us the good news, Arlo," he said, and Dr. Spici put down the papers.

"Well, good news and bad, I guess," Arlo said. "But it's nothing too serious; just something to monitor…"

"Go on," Fisher said. He was irritated by scientists. They couldn't just tell him anything straight out.

"The good news first," he said as he led them over to the ISIS. "The ISIS has been test-trialed in a closed system, and passed successfully. It now only requires enough target DNA to form a template."

"How much will that be?" Fisher asked.

"Four grams," Dr. Spici said, "and it can't be created through PCR analysis."

"What would taking that much DNA do to the target donor?" Wayland asked.

"Kill them," Arlo said. "You couldn't extract that much DNA without taking most of their blood, or a large chunk out of them."

"We're sitting on this until further notice," Fisher said. "As for you…" he looked at Arlo, "…keep it ready."

"Will do. Thank you, Mr. Fisher," he replied.

"What about the bad news?" Wayland reminded Arlo. "You said there was good and bad news."

"Oh, yes, well there seems to be a small disturbance in the Baton Rouge area of Louisiana," Arlo responded. "As I said, it's nothing serious. But if it continues, there's the chance of it getting worse."

"Spit it out, Arlo!" Fisher said. "What are you talking about? What kind of disturbance?"

"The Essence output, in the greater Baton Rouge area; it appears to be polarizing," Arlo explained. "The local effect is small at this point, and the net effect on the system is nil. But there are two areas that I've isolated that seem to be the poles."

"Where?" asked Fisher.

"They're both within the Elayn Hunt Correctional Center," Spici said, " ... at opposite ends of the facility."

●

We ate well; Rosita was an excellent cook. We talked over dinner. I told everyone more about our trip abroad, and we talked about Vic Tanner. I stopped shy of mentioning Yashua to her, but I knew I'd have to tell Alejandro the truth. We'd need him. We also talked about Anno Luce, and HIPPO, which was pretty much a main topic anywhere you went at that point. Rosita's opinions were reflective of the prevailing opinion; HIPPO was a vile invention, but a necessary evil. She thought Biggs was a fool, chasing a fantasy world. She used to buy into his whole "Righteous Brigade" bullshit, but it didn't last long. When she found out about his plant in India, she was disgusted, and she cancelled her membership. She even went as far as writing a letter to him expressing her disgust. That's Rosita, full of fire, fueled by piss and vinegar. Now she feared that he'd be elected President.

"What happens to all the HIPPO votes?" I asked, kind of jokingly, but kinda' not.

"They're talking about counting them as one vote or something," Alejandro said.

"What?" I said. "People are gonna let 'em do that?" I asked.

"Technically," Hernando said, "they're all of one mind. That's what HIPPO does. It runs a people's minds; every one gets the same thoughts and feelings."

"What about the essential people?" I asked. "What will they say about it?"

"There's not much *to* say," Katherine said. "It wasn't easy for people to air their grievances *before* HIPPO. Now it's impossible. You can't rally Washington when you're essential."

"Is there any kind of organized opposition at this point?" I asked.

"There's opposition," Hernando replied, "but it's certainly not organized. Just groups here and there, either in hiding or on the run."

"Has there been any resistance since we've been gone?" I asked. "You know, like, incidents or anything?"

"Just small, local, isolated stuff," Hernando said. "They know a major attack wouldn't work. A resistance would need an audience to be effective. There's no audience anymore. They mainly go after essentials in small skirmishes, really random stuff."

I thought about Jonesy, knowing I needed to find him. Ale' knew Jonesy.

"What about Jonesy?"

"I haven't heard from him in months," Ale' said. "You've probably heard from him since I have."

"Yeah, I saw him around my birthday. That'll be a month ago tomorrow, actually."

"Ya' ain't gettin' another cake," Rosita joked.

I laughed. "That last cake was so good ma'," I said. "I want to preserve its memory anyways."

Rosita laughed, and we continued on our conversation. And Rosita, dear that she was, asked; "So, Barney, are you and Katherine, you know," she paused with that look in her eye, "boyfriend and girlfriend?"

'Aaaargh!'

"Um, ah," I stalled. "Well, we haven't ..."

"told anyone yet, but yes, we're boyfriend and girlfriend."

Katherine tossed out that surprising life-raft to my sinking ship. And the only thing I could think to do was lay a kiss on her right there, hot enough to make *Rosita* blush. And that's tough, believe me.

I felt great. Katherine was with me, and we spent many side conversations getting to know each other better. I found out that she had been overseas before herself. When she was ten, she wanted to help starving people in Africa. And at that time her parents were well off enough to be able to spend six months of their own time taking Katherine to Ethiopia with a relief organization. Katherine's father was a surgeon, and so they went with 'Doctors without Borders.' Katherine helped out with what she could, and the experience was one of her most cherished. I asked her where she was, and she said they were about fifteen miles away from Addis Ababa, and from her description, I knew she was near the steppes of the Entotos Mountains.

'*She was near the Sanctuary*,' I thought.

She also told me how her parents had died, and how she'd had to deal with it. I couldn't say much; I knew that because no one could say anything to me about Anna's loss. But I held her tighter when she quietened up. I'd hoped it helped her. I knew what it was like to lose someone.

"Katherine," I said, as we held each other close on the couch after dinner.

"Yes Barney?"

"I love you."

"I love you too," she said.

We kissed, and my face turned red slightly. I'd already told her I loved her, but I was still nervous. We stayed at Rosita's that night, and we each had our own rooms. Rosita's house was large enough to accommodate. We awoke the next day to go look for Jonesy. But I had to go see Joe McGee. I hadn't even thought about him until that morning, and I felt bad about it. Joe was a good friend. So I told Alejandro about goin' to the Coffeehouse.

"Oh Jesus," Alejandro said. "I didn't even realize!"

"What?" I asked.

"Barney, sit down."

"Ale', what?" I asked, alarmed, and not about to sit down.

"There was an accident," Alejandro said, after an uncomfortably long pause. "Joe's dead, Barney. I'm sorry."

"What?" I asked rhetorically, but I knew what he'd said.

"It was a car accident," Alejandro continued. "It was storming, and he lost control. They said he died instantly."

I broke down. I didn't cry, sob or choke up. Shock kept me from all of those things. I just had to blankly accept it right then. I couldn't afford to let it hit me. I had to shelf it. I had to reserve the immediate future for saving a life, not mourning the loss of one. But, if Alejandro right then had punched into me, and ripped out a part of my insides, the effect would've been the same. All I could do was stare blankly out the window at nothing.

I felt a hand on my back, then wrapping around me. I felt Katherine's warmth against me. She didn't speak, didn't tell me it was going to be okay. She just held me as I sank to the ground. All the psychobabble she could have told me about the 'five stages of grief' that she'd learned in Psych class, they couldn't have done for me what her holding me right then was doing. It helped.

Amidst the chaotic mess of emotions that would eventually turn into grief, I realized that I wasn't afraid to love Katherine. But I was deathly afraid of losing her.

That sort of snapped me out of it. I had to stay focused. There wouldn't be a world for me and Katherine if we couldn't destroy Paradigm and save Yashua. I kissed her hand and I got up. I looked at everybody, and looked up.

"This one's for you then, Joe," I said, and I told them that we needed to do what we had to do. And with a wish of luck from Rosita, we left Mercado. We needed to find Jonesy.

•

Jonesy sat on his ass all that day, working furiously on his computer. He had three cups of coffee under his belt, and two packs of generic cigarettes. He started smoking when he was fourteen, half his life ago. Smokers didn't respond well to mind control techniques like HIPPO programming. It made sense they'd make it hard to get them. And it was getting much harder in the past week, because of HIPPO.

He sat up and looked at the clock. It was twelve-thirty. Everyone was supposed to meet up at two to discuss the next plan. Their last plan was a disaster, and Ed had been detained. Lord knew what he was going through at that moment. Jonesy's spot wouldn't be uncovered; he knew that, but Ed wouldn't be replaceable. And for such a stupid plan too.

They had decided to raid the East Anno Luce relay station, in an attempt to disrupt the flow of Essence going into the facility from the main storage plant in New Orleans. He had grave misgivings about the idea from the start; he knew Paradigm. He also knew that the others had been tired of hiding, laying low, biding their time, and their morale was beginning to slip. So, he reluctantly agreed to go along.

In hindsight, he should have never went along with it. He loved the guys he had picked up along the way. They were all about fucking the system, even back before HIPPO. But they never thought the day would actually come. They used to just party a lot; drink and smoke, play video games and watch TV. They had a lot of learning to do in a short amount of time.

So did Jonesy. Things were changing so fast. He used to pride himself on knowing what was going on in the world. That's why he'd studied programming since he was ten. He knew computers were the future, and he needed to be good with them. And so he *became*. He learned every programming language, devouring books on computers, math and science.

He studied other subjects equally; politics, government, and current affairs. He always wanted to be six months ahead of the news cycle. Sometimes he was years ahead. Sometimes he got slapped in the face by the unexpected. But even he couldn't read fast enough, or watch enough news to have a full handle on the current events.

He knew Paradigm. He'd worked for them once, and one of his team still did. That's the one he never saw; the one the rest of 'em didn't know about. They didn't have to. Tim was the ace up his sleeve.

Mike Jones, aka 'Jonesy', was a programmer. He always told

people that he did low-level stuff. But he wasn't a low-level programmer. He also wasn't doing grunt-work for Paradigm.

He was hired by a recruiter, out of the blue one day. Paradigm had a comprehensive testing process, involving background checks, intelligence and emotional tests, programming tests. Jonesy kept his nose clean in his life; his revolution was always one of thought. His scores were exceptional, and in a short time he was put on one of the first Psionics Development teams, which numbered forty members.

Jonesy enjoyed the work, but he felt like he worked in 'Hell' for six-figures a year. He was disgusted with what he knew was going on there, *and* he couldn't stand J.D. Fisher one bit. Fisher was the definition of an *arrogant asshole*.

But he was uneasy about quitting. He knew things, and they knew he knew things. He had to be careful about getting out. He decided that he would ask for a transfer to the Relay Station. He said the hub was too stressful. They agreed. At that point he was out of the main fray and he chose a job he knew would be mechanized within six months. Paradigm quietly laid Jonesy off, and he loudly celebrated with his friends at the very cabin he now sat in.

He looked out of the window, and the beauty of the day lie in stark contrast to the ugliness of what was happening right then. Jonesy flicked a match lazily, doing his best to light the smoke as coolly as possible, though there was no one there to see it.

Jonesy had a great hiding place. It was out in the desert a bit, off 1-8. It was visible from the highway, back about an eighth of a mile. It was about a thousand square feet, and it sported a worn look. It had a dirt road leading in, and no external power-lines, phone-lines or cable lines.

But Jonesy had electricity, phone, cable and the internet. He had developed friendships over his time in Paradigm, acquiring a whole host of devices that were 'scratch pads' for later prototypes, or the plans thereof. He had turned the cabin into a very comfortable control center.

There was one truly attractive feature that the place had. It was dead to Essence scans. Essence scans were like a million psychics looking around the Earth constantly. But not exactly; the whole thing was impersonal, mechanized and automatic.

Jonesy had been able to manipulate Paradigm's base-map of the Earth in just a small way. The area from the center of the cabin to the road formed a radius that Paradigm couldn't *'see.'* All of this, he did in secrecy. Not even his compatriots knew about it. They didn't know too much about the inner workings of Paradigm, just what they needed to know to evade it.

Jonesy was proud of them though. They'd, in the week since everyone went into hiding, learned a great deal. They were never too stupid to know what was going on; they just didn't have a reason to do the homework. Now that they had to, they were showing the intellect that had made them his friends to begin with. But the delay definitely hurt, and with Ed detained, Jonesy didn't know his next move.

As he sat there pondering, his cigarette ash forming the long column that was his specialty, he saw a van pull into the dirt road. He didn't know who it was, and the guys weren't supposed to be there until two. It was only one. He looked out from the window, crouched at the lower edge. He couldn't make anything out about the van, and he couldn't get a close look at who was inside. He went into the dresser drawer, and pulled out his Smith & Wesson. He didn't want to shoot anyone; he didn't know if he was even capable of it. He also didn't want to get caught with all the 'illegal' equipment he had. That would probably mean death for *him.*

The van pulled up, and the doors opened. He saw a familiar face. It was Barney Sheehan.

'What the fuck is he doing here?' Jonesy thought. *'How does he even know about this place?'*

He was relieved it was Barney. At least it wasn't Paradigm. And then another man stepped out, taller, Hispanic looking. And out of the back came Alejandro and two women. One was older, and Hispanic, one was a younger white girl.

'Well,' he thought as he went to the door. *'At least it ain't Paradigm.'*

He opened the door, putting the Smith & Wesson on the table as he did so. Barney was about a yard from the door, and he looked different. Jonesy couldn't really place it. He hadn't gained or lost weight, and his hair was the same unruly mess it had always been. He had a new tattoo, a strange one. Looked almost like a tribal bird, but it was done real nice. He'd probably paid good cheddar for it.

"Barney," he said. "How've you been?"

"I'm well," Barney said as he looked around. "Just as you described it. Nice work."

"I told you about this?" he asked.

"You were shitty that night," Barney said.

"Oh, Jeez."

"Don't worry," Barney said. "I suspect we're working on the same side."

Jonesy smiled at that. "I suspect we are."

He turned to Alejandro. He said something to him in a language they both knew. Alejandro answered back, and they did the secret handshake.

Barney and Alejandro introduced Jonesy to their companions. The other man was Hernando DeSantis, a former politician, and the older woman was his cousin, Juanita. Katherine was the name of the younger girl, and apparently Barney was with her. Jonesy was happy for him. He'd had some shitty luck with women. This one seemed alright. After Jonesy shook everyone's hand, he looked at I-8, then the van.

"Can you guys pull around back? There's a spot for vehicles," he said, and Hernando hopped back in the van.

Jonesy told him to stop a few yards from the house. He had a garage installed below-ground.

Jonesy, Barney, Katherine and Juanita went inside. Hernando and Alejandro were let into the parking area, and Jonesy showed them around the cabin until everyone was upstairs. Then they sat down to talk.

•

"And we praise the name of Jesus!" the Reverend Biggs said before his televised congregation. "We have seen your signs, and we rejoice your coming!"

The congregation said "Amen" in a monolithic monotone.

"Today has come, the time of Judgment!" he continued. "When the right hand of God will strike the hearts of the wicked, and they will be smote."

The cue-screen before the congregation went to 'Hallelujah', and the congregation blankly droned out a 'Hallelujah.'

"My brothers and Sisters," Biggs said as he grabbed the microphone to walk the stage. "Satan is a devious one, and anyone can be deceived. No one is immune. Not even myself."

The congregation let out little noises, not much.

"I have been deceived," he said, and a trace of a tear caused him to rub his eye. "I have been led to a false light."

The crowd was a little noisier, people whispering among each other.

"The Human Interactive Peripheral Polymorphism," Biggs said. "HIPPO, that I once thought was Christ's gift to us, the kingdom on Earth ..."

The irritant he had on his finger was starting to work, and he felt his eyes begin to water, "...was a deception by the Father of Lies. And I, like so many others, was fooled."

Biggs let out a cry, and sank to one knee. The congregation let out a gasp.

"I have been led astray, Father!" he sobbed. "Please forgive me!"

The crowd was alive with chatter. Some people were angry, those who were already questioning the Reverend's mission. Others went 'aw...' in sympathy with the repentant preacher. Still others were silent.

"HIPPO has been Satan's greatest deception," he continued. "And those who were susceptible to his sway were drawn into it."

He walked to the podium in a carefully rehearsed move, and slammed his palms into the polished mahogany. Everything between his stiffened arms shrank inward.

"I was sought as a man of God and I was swindled," he said softly, but the PA turned up at that moment, making it loud enough to hear.

"We must pray for our brothers and sisters," Biggs said, appearing to regain his composure. "They are trapped, and until we can find a way to cure their addiction, we will need to turn our hearts to God the Almighty Father, and care for our sick brethren. An evil has been unleashed upon the Earth," Biggs said, "and it has now become a necessary evil. I will donate $25 million towards research, to find a cure for this affliction. But for now we must put this in God's hands."

He got booed. Not by everyone, but a few people were not happy with his tearful confession. Biggs felt nervous; he'd never been booed before. He didn't know how to respond. He cut his service short.

"I have to do relief work in Jerusalem on Tuesday, and I need to make preparations," he said. "But I had to take the time today before you and before God to tell the Truth. And I'm sorry."

Biggs gave the subtle cue to the production manager to start the ending procession. The music suddenly came on, as did the 'Applause' screen. Biggs left the stage, and the ending procession was done in almost double-step.

When he got to his changing room, he was nervous. He wasn't afraid of physical attack; he had very good security. He was just nervous about being booed for the first time, and he didn't want to encounter his hecklers. It could show him for what he was. A coward.

Biggs didn't want to make that *confession* but he'd got a phone call from Fisher that morning. He called at six-thirty a.m., just fifteen minutes after Biggs woke up. A little breakfast chat that left Biggs' stomach bitter.

Fisher didn't say it would be wise to tell the flock he had been wrong; He said he'd have Biggs killed if he didn't. Biggs had gotten many threats before, and the feds in turn had gotten many cases. But Fisher was untouchable, and untraceable, as Biggs well knew. His whole Christian Worship Center was funded with Fisher's money. The line Fisher called on was a direct line, and he'd paid to have it put in.

So, Biggs had to do what he'd promised, however unwillingly and insincerely. Fisher was not a man to toy with, and

Biggs wasn't looking to play. But he didn't want to do it; he didn't believe he *was* wrong.

Men like Fisher only saw money, and opportunity. They didn't see the nobler, *higher* purposes. Biggs had been brought to the Light many a year ago. God had given him the sight to see ... and he saw plenty.

He saw the kingdom. Within HIPPO, all minds were directed by the signal to one consciousness. Currently it was being wasted for material things, energy production. Biggs saw this for what it was; the perfect state of human co-existence with the Divine. One day, Biggs overheard Fisher talking about the ISIS Project; he saw it as a sign. ISIS used genetic material to focus the group consciousness. Fisher saw increased production capabilities. Biggs saw a gateway to Communion with God.

Biggs had always seen signs. He saw them in 'random' occurrences, in people's daily goings on. In the eyes of his congregation as they looked to him for guidance. The demonic signs in his critics' eyes. In all the women who'd rejected him and looked upon him with disgust, to hide what he knew was their inner shame.

But he'd seen greater signs. He'd spent years studying the Bible, the Torah, the Talmud, and so many other texts. He knew all Biblical languages, and had been to the holy land ten times. He was heading there soon. Well, he *was* heading there, until he saw the news the other day. A man had been arrested in Baton Rouge, Louisiana, for the attack in Jerusalem. Biggs knew full well how to interpret that sign. The Christ had returned, and was sitting in a prison in Louisiana. His trial was to begin the next day, and if he was convicted, he would be sent to Angola. Louisiana's prison restructuring guaranteed that. That was a SecureCorp prison, one of Fisher's. Biggs needed to get down there by the end of the day. He needed to contact 'Yashua King' before Fisher did.

Biggs knew he and Fisher wanted the same thing for different reasons. The DNA of the Messiah would complete the link, creating the New Kingdom. For Fisher, it would increase the output. But if it worked, Biggs would connect himself, taking the situation out of Fisher's hands.

Biggs left the Worship Center in his sedan. It was an older model, but all decked out; titanium white, bullet-resistant panels and tinted windows, also bullet-resistant. As he took off, people were just starting to come out of the building. Biggs always made sure the procession dragged on long enough for him to get out before everybody else. He was an old pro.

He went to his home in Beverly Hills, a short drive from the Worship Center on South Alvarado Street. As they drove down Wilshire Drive, he called his pilot to have the jet prepared. He'd arrive in Baton Rouge around seven. He knew he could get in to see Yashua at that hour. His own influence ran pretty deep. He arrived at his home, *his castle*, as he knew it, about ten minutes after he'd left the Center. And it was a castle. A replication of one anyways, down to the finest detail. Biggs even had a small moat.

He went into his castle and packed hastily. He was driven. He knew his role in what was to come. He was being called upon to finish the puzzle. When he'd finished packing, he told the driver to step on it, and he took off for LAX.

•

Dan Champere walked into Elayn Hunt to meet with Yashua, pre-trial. He was burdened, but not nervous. He didn't have to worry about losing; Yashua told him, more or less, to just 'go through the motions.'
The night before he'd put blank paper in his trial briefcase.

'*Defending the Son of God with blank paper!*' He had to laugh at that thought.

He went into the same room he had last time, and he opened his other briefcase to get out the court papers. Yashua was brought in, again, overly secured. Dan said something about it, but the guards told him that was orders, and to talk with their boss if he wanted to.

"How are you?" he asked Yashua.

"I'm fine," Yashua said, "and yes, they're treating me okay." He smiled.

"Good, good," Dan said with a laugh. "I just wanted to meet

with you, to tell you what this was going to look like."

"Thank you," Yashua said.

"Okay, tomorrow will be opening arguments, and the prosecution will make their case," Dan said. "The day after tomorrow will be our turn, and then after a break they'll have the closing arguments," Dan said. "I should be able to figure out closing arguments by then."

"Trust in your heart," Yashua said. "My case is there."

"That's a lot to ask," Dan said.

"Has anyone with an easy problem ever come to your door?" Yashua asked jokingly.

Dan laughed. "No," he said, "never."

"The verdict will be held in a special session on Saturday," Dan said. "That's how they do things now."

"Saves them money."

"Yashua," Dan said. "They'll have you in Angola by late Saturday afternoon. Are you prepared for this?"

"No," Yashua said. "I am, right now, a sacrifice, an offering. I am the question of the test. To be answered. God controls my fate now, and preparations are out of my hands."

"Are you scared?" he asked.

"Yes," Yashua said, and he looked blankly off to the side. "That's something you never get used to."

And Dan then thought about the possibility that Yashua *was* the Messiah, and here he was, sitting in a Louisiana jail, experiencing deja vu a millennia old.
Yashua had been through this trial before. Dan saw it in his eyes when they first met. He knew what was going to happen. And Dan shuddered to wonder whether Yashua was scared of facing a second death, and what that would do to the world.

'Daniel,' Yashua's voice appeared in Dan's head. '*I am the sacrifice of the Earth. The lamb led to slaughter. For God so loves you all, he has offered the fate of the Earth for you to decide. An era of true peace and harmony, or immediate, cataclysmic disaster. I have been offered unto you as the direct link to the future of your world. What happens to me happens to you all.*'

Dan was stunned, and panic began to churn his guts.

'*I don't understand,*' Dan thought, and suddenly his head was filled with images, of natural disasters, of wars, things he had seen in the news over years. He saw things from the fifties to recent events, the earthquakes in Greece and Italy and the volcano in Tokyo.

And Dan knew. The doubt he had, the skepticism, the semi-sarcastic jokes that floated through his head in the past two days, gone. He knew the full extent of what rested on the case and he began to despair, for the burden was great.

Yashua put a hand on his shoulder. "Daniel," he said to him. "Through all of this, you will grow, and learn, and love. And no matter my fate, I will be with you."

Dan looked at him, comforted a bit. "I guess I might *not* need a resume after this," he joked.

"Oh, no," said Yashua, smiling.

"For that matter, I could show up in a kilt and it won't make a difference!" Dan said with a smile. "Whattaya say?"

"Not if you fear lightning," Yashua said, seriously at first; then he smiled. They both started laughing.

Chapter Nineteen

Reverend Biggs arrived in Baton Rouge shortly after seven thirty. The flight was late due to weather issues. He was irritated, but he prayed it away. He caught a taxi to St. Gabriel, where he was to meet the Messiah.

Biggs called someone he knew in the Louisiana Department of Corrections, who would get him a pass to see Yashua.
He was in near ecstasy as he faced his destiny. He was being called upon to take responsibility for the transfer of Yashua's DNA, which would unlock the gates of paradise on Earth. He felt blessed.

When he entered the meeting room, he didn't know what to

expect. He'd been given the gift of sight. He'd know it was Him by how He looked.

What came in destroyed his ecstasy and dashed his hopes. It was just a man; an unshaven, greasy *inmate*. This was not the Messiah, The Son of God, *Jesus*. Something wasn't right. Biggs saw *nothing*.

"Good evening, Mr. King," Biggs said, extending his hand. Yashua shook it reluctantly.

"I'm the Reverend Joseph Biggs. Do you know who I am?"

"Yes," Yashua said. "Go on."

"Are you the Son of God?" Biggs asked, as he figured he should just come out with it.

"You could not accept any answer I gave you," Yashua said, his arms folded. "You have spent your life on a fool's errand, fed on delusions, not truths. You have tried to find God through signs and clues, but never in your heart."

How dare he, an *impostor*, question Biggs's path? The man was not Jesus. 'Impostor,' Biggs thought, *or decoy.*

"How were you involved in the attack on Jerusalem?" he asked.

"Your position and your ministry do not give you the right to question me," Yashua said. "Nor me the obligation to answer."

Biggs was angry, but he held his calm.

"A simple test of your DNA could solve the problem," Biggs said.

"And would you be the one pricking my finger?" Yashua said, sarcastically.

Biggs leaned in close to Yashua's face. "I can get your blood, impostor," he said. "One way or another."

"Do as you will," Yashua said. "I fear you not."

"And I will be sure to reveal you as the impostor that you are," Biggs growled in his ear.

"It is as you say," Yashua said. "Or it will be as you tell your flock."

Biggs backed up, and stood there for a second, studying the phony who dared to say the Reverend Joseph Biggs was a fool. Biggs had a personal relationship with God, and Jesus, and it was not Jesus before him.

"Have fun in Angola," he said, and he opened the door.

"Be rested," Yashua said. Biggs ignored him as he left.

•

We all sat at Jonesy's kitchen table, quickly briefing him on what we'd been through, what *I'd* been through with Yashua. We told him (and Alejandro, as I hadn't told him yet) about Yashua, who he was, where he was, and what was happening right then.

At first both Alejandro and Jonesy were incredulous, as we expected.

"Have you all been disconnected?" Jonesy asked. "That's insane!"

"It's true," I said, "It's taken me over a month to come to grips with it myself."

Jonesy looked at us all as if he really believed we were all fucking crazy. Alejandro had a more pensive look. I think it was easier for him to accept.

"I don't believe this shit!" Jonesy said. "I can't deal with this right now. You guys are gonna have to leave."

He went to get up, but I grabbed his, and Alejandro's arm.

"I was in the Noble Sanctuary in Jerusalem," I said to them in a native Peruvian dialect, different than the one they had used. Alejandro grew up in South America, Colombia and Peru. I didn't know the language, but I spoke from my heart, and I knew I'd find the words.

"What?" he said in that language. "How did you…"

"Yashua was in the Dome of the Rock that night," I said. "And I watched the bubbles form in the Jordan as we crossed over it. I didn't see the whale when it beached, because we were using the diversion to get past the border crossing."

Alejandro was stunned that I spoke to him in a language that he'd not heard in twenty years. He knew I couldn't have studied it; two years before he was depressed when the last man who spoke it had died.

Alejandro looked at Jonesy. "I think he's telling the truth,

Jonesy," he said. "That language is dead, and Yashua was a resident at the mission."

"So, you're saying the Son of God is a homeless guy now?"

"Well, technically he's an *inmate* right now," I said.

"Oh, Jesus," Jonesy said. "*Yashua*, whatever...So what does this have to do with me?"

"HIPPO," I said, "and Zygote."

Jonesy had forgotten about Zygote. He'd scrapped that long ago; it was primitive.

"What about 'em?" Jonesy asked.

"HIPPO is feeding the Beast," I said. "We have to figure out a way to cut the Beast off."

"The Beast?" asked Alejandro and Jonesy both.

I had to pause. I knew they weren't gonna believe it anyways, but I had to try to sum up for myself all of the things Yashua told me about it.

"The Beast," I continued, "is a product of man's material desire; his greed, his selfishness, his lust of different things, what have you. It isn't really a being; it's like an energy, created by man. It has consciousness without personality, without conscience."

They listened patiently as I went on. "When people put their energies into material things, they create energy the Beast feeds off of."

"So what, HIPPO's feeding this thing, you're saying?" Jonesy asked.

"Yes, precisely," I said. "HIPPO energy is all material, not spiritual. The Beast is becoming very powerful off of it, and Fisher and those assholes don't have a clue."

"Wouldn't they notice a drain in the Essence levels?" Jonesy asked, and then had to explain to us quickly how HIPPO worked.

"The Beast could leave it in the hub until it needed the stuff," I said. "Spatial rules are different for the Beast. If the Beast has access to it, it can use the Essence at will, unnoticed, untraced."

"So where does, umm, Yashua, right?" Jonesy said, and I nodded. "Where does he fit in?"

Again, another pause on my part.

"The good things people do, the self-sacrifice, the

compassion, the forgiveness, humility and truth in the world; that also powers a being. It's similar to the Beast. It has consciousness *with* personality. And it has conscience. And, like the Beast, it is able to bond to a human life."

"So, if Yashua is the human embodiment of the good, well ...," Ale' asked, scratching his chin, "who's the embodiment of the bad one?"

"His name's Victor Ray Tanner," I said. "And they're on a crash-course."

Alejandro suddenly acquired the thousand-yard stare.

"Did you see him?" I asked. "At the mission?"

"I didn't get a good look," Ale' said. "But on the news they showed him, and I just, like, saw it in his eyes, ya' know?"

"Oh Je-," Jonesy started. "Ah, forget it...'"

I think it was sinking in to Jonesy at this point that we were telling the truth.

He sat there for a while, deep in thought. He wiped his brow more than once.

"So where do I fit in?" he asked.

"We need to work out a solution for Paradigm. And you'll have to lead the team to do it. We need to be with Yashua as soon as we can."

"I don't know if I'm ready for this," he said. "I got a couple of guys, and they're good, but *god-damn.*" He thought about it, and then said, "Sorry; didn't mean to take the Lord's name in vain."

"I wouldn't worry about it," I said. "But Jonesy, your guys are gonna have to do. We gotta' leave by Friday morning. Talk to your guys; you gotta get 'em here tonight. Can you do that?"

"They'll be here in about a half-hour," he told me.

"Good," I said, and we had Jonesy give us a more detailed description of how the HIPPO system operated. We got an earful, and a lot of pieces fell into place for me. Fisher and the rest didn't give a shit if Tanner killed Yashua. They just wanted to be there to scoop up enough DNA to plug into their ISIS device. They didn't know that killing Yashua meant that there'd be no ISIS device, HIPPO, or *themselves.*

Jonesy also talked about transference, which made me

realize that HIPPO was not an isolated system, that it could be influenced by outside events, outside energies. I didn't know the significance of it at the moment, but I knew I should remember it. And I learned about Essence scans, which I'd not known about before then.

We talked more over coffee, and for such a revolutionary as Jonesy, he sure made a fine cup o' Joe.

'But not like Joe, God rest his soul,' I thought to myself.

Before long I saw a car pull in, and then another car shortly after it.

"Those are our guys," Jonesy said, and he activated the entrance to the parking area. In a short while they came in, all decked out in camouflage, pockets bulging, filled with things I had a hunch they'd never used. I saw ammunition on one guy. I saw a flash-grenade attached to another guy's outfit. I almost had to laugh. I didn't, but I came damn close. Those guys had no idea what we were up against, and I rolled up my sleeves. We had some work ahead of us.

I had everyone take a seat. There were six of them, and Jonesy. They called themselves 'The Mighty Seven,' though not to anyone in any kind of serious manner. Aside from Jonesy, there was Cherise, his girlfriend; Jeremy and his sister Alicia, Nick, Bert and Tony.

I got up in front of them, looking at Juanita, Hernando and Katherine. They all nodded me on.

"First and foremost," I said, "we've been told that you all would like to take down Paradigm. That is our intention as well and there's a way to do it." I pointed to the ammunition draped across Tony's shoulder. "Those won't help you here."

He looked pissed that I'd said that, but I paid it no mind, continuing.

"I could tell you a whole lot about what's really going on here," I said, "but you wouldn't believe it, and it would be harder for you to do what you will be called upon to do. You will simply have to trust me on some things."

I had their attention. "We need to infiltrate Paradigm. Not with bullets and flash grenades, but with programming, figures and calculations."

I paced back and forth, continuing my address to the guys.

"Over the next day, none of you will leave," I said, in a voice that said it wasn't up for debate. "You all will sit here, push your grey matter to the limit, and develop a solution to the problem of HIPPO that addresses three things; the safe release of those connected, the destruction of the Paradigm hub, and," I paused, "saving the life of a prisoner in Louisiana."

That drew a questioned look on the faces of those there. I knew I'd have to tell them something.

"He has been sent by God," I said. "He is responsible for the events in Jerusalem in days previous. A man will try to kill him once he's sent to Angola. We must stop this, for the fate of our own lives and that of the entire Earth lay in our success."

I scanned the room. I expected, and saw, many skeptical looks.

"I don't believe in God," Jeremy said.

"Apparently he believes in you, else you wouldn't be here," I said.

"I don't know enough about HIPPO to fuck the thing up," Nick said. "None of us do, except Jonesy."

"Jonesy picked you all for reasons known only to him and God," I said. "You all must have some special talent that'll contribute to the final plan." I paused for a second. "In this game, we all have our place."

"How do we know you're not some whacko?" Jeremy asked. "I mean, you come in here, tellin' us we're gonna topple Paradigm, with pens and pencils, and somebody God sent is in a jail in Louisiana or something? How can we have any credibility with you?"

"What are you doing now?" I asked him. "You're walking around like you're ready for anything. If you were faced with one tenth of the reality I've been through in the past week, you'd shit your pants."

"You don't scare me," Jeremy said. Jonesy put an arm to him to try to shut him up, but he kept going. "I'm not gonna waste time on some God freak, like Biggs who-," Jeremy started, and was cut off as the stack of twenty or so pencils launched from the cup they were in, into the center of the room, in mid-air. I wasn't doing it. I know I wasn't. I couldn't do shit in Anno Luce; it wasn't like Jerusalem.

The pencils spun around furiously at odd angles, no one pencil touching any other. It looked like one of those scrambler rides they used to have at the annual *Anno Luce* festival. A stack of notebooks flew from the top of Jonesy's dresser, and they landed on the kitchen table. The covers flipped open, and the pencils flew to the pages. Three pencils went to each notebook. They began writing, and by that point everyone had backed up away from them. They wrote, or I should say *drew* something small at the top of the first page of each, before falling to rest.

Everyone was silent, probably scared shitless. Except me. I was used to it by then. Katherine didn't seem to have a problem with it either. She looked at me and smiled. I shrugged my shoulders to let her know it wasn't me. I pointed up and smiled, like that was my guess. She giggled.

"What the fuck was that?" Nick asked, and everyone else said 'yeah' or something similar.

"That," I said, "was God. It'll sure freak you out the first couple of times, but you get used to it."

After the pencils fell, a *while* after, we went to the kitchen table to see what had been written. I recognized them as ethereal symbols. I couldn't read them, and I had a guess what they meant.

"My guess," I said, "is that you all should write those formulas and calculations in these notebooks."

Jeremy actually passed out. Cherise started to pray in Spanish. It definitely had an impact on the "Mighty Seven."

They had a very sobering time before them, and I kept quiet. I knew how difficult it was to absorb; I'd been in their shoes a week ago. I went over to Katherine and sat with her. She took my hands in hers, and I felt the comfort she always brought me, rushing in.

After about an hour, I knew we had to get down to business.

"Welcome to the last battle," I said. "Take your positions."

I pointed to the open notebooks. Each one of them went to the notebook they were drawn to, and thus the most important brainstorm in the history of the Mighty Seven, and of humanity itself, commenced.

•

Dan walked to the Parish Courthouse. It was a nice day, and he needed to clear his head. He lived about twenty minutes away on foot, and he felt that would be a good amount of pondering time.

And he had much to ponder. And to worry about. And to fear. But he knew he had to go through with it.
He approached the courthouse, and he noticed that there was extra security.

He entered the courthouse through the metal detector. He had no metal on him; he hated to have to drop anything in the basket other than his keys. Not that it mattered; they knew him there. It was only a minor inconvenience.

He walked down the large hall, and he saw quite a few people there for the trial. Reporters were being allowed in.

'Strange,' Dan thought. '*I thought they didn't allow that anymore.*'

He saw Solomon, so he went over to ask him what he knew.

"Well, not much," Solomon said in that steady, easy manner that had made him such a good detective. "I know everyone and their mother's here. Feds, state and local, a few of my colleagues. They've heightened security, and not just at the courthouse. All throughout Baton Rouge they're doing patrols and roadblocks, I'm surprised you didn't get caught up in one."

"I walked," Dan said.

"They've been keeping LSP out of the loop," Solomon continued, "but I know they're using a mix of military, federal law enforcement and private security."

"Do you think they know?" Dan said softly. "I mean, about Yashua."

"I'm sure some people at the top might know," Solomon

said. "But the consensus I'm overhearing is that they believe he's a terrorist. Victor Ray Tanner's here too today. They say he's takin' a plea."

"Yeah, I heard that," Dan said. They stood there for a moment watching the commotion.

"So, are you ready for the trial?" Solomon asked.

"I don't have a clue, Sol," Dan said. "Yashua doesn't want me to prepare a defense. He said that God would defend him through me and I just have to open my heart."

"I'd trust him," Solomon said.

"I'm surprised to admit that I do," he said. "I gotta get in there, Sol. Meet at recess for lunch, at Mellow Mushroom?"

Solomon laughed at the suggestion of a cop and an attorney eating at a hippie pizzeria, but he agreed. Their pizza was pretty tasty. And with that, Dan walked into the courtroom to prepare for opening arguments.

He set his briefcase on the defense table, and opened it. He pulled out the top paper. When he'd put it in there last night, it was a blank sheet, like all the others. But now it had writing on it, meticulous, but in a language that he couldn't read. It almost looked like hieroglyphs, but he didn't recognize them as Egyptian.

'Oh great,' he thought. 'What am I supposed to do with this?'

He looked at it, studied it, but he still couldn't read a damn thing. Yashua came in, escorted by four armed guards, in shackles. They seated him next to Dan, and he smiled when he saw his defender.

"Good morning, Daniel," Yashua said. "Are you prepared?"

"Lord no!" Dan said, smiling. "But I ain't gonna let that stop me."

"Have faith, brother," Yashua said, letting out a chuckle.

There was a bit of quiet between them, and Dan actually felt confident, though for no particular reason. He still hadn't a clue about the opening argument. He imagined that his defense would revolve around Yashua having a right to be there. But he had no way on God's green Earth of knowing exactly what that would entail. He'd studied the night before, although Yashua said it wouldn't be necessary. He studied mostly the New Testament, which was a first for him in legal work. But he couldn't piece anything together that would be cohesive, and he wasn't exactly drawing from the well right then either.

He looked at the prosecutor. A special prosecutor had been brought in, and Dan didn't recognize him. He was a slick looking fella', with a black designer suit that offset Dan's cotton 'off-the-rack.'

The judge entered, and all rose. Then they sat down to begin the trial to end all trials.

•

J.D. Fisher sat in his luxury suite in an Anno Luce high-rise. The city had become rather wealthy as the HIPPO project went along. Luxury abounded in the midst of a place unknown to most of America. Fisher was turning Anno Luce into America's first 'gated-city.' He had a proposition before the city council, and he'd paid one of them, Teymon, to get it accepted. Aside from a payoff from him, the city would get their payoff as well; twenty-five million in grants for commercial development.

Two TVs were on. One was on BBC, and it was closed caption. The other was on Court TV. Fisher always had the BBC on caption. He couldn't stand 'Limey' accents. They sounded just like some of the snooty bastards at Yale who looked at him as an inferior; as a charity case.

Fisher's parents were poor, and he had gotten into Yale with financial aid - and the other kids *knew it*. He didn't know how, but they did. Well he did know how; financial aid Yale isn't the same as unlimited money Yale. He had to work to support going there, bussing tables at a restaurant that the snooty little brats went to. He remembered many times them spilling something on purpose, knowing he'd have to clean it up.

Not that they didn't have their own reasons for doing it. Fisher was a genius, and he always wrecked the grading curves. He never hesitated to use his intelligence to make them feel stupid.

Fisher saw it as poetic justice. Their money could afford to get them into one of the best schools in the country, and there they were, getting burned by a poor kid from the sticks of Montana. But the hammer swung both ways, and it always found itself landing straight in Fisher's crotch.

He had no social life in school. Any school he went to, he found stupid people. Suckers. And he never, even as a child, had tolerance, or patience. He never had girlfriends; he held impossibly high standards with women, higher than he held himself to. He never had real relationships; only one-night stands, often with atrocious women out of sheer desperation. And in Yale, the other guys saw to it that he never had a chance with the kind of girls that met his standards.

Their money and their wealth made it so easy for them to do. In his sophomore year, Fisher decided that he would beat them at their own game. He decided to change his major, from Psychology to Business, and he studied media production. Studying psychology, he was fascinated by how the media could control human behavior. If one could control what people saw, read and heard, they could control what people thought and felt as well.

Fisher was diligent at that point, driven to achieve what would become his life's goal; to own the media. He worked, picking up the shit the Yale frat boys dropped, and never complained. He kept up a 4.0 in Yale, and eventually graduated valedictorian. His speech was something to behold. In it, he personally belittled and degraded everyone there. He walked off the stage smiling his way into a job with a media company called Synermedia, where he rose through the ranks.

He was ruthless and manipulative. He played competitors against each other, and he always came out smelling like a rose. Within a few short years he became the C.E.O, and was worth just over $300 million.

Under his control, SynerMedia acquired its main competitors, and then it swallowed up the remaining competition. By 2012, SynerMedia owned all media sources, with the exception of some independent presses and internet blogs. But those sources drew their stories from his sources. So, for all intents and purposes, he'd achieved his life's goal by 2012.

By then he'd been well into the Paradigm program. It was a project he'd been brought on to by one of his military contacts; a way of harnessing human psychic energy. Synermedia was instrumental in the beginning of the project. Paradigm was largely responsible for Fisher's windfalls.

Fisher remembered the first time he'd laid eyes on the completed, renovated building with joy. He felt tied to it, *bonded* to it, as if the fate of the Hub was *his* fate. He had gone over every plan, suffered the pitfalls and obstacles over the years and absorbed every detail he could.

Fisher noticed the trial was starting. He turned off the BBC and turned up Court TV.

"They're going through the opening motions right now," the voice-over said. "This is the first time that cameras have been allowed in the courtroom since the Patriot Act 3 was passed. The rules of court procedure have changed, and what you'll see here, Roger, is a faster version of a regular, pre-Patriot Act 3 proceeding."

"Sarah," said Roger, himself now in voice-over. "Can you tell us what we can expect from this trial in terms of time frame, rules of evidence?"

"Yes, Roger," she said. "The trial will take two days; today and tomorrow. This morning will start with opening arguments, and then a recess. After the recess, we'll hear the prosecution's case. Tomorrow morning we'll hear the defense, followed by a recess, and the afternoon will consist of closing arguments."

"Two days doesn't seem like a long time," Roger said. "How will they be able to call all of their witnesses, even?"

"The Patriot Act 3 has changed some of the rules of trial," Sarah said. "The prosecution and defense can call witnesses, but both sides have three minutes for direct and cross-examination. Expert testimony is limited to one expert, for five minutes, and juries have one-hour to deliberate."

"P3 also reversed the need for unanimous verdicts, calling only for a simple majority to find the accused guilty," she added.

"Thanks Sarah. Sarah Canvers, reporting with us from the East Baton Rouge Parish courthouse," Roger said, and the camera took a close-up of Yashua King, the man of the hour.

"We're being told that opening arguments are about to begin. We're going to take you there, live. This is the trial of Yashua King, who's on trial facing charges of conspiracy to commit an International Terrorist Act and Conducting an International Terror Campaign. The International Criminal Court is in formal protest of this trial, their spokesperson stating that they have jurisdiction in the matter."

The camera went to Yashua's lawyer. Dan Champere. Fisher looked him up. Small time, Champere defended poor street thugs, drug suspects mostly. Fisher wasn't worried about him. But he knew Mr. King had someone's help. Champere wasn't court appointed.

Dick Brell was the prosecutor. Fisher's boy. He saw to that one. Brell knew P3. Studied it. The judge, Wanda Forrier, was his too. Fisher reclined, secure in the knowledge that Mr. King would soon find residence on his property in Angola.

"Ladies and gentlemen of the jury," Dick Brell said. "This is not a case about religion, or beliefs, or superstitions. This is a case about facts and evidence, which can be analyzed, evaluated, *given value.*" He leaned into the jury as he said that last one. "And the evidence of this case is simple. We have before the court signed confessions, of six men, who were seen with the defendant during the night of the attack. We also have the defendant's very image on a videotape leaving the scene of the attack. This afternoon you will see witness after witness that has heard him brag about doing it. This is the evidence, and in the eyes of the law, you must see through religions and individual beliefs and look at the facts of the case. Any man can lie." Again Brell leaned into the jury with that last part.

'*Damn, he's good,*' Fisher thought.

"That man right there." He pointed to King. "Yashua King; was seen on videotape, and by witnesses, leading the deadliest attack ever to occur in the city of Jerusalem. And as regards to the Dome of the Rock; no one really knows what happened to it. Guess you'll have to ask him." Brell smiled, pointing to King as he paced the area of the court.

"Now you may be thinking about the signs in Jerusalem," said Brell as he paced, "as am I too. Like many of you, I am a Christian. And none of us may understand what possessed Mr. King to lead such an attack, but by the end of this trial, you *will* know that that man," he pointed to King, "*was* causing death in the Holy City." And with that Brell ended his opener and sat down.

Fisher got a call at about that time, and he turned off the TV. He didn't have any use for hearing Mr. King's defense; he knew it wouldn't mean anything. A third of the jury was in his pocket too. Stacking the deck wasn't cheating; it was winning.

"Yeah," Fisher said as he answered the cell. He knew it was Biggs.

"J.D.," Biggs said. "He isn't the One."

"What are you talking about?" Fisher said.

"I went there last night," Biggs said. "He's a phony."

"You what?!" Fisher said, infuriated.

"I didn't say anything about you," Biggs said. "But I know it wasn't him."

"How do you know?" Fisher snapped, still pissed.

"I've seen him up close and personal," Biggs said. "And I could tell it wasn't him."

"Maybe you've been drinking too much Jesus Juice," Fisher said.

"J.D.," Biggs said, and Fisher cringed. He hated it when Biggs called him J.D.. "If you put his blood in ISIS, it will ruin it."

"Let me worry about that, *Joseph*," Fisher said. "Oh and by the way ..."

"What?" Biggs answered on the other end.

"If you *EVER* do a stupid thing like that again, in my playing field, I'll kill you my fucking *self!*" he snarled, and hung up the phone.

'*Stupid self-righteous imbecile,*' Fisher thought. '*You haven't seen his blood. I have.*'

Fisher had him cut open; they'd sent a test subject after him. They got a blood sample from the hospital he was taken to, and he knew King wasn't an ordinary guy.

There were proteins in his blood the scientists had never

seen before, and they were the best in the world. His DNA sequence couldn't be analyzed either. It 'shifted' whenever an attempt was made to map it out. King was the real deal. He was something anyways. Fisher didn't know what. But he knew that enough of King's DNA would do what he wanted it to. Call it a hunch.

Fisher called to have his jet ready. It usually was. He had a little trip to make, to sunny Louisiana. He wanted to oversee this one personally.

•

Vic sat at his arraignment, bored shitless. The courtroom had been nearly empty. There were victims' family members, but only a few. Vic figured HIPPO had the rest.

'*There were many.*' He smiled. His public defender glanced about nervously.

'*Don't know what he's so nervous about,*' Vic thought. '*I'm the one that's gonna get a needle.*' He looked about, hoping to lick his lips at a camera. But there were none. They didn't allow them.

Vic could sense Yashua King in the building. It was his trial that day too. But he was actually *going* to trial. Vic had other plans.

"How does the defendant plead?" the judge asked his public defender.

"I killed every one of them whiny pussies!" Vic said. "Guilty of all charges!"

The room let out a gasp, and the judge rapped the gavel to restore order.

"Quiet down!" the judge said, and the room fell hush again.

"Mr. Tanner," the judge continued, as impersonally as he could, "do you plead guilty to all of the charges against you, is that correct?"

"I only wish I had more to plead to," he sung.

The judge was rattled, Vic could tell. He cleared his throat, nervously.

"By pleading guilty," said the judge, "under the current law, I am hereby obliged to pass sentence."

Again he cleared his throat. "I hereby sentence you to be sent to the Louisiana State Penitentiary in Angola, to be executed by lethal injection." The judge shuddered to ask the last question.

"Is there anything you'd like to say before this court passes judgment?"

"Yeah," Vic said, and he got up, ripping his shackles in half. The court erupted into screams and commotion.

"I'm gonna be waitin' for ya', *Messiah*!" he screamed, and he threw out a blast of rage. People there felt the building shake. Then the power went out briefly. Vic was suddenly surrounded by armed bailiffs, all of them nervous about what he might do. He so loved that smell. Better than steak sauce. But he sat back down, and put his hands forward. The bailiffs cautiously put a new set of shackles on him before leading him out of the courtroom, onto an awaiting bus.

•

The building shook and the lights went out in the courtroom. Everyone started talking in hushed tones, surprised. Solomon could hear muffled screams coming from somewhere in the building. He suspected it was Tanner's trial, and suddenly he was on alert. He was ready to see Vic burst in, and, unfortunately, he wasn't allowed to bring his gun in. He was nervous, but he kept his calm. He was good at that. He kept his eye on Dan and Yashua, and there didn't seem to be any problem there. Then the lights came back on, and the judge was able to restore order and quiet.

Dan was up. Solomon prayed, but he didn't know how Dan would do. He didn't know what Dan's defense would be, if he'd even *have* a defense. He could hear a pin drop at that point.

"Ladies and Gentlemen of the jury," Dan started, "the prosecution would like to talk to you about the facts. But they've failed to *really* tell you the facts."

He walked around, and Solomon knew Dan well enough to know that he was in control of this argument; just by the way he was walking.

"The facts, in this case, go back two thousand years," he

continued. "The Dome of the Rock, at one time, was the base upon which stood the Temple of Solomon, built for, and by the specifications of, God."

The crowd was stunned, and much whispering erupted. The judge rapped the gavel, and Dan continued.

"Ladies and gentleman, I know this may be hard for you to believe; it's hard for me as well. But though he may look like nothing much, the man sitting at that table ..." He pointed to Yashua, " ...was once the very man in whose name many of you pray to. The Messiah has been reborn; he sits before you. And he is being tried for the crime of performing His sacred duty to God."

The courtroom erupted in gasps and quick chatter. The judge banged his gavel, but no one was paying attention.

"Order!" the judge said. "Order!" The gavel rapped furiously.

Eventually people settled down. The judge looked at Dan.

"Are you honestly implying that this man is ... Jesus?" the judge asked him.

"Yes, your honor," Dan said, and he was greeted with more gasps.

The judge looked at Yashua. "Do you believe that you're Jesus?" the judge asked.

"It is as you say," Yashua said.

Again, the court erupted. Dan had finished his argument, and the judge quickly called the end of court for that day. Everyone piled out quickly, eager to make some noise about what they had just heard. The judge called Dan and Dick Brell into chambers.

"Just what the hell was that?" she asked Dan.

"That's his defense," Dan said. "I can't go against his wishes on this."

"You're not obligated to follow your client's delusion!" the judge said. "You can apply an insanity defense here."

"He's not insane," Dan said, "that's the problem."

"Are you saying you believe he's Jesus?" the judge asked, incredulously.

"I'm saying that he's competent to stand trial," Dan said, not wanting to put his own current belief on the table. "This is the defense he wants, he knows the risks, and I stand by him."

The judge looked at Brell. "Do you have a problem with this?" she asked.

"Not at all, your honor." He smiled.

'*Of course he wouldn't,*' Dan thought. '*He's gotta be lovin' this.*'

"Okay," the judge said, "it's his freedom. *Probably your career.*"

"A risk I'll take," Dan said, and was excused.

Dan left the courthouse with Solomon, who was in uniform, and they were mobbed by the pack of journalists and news-crews out front. He didn't feel the need to 'play the press', so he told them that he didn't have anything to say. They walked to Solomon's cruiser, amazed at how the press followed them, as if he'd suddenly change his mind. They took off from the courthouse, Solomon having to turn on his lights to get the reporters to move out of their way. Onward they cruised to the Mellow Mushroom.

Chapter Twenty

When they got to the Mellow Mushroom, they ordered a large pepperoni-and-meatball pizza, and two sodas. They sat down, and Dan let out a whoosh of breath.

Solomon laughed. "Tough day, I know," he said.

"You ain't kiddin'," Dan said, and when the waitress got the sodas, he took a thirsty sip.

"Ya' did good," Solomon said, "all things considered."

"I don't know where that opening argument came from," Dan said. "It wasn't anything I'd planned."

"Nothing you could've planned woulda' come out any better," Solomon said. "It's a tough sell."

"What happened in the courthouse?" Dan asked. "Did you find out?"

"I know it had to do with Tanner," Solomon said. "But everyone's been tight-lipped, even people I know."

"I'm dreading about an hour from now," Dan said.

"You'll do fine. Just relax, and let it happen."

Dan sat there silent.

Solomon reached out and touched his hand. "You're a good lawyer, Dan," he said. "That's why I called you."

"I just hate it," Dan said. "I feel like I'm being asked to throw the case."

"You're not. Yashua *knows*. If this is meant to happen, your own defense is that you're following the Will of God. Trust His counsel."

Dan laughed. "You're right," he said. "I'm sure I can find as many questions about their case as they can about mine."

"That's the spirit," Solomon said, and they both dug in to their pizza with reckless abandon.

•

They wrote feverishly, maniacally, I even saw a couple of pencils break. They sat there all night, at first staring at the symbol on their page. Then one of them would get an idea and start scribbling, then another; before long the notebooks were being filled with formulas. Calculators were turned on, and the white board Jonesy had was filling up with the different formulae they created.

Hernando, Juanita, and Alejandro went to sleep at one a.m. Katherine and I hit the sack at two; I knew we needed to. The rest of them worked on into the night.

When we awoke the next morning at eight, they were still working. We supplied them with coffee, water, protractors, anything they needed. And as they filled the notebooks, they flipped them over and began writing on the backs of the pages.

I had the TV on, turned to Court TV. It was the first day of Yashua's trial. I saw him sitting at the defendant's table. He didn't look good. He didn't look beat up or anything; just worn and weary. During opening arguments, the lights went out in the courtroom, and I could hear commotion in the background.

"Uh oh!" Katherine said over my shoulder.

"Wish I was there right now," I said.

"I know," she said.

The lights came back on, and I was relieved at that. I didn't suspect that Yashua would be in danger during his trial. I knew it was something he had to go through, God's Will, so to speak, and no one could interfere with that. I'd seen what happened to those who tried.

His lawyer's name was Dan Champere. I felt bad for him. I knew all too well what he was going through right then. But I knew God was probably handing him briefs or something. I knew God wasn't going to let Dan go on empty-handed.

I went to the Mighty Seven as they worked, to check up. The white board was filled, and the different variables and operators had a strange flow to them. Alicia finished first. She basically passed out after that; we had to walk her to the couch to lay down. Then Jeremy finished, and we helped him onto Jonesy's bed. Then Jonesy's girlfriend Cherise finished up, and we found a cot for her. After that, they got the floor and a blanket; nowhere else to put 'em. Jonesy was last up, and when he'd finished, he went to the board, and threw the final formula up. He stepped back to look at it. He chuckled.

"Oh yeah," he said, and just dropped.

They all slept like zombies, and we sat around the TV as the prosecution's case was starting. We knew they'd be out for a while, and I regretted that we'd have to wake 'em up in six hours. But in the light of things, we had no choice.

The special prosecutor was a 'Slick-Willy' kind of guy. Fancy suit, silk tie; I could see the gel in his hair from Cali'. He was a real peach, too. One by one his witnesses were called up. He was leading and coaching each and every one of 'em, right on the stand! But then Champere would get up there and blow 'em to shreds. That guy was every bit as good as I figured he'd be.

It was strange that I could *sense* the Spirit of God and the Beast in the courtroom as I was watching it. I couldn't actually *see* it, as I'd seen it before, but it was just a palpable feeling. Every time Brell or a witness would lie, the Beast swelled up. And every time Champere got up and blew apart their story, I could sense God's Spirit coursing through the room.

Back and forth it went, and eventually the prosecution got to the videotape. They played it for the jury, and I could see the East Gate blowing apart from the outside, and Yashua and I walking through the hole. The jury whispered to each other, and I had a feeling that I'd just seen what the case would rest on.

"That's it right there," Hernando said.

I held onto Katherine tightly. "Yeah," I said, "we gotta go soon."

•

Dan saw Solomon outside the courtroom when the day ended. Again he was mobbed, and again Solomon escorted him to the cruiser and drove him home. They agreed to meet at CC's around seven thirty for coffee. After that, Solomon would have a chance to see Yashua 'below radar'. All the guys working at Hunt that night were friends.

Dan got home and sank into his couch. He knew the video closed the case. He heard the 'death whisper' of the jury when they saw it. No matter what he said or did, apart from having Yashua turn the judge's water into wine (which he was sure Yashua wouldn't do), his case ended with the videotape. Facts, not beliefs. A fact, encoded on a strip of film, replayed in a machine, creating a visual depiction of reality. That's what the jury saw. A fact.

Yet, throughout the trial, Dan knew God spoke through him, gave him the questions to ask, noticed all the subtle lies. He was terrified throughout the prosecution's case, yet, at the same time, he was exhilarated by the feeling of channeling such energy.

As he sat there with a glass of scotch held limp in his hand, barely a twitch away from crashing to the floor, he ran his other hand through his hair and pressed his palm to his forehead. He tightened his grip on the glass and brought it to his lips. The warm rush passed over him, and he understood alcoholism at that moment.

He watched commentary on Court TV. They all sounded pretty confused and he soon realized that he was drawing more of their questions than his client. They must've just assumed Yashua was nuts. They were really questioning *his* sanity. Dan watched in wonder. The irony was hilarious, and he had a good laugh. He would share the joke with Yashua when he saw him later.

•

The bus pulled up to the front gate of the Louisiana State Penitentiary, in Angola. The towers and the buildings were white, as if anything 'pure' went on there.

Vic was twiddling his thumbs the whole ride, fucking with the guards. There were about ten of them, and Vic knew they wouldn't be able to stop him. He was stronger now, faster. And he was getting a handle on using his mind to cause ruckus. He made the ride to Angola *real* bumpy.

The prison didn't intimidate him. No prison did. The time he was in one, he ruled it. The bus stopped, and the men led Vic out and into the receiving area to be processed.

Vic didn't make it difficult. He was actually quite peaceful as they shaved his head, inspected his body cavities for weapons, told him the rules and issued him with his prison uniform. He was put in general population, as he thought he'd be. He placed a call to Fisher on the prison-phone, and it looked like Fisher placed a call himself. That bastard wanted King for something too, but Vic didn't know or care what it was. Fisher was a pussy, always relying on him to do the dirty work. '*But God and Satan both help Fisher if he fucks up my little payback,*' Vic thought. '*He'll be an appetizer.*'

He was led into the cell-block, and, as the door opened, he didn't hear the sound of rowdy inmates that was always so dear to him. As he walked in, the whole building was silent. All eyes turned to him, even those of the guards. Vic noticed that the inmates all had HIPPO connections, but they weren't knocked out. Jails weren't supposed to have 'em, but this was Fisher's jail, and so Vic didn't question it, simply welcoming the opportunity to suck out the anger and rage that the devices were suppressing. Vic smiled, and suddenly he made all the inmates sit down Indian-style wherever they were. On the stairs, along the cell-block, in the cafeteria, everywhere they were - they sat.

The guards tried to get them up but they couldn't. They managed to move the ones from the cell-blocks and the stairs to their cells, but even that was an all-night job. Meanwhile the guards were all shit-scared of Vic. He made no sound, just *breathed*, as he was walked to his cell. He entered it, and sat down Indian style himself. The guards activated the door, and it slid shut with a *clank!*

Vic looked around to the guards, and he could smell how close they were to pissing their pants.

"That'll be all," he said, and let out a cackling laugh. The guards pretty much left it at that, and walked away. Vic saw another clock; the same type of clock that was in Elayn Hunt, and it started doing the same thing, changing all crazy. And Vic suddenly understood what it meant.

"Bring it on," he said, and he made the clock explode.

•

The clock was busted. Dan didn't even notice it at first. He was a frequent clock-watcher whenever he drove. But that day he wasn't paying too much attention. He couldn't tell what time it was, but he knew he was on schedule. He left at ten after six, plenty of time to get to Elayn Hunt by six-thirty. But the clock was acting weird. It wasn't the wrong time; it wasn't any time. The digits kept changing. Just random numbers, it looked like. Dan had never seen that before in a digital clock, but he didn't pay it much mind. He just reminded himself to get a mounted-clock from the dollar store on the way home.

He got to Elayn Hunt around six-twenty, by the clock on their wall. They said all the digital clocks in the jail were messed up too, but the mechanical ones were fine. He talked with the guards for a few minutes; he knew them all pretty well though the years of visits he'd had to make there. When it was six-thirty, he sat down with Yashua in the meeting room.

"Well, I think you know what the video did," Dan said.

"Oh yes," Yashua said. "Nothing more than I've told you."

"I know," Dan said. "I just wish there was more."

"They proved I was there," Yashua said. "Your job is to tell them the reason. And today you did."

"Yeah, now everyone on TV is questioning my sanity for going with this defense."

"Ironic, isn't it?" Yashua said.

"I was thinking that earlier," Dan chuckled.

"You did fine," Yashua said, "and you'll do fine tomorrow."

"Yashua, what's going to happen to you?" Dan said. "To us?"

"Humanity is being given a choice," Yashua said. "You, Dan Champere, are given a choice. Right now you are acting upon that choice." Yashua put his hand over Dan's.

"If I told you what the outcome would be, you would not have that choice," he said, "and you would not be able to do what you'll have to do tomorrow."

"Which is?" Dan said. "I'm still clueless about that."

"You will prove, by a standard that is acceptable to God, that I am the one who was known as Jesus in times past," Yashua said.

"A paternity test?"

"Perhaps," Yashua said. "But have fun getting the DNA sample to match me to."

Dan laughed, and Yashua smiled.

Dan was silent for a while. He wanted to ask something, but he was mindful of what Yashua said about not telling him the outcome.

"Yes, Daniel," Yashua said. "No matter how this ends, I *will* see you again."

Dan put his hand on Yashua's shoulder. "I'll be looking forward to it."

"As will I," Yashua said.

They sat there and talked for a few minutes about things,

and Daniel was surprised that most of it was about things in *his* life; his past, memories and issues.

Dan found it so surprising that in the midst of what Yashua was going through, he would rather sit there and help Dan solve problems in his love life.

Dan knew then that Yashua had to be sent by God. God didn't just make people like him those days. Dan left there at quarter after seven. He'd be late to CC's by a few minutes, but he knew Sol would wait.

Chapter Twenty-one

They sat outside of CC's, Solomon and Daniel. They each had a coffee, and the non-existent traffic down Perkin's was something that neither had gotten used to.

"This is it, Sol," Dan said.

"I know," Solomon said, stirring the outer edges of his cup with the stirrer. "Ya' did good out there, Dan. Ya' didn't let 'em rattle ya'."

"The videotape killed the case," Dan said.

"Yeah, probably," Solomon said. "But your turn's tomorrow. Got anything?"

"Right now, a bunch of blank papers in my briefcase," Dan said. "Tomorrow, my defense will be on 'em."

"The Lord works in mysterious ways," Solomon said.

He stared out across Perkins, which had been turned from residential to commercial, a few years ago. He was looking at a strip mall. A friend of his used to live where it now stood.

"Dan, you did good," Solomon said. "I mean that. Just put this in God's hands."

"I know," Dan said. "It's just hard to do sometimes."

"You went in there today and presented that case, it was probably the hardest thing you've ever had to do, but you got through it. Ya' only got one more day." He patted him on the arm. "You'll do what's right by God, and in the end, that's all that matters."

"You're right," Dan said, and then he sat there for a second, and chuckled to himself. He raised his coffee.

"To this, the end of days," Dan said, and they toasted.

•

J.D. Fisher was in the air by early dusk. There was a problem with the instrumentation. The digital equipment was goin' nuts, the pilot told him. He had to get there, and he told the pilot to 'fly by eye.' He didn't know what to make of it; his own watch was doing it. '*Probably something to do with the hub,*' he thought. '*I'm gonna have to call Arlo once I'm airborne.*'

He was headed for Baton Rouge. He wanted to be there for the defense phase of the trial. Not that he was planning on attending. He had business elsewhere, behind the scenes. He had to attend to the details, which is what his life seemed all about those days.

He didn't like having to actually *attend* to details; he just liked *knowing* them. He hired people that were qualified enough to handle most details. Though he knew every component and every function of the hub, he wasn't very 'hands-on' with it. But, this was politics, and if this trial was to go the way he wanted it to, he knew he'd have to make his presence felt.

He hopped on the phone and called Arlo, who was in Baton Rouge himself right then, attending to Essence issues. Arlo sounded uneasy when he answered.

"J.D., what the fuck is Tanner doing here?" Arlo asked him.

"He's been activated," J.D. Said. "What the fuck do you *think* he's doing down there?"

"Are you crazy?!" Arlo said.

"If King lives, he can stop us," Fisher said as the jet reached cruising altitude. "Tanner will ensure that he doesn't live."

"Tanner could also make sure that there's no sample left for us to use!" Arlo protested.

"Let's get something straight," Fisher said harshly. "This is *my* project, and it will be done in the manner I see fit. There is no *us* right now, understand?"

"I'm sorry," Arlo said. "...Jesus."

"...will be in my hands within two days," Fisher said.

"You better hope you can control Tanner, J.D.," Arlo said. "He's getting a whole lot stronger."

"I'm not concerned."

"Well, you should be," Arlo said. "He caused a disturbance today in Baton Rouge that went across the global spectrum. It destroyed three nodes in Europe, and two in Africa."

"We can deal with that," Fisher said. "Be useful for a second, and tell me what's going on with this electronics malfunction. Is it affecting the hub?"

"No," Arlo said. "No electronics there. As for what's causing it," he paused. "Your guess is as good as mine. We're not doing it, not that I can tell anyways."

"Thanks," J.D. Said. "We'll talk when I get there."

Fisher hung up the phone. He looked at his watch, and it was still haywire, the numbers changing all over the place. He couldn't figure it out, but he noticed that they were changing faster now. Not by much, but they were. A minor detail.

•

Solomon went to Elayn Hunt around nine-thirty, right after he'd left Dan. He didn't know what he was gonna say to Yashua, but he knew he needed to say his goodbyes. He didn't know what was going to happen after tomorrow. He wouldn't have another chance to see him, and he needed to know something.

Solomon was let in by Officer Greenberg, who he was friends with *off-duty.*

"Hey, Sol," he said. "I can get ya' about a half hour. After that, the warden'll be back, and you know the deal there."

"I only need a couple minutes," Solomon said. "Thanks, Jim."

"Any time, Sol," Jim said, and he leaned close. "If ya' ask

me, they ain't got a case against him. Video or not."

"Thanks," Solomon said.

"Ya know, I'd be half inclined to believe it," Jim said in a hushed tone.

"Believe what?" Solomon asked.

"Ya' know, what Champere said about him being, ya' know…" Jim said.

Solomon laughed a little. He was nervous not to say too much.

"This day and age, ya' never know," Solomon said.

"He's a good guy anyways," Jim said. "He shouldn't be here."

"I know, Jim," Solomon said. "But that's how it has to be. Thanks for lookin' over him."

"Glad to," Jim said, and Solomon went in to meet with Yashua.

Yashua was sitting in the meeting room, and his hands were folded in prayer. Solomon could see brightness all about him, and it radiated from his prison uniform, turning the orange jumpsuit to white. His closed lids eclipsed the light coming from his eyes. In the center of his chest, Solomon could see figures of different people. Sometimes he recognized them; sometimes he did not. The ones he recognized were historical figures, men like Ghandi, Abraham Lincoln and Martin Luther King, Jr. There were many others, and he suspected that they were historical figures too. Some wore priestly vestments; others wore rags. They all had a fire in their spirit, and Solomon could hear their voices in the back of his mind.

Then it ended, and Yashua opened his eyes. They were normal. He smiled.

Jim didn't notice anything when it happened. He just let Solomon in, looked right at Yashua, and shut the door, oblivious.

"Solomon," Yashua said. "I'm glad to see you. Come." He motioned to the seat in front of him. Solomon sat down in amazement still.

"Don't be frightened," Yashua said.

"What was that?" Solomon asked.

"The martyrs have collected unto me," Yashua said. "The time approaches when they will have to bear witness."

"Is that anything I would ever understand?" Solomon said.

"Many things have happened; and a few things yet to come," Yashua said. "That was one of them."

"What about the clocks?" Solomon asked. "Does that have to do with all this?"

"Yes," Yashua said. "They are trying to express God's time."

"What do you mean exactly?"

"God's time is not your own," Yashua said. "He is aligning the Earth to His time, for what is about to come. Your timepieces can't express it. So, they go haywire."

"It's coming, isn't it?" Solomon asked him after a period of silence.

"Yes," Yashua said. "Humanity must choose."

Again Solomon was silent. Then he remembered the other face on the video.

"You said I would meet up with someone who was with you?" Solomon said. "Is that the younger guy on the tape?"

"Yes."

"How will I find him?"

"He'll find you," Yashua said. "Just do your job."

"What's that," Solomon joked, "cracking down on reckless speeders? That's what they'll have me doin' soon."

"If that is your job, do it well," Yashua said.

"Yashua, I'm sorry."

"I know," Yashua replied. "In the short time you've known me, you've been a friend. And God is with you."

They sat there for the rest of the time, and Solomon didn't talk to Yashua about the trial, the video or Jerusalem.

•

At six we woke them up. They were tired, but they all got up. We had coffee on, but no one wanted it. They'd had enough. We all sat around the table after everyone had smacked themselves in the head enough, and talked about the solution they'd developed to the problem of Paradigm.

"Okay," Jonesy said, "basically, what we're dealing with is this."

He walked towards the board. "Three quarters of the world's population is plugged into this thing right now. Anything that happens to the hub will happen to them. If there's a rapid disconnect from the signal, the world will be one big looney bin. We don't want that."

"We also face another problem," Jonesy continued. "The hub is very well shielded. I know personally. There are Essence scans, but we can cover those. There are armed patrols around the perimeter of the building continually, twenty-four hours. Hacking is ineffective; digital programming can't be used. The hub has no electrical components. Everything is programmed chemically until it leaves the hub, where it is converted to an electromagnetic wave. This all happens through a device at the tip. The outer walls of the Paradigm Building are filled with highly-shielded electrical conduits leading up to it."

He walked over to another room, and motioned us to follow. Inside the room was all manner of electrical gadgets and other things that I had no clue about. He walked over to a machine about the size of a jukebox, with hoses of varying sizes all over it.

"This is a Cellular Automata machine," Jonesy said. "This one's chemical, and I modeled it after the one I had to use in there. Zygote, the computer program I gave you," he looked at me, "was part of the programming that went into this. A crude part, I might add."

He turned the machine on, and I could see different-colored liquids of dissimilar consistencies begin to flow through the hoses connecting the different parts. In a few hoses I started to see electrical arcs passing sporadically through.

"With this we can design a program the hub could read," he said, as we all stared with fascination at the machine. He pulled a vial of liquid with a metal seal off of a shelf, and held it up. "A chemical program; something that looks like this," Jonesy passed the vial around to us.

"But we still need to get it in there. I know someone on the inside. He's a solid guy, and he hates Paradigm. He can't do it alone, though. He's gonna need a diversion to get into the hub. That's where we come in." He pointed to the Mighty Seven.

"Originally we wanted to shut it down before it got people hooked," Cherise said, taking it from there. "So we built an 'open-dynamo.' It could produce a very intense electric field in a five-hundred square-foot radius. We were going to try to get it right up on the building. Then as soon as they released HIPPO, so many people hooked in overnight that we couldn't use it like that anymore."

She continued as she walked over to the map.

"Now we'll use it for the diversion. We have a van we can load it into, and we'll have to drive it around. It'll be dangerous, but we're gonna have a cloak." She held up a device that looked like an old mp3 player. "The Essence scans won't pick us up. We'll still have to worry about law enforcement and Paradigm security forces, and they'll be able to pin us to a radius of a few blocks, just by the disturbance."

"Fisher and Spici won't be there," Cherise said. "My uncle's his pilot. He told me he had to be by the plane, 'cause Fisher would be flying out today. He left a page on my cellphone. He always does before he takes off. Good luck thing. My uncle and I are close."

"So when we put the diversion out," Jeremy picked up, "we're gonna buzz by as close as we can, without blowing the hub. Jonesy's guy's gonna have about a fifteen minute window. Security will be distracted, and the boss and main scientist are a few states away."

"It's gonna take him about ten minutes to load the vial," Jonesy said. "It's gonna be tight, but we can make it."

"Skipping the technical details, what this'll create," he said, waving his hand about, "is a five minute burst of receptive "awareness" being pumped out. Then the hub will exceed its capacity to handle it, and it will stress the remaining energy, turning it projective. Which will cause an explosion and a rapid disconnect."

We all thought somberly about the ramifications of that.

"When we get this five-minute burst," he continued, "it needs to be focused on something, somewhere. Barney ..." He threw me a device that looked like one of those old USB drives.

"For the five minutes, that thing will put the focus of everybody connected, wherever *it* is," he said. "I trust you'll have a good place for it."

"Yeah," I said. "Thanks."

"No prob," he said. "As far as saving your friend..." He looked out the window, "we haven't exactly figured that out yet."

"We may not have to," I said, holding up the device. "Trust me on this one. The opportunity will present itself."

"I don't know..." Juanita said, scratching the side of her face. "Do you think five minutes of clarity is gonna be enough?"

"You'd be amazed," Katherine said, and I looked up at her.

She smiled, and I suddenly felt just a little bit more confident. Katherine was *living proof* that it worked.

We sat around and discussed the plan further. Alejandro was going to stay with Jonesy's team, and assist in Anno Luce. He didn't want to leave Rosita alone, and to be honest, I didn't want him to. Besides, I knew he wouldn't be ready for the kind of battle we'd have to face in Angola.

They wanted to begin in synchronization with us. Which was a hard thing to do, 'cause all the clocks were fucked up, doin' that weird thing I saw on the inmate numbers in my dream. I didn't know what caused it, but I knew what it meant. It was coming. What lay beyond this little cabin, hundreds of miles away, in a cell-block in Angola, Louisiana. Every clock was becoming the shot-clock.

Jonesy had two old chronographs, all gears. They both worked. They were synchronized, and we were to call Jonesy when we were within two hours of Angola. He handed me a phone that he'd stolen from Paradigm. It ran off Essence, and was immune to the scans. At that point we had to depart. We all knew we had about 36 hours before holy shit was gonna hit the fan, and they had everything taken care of. We all hugged each other goodbye, and we went down into the parking area to our van. Jonesy had us wait while he emptied our gas tank and replaced it with some different gas, if you'd call it that. It was almost blue.

"This burns at about a tenth of what petroleum fuel does," Jonesy said. "You'll be able to get to Houston before you have to refuel. But get high-octane when you do. Trust me."

With that, Jonesy flicked a switch, the ramp elevated and the cover slid back. We waved at everyone as they waved back, and we were greeted by the cool breeze of the new evening. The sun had just set, and the chill of a desert night was already setting in.

We got back out on I-8, and we found our way to 10 East. And I knew the moment we hit I-10 that, in our own ways, me, Katherine, Hernando and Juanita would spend the next twenty-four hours or so cramming our hearts, minds and spirits for the final exam in Angola.

•

Solomon drove Dan to the courthouse on Friday morning. The same mob of reporters who greeted him the day before were there that day, looking none the worse for wear. Dan knew those guys were pros. Many of them had covered wars, disasters and riots. Part of the reason he didn't want to say anything to them had to do with the off-hand possibility that they wouldn't miss a beat, no matter what he said, and the issue would be thrown back at him so quick that he actually *would*. So, he kept quiet, and Solomon escorted him into the building.

He sat down at the table. He had about twenty minutes before the trial was to begin. Yashua was not yet there. He knew he was supposed to wait another ten minutes before opening his briefcase; well, in the back of his mind he knew. But, right then, he forgot, and almost out of habit he reached to open the locks. As he pressed his fingers onto the metal locks he felt a sharp pain in them, like a shock. He realized they were burning. He pulled 'em back real fast, and they throbbed. He blew on them; it was the only thing he could think to do. Then he remembered he was supposed to wait, and he knew why his fingers were burning. He apologized to God in his head, and the pain instantly subsided.

He looked around the room. The clock above the judge's

bench was spinning. *'That's a new development,'* Dan thought.

Last he knew the manual clocks worked; only the electronic clocks went nutty. The hour hand spun backward at different speeds, and the minute hand did the same thing, but forward. Dan could guess a-million-and-three possible explanations for it, and life was about to get pretty funky in most of those guesses.

Yashua came in about ten minutes later. Dan said hello, and Yashua returned the greeting. He looked at Dan's fingers as he sat down, and laughed.

"Funny," Dan said.

"Laughter's the best medicine," Yashua said.

Dan figured at that point it would be safe to open the briefcase, but he tapped the locks with his fingers a couple of times to test it. It felt normal, so he popped the locks and took out his defense, amidst Yashua's subtle chuckling.

Dan saw names. They filled every inch of space on each paper. They were all different kinds of names; some were in English, others not. On and on they went, down through the pages. He scanned each page, but had no clue how he was supposed to pronounce the names. He didn't even know how to read most of them. *'Oh boy!'* he thought.

He looked at the very last page, hoping for something he may see that would make it all make sense. The last name on the last page put what he held in his hands into perspective.

Yashua King.

Dan realized that he was staring at the genealogy of Yashua. He looked at the first page, and the first name on that page. It was written in a set of symbols, almost. He'd never seen anything like it.

"Yashua," he whispered to his client. "I can't read half these names. How am I gonna tell them to the jury?"

"When you looked upon them, God imprinted them in your heart," Yashua said. "So just speak from it."

"Okay," Dan said. He wasn't exactly nervous about it.

Everyone in the viewing world already thought he was crazy.

The judge was let in, and all rose.

When everyone was seated, Dan got up to begin the defense of Yashua King. He started to gather his thoughts, his rhetoric, plan how he'd set up the jury, and suddenly his mind went blank. He felt woozy, and then the world went white.

He awoke to a stunned jury. He could see the slight gape of the mouths of people who couldn't process what they'd just experienced. Then he realized that he was still standing.

"Does the defense rest?" Judge Forrier asked him.

Dan was confused. He hadn't even started the defense. He looked at the clock, which wasn't much help. He looked at Yashua.

'What do I do?' he thought.

'Rest,' he heard Yashua's voice say in his head. He paused, and the judge asked again. He looked at Yashua, who nodded.

"The defense rests, your honor," he said, and returned to his table. Yashua smiled.

"You did well," Yashua said.

"I don't remember," Dan said.

"Don't worry about it," Yashua said. "That's been known to happen." He smiled again.

The judge called recess, and Dan met Solomon outside. They'd have to go to the CC's to get coffee and pastries that day. The Mellow Mushroom was filled with reporters, Sol had told him.

While they ate, Sol told him what the defense looked like from his perspective. All of which was news to Dan. He didn't remember any of it. He had to laugh on a few occasions. He was nervous about closing arguments, but Solomon reassured him that he was doing the best anyone could with the defense he was trying to present. Dan left CC's with Solomon, filled with just enough strength to bring Yashua's trial to a close.

•

The Reverend Biggs ate sushi at a restaurant overlooking the Mississippi River. He was furious about wasting his time on such a sham trial. As he ate, he seethed. It was bad enough that this *man* was being defended as the Son of God. But then to disrespect the name of the Lord, Jesus Christ, by insinuating that he was part black, part Asian, part Hispanic, part Arab… Hell, that lawyer of his called out names of every race, calling it the 'lineage of the Son of Man'. When Biggs thought about the sheer nerve of that, his blood boiled.

Biggs knew from the get-go that Yashua King wasn't white. He didn't exactly look black, but he looked 'non-white.' And Biggs knew that when the Son of Man returned, he would be 'bathed in white.' He would *be* white. Not some kind of … mongrel.

Biggs wondered if this Yashua King had ever been on welfare, eating his tax dollars. Well, not exactly *his* tax dollars. He was given wisdom by the Lord on how to not have to pay them. But King was probably a leech of the system at some point in his life. *Those people* usually were.

Biggs would stay in Baton Rouge for the verdict, and sentencing. He knew they'd find King guilty, how could they not? After the trial, Biggs would travel to Jerusalem, to find the *real* Messiah. But he wanted to see the look on the impostor's face when they threw the book at him.

•

Jonesy and the Mighty Seven sat around staring at a vial of chemicals. It was the 'program' that they had worked feverishly to produce. It had taken them all hours the night before to actually make it. It was tense. But they held together.
As they sat there around the vial, they knew that they had a full day to prepare for what they would have to do. They also knew a day wouldn't be near enough. They decided to relax for an hour, and spend this evening planning the attack. The day it was gonna go down, they'd all be busy with their own little missions.

"Dude," Jeremy said. "This is fucked up."

"Whattaya' mean?" Jonesy said.

"Just this whole situation," Jeremy said. "I mean, does anyone here feel any … different?"

Everyone in the room acknowledged that they were confused too. Eyes turned to Alejandro, who was still dealing with Yashua's identity.

"Don't look at me," Alejandro said. "I don't have any answers for you. I doubt Barney had many more answers than me, and he was in Jerusalem."

"So is this it?" Alicia said. "The end of the world?"

"I don't know," Alejandro replied, "but it's something."

"It's fucked up, whatever it is!" Tony said. "That whole thing with the pencils, and the symbols. Could it have been Paradigm fucking with our heads?"

"No!" Jonesy said. "Those symbols are too perfect. Geometrical, ya' know? Paradigm can't create shit like that with the energy they use. I've seen them try to create drawn images. The shapes, the curves, the lines; they're always jagged."

"Yeah, but couldn't Barney have done it with his mind," Jeremy said. "Using Paradigm's energy?"

"You don't know how hard that would be to do. I've known Barney for a while. He can't draw like that on *paper*, with his *hand*."

"I *felt* it," Cherise said. "It was God."

"The funny thing is," Jeremy said, "is that I felt it too. And I don't even believe in God!"

"I bet ya' do now!" Bert chimed in from the background.

"Can ya' blame me?"

"Hell, I always believed," Bert replied. "Welcome to the flock."

"I hope Jesus fucks that Reverend Biggs up!" Nick said, "That would be bad-ass!"

"Okay, first," Alejandro said, "his name's Yashua. Second ..." He pointed to the notebooks. "We just had God flyin' through here about forty-eight hours ago. Let's try to refrain from talkin' about his only kid kickin' somebody's ass."

Everybody cracked up, including Jonesy.

"All right, dudes and dudettes." Jonesy picked it up. "This is how it's gonna roll." He walked over to the map of Anno Luce, with push pins marking their location, as well as all locations that made up the Paradigm presence in the city.

"Cherise dear," Jonesy said. "You and I will be here. We're gonna have to co-ordinate what we do with what they're doing in Louisiana."

"Why do you guys get to stay here?" Nick complained.

"We need two people to operate the scan-viewers; one for what's goin' on here and one for what's goin' on in Angola," Jonesy explained.

"Wait," Jeremy said. "I thought we couldn't use those. Won't they put you on Paradigm's radar?"

"Yeah, it will," Jonesy said. "But it takes the scan fifteen minutes to sweep. It spends ten minutes monitoring something it picks up. Then if it deems that thing a threat, it alerts Paradigm, who then calls either the cops, or security. In any case it will take *them* twenty minutes to respond. That's about a forty-five minute window. By the time they alert security, my hope is that they'll have other things to worry about."

"We're not gettin' a safe ride here, Nick," Jonesy added.

"Sorry bro'," Nick said. "I was just wonderin',"

"I know," Jonesy said, and went on with the prep.

"Jeremy and Alicia, you'll be driving our little 'disturbance' through the streets of Anno Luce. Alejandro, you'll be driving a smaller version of the dynamo in a separate car. We can hopefully confuse them."

Alejandro and Jeremy nodded. "Jeremy and Alicia will take Marson to Belverde, to Anno Luce West and then to Sindell," Jonesy continued. "That roughly encircles Paradigm at a distance that'll surely get their attention, without blowing up the hub and most of the city. Alejandro, you'll take the parallel roads, a few blocks up in the opposite direction. When you get back to Marson, drive one block away from Paradigm, and basically do the same thing." Jonesy pointed to the map. "Ale', you should come down."

"About how long do you think we'll have?" Alicia asked.

"About ten ... fifteen minutes," Jonesy answered.

"Then what?" Jeremy asked. "Turn ourselves in?"

"No," Jonesy said laughing. "Just turn off the dynamos. The vans will have a cloak. They're not gonna be able to get a good lock on you to begin with, and if you're careful, you can disappear."

"Which may be easier," Jonesy went on, "when the third part of this plan kicks in." He looked at Nick and smiled.

"What?" Nick asked.

"You remember that shit you guys used to talk about," Jonesy said. "That 'Project Chaos' thing I always thought was corny?"

Nick laughed. "Yeah," he said.

"That's phase three."

"Whattaya' mean?" Nick asked.

"You told me you know people out here in the scratch. People like us. How many did you say, Nick, about fifty?"

"Yeah, somethin' like that," Nick said.

"Tomorrow, you, Tony and Bert are gonna go out with that gray truck full of toys, and your mission's to drive to every place you all know, and get as many fellow runaways as you can."

Jonesy walked over to the map.

"The dynamo is a diversion for Paradigm. 'Project Chaos' is a diversion for the whole city."

"You better not be fuckin' with me!" Nick said.

"No way," Jonesy said. "And I don't care what you do, as long as you're between a hundred and a thousand yards away from the building."

"Don't tell anyone about God or Yashua. They don't need to know. Just tell 'em they'll have a chance to fuck shit up in Anno Luce that night."

Everyone laughed.

"So, I'm gonna get to use my flash grenade after all," Nick said.

"Yeah ... carefully," Jonesy said.

•

Solomon watched the closing arguments from the back. He didn't sit; he was in uniform, and he fit in better standing at attention in the back. No one seemed to notice him.

Brell closed on basically the same thing his case rested on. The videotape. He went on about separation of church and state, and that in a court of law, the separation demanded that a case be tried on the evidence and the facts, rather than on beliefs.

Dan did his best. He summed up his side with vivacity and

flair. Dan was always a kindly, soft-spoken man. He usually won trials because he could get juries to feel comfortable around him. He often lost trials because he couldn't overpower a domineering prosecutor. This trial showed Solomon a very different side of Dan.

He was still warm and caring, and his voice didn't change, but Solomon felt projection. He'd been at trials where he couldn't hear Dan if he sat in the back row. This day Dan was loud and clear. This was the trial that Dan was least confident about, but he had never seen Dan with the confidence he showed throughout it. He'd not seen Dan stumble once.

Dan's, or rather, *God's* defense, was more amazing to Solomon than if Moses and Abraham themselves had taken the witness stand. Dan traced Yashua's lineage from Adam. But the first name he only *felt* was Adam. It was something in a language he'd never heard before. He was positive that neither the judge, Dan, the jury, or the viewing public, had either.

The diversity of Yashua's lineage explained a lot to Solomon; why Yashua had looked strange to him. He lived in a world of suspect descriptions, so knowing racial characteristics came with the territory. Solomon was usually good at pinning nationalities; even in people of mixed nationalities, he could spot the mix. Yet Yashua had confounded him. Now he realized that Yashua's lineage was that of every race combined.

'*The Son of Man, in every way,*' Solomon thought as the court was adjourned. There would be special session the next day, where the verdict would be read, and the sentence passed. He met Dan as he walked back.

"How'd I do?" Dan said. "I blacked out again."

"Great," Solomon said. "Maybe you should quit drinkin' that Scotch."

Dan laughed. "I just slept last night," he said as they left the courtroom. "As soon as I got home from CC's. I was tired as hell."

"I can only imagine," Solomon said as they opened the door to a mob of journalists, swimming in a sea of cameras, tripods and cables.

•

"Shit!" I said.

"What is it?" asked Katherine, pressing up close to me. I was looking at the chronograph Jonesy gave me, which was spinning like mad at that point.

"Oh," she said. "Uh-Oh…"

"I'll have to call Jonesy. We have the cell, but I don't know if it'll be up then. We're gonna have to figure out a plan B."

"It's coming," Juanita said. "I'm getting a sense of that."

I hugged Katherine tight to me. "This time tomorrow," I said. "It's coming real soon."

We drove on in silence, and I noticed I was starting to pick up things. Almost like Jerusalem; I was beginning to 'see the field.' Nowhere near to the degree of the battle, but it was there. We were just about to leave New Mexico, and I could feel that the energies in the air were polarizing, and the flow of these energies seemed to be at our backs. Not that it could affect us driving, but it was heading in the same direction we were. To Yashua, Tanner and the inevitable showdown.

•

Dan had a light dinner with Solomon at a Mexican restaurant on Government Street. They both agreed that they would see him. Dan had to. Solomon just wanted to.

At six o'clock Dan went to see Yashua.
Yashua, as always, smiled when he saw him. Dan smiled back, but his gut was churning. He was not happy to ever have to visit a client he knew was gonna be convicted the next day. And it wasn't just any client. It was the Son of God, the Messiah.
As he sat up there, he realized what hurt him more was that it was Yashua. A man he wished he could've counted as a friend for much longer than he could.

"Yashua, I did what I could," Dan said. "But you know what they're gonna' do."

"Send me to Angola," Yashua said. "Yes, I know. I was the one who told *you*."

"I still feel like I let you down though," Dan said.

"You've done God's will, Daniel," Yashua said. "He, and *I*, thank you." He put his hand reassuringly on Dan's, which were shaking a bit.

"I don't know what to do now," Dan said. "I don't mean about tomorrow, but about *everything*."

"Daniel," Yashua said. "When you were conceived, God was there, as was I, in a sense. You're parents asked for Us both. And God put this trial in your heart then. When you looked at the papers, what you saw sparked a deep memory that was hidden from you until right then."

Dan looked at him. "So, I was destined for this all along?"

"Daniel, God is with everyone when they are born, even when the parents don't call for Him. A newborn naturally calls out to God. It's a call of Spirit; the first call they give before their birth cries. And God has a task for every one that is sunk into their memory. It drives us."

"Why do people act like retards and kill each other then? God doesn't make *that* anyone's task!" Dan said. "Does He?"

"When you follow God's path," Yashua said. "Your conscience, your common sense, your heart; it will lead you to complete the task God set for you. You will then feel true satisfaction, and true peace."

"Completing your purpose on Earth is the only way to feel that continuous, self-renewing sense of gratification," Yashua continued. "If you ignore God's call, you'll spend your life searching for outside attempts to achieve it. You build a tolerance to any other attempt to satisfy yourself. Like a drug."

"I understand," Dan said. "But I don't feel very gratified right now."

"You're not quite done," Yashua said.

"You mean after the verdict?" Dan said.

"Yes, after."

They sat there, silent for a second. Dan looked around, not at anything really. He looked at Yashua.

"I just want to say, ya' know ..." Dan said. "Thank you, and thank God, for giving me this opportunity. I know we're not gonna win, but ..."

"You have been a good friend," Yashua said. "And I would have had no other defend me."

Dan laughed, but he was nearly crying inside. He didn't want it to end that way. He didn't want right then to be the last time he'd have a chance to talk to Yashua.

"We'll talk again, Daniel," Yashua said. "Here, or *there*."

That was just what Dan needed to hear right then. He smiled, and tears rolled down his cheeks.

Yashua reached over and wiped his tears to the side.

"It's okay, Dan," Yashua said, and Dan saw his face light up just a little. "When the trial ends, and they take me to Angola ..." He paused.

"Yes, Yashua," Dan said. "What is it?"

"Go directly to New Orleans."

"Is there something I need to do there?" he asked.

"Yes," Yashua said. "Have a scotch for me during Mardi Gras."

•

Solomon walked into Elayn Hunt that night, knowing full well he'd have hell to pay for it the next day. He had to. He knew it would be the last time he would ever be able to talk to Yashua. Solomon had something to talk about.

The guards let him in without saying anything, but he had to sign the visitor's log, and the warden would see it. Yashua looked tired when he saw Solomon, but he smiled as he always did.

They exchanged greetings. Solomon asked him how the accommodations were, and Yashua had nothing to say in complaint.

"Yashua," Solomon said. "There's something I want to talk with you about."

"Gerard Martinez," Yashua said. "I'd wondered if you

would want to talk about it."

"What could I have done?" Solomon said. "I've spent all these years asking myself this, asking God, even. And I never got an answer."

"You could have shot him in one area of his temple, a target no bigger than a half of an inch in diameter," Yashua told him. "A moving target. This would have put the bullet on a course to an area in the middle of his brain, where impulse signals are inhibited. This would have kept his finger from pulling the trigger when you shot him. But, of course," Yashua said, "you didn't have that knowledge. Only God knew at that exact moment what would have stopped him."

"But what if I didn't shoot?" he said. "What if I negotiated, or tried to piss him off, so he'd turn the gun on *me* for that one second I needed…"

"He had the intent, walking in there," Yashua said, "of shooting the first human being he saw in the throat. He was gripping the trigger tight enough so that it would go off, even if you shot him. He was about to draw the gun from her head, down her jaw-line to her throat when you shot him."

Solomon was silent.

"God needed that little girl to be with Him that day," Yashua said. "And you were called upon so that she could die instantly, without pain."

"Will I ever stop seeing her?" he asked. "When I dream, or when I see a little girl who looks like her?"

"Until you see her *again*," Yashua said. "You will see her."

Solomon lowered his head.

"It won't always hurt," Yashua said, putting his hand on Solomon's shoulder.

"I'm gonna miss you," Solomon said.

"Not for long," Yashua said. "Our paths will cross."

•

The Reverend Biggs sat in the first row of the courthouse that Saturday, bright and early. He wanted his congregation to see him, on live television, at the trial. They had to know not to trust the impostor. They had to know that justice was being served there.

They brought out Mr. King, though he thought *Mr.* was a bit too much respect for a fake blasphemer. He was weary looking and unshaven. 'Good,' Biggs thought. '*Hope he didn't sleep a wink last night.*'

Champere looked like shit too. Biggs knew he'd be damned for sure from all of it. He was a Christian; Biggs could tell. He knew he wasn't supposed to help blasphemers and false prophets. It was a sin. And the wages of sin were death.

The judge walked in, and the court was brought into session. Like a big, protracted wave, all rose and all sat. The jury was led in, and Biggs could tell by the worried looks on their faces that the verdict was guilty. He'd seen enough Court TV to know that only guilty verdicts came with worried looks.

The jury settled down, and the room became silent, except for the sounds of paper-shuffling escaping from both tables.

"Has the jury reached a verdict?" the judge asked the foreperson.

"We have, your honor," said the foreperson as she rose.

It was just a formality for the judge to ask that question, as Biggs knew; juries had to reach a verdict in the time allotted.

"Will you please read your verdict for the court?" the judge said.

The foreperson looked at Yashua nervously. "We the jury find the defendant, Yashua King..." she said, and then cleared her throat, " ... guilty on all charges."

Biggs never felt such delight. Seeing the look on Champere's face, hearing the gasps of the nut-cases who'd shown up because they actually believed in King's snake oil was ecstatic. He could barely contain himself, and he had a press conference waiting outside.

As he watched Yashua being escorted to what he knew was the bus to Angola, Yashua turned to look at him. Biggs put his hands together, as if to say he'd pray for him. He knew he never would.

He walked outside to a podium he had prepared for him on

the courthouse steps. He was greeted by the mob he so loved to play with, taking his position behind a sprig of microphones.

"Today, justice has been done," he said as flash-bulbs filled his eyes and the cameras rolled. "This man claimed to be the Lord Jesus Christ. But he was not. And a jury today saw him for what he was; a terrorist, a murderer and a false prophet. He is out there, and I believe he walks the Earth. But Satan has many out there who will claim to be Him, to deceive you. Don't be fooled."

The reporters started asking him questions about whether or not he thought Yashua King was insane.

"I don't think so," he said. "He knows what he's doing."

They also asked him about the connection between Yashua and the miracles in Jerusalem.

"I'm going to Jerusalem after I leave this podium," he said, "to find the *real* Messiah."

Then they started asking him questions about the reversal of his position on HIPPO, and if PRD would still underwrite it.

He thanked them, and then had his security detail walk him to his car. They sped off for Baton Rouge airport, where the Reverend had a private jet waiting. He was tired of commercial flights. He only took them sometimes to show humility. Besides, right then commercial airlines couldn't fly because of their instrumentation 'issues.' Biggs knew it was another sign, the clocks, but he didn't yet know what it meant. He would fly to New York directly himself, and refuel for a flight to Tel Aviv.

•

"Guilty on all charges," the jury forewoman said.

Dan's heart dropped. Fell to the floor. He didn't expect anything else. He knew he was going to hear it. Yet he still held that last bit of hope, that somehow the jury would defy fate and return a 'not-guilty' verdict. But hearing it cemented his hopes into the cell blocks of Angola.

He looked at Yashua. He looked like hell. Dan couldn't even imagine what was going through his head right then. Yashua may have been the Messiah returned, and he may have had God's work to do, but right then, Dan saw a human, alone in the world, destined to suffer a fate that Dan couldn't fathom. One he'd already had to suffer once.

The judge spoke. "Will the defendant please rise?"

Yashua rose. There was a scattering of hushed voices.

"You have been found guilty of Conspiracy to Commit a Terrorist Act and conducting an International Terror Campaign," the judge started. "This court hereby sentences you to serve the rest of your natural life in prison. At the conclusion of this proceeding, you will be transferred to the custody of the Louisiana State Penitentiary, in Angola."

"Does the defense wish to make any final motions before we conclude?" the judge asked. Dan knew none of them would be granted. But he went ahead anyway.

"Just one, your honor," he said, standing up. "My client in no manner has expressed even the slightest hint of aggression, but they send him in here in shackles and chains. Can he at least ride to Angola in hand-cuffs only?"

The judge thought about it. "Okay," she said, looking at Yashua. "Shackles are overkill, I agree. Bailiff, please remove Mr. King's shackles."

The bailiff removed them, and Yashua could move his legs around a little. He smiled.

"Mr. King," the judge asked Yashua. "Is there anything you would like to say before we conclude this hearing?"

"No, your Honor," Yashua said. "My counsel has defended me adequately. But thank you for asking."

The judge looked weirdly at this. "Well okay," the judge said. She rapped her gavel. "This court session is adjourned."

The noise picked up, and the bailiffs came to bring Yashua to the bus. As they led him away he looked back at Dan. He smiled. Dan almost lost it.

•

An expanse of Texas desert surrounded us. We were about an hour away from Houston. Still no luck with the chronographs, and I called Jonesy. I didn't get an answer. I'd hoped he just had his phone off, but I was nervous about it. I didn't know if Paradigm was onto them or not, if they'd been watching Jonesy, letting him think he was off-radar. But I knew there was nothing I could do about it at that point, so I just told myself to keep calling him periodically, until I got through.

We had the radio on, which was covering the trial. The guy doing the show didn't sound like he cared much. He probably had it on because cameras and tape recorders hadn't been allowed in a courtroom in a while. It was just a novelty, nostalgia thing for him, I could tell.

"We find the defendant guilty of all charges," I heard over the radio.

Everybody was bummed, but we were expecting it. Just sucked to hear it.

"So, how long is it gonna take for them to put him in Angola?" Katherine asked.

"Not long," I said. "A little over an hour from now, he'll be in there. It'll take them a while to process him, but, after that, it's only a matter of time and opportunity before Tanner gets to him."

Katherine squeezed on to me. "Barney, I'm scared."

"Me too," I said, squeezing back.

•

Vic sat in his cell, enjoying the quiet he had created. He had never felt this way before, so strong, so *mighty*. He could kill every one of the guards and inmates in here with a thought. Or not. It was his choice. And he was saving that choice for a bigger fish.

He could feel King getting closer. It was a feeling so revolting that it burned him to feel it. This man who walked as God would meet the god who would kill him. The god known only as Victor.

He stared at the spot on the wall where the clock used to be. He had shattered it, along with all the other clocks in the prison. And that's not the only fun he'd had there. He thought it would be interesting to fool with the guards by having all the inmates convulse. That was hilarious, as he'd heard the guards shouting in that deliciously confused manner that occurred when life went haywire. He licked his lips, savoring the tastes of disorder.

He picked up a marker he lifted from somewhere in the building. He just wanted one, and one flew to him. He continued writing his symbols, his 'signatures', he called them. He wasn't much of an artist though. They were all jagged.

'*Fuck it,*' Vic thought. '*When I carve them into God-boy, they'll hurt more.*' He laughed maniacally, and projected his voice so that it filled the entire prison with an eerie resonance.

●

"Fuck!" Jonesy said.

"What?" Cherise asked him. He was holding the wildly spinning chronograph.

"Fuckin' thing's goin' crazy, just like the digitals," he said. "How are we gonna synchronize?"

"Call him," she said.

"I tried, can't get through," he said. "We're gonna need another way to know what's going on there."

"The scans?" Bert suggested.

"No go," Jonesy said. "We'd have too small a window with those. It'll take us longer to find them than Paradigm will take to find us."

"We gotta know when to kick this off," Nick said. "And I mean soon. We should be outta here in about a half-hour to get our guys."

"Alright, hold up…" Jonesy said, "let's think this through. They just read the verdict ten minutes ago. He's probably takin' a seat on the bus now. It's about an hour from there to Angola, and he'll have to be processed when he gets there. That'll take another hour or two. We'll say two."

"They're probably gonna bring him to his cell, and that'll be about a quarter of two, something like that. If I'm guessing correctly, Tanner will try to get Yashua during dinner. When is that?"

"I don't know," Nick said. "Do you think we can find out on-line?"

Jonesy went over to the computer, and typed in 'Louisiana State Penitentiary' in the search bar. A list of links came up.

"Five o'clock," Alicia said.

"Huh?" Jonesy said.

"They serve dinner at five o'clock," Alicia said.

"How do you know?" Jonesy asked.

"I used to live in Shreveport when I was a girl. My father was a CO in Angola," she said. "He used to have to be in work by the first dinner shift, which was five o'clock."

"That means we gotta kick it into gear around four. So everybody needs to be in place in four hours. Anything we need to talk about before you guys take off?" He motioned to Nick, Bert and Tony.

"Where do we go after all this?" Nick asked. "Here?"

"Yeah," Jonesy replied. "If, for some reason or another, you can't get here, you need to be as far away from that thing as possible before it blows. Like a mile, to be safe."

"How are we gonna know when it's going critical?" Bert asked.

"As soon as you hear an audible hum from the building, take off," Jonesy said. "You'll know what it is when you hear it."

"Anything else?" he asked.

"Ya' gonna have any beer for us when we get back?" Nick asked.

"We'll break out the gin," Jonesy said, and he sent everyone on their merry way.

•

Dan drove down Perkins to CC's. He usually went there only with Sol; CC's was his place, really. Solomon couldn't meet him; his boss reamed him out for visiting Yashua last night, and he got thrown on patrols. 'Sol was lucky,' Dan thought. 'They could've canned him.'

Dan would leave for New Orleans at one o'clock, around there. He didn't have a clue about what Yashua told him. Mardi

Gras ended a week and a half ago, on 'Fat Tuesday'. Was he being figurative? It didn't make sense, but having a scotch in the French Quarter for Yashua sounded like a perfect way to top off the bizarre trial.

So, he finished his coffee, and pulled next door to the gas station, where he filled up. As hard as the past week had been, he could use some 'Big Easy.'

Chapter Twenty-two

We reached Houston around twelve-thirty, and gassed up. I put the high-octane stuff in, as Jonesy advised me to. From Houston we drove for four hours, watching dusty desert turn to bayous and swamps, in western Louisiana. It was a pretty quiet drive; we all had things on our mind. We arrived in Baton Rouge at four o'clock, and stopped at a gas station for snacks and a bathroom break.

In Baton Rouge, the energies were pulsating, blanketing the Earth. Wisps of semi-opaque color floated off of things, flittering around in a wind that wasn't blowing.

I noticed that these energies were competing with each other. Colors that countered each other danced in the air. I could sense this great tension between them. It was familiar. All of a sudden I was feeling déjà vu. I'd seen something like this before. In the dream I had; the battle on the ethereal plains. This wasn't exact, but it was close. It *felt* like it.

I noticed a change in the lines coming from houses, the HIPPO lines. They were taut, and seemed to be bulging. Wisps of darker-colored energy would come close to touching them, and where they did, the light in the pipes would brighten a little bit in that area.

The energies in the air were flowing, and again, it was in the direction that we were about to travel. It was all going to Angola, I suspected. I knew we didn't have much time. We were going to have to speed up there, and pray we didn't get pulled over.

That is, of course, exactly what happened. We were so close. We couldn't have been more than twenty minutes from Angola when the cruiser pulled behind us and the berries flashed.

"Shit!" I exclaimed. "Keep going!"

"He's just gonna' have a gun on us when we get there if we do that!" Hernando said.

"Fuck!" I said. "Alright, fuck it, pull over."

"What if he becomes a problem?" Katherine said.

"We're not gonna kill him," I said. "We don't work for that side."

"I wasn't saying that, Barney!" she said. "But I mean, can we incapacitate him?"

"I don't know," I answered. I could see into the driver's side mirror, and he was walking up with his clip-board. 'Maybe he'll just give us a ticket?' I thought. Well, I hoped.

Older cop; he looked more like a State Trooper than a sheriff. Then I realized he probably knew what I looked like. I was sure he'd seen the video-tape of us on the news. Hell, maybe in the courtroom for all I knew.

'Shit!'

•

Solomon sat in the cruiser, waiting off the side of the road for an unfortunate speeder. He had to expect it; he knew seeing Yashua could've gotten him fired. He was lucky it hadn't. He'd probably be doing patrols 'till the Apocalypse. But Yashua told him to do his job, so he resigned to bring justice to the speed limit for right then.

He was positioned strategically on Tunica Terrace, about five miles south of where Rte. 969 cuts off from it. He was about twenty five minutes from Angola. They told him to patrol, but they never said where. He didn't want to get any closer than that. He knew it was a risk being that close even. But, he had to.

He needed to be near Yashua, even though he knew he

couldn't help. He just needed to be close, to feel his *presence*. He didn't know what Tanner was going to do, or when he'd do it. But he knew Tanner was waiting for him. It dawned on him the night before that Tanner gave himself up, murdering those people in Baton Rouge for the express purpose of getting thrown in Angola. Now he understood why.

Just then an old, white Econoline van flew by him. The radar picked up 120 miles-per-hour. *'Jesus!'* Solomon thought. *'This guy's gonna kill somebody!'*

He pulled out and threw on the sirens. It took him a few seconds to catch up, then he was right behind them.

They kept going, then they slowed down to fifty-five. He didn't know what to think, if they were on drugs, or if they were about to take off. Then the van pulled over. He didn't call it in; he didn't want his boss to know where he was.

He got out, unfastening the harness on his service pistol. He wasn't taking any chances. He didn't call for back-up, so he was on his own there. And with Tanner and Yashua in Angola, and all the craziness that was going on, he needed to be safe.

He walked over to the vehicle. He would have done a felony stop, but there hadn't been a chase; the van just pulled over. Solomon knew full well that a felony stop could make the situation worse if it wasn't needed.

He glanced in the car quickly. There was a man and woman in the back, likewise in the front. The man driving the van was Hispanic, older, and looked somewhat familiar. Solomon thought he might have seen him on television before.

"Can I see your license and registration please, sir?" he said.

The man handed Solomon his license, and fished for the registration. Solomon looked at the young man in the back, and he looked a whole lot more familiar. The name on the license was Hernando DeSantis.

"You ran for mayor in LA, right?" he asked the driver.

"Yes, yes I did," Hernando replied.

"Can I just have y'all step out of the car please?" Solomon said. They all looked nervous when he said that.

They all got out, and Solomon had them walk to the back.

As they stood there, Solomon recognized the young man. He was on the video-tape at Yashua's trial.

•

'We're fucked!' I thought to myself.

Carroll, his name plate said. He made us get out, and stand along the rear of the van. He didn't look like an asshole or anything, just a regular trooper. He must've recognized me. That's the only reason he would've made us get out.

He stared at us all as we were lined up. I looked over at Katherine, and realized I was worried more about her being thrown in jail than me.

"You," Carroll said, pointing to me. "Walk over to me. Slowly."

I did as he asked. I'm sure he noticed that I was starting to sweat.

"You're a friend of Yashua's, aren't you?" he said.

"No-," I started to say, and he cut me off.

"He told me I'd meet you."

"Waitaminit," I said. "You know him?"

"I do," he said, and I saw him smile a little.

"You were with Yashua?" I asked. "I mean, in Baton Rouge..."

"Yeah," he said, easing up. "That's why I'm out here patrolling." He then told everyone else to relax. "My name's Solomon."

"Do they know who he is?" he asked.

"Yeah," I said. "Look, we gotta get to Angola, Yashua's in grave danger."

Solomon looked around for a second. He knew if he let them go, or if he took them, he'd lose his job. He looked down at his badge. How it shined. How he'd always respected it. With a heavy heart, he popped the pin and it flew to the ground.

"Follow me."

•

Vic had the inmates standing for three hours, stiff as a board. They looked directly forward, wherever they were. In each one of their hands was a pencil or a pen or marker, anything that could write. And he set them to the arduous task of signing Angola; every cell, every hallway, and pre-fabricated steel canvas in the place. The guards were powerless to stop it; one actually committed suicide. Vic didn't miss him.

The moment King came in, he felt it. His perfect adversary, the positive to his negative, the yin to his yang. He had just entered Vic's playground. And what a game he had in store.

But he wanted a stage, and an audience. So he waited, for the first time in his life, patiently. He just sat in one place, collecting all the rage impulses he'd stored in his soul since birth, and he gave them form in raw, visceral energy. In this power he wrapped himself, tasting it like blood on his lips.

When the dinner bell rang, he made every inmate go, regardless of whether or not it was their shift. When he knew that the last one had entered, he sat them all down in unison, at tables and against the wall on the floor. He could see King, who didn't seem phased by it.

Victor had plenty of things in store for King that would do more than phase him. He rose and floated, inches from the ground. He took himself like wind through the prison, past incredulous guards and to the main door of the cafeteria. Not wanting to skimp on a grand entrance, he blew the doors, and part of the surrounding walls, into shards. Then, he calmly stepped through.

The men who had sat were silent, motionless. Vic had all their energy. The only thing keeping them alive right then was Vic's insatiable need for an audience. Vic stared at King with bitterness and hatred, the sum of all of his misfortunes and misdeeds.

"Better pray," Vic said as he lunged forward.

•

We had gotten back in the van, and Solomon had almost gotten in the door of his cruiser when the ground shook violently. It kept shaking, and we got out quickly. Solomon ran back over to us. I fell, hitting my chin pretty hard, and everyone else had to crouch down to keep from falling. I found Katherine and crawled over to her, grabbing her tight.

It just didn't stop. On and on the ground shook. A power line ahead came down, as did a few trees. One blocked the road.

'*Shit!*' I thought. "Shit!" I cried. "How are we gonna get there now?"

"Are we too late?" Katherine asked.

"Let's hope not!" The rumbling kept on, but it lessened. We could get up after about ten minutes. The worst of it had passed. The road was intact, but blocked by power lines and trees. To the west, I could see an odd-colored cloud. It was getting bigger from where I was looking, and fast.

"What is that?" I asked Solomon.

"Ya' got me," he said.

"Anybody?" I asked.

"A nuke?" Katherine said.

"God I hope not," I said. "If it is, we're already too late."

We walked down the road to where the tree had landed. There was no way to move it, and there was swamp on either side. Going around would be impossible too.

We sat there, trying to think of something for a good half-hour, until the cloud that we had seen growing earlier enveloped us in thick gray ash.

•

"What the fuck was that?" Jonesy said to Cherise. That's about all he had time to say before he and Cherise both were thrown violently to the floor. He hit his head hard enough to blur his vision for a few seconds.

The whole cabin was being tossed around. Jonesy's equipment was being thrown off the different tables it was on, and any object not nailed down was tossed to the floor.

Jonesy thought it was the big one. The great quake that California was always destined for. Happening at the worst possible moment. The ground continuously shook, and it was twenty minutes before he could get a footing. By that time, all he could see was ash outside the windows. It definitely wasn't an earthquake.

Jonesy checked the generator - it worked. He turned it on and used it to operate the air system he had put in two years ago. He just hoped *that* worked.
The generator roared to life, and he put his hand to the vent. He felt the pale, cool rush of generated air, a mix of oxygen and nitrogen, fed by two tanks in the parking area.

He didn't fear any structural issues. He'd designed the cabin to withstand 'the Big One'. He knew that it, and the air system, would hold.

He looked at his computer. Dead. Everything connected to the outside was dead. His cell-phone worked; it ran off Essence, which was immune to most environmental hazards. That told Jonesy that the hub was still functioning. He tried calling Barney again, but he got nothing.

He'd given the program to his guy, Tim Malern, who was a low-level programmer in Paradigm. He could get in the door anyways. In fact, he had to be there that day. He had to work overtime that weekend to finish a project. Jonesy called him to find out what was going on down there.

He masked his number with Tim's sister's number, a clever little code he'd come up with, and dialed Tim's cell-phone.

"Hey sis," said the answering voice.

"Tim, it's Jonesy. What's goin' on over there?" he asked.

"A big ole' shitstorm!" he said in a lowered, hushed voice. "It's like it's the end of the friggin' world. Earthquakes, volcanoes; the big thing was Yellowstone, dude."

"Yellowstone?" Jonesy asked.

"Yeah, Yellowstone!" Tim said. "It erupted. Plus one in New

Mexico. That's what that just was."

"Oh my God!" Jonesy said, stunned. He knew Yellowstone was a caldera, but they said it would give plenty of warning signs before it erupted. That thing was massive. He sat there for a second, processing.

"What about San Andreas?"

"That took a hit too…" Tim said. "Honestly, there's so much shit goin' on right now, we can't keep up…"

"They're also trying to deal with some, umm, disturbances around here." He wasn't gonna say it, but Jonesy knew he meant the Mighty Seven had struck.

"Is it a go?" Jonesy asked.

"They've got two armed guards in the hub, I can't," Tim said. "I'm sorry. I'll try if they leave, but they won't let me get very far."

"Shit!" Jonesy said. "We need that program, like, now."

"I can't right now!" he said. "But I'll do what I can. I promise you."

"Alright," Jonesy said, "keep me posted."

"Will do," Tim said, and hung up.

"Fuck!" Jonesy shouted, and threw the only table still standing to the floor.

•

Fisher looked around the control room of the Louisiana State Penitentiary in Angola, and he watched all the monitors go black. The facility lost power temporarily, but it came back on. Then it went off again as the ground shook with tremendous force. It knocked him off his feet, and he hit the ground with a hard *thud*.

"What the hell was that?" he asked the warden.

"I don't know, Mr. Fisher, sir," the warden said.

"The prison has no power," the deputy warden said. "I'm not getting any responses."

"Shit!" the warden shouted. "Full lock-down!"

"Impossible, sir!" the deputy said. "The doors were open for dinner, and we can't close 'em now."

"Yellowstone National Park erupted!" Arlo said, with his cell-phone to his ear. "That's what just happened."

"Jesus!" Fisher said. "What else?"

Arlo kept listening. "Not just that, J.D.," he said. "They're getting reports all over the world. Multiple eruptions, earthquakes, storms… it's like an environmental meltdown!"

Then, Fisher's phone rang. He knew the ring-tone to be that of the Secretary of Defense.

'What now?' Fisher thought as he answered it. "Fisher," he said.

"Mr. Fisher," Secretary Caraway said. "We're having a problem over here."

"The environment, I know…" Fisher said.

"That's a problem, but not *this* problem," Caraway said. "Our missiles are aiming."

"What?!" Fisher exclaimed.

"Not just ours; everybody's. Russia's, China's, every nation that *has* nuclear weapons. They're all aiming."

"At what?" he asked.

"We don't honestly know," Caraway said. "The co-ordinates keep changing. Just like the clocks have been doing. Almost exactly the same."

Fisher let out an exasperated groan. "What's the President gonna say?" Fisher asked after a pause.

"About which particular crisis?" Caraway asked sarcastically.

Don't be a dick," Fisher responded, "you know what I mean…"

"The nations have agreed to keep quiet about it until they can figure out why it's happening."

"And if they can't?" Fisher asked.

"All I can tell you is this," Caraway said. "If they all launch at the same time, no matter where they're headed, the Earth will be uninhabitable within the space of an hour."

"Jesus!" Fisher said. "Thanks." He hung up. A lot of strange shit was happening. But Fisher wasn't impressed upon that it was anything paranormal.

To Fisher, it was the product of a normal element that was currently unknown to him, and right then the only unknown element in what should've been a normal sample collection was downstairs beating the piss out of his sample.

'*Tanner's behind this, I bet,*' Fisher thought as he started out of the control room door. '*He's had his fun, time for him to earn his keep.*'

•

"Holy shit!" said Dan as the ground shook the French Quarter. He expected things to start collapsing, it shook so hard, but everything miraculously held. Except him. He tasted the sidewalk dirt on Dumaine Street, where he had been strolling prior. He hugged the ground, not at all willing to take his chances standing. The men he was with were on the ground too. But they were praying. They were Muslim, and they were facing east.

He had met the men, Aziz and Rahiim, shortly after he'd arrived in the French Quarter. They recognized him from the trial. They introduced themselves, and Aziz told him, with a beaming smile, that he was the one who flew Yashua and Barnabas to the states.

'*Barnabas?*' Dan thought about the video-tape. One of the people looked American to him. Maybe that was Barnabas. It made Dan hopeful that someone else was trying to help Yashua.

More than one, apparently. Aziz and Rahiim had taken him to a club on Frenchman Street. Sweet Jazz billowed from the band, and Dan noticed that the place was packed with musicians. One of them he was introduced to. The guy's name was Paul.

Paul wasn't a trade musician. He didn't live in the community that housed the Mardi Gras performers. He was a trucker, but he played a mean tenor sax. In fact, few of the musicians there were trade. When Rahiim explained to him why they were there rehearsing, Dan understood why Yashua told him to enjoy Mardi Gras. They were planning an impromptu encore that night, under the city's very nose.

Rahiim and Paul filled him in as they sat listening to the melodious wanderings of the juicy New Orleans jazz.

"When Yashua was arrested, Aziz found me," Rahiim said. "He told me of Yashua, and who he was. And of something Yashua told him."

"Yashua told me he would need New Orleans to bring its voice to bear this evening," Aziz picked up. "I had no idea what that meant, but I told Rahiim about it."

"I had a dream the first night my cousin stayed," Rahiim continued. "I saw many marching through the streets, playing instruments. I was looking from the doorway of a large building, and behind me were thousands of living musicians, preparing their instruments. I woke up, and it hit me. We needed another Fat Tuesday."

"The floats were just put in storage after Mardi Gras ended," Rahiim continued. "And I knew Paul, who knew most of the musicians from volunteering with the community in Metairie."

"So they're gonna kick up another Mardi Gras tonight?" Dan asked. "How many musicians are here?"

"Thousands!" said Rahiim, and Dan spit out his soda.

"How?" asked Dan. "This is the most people I've seen since I've been here!"

"They are waiting in different places, like here," said Rahiim. "They're preparing, practicing. We brought them to our homes, two or three at a time, so as not to draw too much attention. We've been doing this for the past week."

"Did you tell anyone about Yashua?" Dan asked.

"We didn't have to," Rahiim said. "People just wanted to play."

They informed Dan of the full plan, more or less. He said he wouldn't reveal one thing, as Yashua had instructed Aziz not to. But the rest was relatively simple. The floats had been taken to the parking area between Decatur and the Mississippi, where the old French Market used to be. They moved them there under the pretense that they needed repairs. The city let the Mardi Gras performers do whatever they needed to do, so they approved it without much thought. The city was usually empty after Fat Tuesday anyways.

From there, the French Quarter would come alive that

evening with the encore of Fat Tuesday.

But now Dan didn't know. The ground was still shaking, but not as bad, and Dan could rise to his feet if he held onto something. It had been about a half-hour since it started, and when Dan looked west he saw a large, off-color cloud. It seemed to be approaching, blooming forward towards the city. He didn't know where it was coming from, but within a half-hour's time, it'd grown enough to block out the receding sunlight, turning all the electric streetlights on. The cloud came very close, and it was like dust or ash, Dan couldn't tell.

But it didn't enter the city. It surrounded it, and when Dan looked around all he saw was the cloud of whatever it was. Except straight up. When he looked directly up, he saw what remained of the daylight. Clear as a bell, brighter than it had been before, even. Dan shook his head and scratched his chin. All he could think of was the eye of a hurricane.

•

Vic felt the thunder he was creating. It rolled through the prison; steel frames buckled and concrete dust rained down. The ground shook, and Vic felt righteous. He laughed at the frail, pathetic loser that God loved so much. Vic mocked him as the blood stung his eye, broken ribs digging into his insides. His prison uniform was torn open, and Vic marveled at his signature, jagged lines of blood that he'd carved into King's chest.

He'd hurt him bad. But not fatally. Not yet. He had a little game in store for the broken King. He called it *this is your life*. And what a life he'd enjoy picking at.

He looked around, marveling at his handiwork. He had changed his mind at the last minute, and when he'd beaten King, he threw him into the main cell block. He had a better idea for his twisted little game. He made the inmates leave the dining room for the cell block and stand in a row, positioned between every cell.

"Tanner, that's it!" Fisher said as he walked down one of the staircases. "He's had enough. We don't need you fucking up the sample."

"Fisher," Vic shouted. "If ya' know what's good for ya', you'll leave here alive."

Fisher pulled out what looked like a remote control. "If I press this button..." He waved it at him. "You'll die. Just like that. Do you understand me?"

Fisher barely got that out of his mouth before the control device he was waving flew out of his hand and into Vic's.

"Well that's interesting isn't it?" Vic said. "You should've pressed the button *before* telling me what it did, J.D., honestly, you know better than that." Vic make a *tsk, tsk* sound, and immediately J.D. was surrounded by sharp, jagged shards of steel hovering in the air pointed at him, once some part of the prison infrastructure.

"Wait, Vic!" J.D. said. "We can talk!"

"Now I've graduated to Vic? That's good ta' know," Vic said. "Sorry J.D., I have an important meeting to attend to."

The shards flew into J.D. from every direction, severing most of his body. The pieces fell, slopping onto the floor. Spici came running downstairs, but Vic caused his neck to break before he hit the last step. He simply fell as dead weight to the main hallway.

'*Spici was a pussy,*' Vic thought to himself. '*He didn't deserve a good killin'.*'

Vic laughed as he looked at the 'King of the Angola hallway floor.' He flashed his splintered grin and commenced the show.

•

We were surrounded by ash. I couldn't see anyone, and had no idea where they were. I wasn't choking on it, though. It wasn't even touching me. It came to about six inches away, but something was holding it back. I didn't have to guess what, rather who. *God.*

I called out to the others, and I heard Katherine call out in a muffled voice. Then I heard Hernando and Juanita. Then Solomon. I told them all to keep talking, and I went for Katherine. I bumped into her, and grabbed on. When I did the ash receded even further. We had about a foot-and-a-half of breathing room. We held hands and followed the sounds of the others. They were collecting in the same area. When we found them, we all grabbed each others hands, so we wouldn't lose ourselves again.

When we did that, instantly we felt this strange, I'd almost say a 'sucking wind' sound. And a large area around us cleared up. We could see somehow, something was illuminating the road around us. I looked up to see the bright sky, and it looked like we were in the bottom of a tunnel of dust. Or like the eye of a hurricane, or something. And I wasn't the only one that could see it.

"Where's that coming from?" Katherine asked.

"I don't know," I said. I stood there for a second, and I came upon the realization that we had the power of God with us; a power that could illuminate, a power that could clear the air. A power that could clear our path.

As we stood in that circle, with the illumination about us, I suggested that we pray for God to clear our path. We sat in silence for a minute before we all looked around. Nothing. I felt discouraged.

But then it happened. Just like that. The area around us became a broad column, moving forward to reveal the road ahead. The tree came in view for a second before it smashed in half, and the debris launched into the swamps on the side of the road. The column stopped. We watched it. Then it went a little bit, and stopped.

"I think God wants us to follow it," Solomon said. We hopped in the van, Solomon hopped in his cruiser, and we did just that.

•

We drove slowly at first. The column always kept about twenty yards ahead. When a tree or power line was in the road, it would be snapped and pushed out of the way by an unseen hand. We eventually went faster, and it kept pace. By the time we reached Angola, we were trucking.

The main gates were destroyed. We saw the twisted metal and razor wire as God led us through the area they used to secure.

That's how we knew we had arrived. The column led us to a building, and an open doorway. We couldn't get a bearing on where we were, what was around us, the size of the building we were about to enter. We just knew that God had led us to a door that we needed to enter. And we did.

I was horrified by what I was seeing. The building had taken extensive damage during the quake, or whatever that was, but that wasn't what horrified me. There were jagged symbols everywhere. They were like the ethereal symbols I'd seen, only the opposite. They were creepy.

We could see to the door of the main cell-block. It was then that we heard the maniacal laughter that we all knew was Tanner. We ran as fast as we could towards the door, and we entered the fight.

Vic was lovin' the show. Surrounding him and his guest, in each cell, were images. Images of emaciated bodies with tattoos on their wrists. Images of gas chamber doors, thick, greasy smoke pouring out in erratic paths, inevitably passing in front of King's nose. How he was suffering! Vic was in a state of ecstatic overload.

"They were your own children, Mr. King," Vic said. "*Your own people!* Doesn't it just burn you that you had ta' sit by and let it happen, 'cause ya' weren't even born yet?!" He laughed crazy.

Then he sent out a thought, and every inmate picked up anything they could that was sharp on the ground around them, and began to carve into their foreheads. The bleeding lines came together to form the shapes of swastikas.

"Doesn't it just burn you?" he asked gleefully. "Where was your God then? Where is He now?"

'*Yeah,*' Vic thought. '*He's sufferin', but why ain't he crying?*'

He was broken, bleeding and being mentally tortured, but he wouldn't give Vic one tear. That was really pissing him off, too. He was about to turn on the heat in a big way.

Just then he heard the door at the other end of the hall blow open, shattering in pieces. Five people came in. He hadn't even sensed 'em, he'd been so focused on getting off.

And then he saw her. Katherine Willis. *The bitch.* Vic

recognized the two she was stayin' with in L.A. And that asshole cop Solomon was there, too.

There was another guy with her that he didn't know, probably her boyfriend. And somethin' wasn't right with him. He was like her. Strong like her. And he had something on his arm that burned Vic's eyes when he looked at it.

'No matter,' Vic thought sadistically. 'The two of 'em combined can't wipe my ass right now. This is just icing on the cake.'

"Welcome to the show, ladies and gentlemen!" Vic said, and all the inmates clapped stiffly and hollowly on Vic's thought.

•

Katherine was in a state of near shock. There was Tanner, the man who'd attacked her, standing over Yashua. She'd not seen him in near two weeks, and he looked terrible. He was bleeding, and his face was swelled. His chest was lacerated in jagged symbols. He was on the floor, almost in the fetal position, clutching his side. He made not a sound but she knew he was in agony. She wanted to run right over to him and hold him, but Tanner was stronger. She had a strange perception in here. She was seeing energies, as she knew Barnabas could. She looked at him, and he looked back. The look in his eyes told her that he was seeing what she was seeing.

Tanner had absorbed an enormous amount of dark energy. His skin pulsated with it. It fell as wisps from his body along the ground, and tendrils of it surrounded Yashua, swirling about him, tormenting him with God knows what horrific imagery.

Katherine knew she couldn't take him. She knew that she and Barney combined couldn't take him. He had assumed the presence of death incarnate.

"Hey bitch!" he said to her, and she felt Barney getting real angry. She realized then how much Barney loved her, and how easy it would be for Barney to end up losing control of himself over her. She had to think of something fast.

She figured out that Vic was controlling the inmates through their HIPPO links. She knew he was feeding off it; it was the source of his strength right then. It had made him so powerful that he would soon destroy all of them, including Yashua. He couldn't be taken out in the prison. But she knew where he *could* be taken out.

'God forgive me,' she said. 'Barney, forgive me.'

She then went to one of the inmates and ripped off his HIPPO link. She put it on herself and dove into what it took Yashua himself to get her out of the first time.

●

Dan stood there on Dumaine Street with Rahiim and Aziz. They didn't know what time it was; the light coming in through the top had just turned to intense starlight. Rahiim told Dan to go to a restaurant that had a balcony facing Jackson Square.

"Have a drink," Rahiim said. "Enjoy the show. We have to do what is needed of us."

"Thanks, Guys," Dan said as they walked away. Dan made his way towards Chartres St., and he saw Paul on the corner, with his saxophone in a case. He must've been getting ready. He walked with Paul to the square, where he'd watch the show from behind the balustrades. When they approached Jackson Square though, what they saw froze them in mid-sentence.

There were ghosts. Spirits, apparitions; whatever they were, they weren't living things. They didn't look like movie ghosts, all decomposed and falling apart. They looked like people, but they weren't solid. They were dressed up in suits, and they had instruments.

Dan could hear the sounds that they were producing; somber, sorrowful compositions. They walked in lock-step down St. Ann, and turned up Decatur. They walked right past Paul and Dan, and not one of the spirits looked at them. Dan would have probably died from fright if one had come up to him.

"Who are they?" Dan asked Paul, as if he'd know. "*What* are they?"

Paul's voice was choked. "They're the victims."

"Of Katrina?" Dan whispered, though the ghosts were paying them no mind.

"Yes." Paul was staring at the spirit that led the group.

"How do you know that?"

Paul pointed to the leader. "I found him when we searched the city, after it was drained," he said, and paused. "He almost got away." Tears started running down his cheek.

There were many, but they went by incredibly fast. In ten minutes Dan and Paul were watching the end of their procession. Then they parted ways. Dan walked in to the restaurant he was told about. The owner was talking furiously in Cajun to a waitress. He went into the restroom and promptly vomited. He ran water over his head for about ten minutes, sobbing, praying to God that it wasn't true.

He looked in the mirror when he raised his head. He looked like shit. 'I need a scotch,' he thought, and he thought of Yashua. He started laughing, and then he felt it; all that Yashua had told him about. Right then, at that precise moment, he had found what Yashua said would come. He felt satisfaction. By puking in a polished marble sink, he'd accomplished his life's work.

"Only you, Dan," he said to himself as he cleaned up. He walked back into the restaurant, ordered his scotch and went up to the balcony on the second floor. There was a couple sitting at a table next to him, chattering away nervously, obviously freaked out by seeing the ghosts, or whatever they were. Dan sipped his scotch, and it went down smoother than any prior scotch.

He bought a cigar. Yashua didn't tell him to, but he figured it would go good with the scotch. He lit it up to the sounds of sax and muted trumpets, horns and tubas, triangles and washboards, acoustic guitars and harmonica's.

People seemed to come out of every building, walking out into the street, but they all played harmoniously, rhythms and melodies passing back and forth between musicians, between groups of musicians. Dan then heard the clops of horse hooves from down Decatur, and he saw the floats leaving the parking area. He cracked a smile and marveled at it all.

"What's going on?" the woman sitting at the table asked him.

"I could be wrong," Dan said, taking a sip, "but I believe

that's the Second Line."

•

I screamed "Nooooo!!!" as Katherine put the HIPPO links on her forehead and wrist. She froze, and the consciousness left her eyes. Vic suddenly had a look of confusion on his face, and his power faded a little. He cried out, and buckled over for a moment. I ran to Katherine, putting my hands on her shoulders and shaking her, but I knew it wouldn't do any good.

The inmate she cut loose was running around insane. This apparently created a mental problem for Vic, because when he regained his composure, he sent a steel splinter through the man's chest, dropping him. I saw Hernando and Juanita look at each other, and then at Solomon. The three of them ran down the rows of inmates and started disconnecting them.

"What the fuck are you doing?!" Vic screamed, and he dug his palms into his head. He looked over in our direction with a look of utter hatred, and suddenly I felt a tremor in Katherine. She began to shake, and Vic's laughter filled the block. I turned to him in a rage and directed a steel shard at him. He deflected it, sending it through an inmate. Then I realized the inmate wasn't his target. It was Hernando, standing behind the inmate, who fell to the ground in a slump.

I screamed; I was by his side without a second passing. He was mortally wounded. The spike had pierced his chest, and he was losing a lot of blood, too much. He looked at me and coughed. Blood shot up into my face, and I didn't wipe it. Right then I felt that it *needed* to be on me. His blood was on my hands.

'*I forgive you.*' Hernando's voice came into my head. '*Go save her.*'

I looked at him, saw the light of vitality dim, and then extinguish. I looked at Katherine, who was convulsing. I looked at Victor, who was hysterical, and I looked at Yashua, who suddenly looked his age, and I could tell he needed me then, more than he ever had.

I did the only thing I could think to do. I grabbed a HIPPO

link that Hernando had taken off one of the inmates, and I dove in after her.

•

Tim found his chance. Everything was going haywire at Paradigm. Between the earthquakes, volcanoes and what Jonesy's boys were doing before; Tim heard people yelling about two massive disturbances in Louisiana. He picked up that one was in Angola, and one was in New Orleans. The hub was starting to lose control of the Essence flow, and there was no one there who knew enough about it to stabilize it. Spici went with Fisher, and both were incommunicado. The managing scientist had fallen down a stairwell when Yellowstone had erupted.

They couldn't bring anyone in. The ash covering, and still raining, on Anno Luce made calling in help impossible. So Bob Baker, the head guy and coordinator of operations, was in a panic. And Tim saw an opportunity.

"I know how to program Essence," he said to Bob as he saw him walking around frantically.

"How?"

"Spici had me working special projects before." Tim replied, lying through his teeth. "It was need to know."

"If you can get in there and stabilize this mess," Baker said, "you can have *my* job."

"Okay, suit yourself," Tim said, and Baker led him to the secure elevator. He scanned his retina, and the door opened. They got in, and the pneumatic lift gasped to life as it took them to Floor A.

Tim did know how to program Essence chemicals. Jonesy taught him a lot, and he was decent at it. He'd never had a thing this big to practice on, but no better time than the present. Besides, he didn't need to actually fix it, only introduce the program Jonesy gave him and hold the problem off until the thing could kick in. He knew how to do that.

Baker watched as Tim worked. He wasn't going to let Tim have time alone, so he had to think quickly.

"Do you have an isolator program-vial?" he asked.

"An isolator what?" Baker asked, obviously clueless. He should've been. It didn't exist. But Tim knew Baker well enough to know that he wouldn't know that.

"No time to explain," Tim said. "Where do they keep the program-vials?"

"In the storage refrigerator, but it's locked," Baker said.

"If you want to live past midnight," Tim said, "you better break that lock. This whole thing's about to blow."

Baker took that very seriously, and he broke the lock, allowing Tim to grab a vial. Tim didn't even know what particular vial he grabbed, but it didn't matter. He wasn't planning on using it.

Tim walked over with the vial in his grip. When Baker wasn't looking, he switched vials. He walked to the main control element, *the panel,* as he'd heard it referred to, and he slid Jonesy's vial into the acceptor. It started a programming sequence the likes of which he didn't understand. But he pretended to. He then switched the shunt, which drained some of the more frenetic activity. The hub appeared to stabilize. It would be temporary; eventually the shunt would disengage. That would occur in about seven minutes. Jonesy said it would take ten minutes for his program to kick in. That left three minutes for Baker to go *'What the fuck!'* before something happened that Tim was sure would be interesting. And by that time, Tim would be walking through Anno Luce, with a rag over his mouth, taking his chances with the ash.

•

I was surrounded by energy; I was energy. My being was joined with that of everything. I was one with Katherine. I saw her, I felt her, next to me. My reason told me that she was being destroyed by Victor, but I was him too. I was one with him. And her. And images of beauty, and pleasure filled me. I was in ecstasy, floating through life in a cloud of my choosing. I could give away my will, for I didn't need it. I could hear Katherine crying out 'no', but I didn't care. I didn't care about anything.

I just wanted to take it all in, let it become me. If only Yashua could feel this.

And suddenly it changed. I saw the turbulence. Yashua wasn't there to experience it. He couldn't. It was killing him slowly, draining his youth, drawing the life from him. I felt sick. And my revulsion created a wave that Tanner himself felt. I could see him now, as distinct from the rest of the sea of energy I was soaking in. Malevolence, brutality and sadistic glee surrounded him, but I saw into his core, and saw fear. Deep, repressed fear, bundled into his nerve endings. Fear drove him, and for the first time I saw the very center of it. He looked at me. Then he looked down at my arm. It hurt him to see the tattoo. Ethereal images hurt him.

Katherine stopped convulsing. I could see everything, the cell-block, the surrounding ash-choked swamps, and then I could see Anno Luce, and the irradiated black vibes that emanated from the Paradigm building. It looked like Tanner, or rather, Tanner looked like it. I couldn't see a connection but I could sense it between the two evils.

And I could see New Orleans. Ethereal energy was dancing along the streets of the French Quarter in a maelstrom of beats, melodies and rhythms, and each note was an ethereal symbol, combining and recombining to create equations, formulas. I was connected to it, and it invigorated me.

I turned to Katherine, and she saw it too. I smiled at her, and I intimated my love to her in a way that I could only have done in there. For one brief moment our spirits made love, and we shared our minds with each other, our beings, in a sea of pure energy. And we contemplated in unison what we had to do.

We both turned to Vic's energy, and we connected him to us. Our energy to his; our perspective in his eyes. He saw what we saw. And in an instant we turned to watch the ethereal New Orleans. And it burned him horribly. He shrieked, and we had to let him go.

He staggered back physically, screaming. The prison shook with the force of it. He stared at us in rage. But he took it out on Katherine, and I felt her HIPPO link dissolve as he tele-kinetically ripped the device from her head and her wrist. I saw her go limp in the prison. She fell onto the floor, and I saw Juanita run to her.

•

Jonesy and Cherise sat in silence. The ground was trembling, but only slightly. Nothing had come back on-line; nothing could. The ash had collected on the windows, and Jonesy didn't know what was going on out there. It could've been snowing chicken-shit right then and he would've had no clue. He didn't dare open the door. The ash could've been covering the whole house right then; he didn't know.

"I'm scared," Cherise said. "What the fuck are we gonna do?"

"I'm gonna call Tim, that's what I'm gonna do," Jonesy said, and he pressed the digits with shaky hands. He tried three times to even get it right, and he couldn't. He stopped trying and cried, holding his head in his hand. Then it rang.

"Jonesy," Tim's voice said when he answered it. "It's a go."

"You got in?" Jonesy said, snapped immediately back to attention.

Yeah, about five minutes ago," Tim said. "I'm on the first floor right now, by the front doors."

"How are you gonna get outta there?" Jonesy asked.

"I don't know," Tim said. "I can't see anything out there."

"Waitaminit," Jonesy said. "Take the right corridor past the first set of security doors, *right now*, do it."

"Okay," Tim said. "Where?"

"Second door to the left after the security doors," Jonesy replied. "Kick it open if you have to."

"Okay," Tim said, winded. He must have been trucking. He should've been. Jonesy heard the sound of wood cracking.

"Okay, I'm in," Tim said. "Now what?"

"The red locker on the back wall," Jonesy said. "It's always open. It has gas masks for chemical spills. Grab one."

"Alright," Tim said, "got one."

"Do you know how to put it on?" Jonesy asked.

"Yeah, we went through that in training," Tim said. "I never thought I'd have to actually do it."

"It will only buy you a few minutes, Tim," Jonesy said. "It might not be much help at all. Get to a car if you can. Try to drive; I don't know what else to tell you."

"I will, Jonesy."

"Hey Tim," Jonesy said.

"What?"

"I didn't want to say this, because I figured you would think I was nuts," Jonesy said. "But ya' know what happened in Jerusalem?"

"Yeah," Tim said, "what about it?"

"Jesus is back. But is name is Yashua now."

"You're not kidding, Jonesy, are you…" he said.

"We're working to save his life right now," Jonesy replied, "and you may have just helped."

•

Dan watched as the musicians filled the night with sonic joy. He even danced a little. But then he noticed something strange. As strange, if not stranger, than the ghostly 'first-line' he'd seen earlier. There was a glow emanating from the musicians to their instruments, as a line of thought, almost. It was a subtle glow at first, but as the night went on it grew too large to be contained within, and it wisped into the air as strange symbols. Dan didn't know what they meant, but he'd seen them before; on the briefs. They were God's. He could also hear a low rumbling from where the Lakeview Refinery was. He left the restaurant to follow the procession.

Dan followed the second line to North Rampart Street, and he could see the symbols concentrating as they rose in the air. They combined, forming arrangements whose complexity awed Dan. Occasionally this energy would fly jet-fast into the air, and over the column of ash surrounding the city. He also saw a raw, blue energy, like the flame from a Bunsen burner, flowing through the streets before it was sucked up by the musicians. After a few moments, he realized it was coming from the direction of the refinery.

Dan marveled at this. He saw the floats, and they weren't driving down the street; they were *floating* down it, suspended in the air a few inches. Dan also saw the same spirits that had tapped the First Line on North Rampart. They were in the patch of grass separating the two lanes. Dan could've been mistaken, but he believed they were partying. He saw them reaching for beads and throws, and when they were tossed, they fell right through their fingers. They didn't seem to care though. Dan looked to the other end of the street and he saw the leader of the line that had brought Paul to tears. He was smiling.

•

I screamed. If you could call it that, but I didn't rage. I knew Victor could turn it against me. And suddenly I remembered New Orleans; the Second Line. I felt a rush of energy from the French Quarter that was not bound by the distance between us. It was mine to dispense, just like in Jerusalem. And Vic was a side battle. It was the Beast we fought. Tanner was just a tool.

I absorbed the symbols, the formulas, the equations, and they exploded from me. I didn't aim them at Vic. I aimed them at the hub.

Vic bellowed "No!" His energy source was now under attack. He turned in rage, not to me, but to Yashua.

"You gotta die now!" he shrieked, and he grabbed a steel spike. I couldn't stop him; I could barely keep afloat doing what I was. But Juanita and Solomon both tried, running at him from opposite directions. He threw them both across the room. Juanita fell unconscious, and Solomon got up, pulling out his service pistol. He fired a shot clear through Vic's shoulder, sending a spray of blood out of both sides of it. Victor screamed and dropped the spike. He fell back, almost hitting the ground.

He didn't though. Instead he launched Solomon to the ceiling of the cell block, pinning him there. I screamed "No!" but I knew there wasn't anything I could do right then. I was unable to rescue him.

Then, suddenly, I felt them. Eyes, millions of them. Billions of them. All of these eyes looking aimlessly, as if they were lost and trying to get their bearing. They were connected. But they were aware and confused, bringing an incredible amount of stress on Victor. Hell, on me as well.

Jonesy's program. They got it working.

Just then I felt a burning in my pocket. The USB device that Jonesy gave me. I couldn't move, but with all of the force I could bring to bear, I launched it out of my pocket, and toward Yashua.

And now all of the eyes saw. They saw the situation. And they saw Yashua, and what was about to happen. But they did not know what to do, or if they should do anything at all. I wanted to scream at them. They had the power to stop Vic, stop Yashua's death; stop the death of us all. But I couldn't say anything. Nothing came from me. I was frozen.

I began to hear thoughts, a few at first.

"What happened?"
"Where am I?"
"How long have I been out? What day is it?"
"What am I seeing?"
"Who is that man?"
"Why is that other man trying to kill him?"
"Is this really happening?"
"Is this for real?"
"Who is that man?"
"Why is he glowing in the center?"
"Can we stop that other man?"
"How do we stop that man from killing Him?"
"Can we stop this?"

And suddenly we were not alone in the cell-block. There were spirits surrounding us. Many spirits, dressed in different types of clothing. Some looked like historical figures. Martyrs. I saw Mahatma Ghandi, and Martin Luther King. I became flooded with the names Jesus, Yashua and Isa. In the space of a few seconds, the millions or billions of people plugged in suddenly realized that they were about to see the second death of the Messiah, if they couldn't stop it. I didn't know what to do, and I was in such a state of panicked hyper-arousal at that moment that I could only do one thing. Pray.

'God stop Victor,' I pleaded. 'For all the power is yours, Almighty God.' Over and over in my head I projected this one thought. I let it consume every ounce of my energy.

And then Anna appeared. She was radiant. She wore a white dress with yellow sunflowers along the seam. She was glowing, and the only thing keeping me from tears just then was the fact that I was plugged in. And she was praying; as all of the spirits were.

Victor looked uneasy, and I saw a small sliver of energy leave his body. And I saw a sliver of that same energy emanate from my body. It traveled through Anna, and when it passed through her it became stronger, brighter. It then traveled to Yashua, and went into the symbol Vic had carved into him. I kept doing it, and more slivers of energy left Victor. I felt like I would run out of energy soon. But I didn't. Every time it was drained, I felt New Orleans, and I was filled with its ethereal energy. They were creating an inexhaustible supply.

Then my small stream of prayer was joined by Solomon's, who was still conscious, and then another, and then a few others of unknown origin. And all the millions and billions of eyes saw it, and they knew.

The few became a torrent, almost instantly, draining Victor, yanking him off his feet, sending him into the back wall of the cell-block, where he collided with the already broken concrete and fell limp. Solomon fell instantly and crashed onto the floor. I thought it had killed him, and I still couldn't move.

Yashua glowed white hot. The slivers of energy traveling into him had corrected the jagged lines carved into his chest, and the symbol became ethereal. His bruising and swelling reversed, and I watched youth return to his face. And it was beautiful. He was younger than before. He was younger looking than me.

He got up and stood there, radiating ethereal energy. All the millions of eyes saw Him, as He truly was, and He reached out to them with His heart, and with His spirit. And I could see homes in America, in Europe, Africa, Russia, and in Israel; in Bethlehem where we had just been a week ago. People were opening their eyes. They were plugged into HIPPO, but they were no longer connected. And those who'd not been connected as well were drawn to gaze upon Yashua. And they understood.

I looked over at Katherine. Her eyes were open, as were mine. I

*found that I could move, and I ran to her side. She saw me and smiled. I
smiled back. And I kissed her passionately. God could've punished me
right then and I would have taken it.*

*We rushed over to Solomon with the speed that I had on
consecrated ground. He was in bad shape, but he was breathing. I looked
to Yashua. He smiled, and a small whirlwind of energy passed from him
to Solomon. When it cleared, Solomon slowly got up and scratched his
head, quite confused.*

"What just happened?" he asked, and neither Katherine nor
I had an answer.

Yashua then walked over to Juanita, who was still
unconscious. He stretched out his hand and grabbed hers. She
awoke instantly, and he helped her to her feet. She looked at him in
wonder. They walked to us. Yashua reached out his hands.

"Come," he said.

We walked out of the cell-block the way we came in, and
down through the hallway. As we walked outside, we were
surrounded by sparkling color. I looked at Yashua curiously.

"There were a few prayers left over," he said, smiling as he
pointed up. "Waste not, want not."

I saw what he was pointing at. It was cleaning the dust out
of the air, taking away the impurities. I could soon see a brilliant
night sky peeking between the sparkling snaps of energy. The
HIPPO link on my neck suddenly went cold, and it disconnected,
falling to the ground. I lost my connection to the world, but that
was a good thing. Just then I could've sworn I heard the distinct
sound of bagpipes coming from the open door of the prison.

"Good ole' Joe," I said to Katherine. "Gone but not
forgotten."

•

Vic got up with a headache from hell. He felt like shit. His
head was in a fog. Where the fuck was he? What the fuck just
happened. He looked around, and he saw a bright-assed dude
walking out the door with four other people. He didn't know who

they were, but he didn't have time to think about it. He had to get the fuck out of there.

He looked away from the door and glanced around. Everywhere he saw eyes on him. *Angry* eyes. Eyes like his. The eyes of killers. He saw one that looked familiar. It was that Nazi punk, Carerra. Suddenly the HIPPO links went dead and the sound of them all hitting the tiled floor was deafening. They got closer. Carerra had a spike in his hand. He smiled.

"Payback time, motherfucker!" he said before they rushed him. Vic left the world feeling just like one of his victims. *Terrified.* As he was torn to shreds, the sound of bagpipes appeared, echoing eerily in the cell block.

Epilogue

It's been six months since that day in Angola. The damage done by the earthquakes and eruptions remained, but the air was cleansed of ash, averting the greater disaster.
Still, millions lost their lives. Though the dust choked the air for a little over an hour, those who were exposed to it suffocated. Those who survived faced the monumental task of rebuilding the shattered landscape.

There has been a global moratorium on violence, more or less. The cloud of being connected to HIPPO did carry a silver lining; it makes racism, sexism and other 'isms' pointless. People of all different religions, races, nationalities and sexual orientations shared a brain for two weeks. Thus the world is having a hard time being divided over our differences. On the horizon, now blooms an era of peace.

The demand for materialistic fulfillment has decreased, causing a dramatic shift in the world's economy. There has been a pervading sense of global equality. People in impoverished nations, also being connected, shared their first-hand, direct experience of poverty with the entire world, as if all had lived it. As a result, the disparity of wealth in the world has evened out. What surprised me most was that money was not taken from the rich; rather they gave it willingly. Some had been plugged in and felt what the others felt, but many had come to the realization that the world didn't value material things anymore, and the wealth was without any status. It was simply no longer worth pursuing.

Yashua rested for three days. Then he began his ministry. He didn't preach the Word. He didn't have to. Most of the world had shared his consciousness, and the Word was now indelibly printed on the hearts of humankind. He taught humanity things that were practical; herbal remedies, crystals, Reiki and *feng shui*, even. He also taught about science and history, and the peoples of the Earth, for the first time, knew the possibilities of science and their true history.

Yashua is well. I've spent many days with him, but not every day. Not that I don't want to. He tells me that he wants me to have a life of my own. I know he wants what's best for me, and he's got a cell-phone now (I know, weird right?), so he's only a phone call away.

Katherine and I got married the week after what we've simply come to call; 'Angola'. I won't feel embarrassed to tell you we didn't leave the hotel room much in the five days and four nights of our honeymoon.

Juanita is still mourning Hernando's loss. It troubles me still; Tanner killed him with my anger. But Juanita doesn't blame me, and gets annoyed when I keep apologizing about it. I know she loves me. She said she'll honor Hernando's memory by running for a higher office. Senate, perhaps, or even President, she said. I hope she gets it, too. 'President Tierrez'. I can see the bumper stickers now.

Solomon Carroll now travels with Yashua. He's more or less agreed to work as Yashua's assistant, though there's no pay involved. Solomon wouldn't accept it if it was offered. He would've been Yashua's bodyguard, but there's simply no need.

Dan Champere, Yashua's attorney, stayed in New Orleans after all of it. He lives on Dumaine Street, across the street from where Aziz and his cousin now live. Turns out he didn't need a resume after all; crime has dropped to zero, and there aren't any people to defend, so, Dan became a sax player. He met Aziz, Rahiim and Paul down there, and they got him on the path of the staff-lines and notes.

Yashua told me about Paradigm's destruction. He sat me down when he told me that Jonesy and Cherise were the only two left of the Mighty Seven. The rest had given their lives during the attack on Paradigm, still driving, still raising hell as they choked to death on ash. When the building went up, the blast covered a radius of one mile, and a bare exposed blister was all that remained of most of Anno Luce.

Alejandro's mom survived, of course. Alejandro did not. He

wanted to come with us, but something told me that he had performed his life's task in Anno Luce, and part of that included telling a good friend of the passing of another good friend – 'Ol Joe. If I had heard it from anyone but Ale', I would have broken down.

Zee survived, I am told. It saddened me when Yashua told me that Zee had turned to HIPPO after the mission burned down. That depressed me, but I didn't blame him. That place was his whole life. What would I have done? I don't know.

J.D. Fisher was killed gruesomely by the late Victor Ray Tanner, who himself was killed gruesomely by a mob of angry inmates, both executed in manners I won't repeat here.

The Reverend Joseph Biggs crashed in to the Atlantic Ocean as he tried to fly his private jet to Tel Aviv, Israel. He had not slept in a day, and he had foolishly decided to fly it himself over the Atlantic. He was barely awake when Yashua was attacked. The shock-wave of the various eruptions sent the plane into a tailspin, and Biggs wasn't alert enough to recover. He passed out from the G-forces, unable to pray to a God he never cared to know. Yashua told me he warned him to be rested. I had to laugh at that, even though it was disrespectful to another human being.

Katherine and I are meeting Yashua today. We are going to New Orleans, to the French Quarter, to spend the day with Solomon, Dan and Rosita. Jonesy and Cherise are supposed to meet us there too. They're flying in from Cali, where they still live in that cabin. That thing is a beast.

We'll probably say a prayer, and enjoy each other's company for the day. Plus, Katherine and I got a permit to grab a spot on the sidewalk to play. Yashua told me we'd meet Marcel Lyon, who's one of the greatest jazz players going. He said not to worry about 'sucking' around him, but I'm sure I will. Oh well. I'm goin' acoustic, and Katherine's got a small battery-powered amp. She smokes on guitar. She's better than me, and I can't tell you how frustrating that is.

I'm psyched and so is Katherine, even though neither of us can drink. She's pregnant, and I'm a sympathetic, soon-to-be-father. We've agreed that if it's a boy, we'll name him Yashua. And if it's a girl, Katherine's suggesting we name her Anna. That's one of the reasons why I love her so much.

Of course I've asked Yashua how it will end, when it ends. And, of course, he won't tell me. He's now younger than me, physically anyways. He says that he will live all the life that he can. He assures me and Katherine both that he'll outlive us; he's mentioned something about a *Biblical life-span,* but he won't go into detail on that one, believe me. He also guaranteed us that when he goes, and with him the Earth, years from now; however many years it will be, the Earth won't know, nor will anyone feel a thing. He won't tell us exactly how it will happen. But we don't need to know.

Two weeks ago I was talking with Yashua on the phone, and I was telling him that I regretted not being able to have that last cup of coffee with Joe. That night I did, in a dream that was more vivid than any I'd ever had. It was as if it had actually happened. I woke up the next morning with the taste of a strong cup of Kenyan coffee on my lips.

There are so many things I could say right now. Ways in which this has changed me, changed Katherine. The way humanity has changed.

Everyone that walks these days knows that there will be a finite time left to the 'Age of Man.' And we have never known peace like this. It is a strange transition for nations, I'm sure, to have to dismantle their entire militaries. But an 'aiming error' in the world's nuclear arsenal showed even the generals that the destruction of the planet could happen - without their orders. Kinda' took the fun out of everything. The planet is in the process of disarmament as I write this.

Humanity had been given the final exam that day in Angola. Quite to everybody's astonishment, humanity passed.

The End.

Acknowledgments

My grandparents, Hugh and Aileen Sweeny; My uncle Jimmy and aunt
Sophia and my cousin Michael; My uncle Tommy; My aunts Noreen and
Kathleen and my uncle Walt; My cousins Erin, Andrew and Matthew; My
aunt Pat and my uncle Al (R.I.P.), My aunt Christine and my cousins,
Stephanie and Angel

(alphabetically)

Abe Addy; Yacub and Amina Addy; Sr. Mary Aiden; Ashley Boyle; Les
Bristol and the boys (Eric, David, Leonard and Jerith); Tom Bullis;
Catholic Charities of Albany; Catholic Community Services of Baton
Rouge; my fellow volunteers; Kent, Joyce and Jerry; our most gracious
host Juan Calix; Chris Cates; Brian Casey; Eddy Cook; Crimson007; Chip
DePew; Michael Earnshaw; Kelly Fonda; Shirley Foskey; Archie
Goodbee; Stephen Marlowe; J.R. Maston; Paradise Merrow; Himer T.
Morgan; Charlene Nesbitt; Amanda Jo Newer (R.I.P.); Rob Omura; Sean
Palladino; Shaine Parker; Chris Pimental; Billy Pitcher; Bill "Critter"
Reilly; Katrina Rivera; Al Rogers; Fr. John Rooney; Judson "Ever"
Sanford; Amanda Sass; Mike Shaftic; David Soares; Bob Stachowiak; The
Lansing Inn Staff and Residents; James Travers. The Mechanic Street
crew. Rich and Pat VanWicklen

And Jason Ellis.

*And for those of you whom I forgot to mention. I will bang my head
against the wall, and include you in the next one. Get a'hold of me.*

Liam.

Breinigsville, PA USA
03 June 2010
239252BV00005B/1/P